THE LAMB AMONG ✦ THE STARS SERIES

The Power of the Night

BOOK TWO

CHRIS WALLEY

thirsty™

Tyndale House Publishers, Inc.

WHEATON, ILLINOIS

Visit Tyndale's exciting Web site at www.tyndale.com

www.areUthirsty.com

thirsty(?) is a trademark of Tyndale House Publishers, Inc.

Copyright © 2002, 2004 Chris Walley

Cover illustration © 2004 by Mel Grant. All rights reserved.
Title type treatment © 2004 by Nancy Ogami. All rights reserved.

Edited by Linda Washington

Designed by Ron Kaufmann

First published © 2002 by Authentic Publishing, Milton Keynes, England

Library of Congress Cataloging-in-Publication Data

Walley, Chris.
    The power of the night / Chris Walley.
        p. cm. — (The lamb among the stars ; bk. 2)
    "Thirsty."
    ISBN 1-4143-0068-9 (sc)
    I. Title.
    PZ7.W159315Po   2004012695

Printed in the United States of America

08 07 06 05 04
 7   6   5   4   3   2   1

For my parents-in-law,
with gratitude

Fear death?—to feel the fog in my throat,
The mist in my face,
When the snows begin, and the blasts denote
I am nearing the place,
The power of the night, the press of the storm,
The post of the foe;
Where he stands, the Arch Fear in a visible form;
Yet the strong man must go:
For the journey is done and the summit attained,
And the barriers fall.

ROBERT BROWNING, *PROSPICE*

ACKNOWLEDGMENTS

As before, thanks are due to my wife, Alison, for her long-standing assistance and support, and to my sons, Mark and John, for their encouragement. Thanks are also due to Malcolm Down and many other people for, in one way or another, helping to ensure that this book made it through to publication. I specifically want to thank Angharad Brown for remedying my lamentable deficiencies in Welsh—Diolch yn fawr.

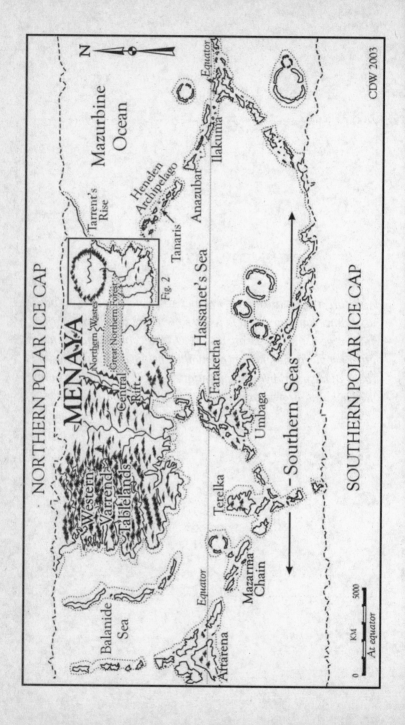

CHAPTER I

It is like being at the prow of a ship, thought Merral Stefan D'Avanos, as he gazed southward out of the rain-drenched windows of the Planetary Affairs building at the sodden houses, roads, and parks of Isterrane below.

Beyond the high gray wall that protected the city from storm and earthquake waves, he could faintly make out the angry white breakers of the ocean's edge. *A storm. How appropriate. A storm has been unleashed on this planet—the Gate has been destroyed and Farholme is isolated from the rest of the Assembly. And we must face what it brings. Do the others feel this?* Merral turned around slowly to stare at the three figures who sat round the dark wood table, awaiting the arrival of Representative Corradon. Vero, dressed in a green jacket and trousers with a definite non-Farholme cut, sat at the far end of the table, staring abstractedly at the large mural of the woodlands of the High Varrend that filled the end wall. Merral sensed that the bland expression on his face barely concealed a profound dejection. Vero reminded him of a lost child. But then, wasn't that exactly what he was? It would take forty years for any message to reach them from the Assembly, fifty years for a ship to come. In what sense did a family continue to exist after half a century of total separation? To the right of Vero sat the slight but erect figure of Perena Lewitz with her cropped auburn hair. Dressed in a deep blue space pilot's uniform, she was staring out of the windows, her expression unreadable. Merral knew the uniform was unnecessary for this meeting and suspected that it was an act of defiance against events. The Gate might be gone and, consequently, her flying curtailed, but Perena would wear the uniform nonetheless.

There was always something insubstantial and reserved about Perena, and here, amid the gathering storm, both qualities seemed emphasized.

Perena's sister, Anya, sat next to her, and Merral noted the contrasts between them. Anya, with a heavier build and longer, redder hair, wore a beige pullover and trousers that teetered on the edge of informality. She was staring at a pile of papers with a deep frown, and as she shuffled them in evident consternation, he felt a longing to put his hand on her shoulder to reassure her. Vero rose and joined Merral at the window.

"My friend," he said lightly, the accent of Ancient Earth plain in his voice, "I have made a decision to keep some of my suspicions quiet."

"Which?" Merral was aware of the others listening.

"Up there," Vero said, gesturing skyward to where the hexagon of the Gate had hung, "I made guesses. I guessed that, despite everything that our history has told us, elements of Jannafy's rebellion somehow escaped destruction at Centauri in 2110. I guessed that they survived, fled, developed in ways we cannot imagine, and now, over eleven thousand years later, they have come back."

"Where, on the very edge of the Assembly, we have encountered them."

"Perhaps."

Perena had joined them now, her lean, tanned face showing curiosity. "But why do you wish to keep these guesses silent?"

"I simply have no proof. It is all speculation." Vero shook his head. "Our tale is extraordinary enough without my adding to it. I think we had best stick to facts. Theories can wait."

Anya leaned back in her chair. "Makes sense, Vero. I barely believe it myself. But, Merral, reassure me—you will take the lead in any discussion? Please?"

Merral hesitated. "I think it is Vero who should speak. He has had suspicions longer than any of us that something was wrong. He is a sentinel."

"No," Anya replied, the ghost of a grin on her face. "Be realistic. The story of your meeting with the intruders is so incredible that they will only believe it if it's told by someone with as little imagination as a forester. This is *your* job, Tree Man."

Vero turned to Merral, a faint smile trying—and failing—to break through his dejected expression. "Yes, you, Merral, should lead. I am both a stranger to Farholme and a sentinel."

Merral noted a slight gesture of accord from Perena. "Very well," he said.

There was the sound of echoing footsteps outside the room. The door slid open, and a tall man wearing a dark gray suit entered, paused, and looked around with alert blue eyes. Merral instantly recognized Anwar Corradon, representative for northeastern Menaya and the current Chairman of the Farholme Committee of Representatives. He had heard the representative speak at ceremonies and conferences, and along with all of Farholme, he had watched his short but momentous broadcast the previous night.

This close, Merral was suddenly struck by how much Corradon looked the part. In his midsixties, he had the sort of face that sculptors and painters liked: long and rather angular, dominated by a well-defined, almost aquiline nose, and thick, wavy black hair with silver streaks. With his looks and bearing, Corradon would have stood out in a room full of people. There was something about his calm, positive manner that seemed to reassure that, however bad things were, they could be sorted out.

"Good afternoon," he announced in a precise and resonant voice as he looked around. He gave a rather sad smile, and for the first time Merral felt there was a hint of the strain he must be feeling. "In the last few hours, I have wished, for the first time in my life, that I was neither a representative nor chairman of the Farholme Committee. Yet this—" here he raised a hand skyward with a slightly theatrical gesture—"happened on my shift. And we must all do the tasks we are called to."

Corradon smiled at Anya. "Now, Miss—sorry—*Doctor* Lewitz, I

3

know. And I can guess this is your sister, Captain Perena Lewitz, but the others here . . ." He shook his head.

"Let me," Anya said. "This is Sentinel Verofaza Laertes Enand of Ancient Earth."

"Ah, our visiting sentinel," Corradon said as they shook hands. "I'm sorry, Verofaza. It's hard to know what to say, I'm afraid."

"I get abbreviated to Vero, sir." Vero hesitated. "Yes, I'm afraid I will be a guest of Farholme for a long time." He seemed to struggle with his emotions.

"Fifty years." Corradon shook his head. "My deepest commiserations," he said in a voice barely more than a murmur. "Another lamentable story. But if there's anything I can do, let me know."

"Thank you, sir."

The representative turned to Merral.

"And this," said Anya, "is Forester Merral Stefan D'Avanos of Ynysmant."

"A forester?" Bushy eyebrows rose in surprise. "I think I have heard your name." He offered Merral a firm handshake. "It's a small planet." A rueful smile slipped across his face. "I was in agriculture once, before they decided that I was more gifted at management. Until this happened, I had not regretted the change."

The door opened.

"Ah, here is Dr. Clemant."

A younger man, also wearing a gray suit, entered the room, closing the door carefully behind him. He stood in front of the door, looking around with deep-set dark gray eyes as if he was trying to fully evaluate the situation before taking another step into the room. The newcomer was shorter than Corradon and had a pale, round face accentuated by neat, pitch black hair parted precisely down the middle.

Merral, who judged the newcomer to be in his forties, felt struck by his watchful and reserved expression.

"And may I introduce," said the representative, "Dr. Lucian

Clemant. Until yesterday, Dr. Clemant advised me on planetary social trends. He has now been given the role of crisis advisor."

Doctor Clemant bowed formally and gave a stiff smile. "An unprecedented title for an unprecedented situation," he said in a deep but rather unemotional voice. *He is a private man,* Merral decided. *You couldn't fail to notice Corradon, but you could easily overlook his advisor.*

"I have no idea of the purpose of this meeting," Corradon said. "Anya insisted it was vital. So I took the liberty of inviting Lucian. Please, everybody, introduce yourselves to him and then—without further ado—let's take our seats. As you can imagine, we are busy people at the moment."

Clemant nodded and moved around rapidly, giving brief handshakes, repeating each name carefully as he heard it.

When all were seated, Corradon nodded to Anya.

"Representative, Advisor," Anya began awkwardly, "thank you both for seeing us—"

"Oh, Anya, we can be on first-name terms."

"Thank you, sir. But this is a serious matter. We seek you as Representative. Formality is appropriate."

Corradon and Clemant exchanged glances, and Merral felt that the advisor's watchful gaze suddenly seemed to become sharper.

"Formal it is then, Dr. Lewitz," Corradon said. "But before you begin, let me give you a status report, so you know where we stand. We have, by the grace of God, weathered the immediate crisis. Communications across Farholme, for example, will shortly be fully restored. The shock of the blast weakened the diary network, and the inevitable usage surge in the wake of the accident overloaded what was left. But it should be back up in an hour."

He glanced at Clemant and got a nod of confirmation. "And, thankfully, the Admin-Net has stayed up." Merral sensed relief in his voice. It was understandable; almost everything to do with running the planet, from the registration of births to the requisitioning of road repairs, went through the Admin-Net. If that had been wrecked, Farholme would have been incapacitated.

"May I ask, sir," Vero said, "about the state of the Library?"

Merral remembered that Vero hoped to use the Assembly's vast store of information to try to obtain clues to the mystery of the intruders.

"Lucian?"

Clemant, who was sitting with his hands placed neatly before him on the table, gazed at his fingers for a moment before looking up at Vero. "The Library? Well, we hold copies of about 63 percent of the Assembly data stock here. Those files are, of course, intact. I have ordered an inventory of what is missing. I suspect the losses will mostly be specialist files to do with other worlds. It will not be back on line today, and tomorrow is, of course, the day of prayer and fasting. But it will—I am told—be back on line the day afterward. Does that help?" The advisor turned toward Corradon to indicate he had finished and then returned to staring at his fingers.

"Thank you," Vero said.

Corradon looked around. "So, that is encouraging. Long term— well that's another matter. A whole new global set of priorities will have to be sorted out. There are endless meetings being arranged, and I can only hope that tomorrow will help clear all our minds. But there are grounds for optimism."

Corradon paused and stared at the end wall. "I have to say that I sympathize with those who have found this event personally traumatic. Our youngest son . . ." He paused, struggling against some deep emotion. "His fiancée was on agricultural training on Pananaret. . . ." The public persona seemed to crumble slightly. "The wedding was to have been this autumn. It is almost unimaginable. Already you can see the problem that is emerging." His voice was slow and strained. "Does he stay engaged to her for the next fifty years? Or does he treat it like a death?"

Corradon continued to stare out at the rain a moment longer and then turned back to them, his face once more the picture of assurance.

"But such decisions *will* be made." Then he looked sharply at Anya. "So, Dr. Lewitz, if, as you say, you and your friends can cast light on this calamitous accident, we will hear you out. But otherwise—if you will excuse me for saying so—other needs are pressing."

"Sir, it was not an accident."

Corradon's eyebrow shot upward. The advisor stiffened.

"Not an accident?" The representative frowned. "I hope you can both clarify *and* justify that statement."

Anya nodded. "Yes. But, please, let me hand you over to Forester D'Avanos, who has been involved from the start. I will let him tell the story."

Merral, aware of the intense and unfaltering gaze of both the representative and his advisor, began his account. He started four months earlier, just before the Nativity celebrations, when he had visited the Forward Colony of Herrandown and seen what he had taken to be a large meteor going northward, toward the area of the Lannar Crater.

Here Clemant silently raised a finger to pause him, drew a control pad out from the table, and pressed buttons. The woodland scene on the far wall disappeared, to be replaced by an image of the whole of Menaya. Merral, recognizing it as a customized digital composite, was struck by how the green areas of woods and cultivation seemed no more than some artist's daubs over the blacks, grays, and dirty browns of the lava fields, ash flows, and sand deserts.

Feeling conscious of the shortage of time, Merral quickly continued. "While I was at Herrandown I felt there was something wrong— something I couldn't identify. Anyway, I returned on the eve of Nativity to Ynysmant to find that Vero had arrived at my parents' house."

At Vero's name, the advisor again raised a finger in interruption. "Sentinel Enand, if I may ask . . . why are you on Farholme? Isn't Brenito Camsar our sentinel?" His tone was cool.

Vero's gaze seemed as steady as the advisor's. "Yes, Brenito Camsar has been your official sentinel for—I think—twenty-two years. He requested help. He had had a vision that Farholme was under threat. I was sent in response."

Clemant, still staring at Vero, tapped his chin thoughtfully. "A threat? As long ago as Nativity? Remarkable. . . . Anyway, please continue."

Choosing his words, Merral explained how, two weeks ago, his cousin Elana had reported seeing a creature that she described as half insect and half human above the Herrandown colony and how his own brief investigation had suggested that there had indeed been something there. As he spoke, Merral saw how the expressions on the faces of the representative and his advisor began to shift from puzzled interest to marked unease. Merral then mentioned results Anya had obtained from the DNA analysis of the strange fur sample he had found and how the results implied that, in total contravention of all Assembly practice, the creature had an apparent mixture of animal and human DNA. As he spoke, Merral found himself comparing the faces of Corradon and Clemant; while Corradon's expression displayed alarm, horror, and shock, his advisor's face simply showed a cool astonishment. *Corradon is outraged,* Merral noted. *His advisor seems to see this as nothing more than some extreme intellectual challenge.*

Then, as Merral went on to mention Vero's discovery that his uncle had apparently willfully altered a re-created voice, the advisor leaned over and whispered something into the representative's ear. Merral caught the word *miriam* or something like it, but it made no sense.

Corradon paused as if in thought, turned to the map, nodded, and then motioned Merral on with his account.

As Merral recounted the story of his trip north up the Lannar River with Vero, Clemant smoothly enlarged the wall image to show the river's path. When, with halting words, Merral described the discovery of the two types of intruders, the representative suddenly strained forward over the table toward Merral.

"You are *serious?*" he asked, his blue eyes strangely wide. "This is not some vision or illusion? There really *are* strange creatures loose on our world?"

"I am afraid so," Merral answered, suddenly aware of the tension in the room. "I wish it were a vision. But we saw them clearly. And I have a wound from one, and we have provisional genetic results from blood samples of both and images."

Corradon shook his head in bewilderment, looked at Clemant as if for reassurance, found none, and leaned back in his chair. "Continue," he said in a tone that indicated he had been badly shaken. "I did not mean to interrupt. Nor, of course, to suggest that you had not got your facts right. However, I had no idea that you were going to tell us anything of such appalling importance."

Mindful of the passing time, Merral rapidly told the account of how they had spent the day on the hilltop at Carson's Sill. Here, although he was inclined to skim over the violent and bloody encounter with the intruders, Vero kept interrupting him and prompting him to expand on various details. Then, alarmed by the intensity of his memories, Merral recounted how they were attacked at nightfall and, at the last minute, rescued by Perena with her ship. He then explained—as economically as he could—how, once back at Isterrane, Perena had arranged for them to join the inter-system liner *Heinrich Schütz* in order to leave the system and get to Earth rapidly. Perena took over and showed her satellite image of the intruder ferry craft near Carson's Sill before outlining the appearance of the mysterious envoy and his warning to her. Finally, Merral concluded with how the inter-system liner had narrowly escaped being destroyed.

"And that is our tale," he said. "We felt you ought to hear it."

The representative took a deep breath, placed his head in his hands, and stared silently at the table in front of him. Merral found himself impressed by the man's control. In the silence, he was aware of the gusts of rain being flung at the window. Then Corradon looked up at Perena, his face pale. "This envoy, this strangest of figures, can you repeat what he said to you? His words were . . . ?"

Perena gave the tiniest of nods. "'Captain Lewitz, *night is falling. The war begins.*' The words will not easily be forgotten."

"Excuse me, Captain Lewitz," Clemant said, his dark eyes scrutinizing her, "can we be sure that this was an *objective* occurrence?"

Perena returned his gaze, her face revealing no emotion. "As opposed to a subjective vision? *No.* It *could* have been a hallucination. But as it preceded—and predicted—one of the most dramatic events in Assembly history, I think we ought to treat it seriously."

The representative nodded.

"You have never had anything like this before?" continued the advisor.

"No," said Perena. "Space Affairs gives me a yearly psycho—"

"Lucian, what's your point?" Corradon's tone was sharp.

"Sir, I just want to distinguish qualitatively between the biological data and the ship damage, which can be considered as hard data, and this report. Which is of . . . of an *appearance*. It could be a vision."

Perena looked across at Clemant with what Merral felt was a gentle curiosity. "I considered the vision hypothesis myself, sir, but after examining the evidence I felt it was an objective appearance. And I do not feel that the creature I met with was human." Her voice remained even toned.

Corradon looked up at the wall clock. "Please," he said, "discussion of exactly what, or *who,* Captain Lewitz saw can wait. The fact that this envoy predicted the Gate loss and allowed us to save almost everyone on an inter-system liner validates it for me. Whatever, or whoever, it was. And it makes the announcement of a war and 'night' worrying in the extreme."

"There was another warning." Vero's voice was quiet but firm. "From a man who dreams and who has visions. He told Merral and me—independently—that he had foreseen the testing of the Assembly and a storm unleashed on Farholme. He gave us a command 'to watch, stand firm, and to hope.'"

"To watch, stand firm, and to hope," Clemant echoed slowly, his round face a mask. Then he looked at Merral with something that hinted at a frown. "Forester, I wish we had known these things. Had these anomalies been reported . . ."

"In hindsight, sir, I erred. But—"

Corradon waved a hand in dismissal. "Never mind now. I'm afraid we have another meeting in five minutes with the Epidemiology Council. Anya—Dr. Lewitz—please tell me more about the biology of these creatures."

"Sir," Anya said, slipping her diary off her belt and putting it on the table, "there are two sorts of organisms that we have evidence for. Both seem, I'm afraid, to be heavily modified humans."

She clicked on her diary, and after a terse command, the map on the wall was replaced by the images Merral and Vero had obtained through the fieldscope. Merral stared again at the strange creatures with their brown, polished-woodlike carapaces, their weirdly jointed limbs, and the platelike covering of their heads and chests. As he watched, the horror of them came back to him, and he was barely able to suppress a shudder. He heard a sharp, appalled intake of breath from Corradon and saw his advisor shaking his head in incomprehension.

"These," said Anya, her voice dark-edged with a note of disgust, "are the ones that we call cockroach-beasts. About 1.5 meters high, with a chitin-rich, rigid outer skin casing. I thought it might be like fingernail cuticle but it's different, apparently generated from insect DNA segments. It's not actually a true exoskeleton, as apparently they do have a vaguely hominid bone structure underneath. It's more an organic armor."

The advisor opened his mouth and closed it again sharply.

Anya showed a few more images. "You can see they are bipedal; they have stereoscopic, forward-facing vision. The insect appearance is purely superficial; they are mammals. Not arthropod eyes either, which is consistent with Elana Antalfer's report that one was watching Herrandown. Distance vision, you see. The hands are strange; the finger and thumb give a scissorlike cutting blade. It's apparently efficient, as Merral found out."

Merral, trying to suppress his memories of the attack, observed a look of stunned incomprehension on the face of the representative and his advisor.

"These we just call ape-creatures," she said, flicking a new image on the screen. Merral felt his stomach squirm again at the sight of the tall, dark-furred beasts with their strange, backward, displaced heads and their peculiar stooping stance. "Bigger, around 2.2 meters tall. These seem to have a mixture of ape and human DNA, but with some innovations. The data is preliminary."

The representative, his jaw moving up and down, gestured at the image. "Ape and human DNA *intermixed*. I find the concept appalling and the reality, well . . . are there *no* limits?"

"A profound question," Vero said in a low but insistent voice.

"This data has not gone to Ancient Earth?" Merral turned to see the advisor staring at him.

"No," Merral answered. "We were taking it with us when the Gate exploded."

Clemant shook his head. "Putting aside—for the moment—the extraordinary irregularity of your journey, why didn't you just transmit all this data as soon as you had it?"

Vero spoke before Merral could answer. "S-sir, I take responsibility. It was because we found out that the signals through the Gate were being intercepted."

"*Intercepted?*"

"I'm afraid so," Merral said, feeling he needed to protect Vero. "We can show you the evidence, but the intruders were able to intercept and modify Gate signals and diary calls."

Vero raised dark, mobile fingers. "A-and if I may interrupt. Please, we must all assume from now on that all our calls can be overheard. Nothing of what we have said here today must be transmitted."

Corradon and Clemant exchanged wide-eyed glances.

The silence was broken by the advisor's deep voice. "Let me summarize. *One:* you believe that non-human—or modified human—creatures have landed in northeastern Menaya. *Two:* they have at their disposal technologies beyond us: in communications, genetics, and weapons. *Three:* they are hostile. And *four:* they are behind the destruction of the Gate. Is that a fair summary?"

Merral was conscious of nods of agreement around him.

"But *f-five*—" there was determination in Vero's voice—"we must not neglect the spiritual dimension. The disturbances in Herrandown, the modified re-created voice. The feeling of evil we have felt. Above all, the warnings of this envoy. Indeed, the very fact of his presence."

Clemant, his face inscrutable, said nothing.

The representative rose. "We must go," Corradon said. "Although after this, I do not feel like another meeting. I need a chance to think and pray."

He stared at Vero for a moment before shifting his gaze to Merral. "But I have, of course, one more question: What do you suggest I do? You have had more time to think about things."

Merral, suddenly finding himself unclear about what he was to say, looked at Vero.

"To be honest, sir," Vero replied, "I think that, at this precise moment, you should do nothing. Until we can meet again the day after tomorrow."

"Nothing?"

"Yes; we too need time to think and pray. I do not think a day's delay will make any difference. I also fear there is a real danger that we may make a wrong decision."

"But surely," Corradon asked, "it could be dangerous to delay?"

"Possibly, sir, but we do not know where the intruders are. And your north looks very big to me."

"I agree with Vero," Merral said. "We need to keep quiet. For the moment."

Corradon looked at Clemant, who gave an unhappy shrug. "Sir, I agree," he said in a low voice. "We need to be very careful. There are issues here that we need to discuss before we act."

"But shouldn't people be warned?" Corradon asked, smoothing his streaked hair. "I have a responsibility."

"Ah, but warned against what, sir?" Vero was frowning. "We do not know how many intruders there are. Or even whether they are a threat beyond the Lannar Crater area. Besides, everyone is so shaken at the loss of the Gate that another shock may cause panic."

An intense expression of alarm briefly appeared on Clemant's face before vanishing.

"Hmm. What about the other representatives?" Corradon asked. "I must talk with them. Can I call them?"

Vero shook his head. "Sir, I do not think you should use diary transmission to talk of such things. None of us should; it may be intercepted. Are you meeting them soon?"

"They are all gathering here in two days for what are scheduled as several days of crisis meetings."

"Sir," Merral said, catching a nod from Vero, "I suggest we meet with you earlier that day. Would that be possible?"

Corradon looked carefully at him and then glanced at Clemant for support. "Yes."

"And, sir," Vero interjected, "if I might make a request, can we meet somewhere more isolated? We have no idea what the power of the intruders is, but we cannot rule out being overheard or noticed here. It was an old rule for meetings to do with strategy to be carried out in secret places."

Corradon shook his head with wearied astonishment. "I had not thought that it was possible to get worse news than the loss of our Gate. But *this* clearly is. This event . . . no, these *events*, are almost too terrible for words. Indeed, the combination of this and our isolation . . ." He paused as if reluctant to finish the sentence. Finally, a degree of composure returned to his face. "I'm sure we can find somewhere suitable to meet. Can't we, Lucian?"

Clemant gave a slight nod of agreement.

The representative walked to the door with a determined step. "Come, Dr. Clemant, we must leave or we may have to make an explanation. And that would not do. Everybody, nine o'clock the day after tomorrow. And then we must take some action." Then he gave a small bow of his head and swept his gaze around the table. "Forester, Sentinel, Doctor, and Captain—my greatest thanks."

Then, with his advisor following him, Representative Corradon left the room.

•—◆—•

Perena, anxious to get back to her ship to oversee the repairs, drove them back in her borrowed Space Affairs four-seater. She dropped Anya at the Planetary Ecology Center and Merral and Vero at Narreza Tower, where she and Anya had their apartments. Perena had found Merral and Vero an empty fourth-floor two-bedroom apartment there; an out-of-system visitor was going to occupy it in a fortnight's time, but that wasn't going to happen now.

As they drove, there was almost total silence in the vehicle. *Somehow,* thought Merral, gazing at the somber, wet streets that seemed to echo his mood, *we have crossed another boundary. Until just now, only four of us really knew what was happening. Now we are six, and the two new people have the power to act.*

Now we need to decide what to do.

Vero sank heavily onto a sofa and leaned forward, squeezing his head between his hands. Then he looked at Merral with urgent eyes.

"Tell me, my friend, did I make the right decision?"

"About what?"

"Telling Corradon not to do anything. For the moment."

"I think so. We all need time to consider matters. And I can't think of anything we can do at the moment."

"I suppose so." Vero sighed. "But God grant we make the right decision when we do meet again." He stared out of the window at the rain and then shook himself. "I need to talk to Brenito. I have some ideas I need to bounce off him. But what do you propose to do this afternoon?"

Merral thought for a moment. "Now that the diary network is apparently operating properly, call up various people."

"Okay, but from now on we must always watch what we say."

"Of course," Merral answered, reminded of his own incautious conversation with Isabella just before their flight.

Vero paused, as if in thought. After a while he said, "Are you going to call Barrand?"

"Yes. The last thing he heard from us, we were walking northward. I don't want him trying to follow. Any suggestions as to what I say?"

"You can't say much. But—I suppose—you could suggest that he and the other families don't stray into the woods, that they take the dogs with them, and that they stay indoors at night. They might want to have the quarry team move closer. Into the settlement."

"Do you think there's a risk to them?"

Vero shrugged. "Oh, my friend, you know as much as I do. If the intruders can destroy a Gate, they are powerful enough to put us all at risk. But it may not be so simple. . . ." He paused. "Look, I'd better go. I hope Brenito may have some ideas. I have no idea when I will be back."

As Vero rose and left, Merral watched him, feeling that his thin figure was visibly bowed under the weight of events.

•—•

Alone in the bare apartment, Merral sat on a chair by the window and gazed across at the wet orchards; shiny, red-tiled roofs; and thick gray clouds that twisted across the sky. He checked his diary and found that, as Corradon had promised, the network was now working. For a moment, he stared at the screen, wondering again what to say if anybody asked him where he had been when he had heard about the Gate explosion. Because he and Vero had been on the *Heinrich Schütz* under the names of other men, only a handful of people knew that they had nearly been caught in the Gate's explosion. Merral realized that he could not now admit to having been on his way secretly out of the Alahir System without raising more questions.

For some time, he pondered the novel and rather unnerving problems that this raised. His only real knowledge of being less than totally honest came from the old literature, and he realized that he had never appreciated how treacherous untruth was. He now saw that if you merely failed to reveal a particular truth, it could become necessary, simply in order to protect that, to tell a new and much stronger untruth. And then to protect *that*, still further duplicity was needed. And so on. One small misdeed bred others until there was a whole swarm of multiplying complications that seemed to have no limit. In the end, he simply prayed that he would not have to reveal too much.

He called his uncle first. Barrand was glad to hear from Merral and seemed satisfied by Merral's statement that they had finished the trip safely and now had a lot of data to analyze. When Merral suggested the precautions that Vero had proposed, his uncle hesitated.

"Since you passed through," Barrand said, "the air seems to have cleared. But better play safe; I will do as you suggest."

Merral then called his mother, who was plainly thrilled to hear from him. The implications of the Gate loss to her seemed to go no wider than how that event had affected Ynysmant, and with her usual gusto, she recounted how two neighbors had relatives caught beyond the Gate. It was all "just so *dreadfully* sad." His father was well, she said, but was now going to be even busier at work repairing things. Then his mother inquired after Vero, sent her sympathy, and made Merral promise to tell him that he could be considered part of the family. "We could sort of *adopt* him, really," she said breezily, "for the duration."

"Mother," Merral replied, trying not to laugh, "that's a nice idea, but he hardly needs adopting. And 'the duration' is fifty years plus. But I'll pass on your concern."

He then called Henri, his director at the Planning Institute. When Merral began to give his careful summary of the trip, Henri cut him short. "*Ach,* it probably doesn't matter now," he said, giving his beard a sharp tug. "Man, even keeping Forward Colonies like Herrandown going is now open to question."

Finally, and with a strange reluctance, Merral called Isabella. She was in her office. Straightening her long black hair, she beamed at him with a tired face.

"Merral!" she cried. "So you are still in Isterrane? I thought you were going away."

He caught a sharp gaze of inquiry in her dark eyes.

"Ah. Isabella, the loss of the Gate has changed everything. So I'm here for a few more days. Then back home, I presume." He paused. "Anyway, how are you?"

She shook her head and breathed out heavily, as if unable to express her feelings. "Shaken, in a word. Coming to terms with being out of a vocation."

The realization that Isabella could indeed hardly assess educational progress against Assembly standards when there was no link to the other worlds struck Merral sharply. It was yet another area in which he hadn't given thought to the implications of the Gate loss.

"Yes, I suppose that's true—"

"You mean you hadn't realized it?" Isabella stared at him, as if offended that it hadn't been at the forefront of his mind.

"Sorry," Merral replied, feeling embarrassed. "I suppose there are just so many areas that the Gate loss has had an impact on that I hadn't thought of that. And I'm afraid I've been busy on other things too—"

She shook her head ruefully. "Oh well. Anyway, I'm sitting here thinking the unthinkable. What do I do? Now we are separate. Isolated." She threw her hands up in a gesture of uncertainty and insecurity.

"Isabella, we are all having to come to terms with that. It's not going to be easy."

"Absolutely, and there's the whole psychological dimension. It's potentially scary."

It's even scarier than you think. "I can sense that, but tell me what you believe."

"It's stood everything on its head. We all grow up with the same sort of mental picture of the Assembly. It's like some great, spiky, three-dimensional shape amid the darkness of the stars, and we at Farholme are on the very tip of one of the protrusions. Yet we are always part of it; that's what the word *Assembly* means. Worlds' End we may have been, but we always looked in to the center, and we always belonged. . . ." She paused. "But no longer. We are *isolated*. We will have to come to terms with that. Psychologically, it's going to be a very interesting fifty years. *Very* interesting."

I might have known that Isabella would see more deeply than me. He picked his words carefully before he answered her. "Isabella, you have to say to yourself that it's temporary. It's not permanent. And ultimately nothing has changed in the great scheme of things. That's what we have to hold on to." He paused. "The King still reigns." *Perena said that,* he reminded himself.

Isabella seemed to think over his words, and then her face brightened. "Yes, you are right. But it may be difficult for some to adjust. Anyway, when will I see you here?"

"I may be back in Ynysmant the day after tomorrow. Or the day after that, all being well. There's a lot of things to be done here."

"We must meet up as soon as you get back. There's a lot to talk about. About *us.*"

"Yes," Merral said, trying to disguise an unwelcome feeling of apprehension as he closed the link.

•—◆—•

Merral was sitting at the table, eating and trying to find a new angle on events, when Vero came in. He took off his wet outdoor jacket and, wiping the water off his dark curly hair, came and sat down gently on the chair on the other side of the table. Without explanation, he took a small package out of his pocket and put it down beside him.

Merral pointed to the pasta he had recently made, and Vero found a plate and helped himself.

"So, have you been outside?" Vero asked after giving thanks.

"Briefly, a walk around the block. I thought it might help me think."

"You've got the picture of what people are feeling then?"

"I was quite impressed. The crowds I met seemed to be taking a positive attitude to it all, really. Is that what you found?"

"Pretty much," Vero said, "but it's early days. I'm not sure how deep or long-lasting the resilience will be."

"Isabella was saying that there's got to be a massive psychological adjustment."

"Indeed," Vero said, midmouthful. "And that makes our dealing with the intruder situation even harder. We must tread warily."

"Yes. And how was your meeting with Brenito?"

Vero swallowed and frowned. "He sends his greetings. He is more shaken by the loss of the Gate than I expected. He feels—as I do— responsible for not sending the warning while we had a chance. But we had—I suppose—a profitable meeting. . . ." He wiped his mouth with a napkin and seemed to stare at the wall.

"You don't seem very convinced."

"Hmm. Oh, I suppose I had my hopes too high. He wants me to set up a meeting with Jorgio. Fine, we will travel out to meet him at Ynysmant. But otherwise—"

"He wasn't much help?"

Vero frowned. "Exactly. . . . In the end he said, 'Well, I shall be interested to see how you handle *this*,' and just looked at me."

"I thought *he* was the official sentinel for Farholme? The point that Dr. Clemant was making this morning."

"I know. But Brenito is a hundred and five and ailing. He also talked about you. 'You know,' he said to me, 'I sensed that Merral would be a warrior; I was puzzled when I saw him head to Earth.'"

"I don't much care for that."

"Didn't think you would. 'That forester and this Jorgio are your assets,' he said."

"Jorgio, maybe. I'm less sure I fit in the asset category. But did he have any solid ideas?"

Vero's face creased into a deeper frown. "Sadly, no. I tentatively outlined some possible actions, and he thought that they were reasonable under the circumstances."

"What possible actions?"

Vero looked away briefly. "I'd rather not say now, Merral. Not just yet. I need to think and pray over them before we see Corradon and Clemant again. At the moment, I'm not even sure that I agree with them." His face became overcast with uncertainty, and for some time he poked at the pasta. Then he looked at Merral. "Do you know what I obtained this afternoon?"

"I have no idea."

Vero pulled the paper bag over and, with an ironic flourish, pulled out two small, yellow, hard-backed notebooks. "It was hard to get them. I am just so unsure about how much our diaries can be explored without our knowledge. But I suspect even the intruders will not be able to spy on pen-and-ink notes. One is for you."

Merral gazed at it wordlessly for a moment before he could bring himself to take it.

"Thank you."

"You see," Vero added, "I have decided that when we next meet with Corradon, he will ask us what we want. That will be the point to make specific requests. I am now going to spend some time making a list so that when they ask, I can say exactly what we need. But exactly what? . . . What dare I ask? What should I ask?"

Then, after helping himself to more pasta, he went and sat down on the sofa, leaned back, folded his hands behind his head, and began to stare up at the ceiling. Eventually he found a pen and set to writing in the book in a tiny, neat script.

Stimulated by Vero's action, Merral spent some time thinking about what his own role might be in trying to deal with the intruder threat. Not long after nine, both of them acknowledged tiredness and, after washing up the supper things, retired to their rooms.

• ◆ •

Merral had held high hopes that the Solemn Day of Prayer and Fasting would shed some revelation on the questions he had, give some comfort, and grant guidance for the future. But none of these happened. And when, at last, Merral slept on the night of that Solemn Day, his slumber was a turbulent one, interrupted by strange, eerie dreams of a curious intensity. In the last of these, and the only one about which he could remember anything, he became aware that he was standing on a high, bare hill in a vast, arid landscape of browns and grays under a sky as white as bone. As he looked down the slope below him, he could see, working their way up toward him in slow, steady strides that never faltered, two figures in the gray, plated space suits of the early Assembly. Finally, they stood just before him on the summit, and as he peered into the reflective metal visors, he saw that he could see nothing, not even a reflection of himself. Then one visor slid away downward and Merral found himself gazing into the dark, hairy face of an ape-creature with snarling yellow-white teeth. As he leapt back in horror and fear, the visor on the other slid away sideways to reveal the shiny brown, woodlike plates and dark, gleaming eyes of a cockroach-beast. As the creatures raised their arms and closed on him, Merral woke and sat bolt upright, clutching his heaving chest.

Unable—and unwilling—to return to sleep, and with dawn less than an hour away, he rose and quietly showered. Then he sat and watched as the rays of the rising sun shining through torn clouds struck first the highest buildings and masts of Isterrane and then slid lower until the houses, trees, and finally the grass were baptized with a fresh, golden light. And as Merral watched, the horror of his dream seemed to fade into oblivion.

At half past seven he and Vero went up to Perena's apartment to find Anya there, sorting out the breakfast.

"Perena's gone to collect some images," Anya explained. As they helped to make breakfast, Merral found himself intrigued by how different Perena's apartment was from that of her sister. Where Anya's had been crowded to the point of clutter and covered with green and brown wall hangings, Perena's flat was bare and neat with cream walls. Aside from some small abstract sculptures on glass shelves and a large glass chess set, the only decoration in the main room was a large watercolor of a night scene on one of the ice moons of Fenniran, with what Merral took to be Farholme glinting in an upper corner.

As they were about to eat, Perena arrived.

"So," Vero asked as they greeted her, "have you found something new?"

"No," she said, and her face showed unconcealed disappointment. "They have vanished. We have a program for finding a lost ship or its wreckage. I had put all the most recent images of all of northern Menaya through it just after we met the other day, and the machines spent all yesterday scanning them. Nothing. I have that single thermal image of the shuttle taken the morning after your attack and that is all."

Vero grimaced. "I was hoping we would have something concrete for today's meeting."

"I too." She looked at her chess set. "It's hard to make a strategy when you don't know what pieces are in play."

"Agreed. And no idea where they have gone?"

"None, Vero. They could easily be in an area the size of your Northern America."

"But it can be found? by a manual search?"

She stared at him. "Perhaps. You'd look for thermal, magnetic, gravitational anomalies. Get imagery and scan every square kilometer visually. You'd have to know the area and the terrain. It could take weeks."

"But it could be done?"

"Unless they make themselves invisible."

Merral realized that everyone had turned to look at him. "Are you suggesting I do it?"

"Perhaps," Vero said, waving a hand dismissively. "But we will see what the meeting brings."

•◆•

Over breakfast, Anya asked Vero whether he had had any new thoughts. He paused for a moment before answering. "Only this: I am puzzled about these intruders. They seem both powerful and weak; confident and hesitant at the same time."

"Explain that," said Anya. "They scare me; I'll be honest. To destroy the Gate . . ." She shuddered.

"Yes," said Vero thoughtfully, "they can destroy a Gate and they can modify and fake our communications. We mustn't forget that. Yet—" he tapped the table with a finger—"yet, their dealings with us have badly failed so far. Merral and I are alive and well. Their losses were heavy."

"God was good," said Perena.

"Amen and amen," Vero agreed. "But you see what I mean. It's all very odd. It suggests that they may have only a limited power. They may not even know as much as we imagine they know. But what do you think, Merral?"

"Me? I am as puzzled as you are," Merral replied. "But I take your point, Vero. I know nothing of warfare, but I know something of sport. I have a feeling—no, more than that—that what happened was not the carrying out of carefully planned tactics, but rather a desperate response to something going wrong."

"Fair point," muttered Anya, and no one seemed inclined to disagree.

A few minutes later Vero pulled his yellow notebook out of his pocket. "Now," he announced, "we need to decide what we want from our meeting. I think it would be helpful for you, Merral, to lead again, and I think it would also be very helpful if we agreed what we wanted beforehand."

Merral saw nods of accord from Perena and Anya and gestured his assent.

"Thanks," Vero said. "Now, in the few minutes left before we must leave for the meeting, let us decide what it is we wish to ask. I should say that I have my own requests, but for the moment I would prefer to keep them quiet."

"Any reason?" Merral asked.

"They will be controversial." He gave a deep sigh. "So controversial I think it is only fair that I alone bear any blame."

CHAPTER 3

The Planetary Affairs building gleamed like a great white sail in the fresh sunlight. A clerk, who was expecting them, led them down a series of stairs and corridors, ushered them into a small, windowless, white-walled room and closed the door on them.

Merral looked around. Crates and boxes had been neatly piled at the back of the room to make space for a single, long, lightweight table and six white folding chairs, and along one bare wall was hung a huge administrative map of eastern Menaya with towns, roads, and air-strips overlain on the topography.

Merral disliked the room; it was small and seemed to hem him in. His mind slipped away to the open woods and forests depicted on the map, and he found himself heartily wishing that he was back at his old job, with the sound of the wind in the trees and the dappled light breaking through fluttering leaves.

His daydreams were no sooner begun than ended, as the door opened and Representative Corradon and Advisor Clemant joined them and took seats round the table.

Merral found himself looking at Corradon. There was a hint of tiredness in the blue eyes, and the representative's bearing did not seem quite as erect as it had been.

Clemant's face was inscrutable, yet his tense posture and his sharp gaze hinted at a deep concern.

After the briefest of greetings, Corradon stared hard at Merral. "So," he said, "I have had some time to think about matters. First though, have you anything new for us?" His words were slow and seemed to hang in the room.

Merral gestured at Perena. "Sir, Captain Lewitz has looked further for the ship."

"And?"

"All I have," Perena said apologetically, "is what I showed you before. There is no obvious trace of an intruder ship. It could have left Farholme, but I believe we would have spotted that."

"I see," the representative said. "I had hoped we would have a location. But finding it is something we badly need to do." He glanced at Clemant, and Merral saw some look of concern pass between them.

Corradon looked around. "You may be surprised to learn that the information flow in this meeting may not be one way. I—*we*—want to reveal something to you."

Merral saw Vero's face register surprise.

"Just after Easter this year we had a short-lived incident that we could only classify as an extraordinary sociological anomaly. I thought of mentioning it the other day, but Lucian and I needed to think more about it. I believe it is important."

He turned to his advisor. "Lucian, please tell them about the *Miriama*."

Clemant rose, walked to the map, and gestured at a coastal town on the southeastern corner of Menaya. "The *Miriama* is a physical oceanography vessel—Type Six. It operates out of the Oceanography Center at Larrenport."

At the word *Larrenport,* Merral had a sudden image of the town as he remembered it: the serried rows of windswept white houses clinging to the cliffs on either side of the great semicircular scoop of the bay.

Clemant's factual and precise voice drew him back to the present. "It has a crew of ten. Normally it operates in the immediate offshore waters. About a month ago, immediately after Easter, its crew spent two weeks much farther north in the western part of the Mazurbine Ocean." He stretched an arm out to encircle an area just offshore of where the Nannalt Delta system protruded into the sea. "Tarrent's Rise, I think, is the main feature there. It was, for the most part, a routine trip—surveying water temperatures. As most of you know—and certainly Forester D'Avanos—we have been concerned about the trend of falling average winter temperatures over the last five years. Although the weather was unseasonably bad and it was not a pleasant trip, they returned to port safely."

He paused, and Merral sensed that he was watching Corradon carefully, as if taking his cue from him. "At least, physically. Then we had a private message passed to us from the director of the Oceanography Center. The crew had made a curious proposal. It was simply this: Because of hardship, for the duration of such trips, they wanted their allowance to be increased." He paused again, looking around carefully for the reaction.

Vero sat upright with such speed that he nearly fell over. "Increased? Their allowance *increased?*" he said, in a voice whose pitch seemed to have risen several tones. "But the allowance is *fixed*. For everybody in the Assembly . . . For you, for me." He stared around with astonished brown eyes and then, with an "Oh dear, oh dear," fell into a troubled silence.

"Just so," noted the representative, in a tone that conveyed that he too had been shocked.

Clemant nodded. "When we had established it was a serious proposal, I was sent over. I had an interview with the captain, a Daniel Sterknem. He—*they*—apologized and dropped the matter. In fact, he seemed a bit puzzled where the idea had come from. I felt there had been more to the trip than he wanted to mention. But he now no longer wanted to pursue the matter. It worried us for a time."

"As well it might," said Vero. "It could unravel the Assembly very quickly if we started recompensing people by financial means. We would be back in a pre-Intervention mess very fast. How do you decide who deserves what? Who is worth more? A Farholme representative or a park keeper on Ancient Earth?"

"Our thoughts too, of course," Corradon replied. "But to me—to us—it sounded similar to some aspects of what you have described or hinted at."

Merral, trying to come to terms with the unpleasantness of a situation in which everybody was demanding compensation for what they did, was aware of the others' nods of agreement.

As Clemant returned to his seat, Corradon glanced around with a solemn expression. "So, now we need to decide what to do." Then his gaze fixed on Vero. "But before that, I want to ask our sentinel a question. From what I remember of the purpose of the Sentinel Order, you were set up to look for any new outbreak of evil. Correct?"

"Yes, sir. That was Moshe Adlen's desire at the inception of the sentinels. Having served throughout the fighting that ended the Rebellion, his desire was to ensure that such events were avoided."

"Yes. It is as I remember. And this is clearly an outbreak of evil. So, in the light of all the evidence, what do you think we are dealing with?"

Vero stared at his hands for a moment and then looked up at his questioner. "I should say, sir, that most of my guesses have been badly wrong. And some of my actions have, it seems, been unwise. But you are right that this is a sentinel matter. Indeed, I am convinced that it was precisely to look out for this sort of thing that we were set up. That I failed to spot it in time to prevent the Gate loss I think reflects badly on me. But it also reflects the fact that these events are not how we as an order had envisaged such a threat."

"If it is in my power to do so, I excuse you." Corradon's voice was little more than a murmur. "Anyway, any evaluation of your role and that of your order must await our reunification with the rest of the Assembly. But please, what do you think is going on?"

Vero opened his notebook, glanced at a page, and then leaned forward. When he spoke, the words seemed to be almost painfully drawn out of him. "I feel there are three elements here. The first is this: there is so much of this matter that suggests the work of our own troubled species."

Corradon's eyebrows lifted in surprise. "With the breach of so many of the Technology Protocols? No one in the Assembly could do this." There was a hint of outrage in his voice. "And there is no other humanity."

"Indeed," Vero agreed, without raising his eyes from his note-book. "That is what we have always known. But, even without Merral feeling that he glimpsed a man, I would still guess that there was something human here."

"The use of human DNA suggests that too," interjected Anya.

"Perhaps," said Corradon as he sat back in his chair and stared at Vero. "So your first element is a human component. But, Sentinel, please continue."

Vero gazed ahead. "Th-the human element is important. I think we can eliminate any idea that we are dealing with aliens here. The second element is also another puzzle. It is that, even before you told us about the request of the crew of the *Miriama,* I felt that there were just so many aspects of this that echoed the times before the Assembly. Or some of the proposals the Rebellion's instigator, William Jannafy, made long ago. It's almost as if something—or *someone*—is turning back the clock."

Vero looked at his notes again. "So that is the second element. I feel that there is an air of lawlessness, of rebellion, about it. Of rebellion . . ." He nodded, as if agreeing with himself, and then went on. "And if it is to do with mankind, then they have pushed beyond all the boundaries we have defined, whether they be in genetics or robotics. . . ." He hesitated, his expression becoming still more solemn. "Or, I fear, in other areas."

"I see," Corradon noted in an unhappy tone. "A terrible thought. Your third strand?"

Vero grimaced and twisted awkwardly on his seat. "Ah. That, sir, is the easiest by far. There is something evil about this. You can see it in the spiritual contagion. At its heart, this is evil."

"I see," said Corradon after a long, drawn-out silence. "Yes, I will not argue with that at least. Human, rebellious, and evil—worrying verdict. Lucian, what do you say?"

The advisor stared at his fingernails for a moment as if thinking carefully. Then he looked up at Corradon with his unfathomable eyes and said in his low, dark voice, "Sir, I would not argue with that view.

But I would say that—by themselves—the adjectives *human*, *rebellious*, and *evil* do not greatly help us. Not without defining exactly what the nature of the threat is."

Merral was troubled by the brittle, almost antagonistic, edge to Clemant's words.

Vero looked hard at the advisor and then flung his hands wide. "D-Dr. Clemant, I do not dare be more precise. I was asked to comment and that I have done."

"Please," Corradon said, rubbing his forehead. "I take Sentinel Enand's comments in the spirit they were offered. But I have a more practical question for our forester here." He sighed. "You see, we meet with the other representatives tonight and tomorrow. Do I pass on to them what you have told us over these meetings? What do you say?"

"I would think so," Merral answered, "but I am open to other advice."

"I would agree," Vero said, "but it should be done privately and face-to-face. They must be told not to tell anything about this matter to anybody else. And not to use a diary to talk about it or to store anything about it."

"To keep it private." Corradon stared at him with a perturbed expression. "Yes, you think they can read our diaries." He cast a brief, unhappy glance at his advisor. "This is very difficult, Vero. You think all our lines of communication are being intercepted?"

"No. But for the moment, I think it is wisest to assume so. I want to research how we may make them secure."

Corradon made no reply, and instead Clemant spoke. "Forgive us, Vero," he said, his voice so deep that it almost seemed to rumble, "but perhaps we find it harder to take such a view. To put ourselves in—what shall we say?—a *suspicious* frame of mind."

Vero hesitated. "I can sympathize. If I had not seen what I have seen in the last few days, I would be of a similar mind."

Clemant tilted his head slightly, stroked his chin with a finger, and frowned. "But we are an open society. The idea of not transmitting views is very odd. I mean, we have a policy of transparency here."

Merral felt certain that there was a slight, but unmistakable, emphasis on the word *here*.

"As elsewhere in the Assembly," replied Vero slowly, phrasing his words with an almost deliberate politeness. "But I have to say, from my studies of the ancient past, when faced with enemies, almost the most vital information we could give them is what we know about them."

"Yes, I could see that," Corradon said slowly, "but, Vero, should we not circulate a general warning for people to be on their guard?"

"I have agonized over this and I think not. I think, for myself, there might be a risk of panic."

Merral saw Clemant shift uneasily in his seat, and the representative looked at him. "Lucian?"

"Panic," Clemant said, with a deeply troubled tone of voice, "is the worst of all possible responses." He stared at his hands, neatly extended on the table, for a moment and then looked up with what Merral thought was a barely suppressed expression of alarm. "With widespread panic, Farholme could become ungovernable."

"Sorry, Vero," Corradon said, "what you want really is, I believe, secrecy. *Secrecy*." The representative pronounced the word emphatically and slowly, as if testing an unfamiliar sound. "A term I do not like. Any more than I like a world without a Gate. But I sense its logic. I take it you agree, Merral?"

"Sir, I agree, most reluctantly, with Vero's suggestion of keeping this private. For the moment."

"Very well. Lucian?"

"Reluctantly." Clemant tapped a finger nervously on the table. "*Most* reluctantly."

"I see." Corradon's dislike of the situation was plain from his expression. "Very well. We will tell the other representatives that we have a problem. And that they must keep quiet. But, Forester, what do we actually *do?*"

Merral recognized that the time they had expected had come. "I— we—feel that above all, we need more information. The conclusion we have come to is that we all want to work on this. In different ways." He waited to be sure that his words and tone registered. "I would suggest that you authorize the four of us to investigate various aspects of the problem. We would, of course, report to you."

"I see," Corradon said with a pause. "A sort of research group. And you, Forester, would personally do . . . what?"

"Sir, we have agreed that I should look at the satellite imagery to see if I can find out where the intruders are based. To find the ship they came in. That seems a priority."

"It's an incredibly large area," Corradon said, staring at the map on the wall.

"Around three million square kilometers," Clemant said, with the air of someone who had calculated it.

"That's a maximum. But it is big and rough."

"But you know the area as well as anybody does, I suppose," Corradon said. "And the others? Dr. Lewitz, for instance; what about you?"

"Me?" Anya said, fixing the representative with her lively blue eyes. "I want to rerun those DNA tests. And I want to model and compile everything we know about the two creature types."

Corradon gave a grunt of approval. "Captain Lewitz?"

Perena hesitated a moment and then spoke in her low and intense voice. "Sir, I would like to look at any reports produced by the team investigating the destruction of the Gate."

Corradon stared at her. "We are putting our best people on that. Will you be able to add anything to what they can do? I have no doubt about your piloting abilities, Captain. But this is, surely, Below-Space and gravitational physics?"

Perena's face expressed the gentlest disagreement. "Sir, I know things that they do not. They, I presume, are looking for a mechanical failure. I will be looking for a destructive act from the outset. I also know that Gate calls were being intercepted and modified at least a week ago. I know that there was an incursion into Farholme space as long ago as just before Nativity. In fact, I want to look at the astronomical data for that time to see if we can work out where the ship came from. And, sir," she said, and paused briefly, "I also want to set up a watch."

"A watch?"

"We know one intruder ship entered the Alahir System. But are there other ships there too? We need to scan the skies."

"So we are not caught out again?" said Clemant.

"Exactly."

"Hmm," Corradon said, sharing a knowing look with his advisor. "I can see this has been thought out carefully." He turned to Vero. "And so, what does our sentinel want?"

A good question, Merral thought.

"Sir," Vero said in a cautious voice, "my request is one that I alone am responsible for. It is somewhat radical, and I would be grateful if you and Advisor Clemant would not reject it out of hand."

"You will have our most careful consideration of it."

"Thank you." Vero looked grave. "S-sir, I would like to put together and train a team."

Puzzlement swept across the representative's face. "A team of what?" he asked. "I thought the four of you *were* a team?"

After a moment in which Vero seemed to be summoning courage, he simply said, "Sir, I want a team of people who will work on the defense of Farholme."

There was an interchange of surprised glances, and Corradon turned to Merral. "Do I gather that this is news to you?"

"Er, yes," Merral answered, aware that Clemant was staring at Vero with an expression of open misgiving.

"Hmm, I see," Corradon said. "Vero, *defense?* You'd better expand."

Vero's fingers twitched. "Well, for a start, investigate—and then make—anything that we think will protect us. Against the intruders. I'd like to look at ways of making secure communications." There was uncertainty in his voice, and Merral realized for the first time that for all his cleverness and insight, Vero was not very good at verbal persuasion. "I b-believe, well—for instance—that if the intruders are looking into our diary system, it ought to be possible to detect how it's done. And stop it."

"I can see the value of that," Corradon murmured. "What else?"

Vero looked uncomfortable and bit his lip. "And, sir, I want to research some, well . . . defensive equipment."

"Defensive *equipment?*" The bushy eyebrows nearly met. "Can you elaborate?"

Vero's dark face became strained. "Well—shall we say—er, military things."

"*Military?*" Corradon repeated, leaning forward as if he had misheard something. Merral caught a low gasp from Clemant.

Vero hesitated and then, apparently aware that he had already committed himself, spoke again with more confidence. "Yes, I mean, can we produce weapons? Should we need them."

"*Weapons* . . ." The chair creaked as Corradon sat back in it, looking thoroughly confounded. "I see . . . ," he said, glancing at his advisor, who was staring intently at Vero.

"Well, I agree with Vero," Anya said in a determined tone of voice. "Reluctantly. You can't realistically keep tackling these things with bush knives and exploding diaries."

"But, Anya—Dr. Lewitz," the representative replied with an air of gentle and dignified exasperation, "we are Assembly. Or we were. I remind you what you all know: the time of peace we have had from Jannafy's rebellion to now is over twice as long as that from the building of the Pyramids to the start of the Assembly. We have given up war."

"But, sir, respectfully, our enemies haven't," Merral said and was surprised at the force of his words. "And while, sir, I share your unease, I too agree with Vero and Anya. We need at least the possibility of weapons. Last time we were blessed with an undeserved success. Next time we may not be able to rely so much on a kindly Providence."

Perena's voice, as quiet and undemonstrative as ever, broke the profound silence that followed Merral's words. "And if I must declare my preference—and it seems I must—I also back Vero and Merral. We nearly lost a general survey craft and an inter-system liner the other day. We *did* lose a Gate."

The advisor, who had been staring from one to the other with a look of careful and unhappy evaluation, turned to Vero.

"But, Sentinel," he rumbled, "this issue of weapons. Surely, it does go against every principle of the Assembly?"

Vero shook his head. "No, sir, I would disagree. The Assembly has always had a small defensive force at the insistence of the sentinels."

"It took twenty years of debate for it to be approved," Clemant grunted, "if I remember correctly. We could start that process here if you or Brenito wished."

Vero's dark skin seemed to pale. "No, on the contrary, sir," he answered, his voice unsteady but defiant, "I-I would like it *now*. If you want me to justify it, I would say, if necessary, that Farholme now forms a little Assembly, an offspring of the greater Assembly. And what was decided for the parent applies to the child. And I don't want two frigates in twenty years; I want twenty-four men and women tomorrow. Or the day after. Quietly. But I do want them." Then, as if taken aback by his own boldness, he added, "P-please."

The advisor, apparently surprised by the force of Vero's words, blinked, shook his head sharply, and turned to Corradon, as if seeking his help.

"I note your disapproval, Lucian."

"Sir," he said slowly, "we know so little about these intruders. I mean, we may be misreading their intentions."

Corradon raised an eyebrow. "But surely, Lucian, they don't *seem* friendly. We have the holes in Perena's general survey craft and our forester's wounded ankle as very tangible evidence of that."

Clemant looked around, his face troubled, and shrugged. "Perhaps, sir. But I maintain that we need to be cautious. By everybody's admission—even that of our visiting sentinel—we do not know what is going on. At all. I agree that these things seem hostile. But so might our dogs. There may be other explanations. For us to act in a hostile manner . . . it might be a capital mistake; it could give a misleading impression of the Assembly. Possibly a fatal one. It is a heavy risk."

Corradon put his large hands on either side of his nose and rocked his head backward and forward, clearly weighing up what he was hearing. "Perhaps, Lucian. *Perhaps*. But they *did* destroy the Gate. And as for risk? All our choices have a risk."

There was an awkward silence, and everyone seemed to turn to Vero who, looking discomfited, blinked and then shrugged. "I simply believe," he said, "that it would be wise to prepare for the worst. I am not asking to use weapons, only to have them made ready."

Clemant shook his head. "But the very act of preparing weaponry could destabilize an already precarious situation."

"Maybe," Corradon said. "But only maybe. Anya, Perena, and Merral—do I take it that you are all in agreement that Vero's proposal is the way forward?"

"Reluctantly, yes," Merral said, and as he spoke, he heard agreement from the sisters.

"Very well," Corradon replied. "Lucian, we must leave. We can talk about this later. I can make no decision now, anyway. I have a lot to think about."

The representative rose to his feet stiffly and moved toward the door. Then, his hand on the door handle, he turned to face them. Merral was struck by how hidden any traces of alarm or disquiet had become.

"Thank you all for coming," Corradon said, in such an untroubled tone of voice that Merral felt they might have been discussing nothing more serious than some plan for a forest extension.

Then he caught Vero's eye. "Sentinel, if—and only *if*—I was to authorize this, how many people did you say you would want?"

Vero seemed to take a deep breath. "Twenty-four, sir. W-well, actually I'd prefer thirty-six. Of the best students you have in around twelve disciplines. I have details—"

The representative raised a hand to silence him. "Later, maybe. Well, I will give you my answer as soon as I can. The other representatives are on their way here, and there are many other issues for me to weigh in the balance. I imagine most of you are going to be staying in Isterrane. Merral, now, what are your plans?"

"I hope to take the two o'clock flight back to Ynysmant, sir. Unless I hear from you otherwise, I will return to work as a forester."

"I see," Corradon answered. "Well, whatever happens, I hope that your return to your vocation can be soon. But let me get someone from the office here to take you to the airport. Where are you staying?"

"Narreza Tower."

"Very good. Say twelve-thirty?" He looked around and smiled. "Thank you all again. I would covet your prayers for the decisions I have to make."

Then he and the advisor left, and as the door closed behind them, Merral could hear animated conversation starting up as they walked up the corridor.

There was a long silence in the room.

Finally Anya spoke. "Hey, Earther," she said, looking at Vero with a grin, "next time you want us to agree with you about forming an army, can you give us some warning?"

At Narreza Tower, Merral and Vero parted from the sisters and returned to their apartment. With sunlight pouring in through the windows, the place seemed brighter and more welcoming. Merral persuaded a subdued Vero to sit outside on the balcony.

"Do you think that we will get what we asked for?" Merral asked him.

"Yes," came the response, "I think we will. But I am worried about that discussion."

"Yes. I felt the opposition from Clemant was striking. I put it down to the shock of the loss of the Gate and the seriousness of what we were discussing."

Vero looked at Merral, his brow creased. "Yes. Perhaps that is it. 'The Gate Loss Syndrome'—a state of mind which you have never heard of before because I have just invented it. I think you will soon. But what do you think lay behind Clemant's attitude?"

"I felt he was afraid."

Vero nodded. "I agree. I have started doing a lot of reading in the pre-Intervention files. It is instructive, even if alarming. We tend to think of fear as an isolated evil. But when you go to the past, what is striking is how often it is fear that triggers other things. Anger and hatred, for instance, often come from fear. 'When a man is terribly afraid he may do terrible things.' It's a quote."

Then, after a few moments, Vero looked at Merral. "I was shaken by the news of that ship, though."

"The *Miriama?*"

"Yes. I am wondering if the evil may not be spreading faster than we had feared. And even whether our conversation today may not have reflected something of the decline we are undergoing."

"Maybe."

"Merral, we must watch. Close at hand and far away."

Then he pulled out his notebook and, with a plea that he wanted to think through what had been said at the meeting, leaned back in his chair and closed his eyes.

•—•

Half an hour later, there was a sharp knock at the apartment door. Merral got up from his seat on the balcony and walked to the door. "Come in," he called out.

The door opened and a tall, large-framed woman in her early thirties came in. Merral stared at her, simultaneously struck by her height, the long, wavy mane of black hair that flowed over her shoulders, the bright but rather sad dark brown eyes, and an unusual sense of energy. He instantly decided that he had never met her; she was not a woman you would easily forget.

"Excuse me," the visitor said, in a sharp, no-nonsense voice, "Representative Corradon said to call here. Are you—?"

"Forester Merral Stefan D'Avanos." Merral turned. "And this is—"

But Vero had joined him. "Verofaza Laertes Enand, sentinel. Or Vero."

The visitor's smile was open and toothy. "And I'm Gerrana Anna Habbentz, Research Professor of Physics, Isterrane University. You can call me Gerry."

Vero shook her hand and gestured to the balcony. "Welcome, Gerry. Come and join us; take a seat. I'm afraid my physics is rather decayed. What sort of physics, anyway?"

"Stellar physics," she said, walking out onto the balcony with a grace that seemed surprising for such a large woman. Yet as he looked at her, Merral was aware that, for all her vigor, she was troubled.

"We have a good little department, really," Gerry said, taking in the view. "Or *had* . . . before the Gate went. Fifty years of isolation isn't going to help." Suddenly she looked glum.

"I'm sorry. Can we get you a drink?" Vero said.

"Thanks. Water's fine," Gerry said, lowering herself into a chair and stretching out long legs. "And we will lose lab access. Of course."

"Lab access?" Merral asked.

"Far Station physics lab and solar observatory. Thank you," she said, as Vero offered her a glass of water. "Yes, flight cutbacks."

"Ah," Merral said.

She shrugged wearily. "That's the least of the issues." She sipped the water. "Look, guys, sorry to come here without warning, but I have something that *may* be of value."

Vero smiled—Merral decided that there was something about Gerry that invited smiles—and said, "Let me guess: you have a faster-than-light-speed ship all ready to launch?"

Gerry returned his smile, but Merral felt there was pain in it. "Now wouldn't *that* be nice?" She sipped at the water again. "But you are pretty close. I may—mark the word *may*—have a way for you to contact the Assembly."

"Surely not." The smile left Vero's face and his eyes widened. "You'd need a Gate link of some sort."

"No. We may be able to send a message by quantum-linked photons."

Vero looked at Merral with a baffled expression; Merral felt sure that he returned it.

"Gerry," Vero said, "go slow here, please."

She shrugged. "It's been known since the dawn of physics—well, Einstein anyway—that you can link subatomic particles so that if you separate them, what happens to one happens to the other." She looked inquiringly at them with her big dark eyes. "'Quantum entanglement?' No? 'Spooky action-at-a-distance'?"

"Sorry."

"Oh well . . . Anyway," she said, "trust me. Einstein got a lot wrong, but not this. If you had some linked photons on Ancient Earth and brought some of them here, what you did to those here would instantly be duplicated on Earth. Okay? So, in theory, if you released them as flashes of light here, matching flashes of light would occur on Earth. Instantly. So you could send a message."

"But—," Vero began.

"Why isn't it used? Because it's horribly complex to set up. And there's noise. And conventional Gate links work well, are simple, and 100 percent reliable."

"Until now," Vero added.

"Exactly," she agreed, and Merral heard a tinge of sadness in her voice.

"But, Gerry," Vero said slowly, "if I understand you—you'd need two things: A supply of linked photons here and someone somewhere else watching their—*entangled,* you said?—counterparts."

"Exactly. And it turns out that we have a limite
d supply of the first and we may have the second."

"Go on," said Vero, his face a picture of eagerness.

"As part of advanced physics, post-Einsteinian physics part three—never the most popular course, by the way—we demonstrate the principle. We have a twinned department—at Zacaras University on Tahmolan—two hundred light-years away, and we have a small supply of entangled photons they sent us. And, at a prearranged time, we send them simple messages."

"It works?" Vero asked.

"Of course it works," she said sharply. "That's why we do it. So, theoretically, we could send them a message. And if someone is watching—expecting a signal—then they might see and decode it."

"And *would* anyone be watching?"

Gerry colored slightly. "The professor there, Amin Ryhan, is a good friend. Well, more than that—"

Suddenly, Merral understood exactly why this woman was troubled. "I'm sorry," he said. "I'm very sorry."

Gerry's face wrinkled. "Yeah. Well, it happens. We were committed and going to get engaged. Amin wanted me to leave Farholme. . . .

Sorry, that's all personal stuff—" For a second, Merral thought she was going to cry, but she blinked and began again. "I was going to try to send a message to him. Then I thought that was selfish. So I had a chat with Anwar—Representative Corradon—yesterday; he's a distant relative. And he said to talk to you. Straightaway. I suppose he wants me to send a message to the Assembly saying that we are okay and that the casualties are low. To list the seven dead on the ship."

"No," Vero said, with a fierce shake of his head. "Gerry, we have a far more important message. How much can you send?"

She hesitated. "Not much. Forty words sent a hundred times, or a hundred words sent forty times. And there's no guarantee. We may not even get an acknowledgement. I'd go for repetitions over length. Send them on the hour, Universal Assembly Time."

"Merral," Vero said, his face a confusion of emotions, "we need to talk. Gerry, will you excuse us?"

Merral followed Vero into his bedroom.

Vero closed the door. "My friend, if this works, it's a gift of God," he hissed. "We have to use it now."

"Shouldn't we get it approved by the representatives?"

Vero shook his head. "No. Definitely *no*. Corradon's given us the go-ahead. They could spend months debating the wording. Or that's the way I read it. Besides, the warning needs to be sent now." He clenched his fists. "Merral, my caution caught me out last time. I will not risk another delay."

"But do we let her in on the secret?"

"Of course. We have to. She's a useful ally." Vero pulled out his notebook. "But what to say?"

After a few minutes of scribbling and crossing out, they had agreed on three sentences:

> *Farholme Gate destruction not an accident but sabotage by non-Assembly forces. Evidence of genetically modified humans, superior technology, and hostile intent. Intruder presence associated with a corrupting spiritual evil.*

Vero hesitated, looked at it again, and shook his head.

"No point in messing about, is there?" he said quietly. He took a deep breath and added three words: *Arm the Assembly!*

"I can't believe I wrote that," he said in an awed tone and looked at Merral. "Do you have a better idea?"

"No," answered Merral slowly, feeling—yet again—out of his depth.

Vero signed it. "There," he said. "That will put the cat among the pigeons."

"The what?"

Vero shrugged. "A twentieth-century Ancient English idiom. It was one of their sports; they would chase pigeons with cats. They were odd like that."

"Are you sure?"

"No, not really. But it's a confident guess. They *were* odd—" Vero slapped Merral on the back—"but let's see what the prof says."

They walked out to see Gerry leaning on the balcony rail and staring out to the western headland where the fluffy clouds still hung over the plateau.

"Gerry," said Vero, handing her a sheet of paper from the notebook, "you'd better sit down and read this. You should add some words of your own to Amin."

She sat down and read it, shook her head so her dark hair flew about, and read it again. The color drained from her face. Then, without warning, she slammed her fist down on the table so hard the glass bounced off it, scattering water on the floor.

"I knew it!" she snapped, her voice bitter and angry. "I knew it. It wasn't an accident. These . . . animals!" She glared at the paper again, then looked up with wild and angry eyes. "You'd better tell me what's going on."

•◆•

Over the next ten minutes, Merral and Vero explained to Gerry what had happened. As they did, Merral felt that Gerry's mood seemed to harden. When they had finished, she got up from her chair, paced around for a moment, then stood against the wall and stared at them, a picture of defiance.

"Okay, I get the picture," she said. "It's *war*. I'll send the message this evening. But what else can I do? These things are our enemy. The Assembly's enemy. They are evil."

"I think we can use a physicist," Vero said. "I'd like you to think about how these things got here. These creatures have come a long way. By a ship, not a Gate. Hibernation? Colony ships?"

She nodded. "Or faster-than-light travel. Autonomous Below-Space travel, perhaps." She paused. "Okay. I'll go and send the message. It will take time to set up the equipment. It should go tonight. But no guarantees, right? We may not even get a confirmation back."

"Gerry, do what you can," Vero said. "I'll be in touch."

"I hope so," she said, and there was determination in her voice. "I'd like to do something to fight back."

As they strode to the door, Merral felt Gerry's shoulders had straightened, and her eyes glittered with a new purpose.

"Oh, Gerry," Vero said, "you know Perena Lewitz?"

"The captain? Yeah, she's flown us to the lab before now."

"That's her. Get together and talk with her on the travel issue. She has some orbital data."

"Okay, I'll do just that."

"Anything else you can think of you might want to look at?"

"Yes," she said, fixing Vero with brown eyes from which any softness had fled. "I'm surprised you didn't mention it."

"What?"

"*Weapons.*" There was a cold anger in her words.

"I'm not sure—," Merral began to say, but Vero silenced him with a gesture. Merral said, "Okay, Gerry. You look into that too."

•◆•

As their visitor's footsteps faded away down the corridor, Merral turned to Vero. "Was that wise? To talk of weapons?"

"It was her suggestion," said Vero defensively. "And it's only research."

"And shouldn't we have warned her not to get too deep in exploring Below-Space?"

"My friend, it's only a theory. But I'll mention it when we meet again."

There was a knock at the door. Merral opened it to find a man in an official uniform who introduced himself as the driver sent to collect him.

"My apologies for being early," the man said. "There has been a change in schedule. Are you ready to leave now?"

Vero followed Merral as he went to his bedroom to collect the few things he had.

"I leave it up to you what to say to people in Ynysmant and Herrandown," Vero said with quiet insistence. "Thankfully, in a strange way, the destruction of the Gate has wiped our trip north out of most people's minds."

"True, but I will have to talk to Henri about it at least." *And Isabella will want to know.*

"Yes, it's difficult. But you could, I think, just say that there may be some genetic anomalies up there. If people want to think that they are natural mutations, just let them think so."

"So we tell the partial truth and not the whole truth?"

"Oh, I suppose so." Vero sighed. "It's all so difficult. Remember: what is said cannot be unsaid; what is unsaid can yet be said. But encourage some precautions, though."

"I will."

"I will be in touch as soon as I hear anything. It may not be direct; I will have to find ways of communicating with you securely. But be careful."

It came to Merral that, even without the approval of Corradon and the representatives, Vero was already making plans.

"You are assuming that you are going to get the go-ahead, aren't you?"

"Yes." Vero nodded. "I understand the reluctance, but there is no option. I felt it before the meeting, but with the news of the *Miriama*, I feel it is a certainty. I see their reasons. I feel that both Corradon and Clemant are reluctant to authorize a defensive team. But they have no choice."

"I wish we could have the time to discuss this with everybody."

"I agree. But we do not have that luxury. Indeed, I fear we are already wasting time waiting for the approval. And so, I am making plans already. Gerry is the first. She will not, I think, be the last."

Merral stared at him, sensing an immense determination breaking the surface. "I see. You seem very resolved on this."

"I am." Vero paused. "Merral, if there is one man on this planet who feels responsible for the loss of the Gate, it is me. I made a bad mistake in not bringing in a threat evaluation team earlier." He clenched his fist. "I do not intend that such a mistake will happen again."

— ◆ —

"We'll be early, won't we?" Merral commented to the driver as he got into the vehicle with its neat emblem of Farholme Planetary Affairs on the side.

"I'm to swing by the office with you," the driver said, pulling out into the street. "There's a message for you there."

It was more than a message. As they arrived at a rear entrance, Merral was surprised to see the tall figure of Representative Corradon himself emerge and beckon him over to a porch.

"Forester," he said, with a soft and apologetic tone, "I am sorry to do things this way, but these are odd days." He frowned. "Very odd days. I needed to speak to you. I think I can promise you that you will be getting the approval on those images. But it will take some time to set up. Do nothing until you hear from me in writing."

He paused, another frown sliding over his tanned face. "But, before you get them, I want you to do something for me. I have a task for you."

"Whatever I can do to help," Merral said, puzzled at both the setting and the tone of the meeting.

"Thank you. Instead of going direct to Ynysmant, I would like you to take the early afternoon plane to Larrenport. I want you to talk to this Captain Sterknem about what happened on the *Miriama*."

"Certainly, sir . . ." Merral hesitated. "But I thought that the matter had been handled already by Dr. Clemant."

The expression on the representative's face was one of total noncommitment. "Lucian did a good job. But I'm not sure now he got to the bottom of what caused it. How could he? We had no reason to believe that it was anything other than a rather odd sociological phenomenon. Not *then*."

"I see," answered Merral, realizing that the representative was revealing a gap between himself and his advisor.

"Yes, I want a second opinion and I value your judgment. I've written a letter requesting that the captain tell you everything." He reached into a side pocket of his jacket and carefully pulled out an envelope with a handwritten address on it. "He's in Larrenport. I'd like a written report; send it by courier over to me."

Merral took the letter slowly. "So what do you want me to ask?"

"I want you to find out exactly what happened—from your viewpoint. To see whether it matches with what you have experienced."

"I see. Who am I to tell about this?"

"I'd keep it between us, I think." He paused. "Yes, between the two of us—for the moment." He turned his tired eyes on Merral. "Is that all right?"

Merral hesitated. "Yes. I'll do it. There's a place on the flight?"

"Yes. I took the liberty of booking you on it. It goes at two."

"I see," Merral answered, feeling unhappy about this most irregular commissioning but unable to express his concerns. "Oh, we had a meeting with Professor Habbentz."

Corradon gave a gleaming smile. "I'm glad. Gerry is a remarkable woman. Very determined." Then he glanced at his watch. "More meetings, I'm afraid." He extended a hand. "Thanks, Forester."

"I'll see what I can do, sir."

• ◆ •

As a result of the disruption to flights caused by the suddenly announced Day of Prayer and Fasting, the short-haul flier to Larrenport was full of people and cargo. Merral was pleased to get a seat by a rear window, even if it did mean he was squeezed in next to a crate of engineering equipment.

As he stared out of the window at the view, he realized that he was rather relieved at not having to talk to anyone. It was, he decided, another disturbing implication of no longer being part of an open society: silence and isolation had become desirable.

As they flew on, Merral stared down at the wild and often savagely indented coastline. Despite having just seen his world from space for the first time in his life, he still enjoyed seeing it from this altitude. *Is it,* he wondered, *because from this height, you can see not just the physical features but also the human elements: the farms, homesteads, and orchards?* And yet this was an artificial division. *After all, on the Made Worlds, human beings made everything except the rocks.*

He had been to Larrenport twice before, both times on conferences, and had, each time, been struck by the town's geometry. The town was on a half circle of steep cliffs facing south and was split into two almost symmetrical parts by a sheer-sided gorge. On one of the best-protected bays of eastern Menaya, Larrenport had long served as a port and provided vital ferry links to the few communties scattered around the long Henelen Archipelago of over a thousand jagged-peaked islands that stretched almost as far as the equator. *In other words, it is a quiet town on what was once the quietest part of the Assembly.*

As he thought about Larrenport, Merral remembered that his aged Great-Aunt Namia, having outlived her expectations of dying in early spring, was still in an intensive nursing home there. *Well,* he thought, *if I get the time I will visit her.*

What with two stops and a two-hour time-zone shift, it was just before six o'clock local time when the descent into Larrenport began, and Merral caught a glimpse of the deep and precipitous-sided gorge that bisected the town. The airport was on the western part of the plateau, and after a struggle against wayward wind gusts from the sea, the plane landed gently.

"Felenert Terrace?" Merral asked a blonde clerk at the reception desk, reading the address off the envelope Corradon had given him.

"Top end of Sunset Side," she answered, with a ready smile.

"'Sunset Side'?"

"Oh, sorry," she said, giving him an apologetic look, "you're from out of town. *Sunset* is the eastern side. *Sunrise* is the western side. You're one or the other in Larrenport."

"I see," he replied, feeling that the last phrase sounded like some sort of local idiom, and walked over to where a bus with "Larrenport (East)" marked on its destination screen stood waiting. Ten minutes later, having crossed the five-hundred-meter-long suspension bridge, it paused at the crest of the plateau and Merral got off. He could carry what luggage he had in one hand and felt that after the hours in the plane, he needed the exercise.

As the bus disappeared down the first of the hairpin bends into the town, Merral went over to the stone wall and leaned on it, looking down at the rows of neat, gray-roofed houses broken up by clusters of trees that, in a dozen rows, dropped down to the blue sea nearly three hundred meters below. He looked beyond the houses at the white-flecked waters stretching out ahead, at the clustered shipping in the harbor complex and the white wakes of the vessels entering and leaving. In the middle distance, the great black snake of Fircorta Isle that gave the town its natural protection against storms and tsunami stretched across the waters. Beyond that lay the white-tinged waters of the open ocean that stretched out into the hazy distance, and on the very horizon a dark peak like a broken tooth rose out of the water; Merral recognized the nearest island of the Henelen Archipelago.

I love this world. I've fought for it before and I'll fight for it again.

Then—mindful of his recent ankle wound—he walked slowly down a line of steep steps between the houses, enjoying the early evening warmth and salt air. The steps were almost empty; a gull perched on a wall flew away as he approached and a cat scurried silently for cover at the sound of his feet. As he descended, Merral became conscious of the stillness of the town. He listened harder, hearing only the voices of children playing behind walled gardens, the soft chatter oozing out from behind opened windows, and from far below, the melancholy hoot as a heavy freighter made its way out of the harbor.

Merral felt troubled. There seemed to be something wrong about this town, but he found himself unable to say what it was. There was not the bustle he had expected; for all the brilliant evening sunlight, Larrenport seemed like a town over which a shadow hung.

My own strained imagination, he told himself. *Anyway, why shouldn't a town be subdued days after the greatest calamity in the planet's history?* Yet these thoughts did not reassure him.

Eventually, Merral found a street of three-story, balconied houses labeled "Felenert Terrace" and, at the number he had been given, stepped inside the weather porch and pressed the doorbell. There was no answer. Merral opened the door.

"Anybody home?" he called.

As his words echoed along the white walls of the hallway with its carefully hung seascapes, his eye was caught by a slip of card displayed on a message board. The handwritten note, signed by Daniel Sterknem, simply said, *While my wife is away visiting her family, I'm staying down on the* Miriama.

Closing the door carefully behind him, Merral walked on and turned down a new set of winding steps. After a few minutes of descent, he began to feel again that there was something oppressive in the town's silence. It was almost with relief that he saw four youngsters sitting on a wall at the bottom of the next flight of steps, swinging their feet idly.

"Evening," Merral called out as he approached.

One of the boys, no older, Merral guessed, than thirteen or fourteen, stared inquisitively at him. "You from Rise Side?" he asked in a sharp voice.

Rise Side? It took Merral a moment before he realized that he was being asked if he was from the Sunrise Side, the western half of the bay.

"Does it matter?" he inquired, slightly perturbed at both the nature and the tone of the question.

The answer was sharp. "You're one or the other."

"Actually neither," answered Merral. "I'm from Ynysmant."

"Ah, let 'im pass," muttered one of the other boys, and they returned to kicking their feet against the wall.

Merral shrugged and walked on, his feeling of unease deepening. A few minutes later, he came out by the lowest line of houses. The seafront lay ahead of him. He began walking eastward along the promenade, heading toward the harbor and the boats. He passed a few people walking in the evening sun, but they gave him no greeting other than rather formal nods of acknowledgement and distant, cool smiles. *How strange,* he thought, beginning to wonder more about this town. *Is it subdued, or is there something worse going on?*

In the port area, the first vessels Merral came to were small sail craft, each labeled with the school, street, or even congregation it belonged to. As he walked by them Merral, still troubled by the *something* that hung over the town, caught the sounds of the wind rattling cables and cleats, of the hulls creaking, of the small waves slopping against sides, and of chains clinking. There was, he reflected, something timeless about ports. Jason, Ulysses, Columbus, and Cook would have, with only the slightest adjustment, soon been quite at home here. *True,* he decided, *they would wonder at our sea's lower salinity, marvel at our artificially generated tides, and doubtless be frustrated by the strangeness of our moonless night sky. Yet surely, on whatever world it occurred, the sea is the sea?*

Passing beyond the sail craft area, Merral came to the main part of the harbor. Here larger vessels were moored to a maze of quays and hoverers, and smaller boats lay beached on ramps while an extraordinary array of cranes, gantries, and servicing engines worked on them. Ahead of him, he saw a big, silver, six-legged transporter leaning at an odd angle against a large red cylinder on wheels. There was a cluster of men standing around peering at the interlocked machines, and Merral decided that he would ask them the way to the *Miriama*.

"Evening," he said.

Heads turned toward him, and there was a ragged chorus of greetings in response. Yet despite the words, Merral felt strangely aware of looks that did not seem as welcoming as he would have expected.

"What's up?" he said, trying to make conversation.

"Machine's amiss," a man said. "This spider here hit the tanker."

"That's odd."

"Telling me," a second man said. "Could have been nasty, only Malc here hit the manual override. Shut it off before it did any real damage."

"Has it ever happened before?" Merral asked.

"Nah," the first man said. "Machines always work, don't they? That's what they're designed for."

"That always used to be the case."

How very odd, thought Merral, trying to resist the temptation to look up to where the Gate should have stood if it had not been destroyed. But someone else made the connection for him.

"It's 'cause of the Gate," said a third man.

"What do you mean?" asked someone else.

There was a shrug. "Dunno. But if the Gate can go, so can a spider. Figures, right?"

"An interesting thought," Merral said, oddly anxious to move on. "Anyway, I'm looking for a ship called the *Miriama*. Where can I find it?"

"Can't miss it," someone said, gesturing with a jerk of a large thumb. "Over there. The only orange vessel round here."

Ten minutes later, after skirting the area where the big cargo and passenger ferries for the islands were berthed, Merral came to the *Miriama*. As he got closer, it seemed to him obvious that this dumpy, businesslike ship with *OCEANOGRAPHY* written in man-high black letters on the lurid orange sides could only be a research vessel. The strangely smooth hull—he presumed of some high-strength durapolymer—was broken by a sharp, titanium alloy, ice-breaking prow; the masts had an abundance of strange aerials; and aft of the cabin the deck was covered with an array of drogues, submersible samplers, winches, and davits. A small launch under a pair of davits hung above the ship's stern.

The ship appeared deserted, and Merral climbed up the gangplank onto the deck, feeling the high-friction flooring surface grip his feet and noticing the numerous dents and scratches on the surfaces.

"Hello?" he called out. There was no answer and he looked round, seeing the terraced houses of the town staring down at him.

"Hello?" he called out more loudly.

Suddenly he saw a face at the window of the bridge, and moments later, a doorway swung open. The head of a man with unruly but sparse and receding gray hair, wild turquoise eyes, and a thin, stubbly gray beard peered at him from the top of a stairway.

"I'm looking for Captain Sterknem," Merral shouted.

"Wait," the figure called out. He clumped down the stairway and walked over. The man's bulky frame was dressed in old, stained blue overalls that were held in place by a wide belt from which an array of tools hung.

Merral found himself staring at the man's face, noticing the etched lines round the eyes and mouth, the rough, reddened skin, and the small white scars visible beneath the beard. *He must be in his fifties, and I'll bet he's spent most of those years at sea.*

"Captain Sterknem?"

"I suppose that's me," the man grunted. He came a few steps closer, and Merral saw that his eyes showed both intelligence and caution. *A closed and reserved man,* he thought, suddenly reminded of his troubled uncle, Barrand.

"Merral Stefan D'Avanos, forester," he said, extending his hand.

"Daniel Klaus Sterknem, captain, Farholme Oceanographic Service," was the response, and with it came a brief but powerful handshake. The hands were large and marked with numerous tiny scratches and cuts.

They looked at each other for a moment, and Merral decided that there seemed to be something strangely wintry about the man, as if long years among ice floes had transmitted their character to him.

"Not from these parts, are you?" the captain asked, tilting his head slightly as if to give him a better view.

"Ynysmant," Merral replied. "But does it matter where I come from?"

"Not to me," was the terse response, "but some people seem to think so these days. But how can I help you?"

"I have a message from Isterrane for you."

Merral handed over the letter from Corradon. Shaking his head, Captain Sterknem took the letter with reluctance and slit it open with a knife from his belt. He read the single sheet silently and then, without comment, folded it up and put it in the breast pocket of his overalls.

There was a pause and then he turned to Merral. "Look," he said, his weather-beaten face reminding Merral of some wave-washed piece of driftwood, "excuse me being blunt—even rude. I told Dr. Clemant everything that was significant weeks ago. We, the crew, apologized. It's all over. I'm trying to forget it. It was a bad move."

As the green-blue eyes locked with his, it suddenly came to Merral in a flash of certainty that this man had seen something that had troubled him and still did. Merral uttered a little prayer under his breath and then began talking, groping for words as he went on.

"Look, Captain, I'm here because I know there is a problem. A few of us do. We know that there is something bad up north. Really bad. Something that we in the Assembly have never met before. *Things*. And to counter it—to counter *them*—we need to know. We need to know what you know. Please?"

For a moment, the only acknowledgment that Merral had even been heard was a faint widening of the sea-colored eyes. The big man gave a soft sigh so deep it was almost a groan. Then he gestured toward the cabins. "Follow me," he said. "I suppose we'd better talk."

CHAPTER 5

The captain led Merral through the watertight doorway into the lower part of the bridge, where Merral glimpsed a complexity of screens and consoles that reminded him this ship was as much a laboratory as anything at his own Planning Institute. Then they descended a ladder and went aft along a corridor with the names of the crew on the doors.

As if answering some unspoken question, the captain said over his shoulder, "I have lots of work to do at the moment. We are supposed to be listing all NFS parts that may need replacing in the next fifty years."

"NFS?"

"Not heard it yet? Oh, you will. It will haunt you and me to the end of our working lives. 'Non-Farholme Sourced'—NFS—the problem bits."

The door at the end of the corridor opened to reveal a low-roofed kitchen with a mess room attached. Two open portholes let in light.

Merral glanced around the mess room. In the best Assembly tradition, a good deal of effort had been made to make it pleasant and even homely, with genuine wood paneling and a collection of decent landscape paintings on the walls. He presumed that in the bad weather and short days that the *Miriama*'s more northerly winter voyages must encounter, an attractive eating room was considered a vital feature.

"You hungry?" the captain asked, with an abrupt gesture of a big hand toward the cooker complex. "I normally eat about now, even without having days of fasting. I get up early."

Merral looked at his watch. "Why not?" It felt early, but he hadn't yet adjusted to Eastern Menaya Time.

The captain nodded as if to himself, then turned his rugged face to Merral. "Look, I'll tell you what happened, right? All of it, including the stuff I didn't tell Advisor Clemant. But after supper. Not before. That all right?"

"Fine by me. I may be able to help you."

"Hope so," Captain Sterknem muttered. "It's bugged me." He looked around. "You got somewhere to stay tonight?"

"No. I was going to knock on a few doors when I had finished talking with you. As usual."

"Of course." The captain paused. "Better still, I'll give you a cabin. The company won't hurt me. Meantime, come and choose some food out of the store."

He stopped and twitched his back as if troubled by an old injury. "Personally, I ain't eating any crayfish or lobster, though."

"I've never heard of a sailor refusing to eat invertebrates. We kill them humanely too."

The captain's tight-lipped expression seemed to hint at something hidden. "Forester, I'm just being humane to myself. But let's have a look at what we have."

In the end, they agreed on a bean, vegetable, and cheese casserole recipe, and after finding the ingredients in a well-stocked freezer, Merral started the cooking while the captain went off to close down hatches on deck.

• ◆ •

A quarter of an hour later, just as Merral was deciding that the food was ready, the seaman came back.

"I've closed everything up. Oh, and if you try and leave in the night, I should warn you I've pulled up the gangway."

Merral detected a hint of embarrassment in his voice. "Any reason?"

"Same as the lobsters, Forester," he said with a strange, deep, and injured look. "Let's just say I feel better that way." They sat down at the table and, after giving thanks, began to eat. Captain Sterknem began to thaw out as the meal progressed, and soon it was "Merral" and "Daniel" rather than "Forester" and "Captain." The barriers, though, did not drop entirely, and Merral felt certain that there were things that his host was not ready to talk about. So he let Daniel lead the conversation in his clipped, almost staccato speech, and for a long time they talked only about the loss of the Gate and its probable effects on Farholme life and culture.

Sitting opposite the captain at the other end of the thin table, and aware of the ever-present gentle sway of the ship underneath him, Merral was struck by how nearly it was an enjoyable meal. Yet despite the cozy nature of the room and the increasing openness of his host, he did not feel at ease. *There are shadows about,* he thought, *both around this man and this town.*

As they ate, the sun went down and the evening light flooding in through the west-facing porthole reddened, making the room glow and casting long, distorted shadows across the table. Finally, with the fruit pie dessert over, Daniel began, at last, to talk about the work of the *Miriama*.

"Extraordinary, really. The rest of these ships—" here he gestured with a big hand toward the rest of the harbor—"avoid storms, currents, unstable water masses, gas seeps. We seek them out. That's why she is built like she is. Capable of surviving even if we capsize. Not that I want to try it."

He rubbed his sparse beard, sipped his drink, and stared into the distance. "This is the last ocean, Merral. If there are any oceans beyond here, beyond Worlds' End . . . they will be different. Funny," he sighed, "that idea always used to excite me. To be the sailor navigating the farthermost ocean. To sail the ultimate edgeward sea."

I sympathize, thought Merral, recognizing the common challenge of the Made Worlds. But he noticed the past tense. "Does it still?"

"No," the captain answered after a long time. "Not after what happened. . . . I am now afraid of what I may find."

Then he stood up and, walking heavily, went over to the portholes and slid covers smoothly over them. As the crimson light went and the room slipped into a soft darkness, a low yellow illumination came on around the room.

"Night is coming," the captain said and seemed to shiver.

Then in a slightly unsteady way, he sat on a corner seat. Merral rose from the table, sat opposite him, and waited. Finally, with a grimace, the captain spoke. "The trip. You really want to know all about it?"

"Yes. That's why I'm here. Take your time."

Daniel sipped his drink. "A ten-man crew. No women on this voyage. A two-week trip. Our orders were to sail a precisely defined course—north to the Nannalt Delta and then eastward over Tarrent's Rise. A series of zigzags. No, I don't plan the course. Rassumsen in the Institute does that. *Stop*." He raised a hand. "You know about Made World oceanography?"

"A little."

"The oceans are the most important thing on a Made World. Most overlooked. Transmit energy, water, nutrients. Switch a water current off and the climate goes crazy. Very delicate, almost chaotic. So we have to watch them carefully. That's what we're about. Physical oceanography. The physics and chemistry of seawater and the seafloor. We were mostly looking at seawater chemistry. *Not* biology. Got that? That's important to my story."

"Go ahead."

"So we were up at the delta mouth first. We knew from the color of the water there had been flooding as soon as we got near. So much mud in the water, we were sailing red-brown seas. From the lavas. You've seen it?"

"Only from the air."

"Yes, well, it often occurs at that time of year. But this year, of course, it was particularly bad because of the wet winter. Anyway, our task was to put out a kilometer-long array of sensors. Across the area where the fresh water from the delta was mixing with the seawater.

Thirty-meter-long sensor tubes, each separated by forty-meter gaps, all linked by optic fiber. Leave it out for twenty-four hours. You get the picture?"

"Yes."

"But when we got there we realized there was going to be a problem. There was a lot of debris in the water. Wood, tree trunks. All that stuff washed out to sea." He shrugged. "So we anchored, put out the array in the afternoon, and kept a watch for anything striking it. That was hard, as it was misty. And cold. The only good thing was that it wasn't raining and the sea was smooth."

Daniel paused. "Anyway, I got woken about two in the morning by one of the men on watch. Lemart, Billy Lemart, lives on the Rise Side. A whole tree had got caught in the outer sampling array." For a long time he said nothing, his lips moving silently. "So I dressed and we looked at it. We agreed that we needed to clear it before it wrecked the equipment. So I left the officer on watch in charge, and three of us decided to go and try and free it with the launch.

"I want you to understand what it was like. Cold, mist patches rising off the water. A faint starlight. A cone of silver light from the ship on the water. We get out there—seven hundred meters out—and we see this tree wrapped on the cable. Massive thing, half as long as the ship, big roots. Fir of some sort. . . . Sorry, Forester, I don't know the name." He paused again and closed his eyes for a moment. "The plan was easy. Get out to the far end, free it, and tug it away. I got out the all-purpose cutting-saw tool we have. The combination arc-and-vibration P20 unit. You know the thing?"

"For trees? Never use it. The fire risk is too great."

"Ah—of course. Well, that's not a problem twenty kilometers from land. Anyway there's me, Billy Lemart, and Lawrence Trest. Trest takes the cutting tool, I manage the launch's lighting, and Lemart has the helm. You have to be careful. If he cuts the tree so it rolls the wrong way, we could lose the launch. And us." He stopped, sipped his wine again, and wiped his lips with his tongue. "You've got the picture, then?"

"Yes," Merral answered slowly, feeling a prickling of unease.

"It's dark and cold. Anyway, Trest cuts away one branch. *Splash*. Then suddenly he yells out, 'Cap'n, there's an animal in the branches!'"

Merral felt himself go rigid.

"I point the light at the tree and—" Daniel swallowed and closed his eyes, as if in pain. "In it . . . is a *thing*. Moving. At first I think it's a bear. Then I realize it's like nothing I've ever seen. Perhaps half my size, brown, and shiny."

"Shiny?" Merral heard himself say, his own voice sounding strange.

Daniel opened his eyes wide in a look of acknowledgement. "*Ah*," he said in a long, ragged whisper as their eyes met, "so you have seen it too?"

He stared at his glass, seemed to realize that it was empty, and put it on the floor with an exaggerated carefulness. "It was hard to see really. Ten meters or so away. But it was shiny; glistening in the spotlight. The weirdest, most horrible thing. You could make out plates on it. Brown, gleaming—some sort of strange limbs. An odd brown head. Moving very slowly. Toward us . . ."

"Go on," Merral said as gently as he could.

"Like a big insect. A fifty-kilo cockroach. You could hear the thing hissing. None of us liked what we were seeing.

"Lawrence steps back and starts praying. Weird thing was, I could see its breath. Weird—for an insect, that is."

Suddenly the captain exhaled noisily and the words began running out. "Then, all of a sudden, this *thing* leaps at the boat. Just like that. Weird arms up in the air, clattering. As if they were mechanical. Billy screams. The thing lands in the prow, rocks the boat, and lashes out at Lawrence. An attack. Lawrence runs back, nearly overturns the boat. Drops the cutting tool. Now this thing, brown plates, scales— whatever—is in the boat. Like a lobster the devil's made. Then it's coming at me. So, I do the only thing I can think of and I pick up the cutting tool. And as the thing moves toward me, I flick the beam on."

Merral shuddered, imagining all too clearly the cockroach-beast in the boat held at bay by a meter-long, pencil-thin beam of glowing, high-temperature gas.

"For a moment I thought it was going to back off. Then it jumps. Waves its arms at me and then moves at me. With these weird hands that look like they are crossed with an electrician's wire cutters. And—"

He stopped and stretched out his arms on either side of him as if to brace himself against the cabin walls. Then, with his voice slower, the captain spoke again. "And I hit it with the beam. There's an awful scream and a smell of burning. The flames are all round its face and it leaps in the air, screaming. I keep the beam on it because I'm terrified, and it lands on the edge of the boat. Thrashes around there in flames. Then it crawls over the edge and drops into the water."

His jaw trembled. "And Billy is yowling and Lawrence is yelling at me and I realize I've still got the cutting tool blade on. So I turn it off and I see that we're all shaking like leaves in a gale, and I focus the light into the water where this thing is thrashing about with steam coming off it. And there's blood all over the side of the boat. And then this thing stops moving and just lies there, bobbing up and down. Face down, with this strange corrugated brown back. And there's blood in the water."

Far away a ship's siren sounded. When it had died away, the captain began again. "So we stare at the body. Lawrence is just saying 'mutant insect, mutant insect' over and over again. Billy is gibbering, and I'm wondering what to do."

He sighed. "But I figure now we did the wrong thing. We should have hauled it back onboard, piled it in a big sealable bag, thrown out half our food, and put it in the freezer. Let Biology look at it. Well, you can guess what we did, can't you?"

"Yes. Easily." Merral realized his mouth was dry. "Just let it float away and washed off the blood?"

Daniel nodded, and Merral could see his pink tongue wrap round his lips. "Yes." His voice was thickened and slow now. "We said we were *physical* oceanography, see, not biological. And we just decided that it's some insect thing, right? Some mutant, Made World arthropod, some crustacean monstrosity. That's why I don't eat the things now. Only, as I stare at it, it begins to roll over. 'It's sinking,' says Lawrence, and his teeth are chattering. And as it does I see the head properly."

He rubbed his cheeks with his hands as if rubbing soap into his beard. "This is the worst bit. You see, it's the head—the face—that's burned the most. And as it sinks, slowly, I can see that it has a skull. White bone, braincase, jaws. A skull. Like you and me."

"*Ah.*"

"Yes." A muscle twitched in the side of Daniel's face. "It wasn't an insect. So that's why we decided to keep quiet. We figured—well, I figured—that I'd killed some poor mutated human. We swilled out the boat, got the tree trunk free of the cable in double-quick time. Promised secrecy to each other. By dawn, we were kilometers away. So there you are. I killed it."

Merral stood up and stretched himself, more to give himself a chance to think than because he needed to. He walked to the window and then back to his seat.

"Let me try and put your mind at rest," he said after a moment. He took out his diary, found on it an image of two cockroach-beasts, and showed it to Daniel. "Is this it?"

The seaman gasped. "Two more?"

"Yes. I think there are still others left." He switched the image off and sat down. "I have also met these creatures, and under circumstances like the one you described, I too killed one. It was either him or me."

The eyes widened. "You're serious? You are not just saying that?"

"Can you imagine what a nip from those hands would look like on an ankle?" Merral lifted his right trouser leg and rolled down his sock, exposing the red line of the still-healing wound. "My boot protected me a bit, but it still cut in."

He covered his ankle again and looked at Daniel, who was shaking his head in disbelief. "No, Captain, whatever you killed was not human. It had human elements, but it was, in a way that we do not understand, a fabricated creature. And evil. I think it would have killed you and all your crew if it had had the chance. I think you can rest in peace about your action."

"Thank you. Thank you!" The captain seemed close to tears. "Thank you very much indeed. You have no idea—" He shook his head.

"I do," answered Merral, feeling an intense pity for this man. "Oh, I do. Actually I can guess your feelings better than most people. After all, I did the same as you. But in my case it was very obvious that these were hostile, evil things."

"So . . . what are they?"

Merral hesitated, then decided that this man had earned the right to know far more than he knew already. So, omitting the details of the spiritual malaise that seemed to have affected Barrand and the Herrandown community, he described as much as he knew of the two types of intruders seen near the Lannar Crater. At the end, they agreed that it was perfectly likely that a creature, unfamiliar with the way Farholme's rivers could suddenly rise, might all too easily have been caught in a flash flood and washed out to sea.

Daniel shook his head in disbelief. "I was horrified about what I had done. Now I am less so. Instead, I am appalled at what has been done in the making of these things."

"Yes," answered Merral, "and there many questions lie."

"But are they a danger? with the Gate gone?"

"We do not know. Their losses have been heavy. They have not been reported much beyond the area of the Lannar Crater. We are working on the problem. That is why I came here."

"Altered *humans*," Daniel muttered in disgust. "And the Gate gone. These are strange days."

"Indeed," answered Merral. "But it's as well that as few as possible know how strange they are. And if I may ask you more questions— what happened on the rest of the trip?"

"Ah," Daniel sighed and shook his head. "Yes, well, from then on it seemed like things went wrong. Only the three of us knew, and we said nothing, which was hard. We cleared the delta and then the wind got up. Even with stabilizers running at full compensation it was rough. The wind was from the north and it was bitter out; there was spray lashing over the prow, night and day. The ice covered the deck and the equipment; the antislip surface was useless. Then we got the main submersible sampler snagged on a recovery and had to send a diver down. He got his suit cut and nearly froze from exposure. Then we had a storm and a big wave that almost swamped the ship. And somehow a ventilation hatch was open and we got water all through the ship. And the electrics started playing up. Oh, and everybody started going down with colds. It was a dreadful trip. Worst I've known. And the thing was, they all started blaming me or each other."

"I see." Merral looked around, imagining ten people in this room with the floor tossing and heaving and all arguing with each other. "And that's when the allowance idea came up?"

"Yes."

"Who thought it up?"

"No one will admit it. Each side blames the other."

An insight flickered in Merral's brain and he tried to grasp it, but the captain continued speaking and he lost it. "Anyway, when we got back, someone asked me to raise it as a suggestion and—like a fool—I did. I can't think what came over me."

He gave another deep sigh. "So the rest of the voyage felt like a curse. There is an old sailor's poem, from before the Intervention. I only know it in the Communal translation as 'The Venerable Sailor.' The original is Alt-Dutch or Ancient English."

"English. 'The Rime of the Ancient Mariner.'"

"That's it. Anyway, you remember how in the days of sail, the sailor shoots an albatross with an arrow and the ship gets cursed as a result. Strange poem. You never know with the ancients whether they really believed these things. It kept coming back to me." He gave a tired smile. "But tonight I think I can sleep as a more relieved man. I will tell Lawrence and Billy when I see them. Privately, of course."

"So," Merral asked, as gently as he could, "you think it's all over now?"

"Yes," came the answer. "It was a temporary aberration. A bad voyage. It's over."

I hope so, thought Merral but stayed silent.

The silence that followed was broken by Daniel stifling a yawn. "Excuse me!" he said. "I was up early. But come, let me show you your cabin."

He led Merral beyond the mess room to a cabin so wide that it seemed to extend across the width of the ship. There was a big wallscreen on one side and a variety of sporting and exercise gear.

"The recreation room," Daniel commented. "You can hardly run around the deck in bad weather. Your room is through here."

"Very nice," observed Merral. Then his eye was suddenly caught by a notice board. On it was a large white sheet divided in two, with columns of marks underneath. *A score sheet,* he thought idly, then stopped, his eyes riveted by the twin words at the top: *Sunrise* and *Sunset*.

Trying to make his voice sound unconcerned, Merral turned to the captain. "You divided the crew into two teams?"

"Have done for years."

"And it's easy enough to divide the crew up? I mean on the basis of where they come from?"

"Yes, we've been split neatly into Rise Siders and Sunsetters for some years."

"So 'you're one or the other in Larrenport'?"

The captain smiled back in a tired manner. "That's what they say. I gather you've heard the phrase?"

"Yes."

Daniel shrugged, walked over, and opened a door, revealing a small cabin with a single bed. "I hope it's all right?" he asked.

"Fine," Merral answered, glimpsing the town's lights visible through the porthole. "Can I ask you another question, Captain?"

"Why not?"

"Yes, you see, I couldn't help wondering—really it's none of my business—why you sleep on the boat when you have a home not far away?"

A soft "hmm" was all the answer that Merral received.

"Is it," he suggested as sensitively as he could, "that you feel safer with the gangway up and the hatches closed than in a house with open doors?"

"Yes," came back the tentative answer. "That's it."

Merral, staring at him, discerned a look of embarrassment in his eyes.

"But I think I'll go back tomorrow. My wife will be back then anyway." Then, with a wish that Merral would enjoy a good night's sleep, he left.

•—•—•

By the time that Merral awoke, showered, and dressed the next morning, Daniel was already up and working in one of the cabins beyond the mess room. The captain joined him for coffee and breakfast and then led Merral up into the deck. Above the town the sun was shining between gaps in patchy gray clouds. The captain lowered the gangway and stood by it.

"Thanks, Merral," he said, giving him a firm handshake. "Thanks so much. I guess I can now try to forget what happened on that voyage. I can put it behind me."

Merral stared beyond him at the twin halves of the divided town before them, the left hand side gleaming in the morning light. *Sunrise and Sunset*, he thought, remembering that he had one more question.

"Yes, Daniel, try to do that. Put it behind you. But something comes back to me. Yesterday you said about the crew problems on the voyage—what was it? 'Each side blames the other.' Did you mean that this sports division, well, sort of spread into everyday matters?"

"Yes, I suppose so," Daniel answered, his voice charged with reluctance.

"But only really during the trip we've been talking about? Never before?"

"No—I guess not. All the bad weather seemed to make things worse. We were more cramped. And the colds—but it's over." He hesitated. "Isn't it?"

Merral glanced at the captain and saw he was gazing with a troubled expression at the split town. In a flash of intuition, he realized that Daniel was worried that it wasn't over. Had he, perhaps, sensed something of the atmosphere of the *Miriama*'s voyage in his own town?

"I don't know, Captain," Merral said. "Let's pray that it's so."

•-•-•

As he had expected, Merral found a bus stop at the gate of the harbor. A number of people who looked as if they had come off an overnight shift greeted Merral in an affable fashion and, when they learned he was a visitor from Ynysmant, offered him advice on how to get to the High Cliff Intensive Nursing Center where Great-Aunt Namia was.

"Easy enough to find," said one woman. "Straight off the bridge. Turn right and it's at the top of Rise Side at the cliff edge. Looks down on us. Typical." The tone of disapproval in her voice caught Merral's attention.

"Why, er, typical?"

She waved a hand dismissively to the west. "They don't have the docks and harbor, see. Risers pride themselves on being better because of it."

Merral tried, with difficulty, to bury his alarm. "This feeling they have—or you think they have—of being superior. Has it always been like this?"

She looked at him warily. "Oh no. Only the last two months. Suddenly."

"I see," he said, and he was going to ask whether there was any reason, when a bus turned the corner.

"Here's your bus," the woman said sharply. "Yes. Ever since Easter they have been getting so above themselves. Well, I really don't know where it will end."

As the bus went up over the last of the hairpin bends, Merral looked back down to the ships, trying to see the orange dot of the *Miriama*.

"It's over," the captain had said. But Merral knew he hadn't believed it.

Now *he* didn't either.

High on the western side of Larrenport, Merral bought some lilies from a flower shop and then, his mind preoccupied by events, strolled over to the High Cliff Intensive Nursing Center. The center and its grounds, embraced in a protective semicircle of beech trees and evergreens, lay tucked just below the plateau edge. Looking at it, Merral felt that this elevated setting on the edge of the cliff was almost symbolic, as if it were easier to pass from earth to heaven from up here.

Halfway along the gravel driveway he stopped, gazing beyond the rosebushes and down to the town and the bay far beyond. Far out to sea, beyond multitudes of turning gulls, a belt of cloud was broken at the horizon so that a line of brilliant silver etched out the boundary of the sea and the sky. With an effort, Merral pushed his concerns out of his mind; in this twilight of her long and profitable earthly life, his great-aunt deserved his full attention.

He walked on to the reception office.

"Good morning; I've come to see Mrs. Namia Mena D'Avanos," he said to the fresh-complexioned nurse with a blonde ponytail who sat behind the desk.

She smiled up at him welcomingly with round, nut brown eyes. "Oh yes. Are you a near relative?" she asked, in the sort of smooth and soothing voice that Merral felt was entirely appropriate for dealing with the elderly.

"Fairly," he answered, wondering how near you were when a hundred years separated you. "She's a great-aunt. I bring her family greetings. You know her?"

"Of course. We know them all." She smiled again, but something at the edges of her mouth hinted at some difficulty. "But let me call the doctor to take you over to her," she said and pressed a button.

"Do I need to talk to the doctor?"

Her smile was disarming. "I'll think she'll want to talk to you." She nodded at the flowers Merral was carrying. "Nice bouquet. But you aren't local, are you?"

"No, visiting from Ynysmant. Came in yesterday."

"Ah, up on the lake, eh? Stay anywhere nice last night?"

"On a ship in the docks, funnily enough."

"A pity. You should have stayed over on Rise Side."

There it was again.

"Rise Side. Is it better?" he asked, peering at the smooth face and the brown eyes.

"We think so. Quieter. Of course, they make all the fuss about East Side being the real heart of Larrenport. But West is best."

Reluctant to answer, Merral replied with what he hoped was seen as an equivocal nod.

A paneled door opened and an elegant auburn-haired lady in her forties, wearing a white jacket with a Diagnostic Medical Unit poking out of a pocket, came over and introduced herself. She and Merral exchanged greetings, and then she led him down a covered walkway to a cluster of rooms.

Outside a doorway decorated with hand-painted creeping red roses, she stopped and beckoned Merral close to her.

"It's an odd case," she said, in a low, confiding tone. *"Odd."*

"Is it?" he answered. "I thought she was just, well, *old*. One hundred and twenty-four. I presume all sorts of things start packing up at that age."

"Hmm. Yes and no. Physically, she's remarkable; you'll be blessed if you have some of her genes. No, it's just that Mrs. D'Avanos is suffering from an odd set of psychological symptoms. Very strange . . ."

"What sort of things?" Merral felt a shadow of unease fall across him again. *But this,* he told himself, *must surely be something else. It has to be.*

The doctor frowned and adjusted her jacket. "A sort of depression. Anxiety attacks. The pastor and I have a dossier. . . ." She hesitated. "No, I think it's better you talk to her. Then—if you want—you can talk to me. But I just thought I ought to warn you."

"I see."

She looked at him carefully. "When you last saw her . . . was she fine?"

"Yes. I saw her last autumn. I was here for a conference."

She paused and he was aware of her green eyes scrutinizing him. "May I ask," she said gently, "how did she view her death?"

Merral felt himself staring back at her. "Well, we barely discussed it. But she had a perfectly normal view of it." He was tempted to add *of course,* but somehow *of course* didn't seem to apply as much as it used to.

"Great-Aunt Namia was," he said, remembering what they had talked about, "looking forward to going Home, to going to be with Jesus. Which she expected to be in the spring. She was awaiting the Resurrection and the new heaven and the new earth. And a new body—she was particularly looking forward to that. She had been active well into her nineties, but that was a long time ago."

She nodded sympathetically. "So we have heard. We had her in just after Easter and didn't expect her to stay. Most people come here for the last few days or weeks of life. She was slipping away, as they do, but then something happened. Now she's fighting it." A look of troubled perplexity crossed her face.

"Look, I'll leave you with her. But, if you get any insights, see me on the way out? Please?"

Then she turned and walked up the corridor, looking deep in thought.

Merral knocked and, hearing no answer, slipped into the room. His aunt lay propped up in bed, facing away from the door and apparently staring at a painting of a mountain landscape on a wall.

Hesitating to disturb her, Merral looked around the room, noting the pastel blue walls, the discreetly hidden medical equipment, the read-out panels high above the bed, and the framed family images on the chests. The windows stretching from floor to ceiling at the end of the room looked seaward and were open a fraction, so that the white gauze curtains swayed gently in the breeze.

"Great-Aunt?" Merral called out softly, and as he walked over to her, she turned slowly and stiffly and looked up at him.

He was immediately struck by how delicate and pale she had become. It was her paleness that struck him most, and it occurred to him that an artist could have painted her faithfully using only a palette of grays, whites, and blues.

Her wan lips twitched and tired bleached-blue eyes smiled at him.

"Merral, dear! How lovely. Come and kiss me." The voice was slight and brittle.

Merral carefully put the lilies on the table where she could see them, pulled a chair up to the bed, bent over the fragile figure, and kissed a powder-dry cheek.

"Let me sit up more. Sit back a bit," she whispered between bloodless lips. "Bed, more upright, please."

There was a faint whine of motors and the top part of the bed tilted. "Bed, stop!" she called and the motion ended.

"Merral, now turn off that camera, please." She gestured at a small wall-mounted lens. "I can't order that."

He rose and tapped the switch below it.

"Why, thank you, dear. I don't like being watched all the time."

He was suddenly aware of the sensor bands on her neck and wrist, of the way her white hair was tied back, of the soft embroidered white nightdress.

His great-aunt gave another thin, forced smile. "So tell me all the news. About everything and everybody."

"Are you up to it?" he asked.

"Ah," she said, with almost a snort of amusement. "Look at that book on my side table and tell me what you think of it."

He picked up the white book, opened it, and was faced with pages of strange characters. "Let me guess," he said. "Your Old-Mandarin Bible?"

"Indeed so. And I still read it daily. Keeps my mind going. You have to keep up your Historics. But—" a frown crossed the lined face—"it doesn't help. . . ."

She grimaced as if struck by pain. "Later. Tell me about Ynysmant. And the Gate exploding. I can hardly believe that. The family, though, first . . ."

•—•

After spending twenty minutes recounting matters to do with his father and mother in Ynysmant, his sisters and their families elsewhere, and other news, Merral looked searchingly at his great-aunt. "But how are you?"

She gave a wheezy sigh. "Not good," she whispered in a faint and pitiful voice.

Merral held her fragile, bony hand gently, watching as she screwed her old eyes up in misery. Suddenly the novel thought came to him that in his great-aunt, he saw a malignity in old age. At its best, he had always seen old age as a mellow autumnal ripening, and at its worst, as no more than a gentle fading out. It was the slow, soft draining of physical and mental powers; the yawning and dozing before the onset of that long sleep of the real person that extended until the Great Awakening. But now, as he looked at his great-aunt's pained face with a fierce stab of pity, Merral could see aging as the ancients had seen it: as some cruel force that ripped and gnawed at the very essence of what you were.

Namia spoke slowly. "Merral, I need to be honest with you. Can I?"

"Of course."

"I'm scared." Her hand shook.

"Of what?" he asked.

"Of dying, Merral. Oh, I know it's crazy, but I'm scared."

He squeezed the almost fleshless hand gently. "But you know the truth. Jesus loves you and died for you. Dying is going home to heaven—to the Father's house. He is waiting for you."

Her eyes watered, and he reached for an embroidered handkerchief and dabbed her eyes. There was something contagious about her tears, and he felt like weeping himself.

"I know it in my head," she said to him in a peculiar and distant tone. "But I can't feel it. I have no confidence. Supposing it's just dark forever? or that I just cease to exist?"

Merral stared at her. "It isn't dark. And you go to be with the King of the worlds. But, Great-Aunt, you have trusted him in the past for well over a century."

"Yes," she said weakly.

"I'm puzzled. I've never come across anything like it. You've prayed about it?"

"Yes," she sighed, but it was nearly a sob, "but I seem to get no answer."

"I see," Merral answered, feeling utterly inadequate. "When did it start?"

"I had been here a few days. I was expecting to go. Waiting for him to lift me away. I remember rather looking forward to it. It was the first spring day. It'd been such a long winter. I was sitting down there, in that chair, just watching the ships. Always liked that. One boat attracted my attention. A little thing coming in past the island. *That's like me,* I thought, *nearly ready to get into port.* But as I stared at it I felt there was a dark cloud over it. . . . And then the cloud came and hung over me. And I suddenly had a terrible fear that has never left me since. They gave me tablets for it."

She gave what was almost a whimper, and on the console above the bed Merral saw that a red light was flickering. "The tablets hide it, but it's still there. That's why I've held on till now." Her pale eyes seemed to widen, and her frail hand stiffened in his. "It's worse at night. I sleep with the light on."

There was a tap on the door and a male nurse glided in and came behind him.

"Sorry, Mr. D'Avanos," he whispered in his ear, "metabolic monitors indicate her stress levels are very high. We'd prefer to let them drop a bit. A mild sedative—"

"Very well," Merral answered, feeling suddenly angry with whatever it was that had so terribly afflicted this old woman at the end of her life, "but let me pray with her."

As the nurse retreated to the window, Merral prayed audibly over his great-aunt and was rewarded by a faint "Amen" from the pale lips.

"God bless you, Great-Aunt. Trust him."

She squeezed his hand feebly.

He rose to his feet and gestured the nurse over. Then slowly he walked to the door. Just as he was opening it, a thought struck him. "Oh, Great-Aunt, one question: the boat you watched. What color was it?"

The nurse looked at him, his face full of bewilderment.

"What a *strange* thing to ask, Merral," his great-aunt said slowly and faintly. "It was orange."

• ━ •

At the reception desk the nurse with the blonde ponytail and the round, dark brown eyes looked up at him. "I hope it wasn't too upsetting."

For a moment, Merral felt lost for words. "Yes," he answered. "I mean, it *was* alarming. I think I ought to talk to the doctor about what she said."

She nodded. "Thought so. Follow me."

As they walked along, Merral turned to her. "By the way, Nurse, I was struck by a comment you made earlier. That the Sunset Side believed it was the real heart of Larrenport. Since when have they been making a fuss about that?"

He caught an expression of mild embarrassment. "Six weeks, eight weeks maybe. It just seemed to start as the weather got warmer. But I was going to say to you that I've been wondering whether I should have said that."

"That's interesting. How so?"

"I was just thinking about it and it struck me that—well, if you let the business about one side of town being better or worse continue, then there was no telling where it would end."

Instinctively, Merral patted her gently on the arm. "Nurse, that's about the most sensible thing I've heard all day. You're right. *Don't* pass it on. Try and stop it. We have to fight it."

She turned to him, pale eyebrows raised in something close to alarm. "What's going on? Your great-aunt . . . ? The mood in the town . . . ? And now the Gate?"

"I don't really know," he answered. "But, hard as it may be to believe, the Lord still reigns."

After a moment's thought, she smiled slowly back at him. "I guess so. I never felt I needed reminding of that before." She gestured to another room. "The doctor is in there."

The doctor was reclining in an old armchair, drinking from a mug of coffee and staring into space.

"Ah, Forester D'Avanos. I thought I might see you. Do you want a drink? coffee, tea?"

"No, thanks. I'd better get over to the airport soon."

She scanned his face. "You saw the problem?"

"Oh, indeed. She's scared of dying. No," Merral corrected himself, "not of *dying,* but of being dead. She's scared of *death.*"

"Exactly. It's very sad. Very disturbing."

"Is she the only case?"

There was a long pause in which the doctor sipped her coffee and gazed ahead. Then she looked up at him with a frown. "No, there are others in the town. She was one of the first, but she was—is—an unusual woman. Very sensitive, perceptive, intuitive."

She looked at Merral as if comparing him to his great-aunt. "Yes, you have something of that. But any ideas about treatment? I was intending to call Central Geriatric Care on Ancient Earth." She shrugged. "Not a lot of hurry now. I can find nothing like this in our files. Nothing so deep or so permanent. It's not death as we have known it."

Merral shook his head. "Oh, you can find references to it," he said, and he was aware of her look of surprise. "Go back before the Intervention. You'll find it there. My guess is her symptoms were not atypical then. My memory suggests that there are hints of her mood in the Psalms."

The doctor gave a little start, her face squinting in thought. "Yes . . . I suppose so. But that is *very* odd."

"Yes. It is odd. My suggestion is to get the brightest spiritual advisor or counselor you can find here and let them dig some of the pre-2050 pastoral counseling material out of the Library."

He suddenly realized that he had already told her too much. "Look, I'd better go. You have my details with the nurse. Keep in touch."

She put her coffee down and rose slowly to her feet. "Yes, I think that's a good idea. But, surely—" She looked perplexed. "Surely, that age of humanity is long over?"

"Hmm," Merral said, moving toward the door. "That's what I used to think too."

•—•—•

He got to the airport earlier than he had expected and easily found himself a spare place on an early afternoon ferry flight to Ynysmant. Then, while the freighter was loading and being refueled, he found a quiet corner, took out some sheets of paper, and began writing his letter to Representative Corradon. Unlike his father, Merral had never been one for using pen and paper but now he felt it was time to get used to it.

He began by outlining, as precisely as he could, Captain Sterknem's account and suggested that Anya be informed of the relevant biological details. Then he recounted the curious divisions appearing in Larrenport and mentioned the problem he had heard of with the machines at the dock. Finally, he summarized his visit to

Great-Aunt Namia and her frame of mind. Then, after a long time thinking and choosing his words, he wrote the final sentences:

> *All these phenomena worry me in different ways. If they are interlinked—and the timing suggests that they are—then the implications are extremely disturbing.*
>
> *Yours, in the Service of the Assembly,*
>
> *Forester Merral Stefan D'Avanos*

Then he sealed his letter in an envelope, addressed it to Representative Corradon at Isterrane, marked it "private and personal," and handed it in at the airport office with a request for it to be urgently sent by courier.

• ◆ •

Merral arrived back at Ynysmant in the late afternoon and, deciding it was too late to go into the Planning Institute, walked into town along the causeway. Hearing the energetic chop-chop of the waters against the walls and feeling the wind and sun on his cheeks, Merral stopped to look at his hometown rising on its steep, dark mound out of the lake. Seeing its curving lines of red roofs, spires, and towers bathed in the spring sunshine, he was seized with a sudden, intense affection for Ynysmant. *It's* very *good to be back.* It seemed quite extraordinary that less than two weeks ago he had left there with Vero for Herrandown. His life before then already seemed to be distant and dreamlike.

He walked on, and as he approached Ynysmant, the long, steep-pitched roof of the hospital caught his eye and an idea came to him. Instead of going straight home, he turned up the street that led to the hospital, and walking in through a side entrance, he made his way to Administrative Affairs. There, in his office dominated by potted plants, he found Tomos Daynem, the junior administrator.

Tomos, lean and muscular, seemed to bounce up from his seat when he saw Merral at his doorway.

"Hi, Merral! Come in. Heard you were out of town." He shook hands. "Welcome back. Take a seat."

Merral sat down, stared at his friend, and gestured to the image on the wall of the winning side at last year's Ynysmant Team-Ball championship.

"How have we done lately?" he asked, knowing that particular image well. On it, Tomos, as captain of the Blue Lakers, one of the three best teams in town, was holding the cup high while Merral, who had merely played as a winger in a semifinal match, stood at the back.

Tomos gave a theatrical groan. "Oooh, don't ask. We lost against the Western Lake College First Team. Those boys are good. And we need to improve our passing. You ought to play more."

"I ought to. I just don't seem to be in the right place at the right time. Any repercussions from the loss of the Gate?"

He shook his head. "None I've thought of. I mean, it's hardly as if we had inter-system championships, is it? It's all we can do get a northeastern Menaya tournament organized every three years."

Merral felt a sense of relief that something at least seemed to be unchanged. In fact, it was hardly surprising; Assembly sports were informal, localized, and frequently haphazard.

Tomos leaned back in his chair. "But you didn't come to talk Team-Ball, I presume."

"No," answered Merral, choosing his words, "I have an odd question. I was in Isterrane recently, and there was some discussion about some regional medical anomalies. Then, this morning, I visited a rather aged great-aunt in Larrenport, and I found that she and some others were having problems at the end of their lives. They were fighting it, afraid of death. Anxiety. All very disturbing. It had just started within the last two months. So, I thought I'd ask you if there were any oddities you had heard of concerning the terminally ill."

Tomos's mouth made an expression of surprise. "Odd. I've heard of nothing. Not here. And I meet with all the medical sections regularly, so I'd know. In the last two months?" He shook his head. "No.

Same as usual. A couple of heart attacks when the Gate went, but that's not the same thing."

Merral felt a surge of relief. The idea that his hometown was unaffected was a relief.

"Thanks. I'm glad to hear it. *Very* glad. Forget my question." He rose to leave. "I'll leave you to get on with your work."

"Thanks. In fact, I am pretty busy. The Gate loss has had a major impact on the hospital's work. We'll have to make do without some equipment, some organ replacements, and some drugs." Tomos got out of his chair in a fluid motion and walked to the door. "It's going to be a very challenging half century. About the only plus point is that with no visitors we should have fewer stray viruses."

"Nice to hear something positive."

"Ah, but the difficulties may come when the isolation is over and we get exposed to any new strains that have developed." Tomos smiled. "But that won't be my concern. Anyway, Merral, I'm glad I've put your mind at rest." He opened the door. "Mind you, if you'd asked me about the beginning of life, I'd have had a different story to tell."

"The *beginning?*" Merral asked, suddenly feeling as if a lump of ice had been placed against his back.

"Yes. The delivery problems. But that, I presume, is another thing."

"What?"

"The labor difficulties we seem to be encountering this year."

Merral held on to the doorframe. "We have problems with *babies?*" He was aware that his voice sounded strangely muffled.

There was a nod. "Yes. But you didn't ask about that. You look a bit pale, Merral, are you okay?"

"Sorry. I've had a stressful few days. Can I talk to someone about it?"

•—•

Ten minutes later, Merral was sitting in another office staring across a fussily tidied desk at Dr. Edgar Meridell, a short, plump man with a smooth, bald head framed by tufts of white hair sprouting above his ears and prominent white eyebrows. Just behind him a holographic womb and baby were displayed on a floor stand, but Merral tried to avoid looking at it. He remembered that it was an unease about dissections and anatomy in his early biology courses that had been partly responsible for diverting his career into forestry.

"The best index," the obstetrician was saying in his dry, rather scholarly voice, "is the use of painkillers in childbirth. We use a substance called OA25. That's obstetric anesthetic 25. Do you need the formula?"

"No."

"Assembly standard. Has been for, oh, five hundred plus years. We have it on standby; the mother can ask for it if she feels excessive pain. Now, the figures—" he consulted his diary with slender fingers—"yes, last year, '851, we had just over two hundred babies born here, and it was used twice. Say, less than one percent take-up. Now this year—" he tapped the diary screen carefully—"ah yes. We have the figures for the first four months, as a percentage; January—2 percent; February—6 percent; March—15.8 percent and April, well, 29.4 percent. Our projections for May's figures are looking—" he gave a low whistle— "higher still."

Merral thought about the figures. "Very odd. So it's doubled every month, more or less. You will soon be at over a half take-up."

The doctor gave a reluctant nod of assent.

"So what's happening? Labor is getting more painful?"

"Well, now," came the wary answer, "that's not scientific language, Mr. D'Avanos. It's not easy to measure pain quantitatively. All we can say is that midwives are reporting an increasing demand for painkillers during childbirth. I've done a memo on it."

"I see," Merral answered, trying to keep his emotions from showing on his face. "Can you do me a favor? Send me a copy. No hurry. But by hand, not by diary."

The eyebrows rose. "It's a bit out of the area of forestry, isn't it?"

Merral shrugged. "Yes. I'm collecting oddities. It's becoming a hobby. Any idea why this is happening?"

"Embarrassingly, we have no idea. The possibilities are a virus, but there is no evidence of that. Some dietary issue, perhaps. Some sudden variation in a trace element. Or it might just be some factor to do with the dreadful winter. Lack of exercise . . . that sort of thing." He shrugged his shoulders and looked mystified. "But I'll send you that memo."

Suddenly, feeling that he had taken as much bad news as he could bear, Merral decided that he needed to get out of the hospital. He found a secluded site that looked westward over the inlet of Ynysmere and the rolling ground beyond it and sat down on a sun-warmed bench.

There he sat staring into the distance for some time, his mind distracted by events. Words and phrases seemed to circle round and round in his mind. *Birth and death; Herrandown, Larrenport, and Ynysmant; not death as we have known it; that age of humanity is over.* Linked with the phrases were images: his great-aunt's tears, Daniel Sterknem's face as he remembered his terror, the eyebrows of Dr. Meridell raised in puzzlement. Plainly, some subtle, vague, and spreading evil was abroad in the land, and its occurrence was clearly related to the intruders. And what he needed to do was equally plain: he had to observe and report, and when he was given the go-ahead, do everything he could to find the intruder ship. In the meantime, his duty was to not alarm anyone.

A cooler gust of wind spiraled past him, and to his surprise he realized that it was nearly six o'clock. It was time to see his family. He got up from the bench and walked out of the grounds, up through the sinuous streets to his house.

"I'm back," he called out as entered the house. His father, starting at his voice, stood up suddenly from the general room table where he was writing on sheets of paper. Brushing crumbs off his chest, he came over and hugged Merral.

"Why, Son! Good to see you. Excuse me—" Stefan gestured to a half-eaten sandwich on a plate by him—"I started eating. I wasn't sure when you were coming. Your mother is next door, just having a chat with friends. As she does—"

Merral sat at the table opposite, relishing being back home. "You look tired, Father."

"Me? Oh, it's been a long, weary day," his father said, running his hands through his straggly hair and stroking his unruly silver beard. "We have been making new guidelines about even stricter recycling of anything with rare earth elements."

"So you are working on it now?" Merral pointed to the sheets of paper covered with blocks of neat handwriting, lines, and arrows. It was one of the characteristics of his father, consistent with his often-winding way of thinking, that he preferred to scribble on sheets of paper rather than use a diary.

"This? No, it's my Historic. We Welsh speakers are having a discussion meeting next week." He paused, then read the title. "'*Am fater y Porth a'r oblygiadau ar gyfer dyfodol y Cynulliad a Farholme,*' or 'On the matter of the Gate and its implications for the future of the Assembly and Farholme.' I said I'd open it with a presentation of some of the issues. But oh, Son, it's hard work." He sighed and stroked a rogue strand of hair vaguely back into place over an ear. "It gets harder as you get older. A lot of future tenses. And concepts. I find Welsh so much less *clear-cut than Communal and, of course, a lot more difficult." He sighed* again and his finger intertwined with his beard. "But I wonder really—"

"You wonder really *what?*" asked Merral, feeling almost too scared to ask.

"Well, I don't know. I just feel, somehow, this emphasis on us all pursuing these old languages—sorry, that's not a sentence."

Merral, dismayed by what he was hearing, tried to keep his face blank and nodded encouragement for his father to continue.

"Yes, I've just been thinking now about the whole issue of preserving Historics. Perhaps this business—" he gestured upward to where the Gate would have hung if it had not been in a billion fragments—

"will give us a chance to think things through. . . ." Then, as if struck by the implications of what he was thinking, he fell silent.

Before Merral could make any reply, the door opened and his mother bustled in and surrounded him with her arms.

"Merral *dear*. How *lovely!* Let me look at you."

She clutched him to herself.

"It's been *ages*. And the Gate *gone*. We have missed you. Has your father got you some food?"

"Well, we've just been talking—"

She turned to his father. "Oh, Stefan! The boy's traveled hundreds of kilometers! You could have started getting *something* for him." Merral found her tone strange; jocular, yet also with a sharp and critical edge.

His father's face clouded. "Oh yes, sorry. I mean we were talking, weren't we, Son?"

He rose to his feet, shedding more crumbs off his pullover.

His mother frowned. "Oh, Stefan, just look at you! Those crumbs—all over you! The *men* of this house—" She gave a sigh and then hesitated, as if struck by her own reactions. "Sorry," she said in a quiet, introspective tone. "I'm not feeling quite myself lately. I suppose it's this awful Gate business."

But is it? Merral thought as they ate their supper and his mother discussed the practical repercussions of the loss of the Gate in her life and that of her neighbors and colleagues. Was his mother's critical mood a reaction to that event, or was there something else at work?

•◆•

After supper, Merral called Isabella to apologize for being back a day late. From the diary screen, he could see that she was sitting in her bedroom.

"Can we meet tomorrow?" he asked. "It's the Lord's Day, and we can meet in the afternoon or the evening."

Isabella's face showed an expression that was close to a pout. Then she brightened and turned her head slightly on one side, smiling.

"But you could still come over now," she said in a voice of warm invitation.

Struggling with his emotions, Merral did not immediately answer. *I care for Isabella,* he thought. *I find her invitation appealing, yet I want to keep my distance. Something is going wrong between us. Time was, we controlled our relationship; now it seems to control us.*

Suddenly an excuse came to mind. "Isabella, it's a bit late and I'd like to spend some time with my parents. Tomorrow's better."

The response was a brief moment of silence.

"Yes," Isabella said slowly and smiled again, but Merral felt there was effort rather than spontaneity behind her expression. Then, after making arrangements to meet on the following evening, and further pleasantries, they ended the call.

That night, before he went to sleep, Merral lay awake reviewing the day. What he had worried about on the hospital grounds now seemed terribly confirmed by the hints and nuances from within his own family.

The intangible shadow that had fallen over Herrandown and Larrenport was now falling over his own town.

CHAPTER 7

The following morning, Merral tried to put his concerns out of his mind. He felt it wrong that on the Lord's Day matters of evil should preoccupy him. Yet it was a struggle. Everything seemed to draw his mind back to the nagging shadow that now appeared to loom over everything. Indeed, as he left the Congregation Hall, high at the top of Ynysmant, Merral paused and looked north through the clear air. He could just make out in the far distance the snowcapped summits of the Rim Ranges. *How many days would it take,* he wondered, *for those cockroach-beasts and ape-creatures to reach here?* Could he be certain that, even now, they were not slowly advancing through the greenery of the orchards and woodlands that he could see? In spite of the warm sunshine, he shivered.

In the afternoon, Merral played a full game in the Blue Lakers' B squad. He had no great success, and his injured ankle was throbbing at the end of the match. But it took his mind off matters and gave him some exercise.

That evening Merral and Isabella walked down to the Waterside Center. The sun was setting by the time they got there, and it was still too chilly to sit outside, so they went into the center. Most people were downstairs where a local string-and-wind band was playing, so they went upstairs to an almost deserted lounge. There they got some drinks, found a quiet corner by a window, and made themselves comfortable. As they sat there together, Merral felt his concerns about their relationship slip away. Indeed, he was soon thinking about the kiss they had shared, a recollection that seemed to tingle with promise. Yet, as he thought about it, he realized that while that memory thrilled him, it also troubled him. *There are times and places for every stage in a relationship,* he thought, *and that, somehow, was out of place.*

Then Isabella started speaking, and he pushed his troubled thoughts away. "I have a new job," she said with excitement. "I am starting work this week in Warden Enatus's office. He is setting up a crisis team using people like me who have nothing to do now that the Gate is gone."

"Looking forward to it?" Merral asked.

"Absolutely." There was no mistaking the enthusiasm in her dark eyes. "It's going to be very stimulating. I feel like an explorer."

"I'm glad someone is positive."

"It's not all bad, you know."

She leaned over the table. "So, Merral D'Avanos," she said in a secretive voice, "tell me all about your trip north. You have been very evasive. Did you see that insect man-thing that Elana saw?"

It suddenly came to Merral that this was going to be very different from the conversation with Henri. Isabella would not be content with platitudes. And, as he realized it, he felt a horribly strong temptation to deny everything and to say that he had seen nothing. The attraction of the lie made him feel almost nauseous. Sensing his hesitation, Isabella murmured, "Go on. You can tell me."

"Isabella, dear," Merral said after a moment, "I'd just rather not talk about it. I really would."

The sort of relationship that Isabella and I have, he thought in alarm, *should involve progressively greater openness; that is what the whole sequence of commitment, engagement, and marriage involves. Yet instead of going forward, I find myself wanting to hold back. She demands to know more of me, yet I find I am reluctant to do so.*

A darkness seemed to cloud her face. "But I ought to know, really. It might help you to talk about what happened."

There was the usual gentle softness to her voice, but underneath Merral sensed a hard core of insistence.

"Perhaps," he answered, "in time, I may be able to talk about it fully."

Isabella looked out of the window into the dusk as if trying to hide her impatience and then turned sharply back to Merral, her dark hair swinging over her shoulder. A strand landed across her face, and almost with irritation, she flicked it back.

"Merral," she said softly, "I was up there at Herrandown with you. I *know* the problems already. I really ought to be told the end of the story."

Her tone was gently imploring, and Merral found that somehow it irritated him. And the fact that her insistence irritated him made him feel both miserable and alarmed.

"Well, I said I'd rather not—"

"And at least," she said, giving him a forced smile, "I want to know how you got from presumably well north of Herrandown to Isterrane, over a thousand kilometers away. Oh, come on, tell me!"

After a moment's further hesitation, Merral spoke. "Look, Isabella, all I wish to say—at the moment—is something like this: Over three days, Vero and I walked up the Lannar River as far as Carson's Sill, which is a rock ridge just before the Rim Ranges proper. There . . ." He paused, puzzling exactly what to say. "Well, there, we saw what shouldn't have been there. That we cannot explain. We asked to be pulled out and were picked up by a general survey craft and taken to Isterrane."

Isabella stared at him. "So it does exist. I thought so. From the way Elana talked."

"Well, we think . . . that whatever they are, they are gone. At least from that area."

"*They?*" Her thin eyebrows arched upward.

"There was more than one of them."

"I see." She shuddered. "And you are doing something about it?"

"Of course. There is an informal group of people working on it."

"Who? You and Vero?"

"And Anya Lewitz, the biologist who looked at the samples. And her sister, Perena, who piloted the craft that picked us up."

Isabella took a sip from her glass before speaking. "I see. But how does she fit in? Perena, I mean, to the group? I mean, I can see how you and Vero fit in, and I can see how Anya fits in. But a pilot? And if she's flying a general survey craft, she has got to be a Near-Space pilot."

Merral stared at Isabella, realizing that he had underestimated her.

"Well . . . we think it possible that these things may have come from outside Farholme. By ship."

"You think they are aliens?" Her eyes widened.

Merral hesitated, realizing that he had been dragged into saying more than he had intended. "Well, that may be going too far. We are looking into every possibility, but obviously we need to keep it quiet. We do not want to panic anybody, and as you would be the first to appreciate, now is not the time to release speculations."

As he spoke, it came to Merral as a fresh insight that while he was capable of being firm in his dealings with captains, advisors, and even representatives, in his dealings with Isabella he was weak. The insight irritated him.

"That is *so* scary. But what I want to know—"

Suddenly, Merral felt he had said enough. "Look, Isabella, I've told you as much as I can at the moment. That's all I want to say. The rest is, for the moment, private."

As the words came out, he realized how brusque they sounded and was appalled. "Sorry," he said.

Isabella blinked and then she just reached out and stroked his hand for a second in a placatory gesture.

"I'm sorry; it's been a difficult few days—for us all."

"That," Merral said, sitting back, shaking his head, and sighing, "is what everybody says." *Perhaps,* he thought, *we can work something out between us. What we once had was so good that we ought to be able to get it back.*

"But it's true, Merral. It's an unprecedented shock."

"But is it, in your view," he said, thinking how relieved he was to turn away from the subject of the intruders and his trip north, "an unmitigated evil?"

"What do you mean?"

"Well, I was talking to someone at the hospital who was saying to me that at least we might be free of those viruses that come in with travelers from other worlds."

"Like the Carnathian flu we all had to be inoculated against last year?"

That's it. Stay away from the intruders. "Yes, I suppose so. . . . I mean, have you found any silver linings in the black cloud? I could use them."

"Me? Well, I did have one odd thought—"

"Which was?"

She creased her brow and gave him what he always thought of as one of her intense looks. "Well, the Assembly has always valued stability. As you know, Assembly society doesn't change very much in space or time. It has been said that if you could—somehow—transport one of the founding generation here across those twelve millennia, he or she would fit back into our society with barely a murmur."

"It's almost a truism," Merral said, feeling more relaxed. "Or if our society does change, it changes within only tiny limits."

Applause drifted up from the room below.

"Yes, well, that is partly due to planning. But there are also sociological reasons why that has been the case. The Assembly is just too big and too open for innovations to take hold."

"Yes," he answered, realizing that part of her charm was the way her intelligence and analytical ability stimulated him. "Genetic systems work in the same way. It's hard to modify large populations as the new genes just get swamped."

"That may be where the idea came from. Well, you see . . ." She paused, a slender finger tracing a meandering pattern on the table. "I was thinking that in a small, isolated society, which is what Farholme will be for the next fifty years, change can happen."

"I see. . . ." It was an interesting insight.

"And," she went on, "when we get reconnected, we may be very different."

"And this change . . . ;" Merral asked slowly, watching her delicate face, "would be good?"

A flicker of uncertainty crossed Isabella's face. "Well, of course, not all change is good. We need to be careful. That's what we will be looking at. But—and it's a tentative thought—the Assembly may, for the best reasons, have kept us back."

"Kept us back?" Merral felt suddenly tense.

"Don't sound so surprised, Merral. What I mean is this: To be an adult you need to make choices. We have not had the choices. We have been kept in a moral kindergarten."

"Go on, Isabella," Merral said, feeling unease. "I'm just a plant person really. All this social analysis stuff is new."

She stared at him. "Well, you see, societies may be like people. Perhaps we too need to go beyond kindergarten."

Merral felt cold, as if the lake waters were seeping into his veins.

"I see," he said, trying not to express his disquiet. "I would need to think about that. It's a new idea."

Isabella touched his hand again. Far away, the band struck up a new piece.

"Maybe," she said, in a low voice that seemed somehow to make all Merral's concerns trivial, "maybe *we* need to think about it."

Merral, feeling both longing and alarm in equal and conflicting amounts, tried to speak in as smooth a way as he could manage. "Yes, but not just now. When things settle down."

Then to cover his confusion, he took another sip of his juice. *I wish Vero were here. I need to talk with him about how she perceives the situation.*

Then, in order to restore balance to his mind, he switched the subject to the plans for a new sports tournament for the Ynysmant schools. After an hour, pleading genuine tiredness, he walked her back to her house.

•—•

As he donned his night-suit for bed that night, Merral still found himself troubled. He took down imaging glasses off his shelf, went to the table, and carefully picked up the small crystal egg that was perched on a stand. He placed it on the personal creation reader by his bed, lay down, put on the glasses, and ordered that he be logged on to the castle tree simulation.

He closed his eyes as the optics adjusted and opened them to see that he was standing a few meters above a thick snowfield that was lit by late winter's afternoon sun. Data hanging in the air told him that in the fortnight since he had last visited his world, over three years of simulated time had elapsed.

Merral paused, adjusting himself to the sterile, noise- and odor-free brightness of his world. Then he flew effortlessly over the gleaming ground until the vast, snow-streaked brown bulk of his castle tree loomed up before him. He stared at it, admiring again its towering mass, twice the volume of Ynysmant town, before slowly spiraling up around the outside, examining its surface. At the completion of his survey, he found himself pleased; the simulation was progressing well. There was new growth, and despite the heavy snowfall, only a few branches had snapped under the snow's weight.

Now, at the top of the tree, Merral turned and floated down into its enormous hollow interior. Here, protected by the vast wall of the tree, a quieter, milder climate prevailed, and he found that parts of the lake at the bottom had remained unfrozen. He was not surprised to see no sign of life; the only creatures he had created so far were insects, and they were overwintering as larvae in the crevasses of the trunk.

Satisfied, Merral ascended again until he was high in the air above his creation, and as the sun set, he put himself in a slow circular orbit around the tree. There he toyed with the questions his simulation raised. When should he let the tree breed? Should he make another tree anyway? And what other life-forms should he create? He could, of course, just let the insects evolve, but that would take time.

Normally, unless he was going to make adjustments to the program or take images, Merral would have exited his created world fairly promptly. But today, somehow, things were different. As the darkness gathered under and inside the tree, Merral found himself lingering. He had always been fond of his world and proud of his castle tree, but he had never had any illusions that it was anything more than a pure fiction of electrons and photons created and sustained by enormous processing power. Yet now it held an attraction for him that it had never had before. There was something clean, simple, and undefiled about this world that he found alluring. "If only it was real," Merral said with longing, and he marveled at the strangeness of the thought.

• ◆ •

The following morning Merral walked across the two kilometer causeway and went straight over to the office of his director, wondering what Henri was going to say to him.

Henri gestured him straight to one of the chairs in front of his desk. He flung his own wiry frame into the facing seat.

"Man, I'm glad you are back," he drawled. "*Ach.* You chose a momentous time to be away." He gave Merral a bewildered, almost stunned smile.

"Yes. Pretty momentous."

"Momentous. Isn't it?" Henri toyed with his beard, and Merral noted that it had lost its usual neatness. "A week ago the job of this Institute was to slowly and steadily expand the forest and the settlements. Then, out of the blue, the Gate goes, and everything is changed. Now our job is ensuring survival." He breathed out a heavy sigh. "*Ach,* man, we haven't a clue how to do it. So it's endless meetings. But I think we will have to let much of the north go to wildwood."

Merral groaned. "Wildwood? Oh, let's hope we can avoid that."

Henri looked sympathetic. "I know. Foresters see wildwood as a mark of defeat. But what else can we do? Our overstretched resources won't allow for more. And remember, it's merely a fifty-year setback. Think of the ten thousand years we have already spent on this world."

"I suppose you are right, Henri; take the long view."

"There's no other way." Henri paused, raised an eyebrow in inquiry, and leaned toward Merral. "But we can talk about that later. Your Herrandown trip. What can you tell me?"

Merral thought for a few seconds. "I'm glad you put it like that. The answer is, not a lot yet. . . .We have got a lot of data in Isterrane, and it's being studied. But there does appear to be something up north, beyond Herrandown. Something that is genetically odd."

There was a sharp, quizzical look. "What? The Antalfers may be your family, but they are my responsibility. Some sort of anomaly?"

"Yes, something like that . . ." Merral paused. "A mutation or mutations. Perhaps."

"Hmm. I gather from the quarry team at Herrandown that you sent a message advising more precautions?"

"Yes, people to work in pairs, not to work at night. To avoid the woods."

"Man, I'd like to know more. . . ." Henri's dark eyes seemed questioning.

"I'd like to tell you. But we just want to be careful. I'll tell you when we have firm data and a decision on what to do. But I take it no one is intending to visit the Lannar Crater area?"

"Not for a month. Assuming that the schedule holds. Which I doubt. But you have a suggestion?"

"I think the area should be left alone. We shouldn't send anybody north of Herrandown until things are clearer." Merral heard a sharp edge to his voice.

Henri rapped slender fingers sharply on the chair arms. "Well, I'd normally request your reasons, but it's now an unusual situation right across the board." He sighed. "And to be frank, man, the development of the extreme north was always going to be the first casualty of the Gate loss. Okay, we'll veto the extreme north. We may boost some of the southern colonies instead. They are less demanding."

"Thanks. So tell me, what have I come back to?"

Henri leaned back and gave a chuckle, but it was one without any happiness. "*Ach*, a fluid and fast-moving situation. I don't even know whether your tropics posting is going to come off."

"It can wait," Merral answered, and he meant it.

"Sorry. Anyway, the initial directives are for categorization; we have to look at all our plans in terms of what equipment and resources they need and whether they make use of non-Farholme-sourced material."

"Any specific guidelines?"

"Two specifics: Delete no data files unless you have first checked that the Library holds a copy. And just today I have had a direct order from Representative Corradon's office telling me that we are not to use machines with gravity-modifying engines. All available Farholme GMEs are prioritized for medical, rescue, and other such work. So, if you need a low-impact machine, use a hovercraft, not a GM sled."

"Makes sense," answered Merral, wondering what else would be affected.

"Yes." Henri rubbed his forehead. "I suppose we must be positive and see it as a challenge. There's a pile of things on your desk."

"Yes. I saw it."

Henri rose to his feet. "Yes. But, man, it's good to have you back."

•-◆-•

Seated in his office, Merral began to sort out the memos and files that had accumulated on his desk and on the in-tray of his deskscreen.

A lot of the material awaiting him dated back to before the loss of the Gate, and Merral was able to simply consign it to either a digital or real recycling bin. It was when he stared at his personal calendar with its list of forthcoming virtual conferences across the worlds that he had been planning to attend that the isolation his planet was now under came home to him. He closed his eyes and issued an order. "Diary, delete all reminders re inter-system conferences from today onward."

The metallic tones came back to him. "Diary query: Your request normally requires an end limit. Until when am I to delete them?"

"Diary, unlimited deletion. All of them. Until further notice. Forever."

The words "request completed" echoed around the office.

"Good-bye, my old life," Merral said aloud, and suddenly struck by the enormity of it all, he put his head in his hands.

• ◆ •

For the next few days, Merral threw himself vigorously into his work. He heard nothing from Isterrane and part of him began to hope that Vero's proposal for teams was going to be refused. *Perhaps,* he thought, *I can return to my old life.* Yet every meeting he went to was dominated by the changed priorities they all now faced and reminded him that his old life was gone beyond recall. And at any meeting, whenever a map was produced, he found his glance straying northward to where the broken circle of the Lannar Crater appeared.

• ◆ •

Midmorning on the last day of the working week, there was a knock at his door. Henri walked in carrying a large carton and two long white envelopes, one of which was open.

"Morning, Merral," he said in a strange, unsettled tone. "May I talk to you privately?"

"Of course."

Henri closed the door behind him and, putting the carton down on the floor, pulled up a chair at the other end of the table.

"Our world is changing isn't it?" Henri's voice expressed how uneasy he was with the idea.

"Yes. And it worries me, very much." *I can guess what is about to happen. It is what I have been expecting since I got back.*

Henri waved the letters. "These were couriered to me today. And this carton. Both marked 'urgent.' One letter for me personally and one for me to hand to you. From Representative Corradon."

"Ah."

He handed an envelope to Merral, who glanced at the front, taking in the linked crests of Farholme and Menaya and the embossed emblem of the Assembly, the words *Private and Confidential,* and the two-line address *Forester Merral Stefan D'Avanos, Ynysmant Planning Institute.*

"I think you'd better read it now," Henri said. "*Ach,* it's private, but we need to discuss what it says."

Merral opened the heavy envelope with a knife and unfolded the two sheets of paper. The heading on it said simply *Anwar Corradon, representative for northeastern Menaya,* and underneath the previous day's date was a neatly handwritten message. Merral read it carefully through twice.

> Dear Forester D'Avanos,
>
> I have carefully considered both our discussions and the letter I have just received from you on the state of matters in Larrenport. After meeting with the other representatives, I am hereby authorizing your release from your duties at the Ynysmant Planning Institute to work specifically on some of the questions raised by the appearance of the intruders. I have written separately to your manager requesting your immediate release. You are authorized to use such resources of Farholme as needed. You may wish to use the Planning Institute as your base for the time being.
>
> In an accompanying package you should find the datapaks of all the imagery you need. I would like to be made aware of any significant developments in this matter as soon as possible by personal or written communication alone. No contact of any form with the intruders is to be sought without my permission. I have written similar letters to Captain Perena Schlama Lewitz and Dr. Anya Salema Lewitz.
>
> Furthermore, after further discussion with Sentinel Enand, the other representatives, and Advisor Clemant, I have, most reluctantly, authorized the creation of a Farholme Defense Unit that will interlock with the research work authorized above. Sentinel Enand has been authorized to instigate and organize the development of the Defense

Unit, again with the strict ruling that no contact with the intruders is to be made without my approval.

In a break with Assembly tradition which, we must pray, is a temporary measure, the nature of your research and the existence of the Farholme Defense Unit is not to be made public knowledge.

These arrangements will be reviewed on a monthly basis.

Please keep this document private and secure.

Be assured of all our prayers and support.

Yours in the service of the Assembly,

Anwar Corradon, representative

Merral closed his eyes as the import of the letter sank in.

"You okay, man? You look like you need some fresh air."

For long moments, Merral could not answer. "My responsibilities are now heavier than you can imagine," he said finally. "Sorry, Henri. What do you know?"

"A bit. The representative says that he has appointed you to be—how did it go?" Henri looked at his letter. "'To be in charge of a special project of vital importance to the future of Farholme, centering on some of the oddities that have been occurring within Menaya. Rather uniquely'—*I'll say*—'this is not to be made public. I would ask you to assist him in whatever way you can. If you wish to discuss this matter, please do it either by a hand-couriered document or by face-to-face contact with me. I am anxious that no mention of this matter is made on either diary links or the Admin-Net.'" Henri looked up and shook his head. "I'm still trying to work out the implications of that. And the rest. But I don't like it. Not at all."

"Me neither."

"Anyway, he goes on to say, 'I would be grateful if you would not press Forester D'Avanos on any matters to do with this project. Yours, *et cetera.*'"

"Does it say to keep this document private and secure?"

He smiled ruefully. *"Ach.* Man, it's worse. At the bottom it says, 'Please commit the above to memory and then have it destroyed.'"

Henri looked intently across the table at him. "I have no real idea what this is about. I have never heard of anything like this happening. But, Merral, you have my support. Anything I can do to help, I will do."

He extended his hand and Merral shook it.

"Thanks, Henri," he answered, his mind still adjusting to the arrival of what he had both hoped and feared. Then he walked over to the window and for long moments stood there, resting his fingers on the sill. He looked across the lake where the sun was breaking through thin, ashen clouds and lighting up the tops of waves in the distance. *My days of being a forester are ended,* he thought. He tried to console himself that, weeks or months away, he might be fully able to resume the work he loved. Yet it was a consolation that now seemed hard to believe.

Finally, he turned round to Henri. "Thanks. I need to sit and think. And pray. Then, if I may, I will come back to you, probably with some requests."

"I'll do everything I can, Merral. May God help you."

"May he help us all, Henri."

•—◆—•

An hour later, Merral walked into Henri's office with a piece of paper in his hand.

"Okay," Henri drawled, "tell me what you want."

"I need some things to start with. A big cupboard, big enough for maps and papers."

"Done."

"And I want another computer, able to handle map data for the whole of northeastern Menaya."

"Again, done."

"Thanks. But there may be a problem. I want that machine isolated from the network."

"Isolated?" Henri's jaw sagged slightly. "But, man, to state the obvious, if you do that no one will be able to interface with it."

"That's the point."

"*Ach.* I see," Henri said, his face showing evidence of a brain working double-speed to handle new ideas. "So I get to lose you? That's bad news for me."

"I've been thinking about that. I don't think I can work all day on this project, anyway. I'll need a break. And if I dropped out of all forestry work, everyone would be very curious. So why don't we cut my workload, and I'll see how much I can do?"

Merral found the happy look that came to Henri's face gratifying.

"Excellent. Anything else?"

"I want to see if one of the maintenance people can modify my office door in some way."

"Let me guess. The same as Herrandown. You want a bolt?"

"No. More complex. A device so that I can bolt and unbolt the door, but from the outside."

An uncomprehending stare slid across Henri's face. Merral paused and then reluctantly said, "The design will be in the Library files. It's called a door lock."

"A door lock . . ." Henri stared at the map on his wall for a long minute in a perplexed manner and then turned to Merral. "What, in the name of the Assembly and all it stands for, are we up against?"

There was a long silence, and then Merral said, "The problem is, Henri, I don't know." He paused, struck afresh by the dreadful responsibility that had now been thrust upon him. "And it has become my responsibility to find out before it's too late."

Within hours, Merral had started on his task of finding the ship. And by the end of the day, he had realized that he faced a daunting task. Not only had he a vast area of incredibly rugged terrain to search—his estimate was that the Lannar Crater alone covered around a million square kilometers—but he didn't know what he was looking for. What shape was the ship? What color? What size? Would it show up on gravity or magnetic data? Could he eliminate swamps, screes, and mountain summits? The answer, he realized, was, in every case, that he simply didn't know.

Over the next week, Merral's doubts deepened. One promising technique had failed completely. He tried getting the computer to compare last year's images with this year's and to flag any changes. The problem was that the crater area was so dynamic that every square kilometer turned out to have something new, whether it was a fresh stream, some fallen trees, or a new landslide. So for two days he turned the images into a digitally created landscape, put on imaging glasses, and cruised across it at a variety of altitudes. But he found no trace of any ship.

In the end, Merral divided the imagery into blocks of ten square kilometers and began to look at each in turn, cross-checking the visual data with any geophysical oddities. It was slow work, and he found he could only concentrate for so many minutes at a time before he had to take a break. As a change—and to try and freshen his mind—he took to running along the lake edge at lunchtime. But after a week's work, the verdict was inescapable: he had discovered nothing.

One of the few consolations that emerged during that first week of the search was that Merral found his relationship with Isabella seemed to be running more smoothly. For one thing, her new job seemed to occupy her energies. It soon emerged that she had been made the deputy leader of the warden's crisis team. For another, she seemed to have made a decision not to push Merral to say anything more about the intruders, and he was spared more troubling questions. But the topic didn't go away. Merral felt that, like a rock under the surface of the water, the subject was always there. In the end, Merral found the whole thing so awkward and irritating that he decided to tell Isabella almost everything. So, one evening, they went for a walk in the woods south of Ynysmant and there, in a clearing a long way from anywhere, Merral told her—on the condition she told no one else—what had happened.

"That's as much as I know," he said at the end. "So I'm hunting this ship while Vero is busy organizing things in Isterrane."

Isabella had followed the account in an attentive silence. "Thank you for explaining this," she said. "I could guess the Gate destruction was linked to these intruders. It stands to reason. You don't get oddities in a world like Farholme. When you get two oddities, it figures that they must be related. But I had no idea that it was this bad. It has awesome implications."

She fell silent again, and as they walked back together, he felt he could sense her mind working away, putting the pieces into place.

As he left Isabella at her parents' house, she turned to him and hugged him tightly. "Thank you, Merral. I wanted to ask, but I preferred for you to tell me in your own time. Thank you so much for telling me."

But as Merral walked home, a troubling thought seized him: had he genuinely volunteered the information, or had Isabella somehow manipulated him into giving it?

•◆•

At the start of the next week, he had a terse handwritten note from Vero announcing that Perena would fly him and Brenito out in two days' time to see Jorgio. The letter concluded with *Very busy here; be good to talk with you.*

Merral immediately set about making arrangements for the trip. The real problem turned out to be ensuring Jorgio's presence. In fact, Merral found it frustratingly hard to even find him. The central files listed Jorgio Aneld Serter as a "noncorrespondent," the curious term used for people—like honeymoon couples and those seeking the discipline of solitude—who decided to forgo diary usage for a few days. Only in Jorgio's case, it seemed that he hadn't used it for twenty years. Eventually, Merral got hold of him through Teracy, the assistant manager at Wilamall's Farm, and managed to extract a promise from Jorgio that he would be there. In contrast, arranging to get a rotorcraft and pilot from Henri proved simplicity itself.

• ◆ •

Two days later, Merral was at the strip at nine o'clock peering into the cloudless skies for any sign of the plane. It had crossed his mind that Anya might come with the party as well, and he was disquieted at finding how much he hoped that this was the case. Shortly after nine, a small courier plane flew in from the west, made a perfect landing, taxied toward him, and stopped.

Vero, carrying a briefcase, was the first to get out, followed by a tall, muscular, blond-haired young man who helped the slow and heavy figure of Brenito down the steps. Moments later, Perena and another woman in a pilot's uniform emerged. There was no Anya.

A few steps away from the plane, Brenito stopped and pulled a broad-brimmed hat down over his large head, then extended a hand to Merral.

"Well, we meet again, Forester," he said slowly as they shook hands.

Looking at his pale, drained face, Brenito seemed to Merral to be badly shaken by events.

"Sooner than we had expected, Sentinel Brenito. But I welcome you nonetheless. There's a rotorcraft waiting over here."

Vero came over. They hugged each other and stepped back to look at each other. Merral wondered whether his friend was thinner.

"Oh, it's good to see you, my friend!" Vero said, his brown face displaying transparent pleasure. "It really is. I have missed your insights and your leadership. And there's so much I want to show you." Then he looked at Merral. "Is there any news?" he asked in an urgent tone.

"I'm sorry. No."

Vero bit his lip. "Ah. I was afraid of that." He paused. "We will talk later. Introductions first."

He beckoned the young man forward. "Merral, this is Zachary Larraine. He's one of the team: an aide."

Zachary, who had the sort of physique that Merral associated with those who took their athletics seriously, gave him a knowing smile.

"It's Zak. I'm from Kelendara. Heard a lot about you," he said, his sharp blue eyes radiating a quiet self-assurance. He gave Merral the firmest of handshakes. "I'm just delighted to be involved, sir."

Sir? thought Merral with something approaching alarm, as Zak joined Vero in walking on either side of Brenito as he made his slow way toward the rotorcraft.

Perena then hugged Merral and introduced the second woman as Lucinda, the pilot. Lucinda smiled, shook hands, and said she was staying by the plane.

"So, Perena," Merral said, "whose is the plane?"

She smiled. "It was going to go to the Mazarma geographic survey. It's been reallocated to us."

"Us?"

"The Farholme Defense Unit."

"I see."

"It is useful. We don't have to try and squeeze on existing flights."

"Makes sense. But how did you get it?"

They began walking slowly over to the rotorcraft.

"With some help from Gerry, I persuaded Corradon and Clemant that the intruders almost certainly had some sort of ability to travel faster than light without using a Gate. And as we all face a very tough future, the idea of having access to that ship or its technology is very attractive."

"I can imagine."

"But there was more. They are also fearful of the risk the intruders pose for the Assembly."

"For the rest of the Assembly . . . ?" Then, as an understanding of what she meant came to him, Merral felt a sudden stab of alarm. "Oh! How silly; I hadn't thought of that. I had assumed that, with the destruction of the Gate, the intruders had been stopped from infecting the rest of the Assembly."

"No, we do not have that consolation," Perena said. "If they can achieve, say, just thirty to forty times the speed of light, then they could be at Earth within a decade. Faced with that prospect, they have given Vero more or less everything he has asked for."

"I see. And Dr. Clemant agreed? I'm amazed; I thought we had some serious opposition there."

"Yes, he agreed. Our doctor has taken a long, hard look at the way things are going. And he has realized that, of a number of evils, Vero's approach is the least objectionable."

"Interesting. I am impressed at what he has achieved."

"You have only seen the tip of things," Perena said, gesturing toward Vero. "He's doing an amazing job. Generating orders and paperwork from dawn till late at night. Ten days ago, the FDU was just a few bits of paper and some ideas. But now, it's an organization. I'm impressed." She paused. "Mind you, it's all a bit scary. So much is happening."

Merral looked at her, sensing something. "Do I detect caution?"

"Ah." She glanced at him and he caught a concerned smile. "A bit. I only wish we knew more about what we face. But that's just me. I'd see it as being like playing chess with an unknown opponent; you're careful first. But Vero . . ." She hesitated. "Vero has decided that we must move fast. We can't wait for them to make another move. And actually, I think he's right. This isn't chess."

"No."

The others had reached the rotorcraft, and Perena and Merral stopped just out of earshot behind them.

"And you . . . ?" Perena inquired.

"I'm sorry. Nothing to show. I've just had a long, tiring, and so far fruitless search."

"A pity."

"Yes. And Anya? How is she?"

"Busy. She sends greetings. The intruder genetic code is being unraveled." She shook her head. "Unpleasant."

"It's a pity she wasn't able to come out."

"Yes. It would have done her good. She has been working long hours. They all have."

"So, are you getting much flying done?"

"A little. I've got my first space trip next week. I am taking Gerry and some colleagues out to Far Station."

"I thought her research had been cancelled."

"It's been redirected," Perena said, looking at Vero with an expression in which Merral felt respect and amusement were mixed. "He's got most of the physics department working for him now."

• ◆ •

Half an hour later, they landed at Wilamall's Farm. Merral felt relieved to see the lopsided figure of Jorgio Serter waiting patiently by the landing pad.

Jorgio wore faded green trousers and an old white shirt, and had a single red rose stuck in his breast pocket.

As if the others didn't exist, Jorgio came over to Merral and gave him one of his big and clumsy embraces. "Why, Mister Merral!" he said. "Arriving out of the sky like this." He shook his tanned and twisted head. "*Tut.* You'll forget how to ride like that."

"No, my old friend," Merral answered, "I will not forget how to ride, and one day I'll come up here for a weekend and do nothing but ride."

"And how is Graceful? You're not too busy to look after your horse, are you?"

"She is fine, stabled at the Institute, but she gets little riding from me. But let me introduce you to everyone. Vero, you know."

In turn, Merral introduced Jorgio to Perena, Zachary, and finally to Brenito, who bowed slightly.

"If you please," said Jorgio, with a wave of a large hand, "do come over to my cottage. I have some tea and cake. Mind you, it will be a tight fit for us all. But we will do it."

In the end, after Zak had taken a quick look around the room and volunteered, with quiet tact, to take a walk instead, they did all manage to squeeze into Jorgio's small, sparsely furnished living room with its low wood-beam roof and its walls hung with gentle pastel abstracts.

As they drank tea and ate the cake, Brenito said, "Jorgio, I want to thank you for your help and advice to my friends, Merral and Vero."

"Just part of my service to the King, that's all," Jorgio said in his rough voice. "I just wish I could have saved the Gate. There've been a lot of people I heard of as are separated from loved 'uns."

"Indeed. It's very sad. But, Jorgio, please tell me about your family. Go back as far as you can."

So, for the next ten minutes or so, Jorgio talked in his roundabout way about his father and his grandparents, while Brenito sipped at his tea and listened carefully, occasionally making such comments as "indeed," "really?" or "how interesting."

There was, Merral decided, an odd affinity between the two men. It was as if they were two related plants: Brenito, the cultivated variety; Jorgio, the wild form.

Then, as their host paused for a moment, Brenito raised a finger. "Now tell me, this gift of 'seeing things' you have. Does that run in the family?"

Merral saw Vero stiffen. Perena, squeezed unobtrusively into a corner of the room, tilted her head as if anxious not to miss a word.

"I reckon so. My grandfather—on my dad's side—could sense the weather. So they said. People would go to him 'bout that. Reckoned he was better than the forecasts. Least for this part of Menaya; forecasts don't work right here sometimes."

"So was he considered a prophet?"

Jorgio pouted. "Now, the local congregation did say that. Crops, seasons, missing animals—they felt he knew that sort of thing. In fact, now as you mention it, I remember when I was young him saying as his grandfather had something similar."

Brenito nodded. "So that would take us back, what? Almost two hundred years? Intriguing."

Merral wondered why such an inherited gift should have gone unnoticed. Then it occurred to him that, in a world where nothing much happened, the gift of seeing the future was hardly one to be prized.

"So," Brenito said, his voice oddly resonant in the small room, "Jorgio, Merral, and Vero have told me about your visions, about the Assembly, about what's happening. Can *you* tell me about them?"

Jorgio rubbed his smooth, bald head and stared at the table. "*That.* That's why you're here, isn't it? 'Cause old Jorgio sees things."

"I think God has given you a gift that we need."

"*Tut.* We all 'as gifts," Jorgio said dismissively and looked around. "Lots of gifts here."

"I think so too. But we want to hear about yours. Tell us about your dreams, your visions. We need help and you can give it to us."

So, prompted by Brenito, Jorgio recounted his dreams and visions. Although Merral had already heard what his old friend had to say, he still found his words both compelling and troubling. And from the tense, rapt expressions on the faces of Brenito, Vero, and Perena, he knew that the others were similarly gripped. And as Jorgio told them of his awareness of cold, creeping shadows under the northern woods, Merral felt as if the sunlight somehow faded and the day's warmth left the room. And when Jorgio told of his two specific visions of a threat to Farholme and the Assembly, Merral felt there was an almost electric tension to the room, as if a summer storm were brewing.

"Hmm," Brenito said in the long silence that followed. "Extraordinary. Tell me, when the Gate went, Jorgio—when you heard the news—what did you feel?"

"Now that was odd. I felt anger." Jorgio's forehead creased into a frown. "Yes, if you please, *anger*. It was almost as though it was the Lord's anger, if you like."

"Would it surprise you to know that it wasn't an accident?"

Merral was aware that every eye in the room was turned to Jorgio's face.

"Accident?" His thick lips smacked in indignation. "Surprise me? *Tut*, I knew it weren't that. It was them in the north that was behind it."

"Ah," Brenito said; it was a single, long, slow word of discovery. "And who," he continued, as delicately as if his words were on tiptoe, "are *they*?"

"I don't rightly know." The leathery face wrinkled, revealing uneven teeth. "But I know as they aren't good. That's obvious anyway. And there's something there that ain't flesh and blood either, if my dreams are right. Or, at least, not *natural* flesh and blood. Not warm, living, flesh and red blood, like what you and I have under our skins." He chewed his lip. "And I think this something is old—"

"Old?" Brenito's question was barely a whisper.

"As old as the hills. No—older. Older than the stars."

"I see." Merral caught Vero's glance.

"And they don't like us, Mister Brenito. They hate the King's people. Always have."

"Hmm." Brenito shifted awkwardly in his chair. "What else do you know about them?"

"Know? Oh, I know little. It's what I reckon, really."

The old sentinel smiled. "Go on. I'm very interested."

"We all are," added Vero quietly.

"For instance, where are they?" Brenito asked "Exactly? Do you know?"

"Up north, I reckons. Beyond the mountains." Jorgio shivered. "I get cold at night thinking about the north. The ice, the frost. But it's colder than that now. Now it has them."

Jorgio fell silent, looking at the floor and twisting his gnarled fingers.

"Why are they here?" Brenito asked.

"It's 'cause the barrier is down."

"The barrier is down?" Merral echoed and received a cautionary glance from Brenito.

"Yes," Jorgio said, scratching his uneven nose, "leastways, that's how I look at it."

"What barrier, Jorgio?" Brenito said in a soft voice.

"Well, see, I don't say as I'm right or I'm wrong. But I always reckoned there has been a barrier. Like a wall, see?" He tapped a finger on the masonry beside him. "I expect it's invisible except to the Lord and the angels. It's his handiwork, of course. Round the Assembly. And it keeps 'em out. Or it did."

"Did?"

"Well, I reckon. No, I *knows.* But either they have been let through, or something—*someone*—has made a hole in the barrier. And they're getting through. Now."

"This barrier—where does it lie?"

Jorgio gestured sharply upward at an angle. "Beyond Farholme. We're at the edge. We are Worlds' End."

There was a long silence.

With a loud creak, Brenito leaned back in his chair. "Well, thank you, Jorgio. I think what you have said is very significant. I am delighted to have heard it from you personally."

"Mr. Serter." The sound of Perena's quiet voice made every one turn toward her. "Just before the Gate went . . ." She paused. "I met a strange figure. A man—only he wasn't a man. He warned me that night was falling and the war was beginning. He told me that the Gate was under threat—" she swallowed—"he said he was an 'envoy' sent from 'our Lord the King.' I was wondering if you knew anything about him."

Jorgio looked at her, then broke out into a broad smile. "Well, bless his Holy Name, I am glad to hear that." Jorgio gave a little clap of pleasure. "Best news I heard in a long time. 'Course, it's not surprising. The King never leaves his people on their own."

"So you know who he is?" Brenito asked with a raised eyebrow. "This envoy?"

"Oh, I don't know *who* he is but I can guess *what* he is: one of the King's warriors, he is. There's old stories as all the worlds have angels. He'll be ours."

"Thank you," Perena said quietly. "Thank you very much indeed."

There was a long silence, a silence deep enough for Merral to hear the sound of Brenito's heavy breathing. Suddenly, the old man gave a sharp little gasp. Merral saw the look of concern on Vero's face and understood his expression perfectly; this was not a well man.

Jorgio rose slowly. "Mister Brenito, would you like to lie down on my bed while I prepare lunch?"

"P-please," said Brenito in an unsteady voice. "Thank you—I don't mind if I do. . . . And a glass of water? Thank you."

Helped by Merral and Vero, Brenito managed to get out of his chair and into Jorgio's bedroom, where he lay down. After taking some water, he seemed to improve and asked that he be left on his own.

Perena insisted on helping Jorgio with lunch, so Merral and Vero left the cottage. It was turning out to be one of the first really warm days of the year, and they went and sat down on a grass bank in the shade of a big western oak that faced the cottage.

"Brenito's ill, isn't he?" Merral said.

"Yes," Vero said and shook his head. "It was a risk bringing him today. But, I think, a worthwhile one. What do you think of what Jorgio said?"

Merral thought for a moment. "It's scary. The barrier being down, I mean. But it makes sense, doesn't it? The idea of something outside the Assembly managing to get in."

"Yes. I just think it makes what we are doing even more urgent."

"Perena told me that the FDU is growing."

"Yes, I think it is, gratifyingly fast. And then I hear Jorgio and I wonder what we are up against."

"No news on Gerry's quantum communication device?"

"None." Vero shook his head. "She sent the message repeatedly; we have used up all the linked photons. There was no reply. Gerry wasn't surprised though. I guess I don't understand the physics. 'We will know in fifty years whether it got through,' she said. But Clemant was *not* happy about it. 'It should have been approved, Sentinel.' He didn't care for your account of what had happened at Larrenport either, when that got out." Vero shook his head as if trying to shake off a troublesome fly.

"But he has come around to supporting you?"

"Yes. He is fundamentally a pragmatic man. It took him some days for the gravity of the situation to sink in, but when it did—" Vero shook his head— "he became very helpful. He doesn't care for what we are doing, but he acknowledges it is needed. But, Merral, tell me about your hunt for the ship. You really have found nothing?"

"Nothing."

The look of disappointment on Vero's face was unmistakable. "I had assumed from your silence that that was the case."

"Vero, I'm spending six or seven hours a day on it. I can't do any more. I'm now going over it square by square at a scale where I can make out individual trees. But it's slow."

"How slow?"

"It could take me another three months to do the entire area."

Vero gave a cluck of dismay. "I'm not blaming you, of course, but can it be speeded up?"

Merral explained the difficulties.

"I see," Vero said. "It's like 'looking for a needle in a haystack.'"

"Not heard that one. Is that another of these pre-Assembly sayings?"

"Yes. All my reading is in that period now. When I find time."

" 'A needle in a haystack' raises lots of questions; I mean, why bother trying to find it? Couldn't they have used a magnet?"

"It was probably a ritual." Vero thought for a moment. "But are you staying fit?"

"I try and run every day. Why do you ask?"

Vero frowned. "Because when you—when *we*—find this ship, we will need to mount an expedition to it. You'll have to lead—"

"Vero," Merral interrupted sharply, "you aren't serious?"

"Of course."

"I really don't fancy turning up and knocking on the door, you know. Not at all."

Vero laughed. "My friend, the work of almost my every waking hour is to ensure that if, and when, we do meet them again, we meet them on very different terms than we did before. But let's not talk of that now."

Merral noticed that, by the cottage, Perena and Jorgio were putting out lunch on a table set up outside the door, and Zak was unrolling an awning from the cottage wall.

"Where did you get Zak from?"

"As soon as the FDU was approved I sat down with all the university academic and sports listings and looked up the best of the recent graduates in both areas."

"Why sports?"

"I wanted them fit. If we have to go for the ship—" Vero left the sentence unfinished. "And I was also looking for the good team players. But Zak Larraine's one of the best. He learns fast. I think he could master anything very quickly. He was in the first thirty-six I had."

"The first?"

A sheepish expression crossed Vero's face. "Oh, well. As I got them, we made plans and I realized we needed more than twenty-four. So we recruited another twenty-four. And so on—"

" 'And so on'? How many more are there?"

Vero peered intently down at the ground by his side. "Currently I have around a hundred people—all busier than these ants."

"That was fast."

Vero looked up, his face gloomy. "But we may not be fast enough. Things are happening and it's not good."

"What sort of things?"

"At Larrenport the annual Team-Ball match between the Sunrise and Sunset sides was cancelled last week. There was abusive language between the supporters. Unheard of. 'Stupid Setters.' 'Risers are slugs.' Amazing stuff. And there've been problems in the Library."

"The Library?"

"I'll tell you about it when it is confirmed. But, Merral, I fear that time is not on our side."

• ◆ •

By lunchtime, Brenito seemed to have recovered, and he and Jorgio engaged in quiet and close conversation. After lunch, Merral and the others drifted away to allow them some privacy. As he walked around Wilamall's Farm, Merral was disturbed to find how rapidly the complex was being run down. Shortly after two o'clock, they all returned to the house. The intense conversation between Brenito and Jorgio had ended, and Merral felt that the old sentinel had an oddly subdued air about him. They made their farewells to Jorgio and left.

On the rotorcraft journey back to Ynysmant, Merral noticed that Brenito barely said a thing but instead stared out of the window with a distant expression on his face. *It's his ill health,* Merral decided.

At Ynysmant strip, they clambered out of the rotorcraft and walked over as a group to the courier plane. Midway, Brenito raised a large hand. "A moment," he announced and gestured Merral over. "I need to have a private word with our forester."

The others withdrew out of earshot.

"Hmm," Brenito began, paused, and then began again. "Merral, over lunch and afterward, Jorgio said more than he had said earlier. He told me some things that I did not especially wish to hear." The big man paused again, wiping a bead of sweat from his forehead with the back of his hand. "He is an extraordinary person. There are depths to him that I really cannot fathom. His counsel is of great value. Not always easy to understand, of course. And he may be wrong. . . ."

Brenito paused again, staring at the spires and roofs of Ynysmant. "A pity. A town I never visited—" Then he seemed to focus back on Merral. "Yes, Forester, two things: First, guard and protect Jorgio. I have played my part, but I feel he has yet a great part to play. What part, I do not know. But our stable hand and gardener is not just someone who sees things; like you, Merral—but in a different way—he is a warrior. Do not neglect him, but at the same time do not expose him."

Merral found Brenito's gaze oddly disconcerting.

Brenito's slow voice continued. "You know, if I were the enemy, the person among you I would most fear would be Jorgio. So keep an eye on him."

"I will do that, sir, as best I can," Merral answered, struck by the sentinel's solemn tone.

"Thank you. And secondly, a warning: I fear that you will all have many dangers to face. Jorgio sees the testing of the Assembly as being not just of an organization but also as a testing of people. I think he is right. You will face dangers. Some of those dangers may come from nearer at hand and in stranger fashions than you suspect. Jorgio warned me that not all who are drawn into the fight against the intruders will win. Some, alas, will be lost."

"I see," answered Merral, feeling very uncomfortable.

"That's all, Forester," Brenito said, extending a hand. After they shook hands, he said, "Thank you, Merral, it has been good to see you."

"I hope to see you soon with the results," Merral said.

"Do you now?" A quite unreadable expression crossed the heavy face. "Perhaps—I would appreciate your prayers for the next week. I have much to do. Good-bye, Forester."

Then he turned and, with Zak at his elbow, walked with a slow and unsteady gait to the plane.

Vero came over. "I won't ask what that was about. But he is in a funny mood."

Merral, touched in a way he couldn't understand or express by what Brenito had said, just nodded.

"But thanks, Merral, for arranging this today. And as soon as you get something, get on a plane and fly over."

"I will, trust me."

Vero smiled. "Look, do what you can, as fast as you can, but don't worry. Even if we had a location, we aren't ready for an encounter yet. Realistically, we need three weeks." He turned and looked northward beyond the strip and trees. "And will we be ready even then?" he said in a voice that was barely a whisper.

CHAPTER 9

Eight days passed.

Merral's life remained dominated by the search. There were just two breaks: the Lord's Day and the annual holiday of Landing Day, traditionally marked by the first picnics of the year and a great deal of good-humored fun. This year, though, the picnics were not a success; they were blighted by a sudden rainstorm, and somehow the fun never really happened. And the next day, Merral was back again at his desk and staring at images on the screen.

Midmorning on the ninth day after Vero and Brenito's visit, an envelope was brought to Merral. He recognized Vero's handwriting on it and tore it open with a strange sense of foreboding.

"Oh no," he heard himself say as he read the first line.

Dear Merral,

I'm sad to tell you that Brenito went Home a few hours ago. He was taken into Eastern Isterrane Main Hospital yesterday morning feeling unwell and had a series of heart failures which culminated in his death around three. They could have kept him alive longer, but we all knew it was the end. In the end, death—ever the King's servant— took him Home gently.

I was there, and he said to me toward the end, "Vero, I have done my bit in this business. I would have wished to see the matter through to the end, but that is not to be. You play your part." He said other things, some of relevance to you, that I will pass on to you when we meet.

You can imagine my feelings. Since the loss of the Gate I had come to see him as part of my family. I had hoped that he would continue to be around to help us as we enter difficult days. I shall miss his bluff wisdom and his common sense. He discouraged some of my wilder ideas, and without him around, frankly, I fear for myself.

He told me over the last week that Jorgio had told him—in effect—to put his affairs in order. We agreed therefore that, contrary to usual practice, the funeral would be soon and private. We decided, and Corradon agreed, that as a matter of strategy, news of his death would not be made public. As you know, he had no family here. He will be buried in the Memorial Wood on the headland by his house. I will leave the planting of the tree till later. An oak perhaps?

He fought the fight well. May we do the same.

Yours in the service of the great Shepherd who protects all his sheep,

Vero

Merral sat back in his chair, suddenly realizing how utterly expected the news was. Yet it was a loss, and the idea that there was one less person to offer guidance was a hard blow. He left his office and went for a walk up through woods behind the Institute. There he found a quiet spot and gave thanks to the Lord for the life of Brenito Camsar, sentinel, formerly of Ancient Earth, and the man who, in summoning Vero to Farholme, had set in motion so much.

So much, Merral thought as, half an hour later, he walked back to his office, *but so much unfinished business too.* He wrote Vero a letter of condolence and then, telling himself that it was what Brenito would have wanted, he sat down at his imagery again. Perhaps today, he told himself, he would find what they sought.

But he didn't.

• ◆ •

Over the following days, Merral found that success continued to elude him. A week later, as he stood at the window of his office staring at the grayness of Ynysmere Lake, he realized that he was very close to despair. *Nearly three weeks of searching,* he thought gloomily, *and I have found nothing.*

His unhappiness was not just because the ship was still hidden. It was also because things were changing—and changing for the worse—in Ynysmant. Joylessness and dreariness now seemed widespread, grumbling and criticism were now common to be heard, and even Team-Ball matches were marked by grumpiness and bad temper.

At home too Merral had found things emerging between his mother and father that he was uneasy about. In particular, his mother now seemed—almost as a matter of habit—to be telling his father to tidy up either himself or whatever he was doing. Surely, Merral wondered, she had been more tolerant in the past? Or was his father getting more slovenly? There too something was wrong.

The situation with Isabella also troubled him, although Merral was not sure whether this was part of the general malaise or something purely personal. He had not seen much of Isabella because both she and he had been so busy. But when they did meet there were problems. True, the matter of the intruders was no longer an issue between them, but the matter of their "understanding" with each other had replaced it. Merral preferred to see this as merely an informal agreement that they had a serious relationship. Isabella, though, clearly saw it as something else: as an unofficial statement of commitment, the formal public precursor to engagement and marriage.

It was not that Isabella regularly mentioned the matter of their commitment; it was just that she always seemed to hint at it. Merral preferred not to raise the subject, hoping against hope that it would go away. Yet it didn't; the question of their commitment always seemed to be there between them. In his darker moments, Merral wondered if Isabella was doing, by accident or intent, what she had done with the intruders and employing slow, subtle pressure on him to yield and agree with her point of view. The effect was a renewed tension between them.

One other oddity was that he had spent more time than usual in the simulated world of his castle tree. Frequently, Merral entered the silent realm where his great tree stood before going to bed. He found a strange relaxation in drifting around in between the branches as, in speeded-up time, the clouds flew by overhead and the sun glided across the sky. He had decided that it was time for the tree to breed and had prepared those modifications to the program that would allow his tree to bear male and female flowers that his insects could pollinate. Eventually, he decided, he would make both male and female trees, but for the moment, his only specimen would have to be a hermaphrodite. Yet something about the growing intensity of his involvement with his personal creation troubled him. The sense of relief and release Merral felt as he entered the simulation was something that he had never experienced before. Was it, perhaps, an escape?

"Time is not on our side," Vero had said, and his words seemed to haunt Merral. Yet the one thing he could do that might change matters—find the ship—seemed to be impossible.

Merral frowned. Despite all his hours of poring over images on screens and printouts of various sizes, shapes, colors, and resolutions, he had made no progress. Indeed, in strange and unpleasant moments of mental darkness, he had even begun to wonder if what he sought existed. Clearly, if there was anything, it was hidden. Such a situation was, of course, quite logical; if the intruders were warlike, then one of the skills they would have mastered was camouflage. Satellite surveillance was a very old art and, he presumed, proficiency in avoiding it equally ancient.

Deeply troubled by his thoughts, Merral looked over the water to where, at the edge of his view, the outer houses of Ynysmant clustered round the lake margin. *I'm losing the battle; things are going downhill fast.*

He turned away from the window; this was getting him nowhere. He wondered whether he should travel to Isterrane to talk with Vero. He had heard nothing from him since the announcement of Brenito's death. He needed to clear his mind. Sticking a note on his door, he left the office complex, walked past the stables, and paused at the paddock fence, watching the horses. After a minute, Graceful came over to see him, and he stroked her head for a few minutes, feeling the grit in her mane and wondering at the changes that had happened in the months since he had ridden her into Herrandown that cold winter's evening.

Then Merral walked slowly up the grassy rise, trying to minimize the intake of dust into his lungs. Halfway up the slope he found an empty wooden seat overlooking the lake. He sat on it and tried to think. *What am I doing so wrong that I cannot find this craft?*

As he struggled with his thoughts, his attention was caught by the slow elevation of a hydraulic access platform down by the engineering complex. It was the time of year when the equipment that would be used over the summer was checked. He sighed; all the equipment and technology that he had used had failed him. Then, as he looked over the dust-tinted clouds of white and pink blossoms on the trees below him, the idea came to him that it might be the technology that was the problem. He gnawed away at the idea, progressively becoming more enthusiastic about it. After all, he had to recognize that it was in the area of technology that the intruders were superior. If there was a way of masking a ship's presence, they would know how to do it, and he, novice that he was, was not going to penetrate such a mask.

Merral sensed a glimmer of progress. *Perhaps, I now know what I have been doing wrong.* He tried to think of an alternative.

His thoughts were interrupted by a handsome male Menayan bullfinch that landed on a nearby apple tree bough and began to nip at the blossom. Merral leaned forward to watch it, struck by its confident manner and its glorious breeding plumage of glossy red and black.

The animals could detect them.

Merral sat bolt upright, his discouragement suddenly ebbing away at the thought. He remembered how he and Vero had found the woods so quiet and lifeless on the way up the Lannar River. Other birds had fled the dreadful buzzard—half machine and half corpse—that had watched them as they made their way northward. He remembered how Barrand's dogs had been disturbed at Herrandown and how Spotback had pursued the two creatures northward and paid for

it. *Perhaps,* he asked himself with mounting eagerness, *the intruders'
weakness lay here?*

Agitated, Merral rose and walked to the summit of the hill overlooking the Institute, trying to pursue this line of thought. He smiled at
the idea of leading a team of dogs across the length and breadth of the
Lannar Crater. That was hardly practical, yet there might be something in the principle.

It was a pity, he reflected, as he finally stopped on the smooth,
grassy summit, that the wildlife of the crater area was so poorly
known. He looked northward thoughtfully, hoping to see the Rim
Ranges in the distance, but the grimy air had hidden their peaks. He
went through what he knew: herds of caribou migrated across the
area, their numbers kept in balance by wolves. There were brown
bears, beavers, long-tailed otters, and many other smaller mammals.
Of course, there were also various birds, and many ducks and waders
migrated in and nested in the swamps. The problem was that few people ventured regularly up to study them. There was just too much to do
farther south. Yet there was *some* data and some of that, Merral realized, was in the Institute itself.

He hurried back down and went straight to the office of Lesley
Manalfi, the ornithologist.

Lesley ran his fingers through his wide, straggly, and graying red
moustache as Merral asked him about any bird oddities in the Lannar
Crater. One of his fingers bore a large pink bandage.

On a shelf above them, a female chaffinch hopped about watching
them cautiously. In the background Merral could hear chirping and
cawing from the adjacent room. Lesley had a reputation for being able
to heal injured birds, and in spring and autumn his laboratory was
often the home of exhausted migrants that had been brought in.

"Oddities, my boy? What sort of oddities?" Lesley asked.

"Signs that animals are avoiding an area. Please don't ask why."

"Avoiding an area?" Lesley repeated in perplexed tones. "Well,
the Lannar's not really my patch," he said, looking at Merral with
good-natured puzzlement. "The only studies are by remote means.

But, strange to tell, I did see something from a satellite run only the other day. Where was it?"

He flicked his bandaged finger over the touchpad below the deskscreen. "Yes, that's it. There's a lake; formally unnamed as yet, but it's Fallambet Lake Five on the maps. There's always a lot of *Cygnus cygnus*, that's the Whooper Swan—the Farholme subspecies, of course—breeding around the northern tip. You see, we can keep a tag on them because they are big enough and white enough to be easy to count on remote imagery."

He muttered under his breath quietly as he looked at the screen. Above them, in a flutter of wings, the chaffinch flew unsteadily across to the other side of the room.

"And?" asked Merral, aware that Lesley had turned to watch the bird.

"Now that *is* good; it's only today that she has been flying at all. And what? Oh yes, this year the image shows none breeding. Not there."

Merral felt a tingle of excitement. "Which means what?"

Lesley twirled the end of his moustache and smiled up at Merral. "Well, without checking on the ground, it's hard to say. And you know, probably better than all of us, that the area is rapidly changing. Perhaps the water quality may have altered in some way that has affected the ecology. Whatever the cause, they've moved elsewhere."

"Could it be, perhaps . . . disturbance?"

"Disturbance by *what*, my boy?" The brown eyes glinted.

"Oh, anything," Merral said, realizing as he spoke that he was deliberately trying to sound vague. "A methane seep? hot springs?"

"Hmm. But yes, it's possible."

"How long have they been breeding there?"

"Oh, regular records go back three hundred years. Plus. This is the first year with no breeding pairs."

"And could it be the bad weather?"

"Possibly—" Lesley checked the screen—"but . . . no, elsewhere they are still nesting farther north."

"Do you have an image of the lake there?"

"Yes, certainly. Here." He swung the screen around.

Merral glanced at it, recognizing a dumbbell-shaped lake near the center of the crater that he had already looked at in his search. He checked the scale; along its longer northern axis it was barely ten kilometers long and less than half that at its widest part. In the middle, where a small delta had built out from the western side, it was no more than a kilometer wide. There were extensive reed areas around the northern margins and clumps of firs elsewhere; otherwise the surroundings were rolling sands with coarse grass patches. There was nothing striking in any way about it.

Merral, conscious that Lesley was looking at him, tore his glance away and got to his feet. "Thanks. Well, I must go. . . . Fallambet Lake Five . . . very interesting. And that's the only data you have for the area?"

Lesley looked curiously at him. "Well, we have the bird migration pathways, of course. A lot of species breed in the Lannar area."

"Of course. I should have remembered that."

"Well, we don't do too much with the data. At the moment. We plot them as routine; there're, oh, probably about a thousand tagged birds of a dozen species. As you know, the rings transmit the position fairly accurately, so we have a good idea of the flight paths."

"Could I interpret the data?"

"Even a forester can do it, my boy. It's in standard map format; the routes are for spring and autumn each year. You want the files? I'll send them over to you." His finger moved over the touchpad.

"Yes . . . but wait. I'll call them up from you."

"As you wish. But can I ask—?"

I'd better get used to this. "Sorry, Lesley, it's a special project. It's confidential."

Lesley's expression was suddenly one of surprise. "Confidential? That's a strange word. Who says it's confidential?"

"Uh, I'm probably not supposed to tell you that."

"Huh?" The eyes widened further. "You mean the reason why it's confidential is confidential itself?"

Struck by the logic of the question, Merral hesitated. "Hmm, I hadn't thought about it that way. It is a bit odd. Sorry. I really am." He moved toward the door.

The ornithologist shrugged. "You know, five weeks ago this was a normal Made World. Now I'm really beginning to wonder. Things are going crazy here. The Gate. You. The hawk."

"I'm sorry," Merral said, feeling unhappy that he couldn't explain to a colleague more about what was going on. Suddenly, Lesley's final word registered with him. "The hawk?"

The ornithologist grimaced and waved his bandaged finger. "Oh, I thought everybody knew. One of the Levant sparrow hawks I was checking on yesterday suddenly had a go at me. It took a chunk out of my finger with a claw."

"I'm sorry, Lesley. Serious?"

"No, but I'll have a scar. . . . But I felt stupid, really. Thirty years of handling birds, I know what I'm doing. Or I thought I did. Weird though. It behaved as though it was scared of me. They don't do that."

"They didn't—," Merral sighed. "You know, Lesley, I'm hearing—and using—the past tense far too much these days."

Before he had to explain any more, he left the ornithologist and walked past his office to the empty teaching lab. There, without giving his name to the network, he accessed Lesley's data.

Feeling as if he was holding his breath, Merral scanned the migration routes of the twelve species over the last dozen years. Of the twelve species he had the data for, ten regularly migrated north over the feature labeled Fallambet Lake Five.

But not this year.

This year things were different. Most species had swung west round the lake, while a few had gone east. None had gone over.

An hour later, Merral had acquired from one of the mammal biologists the remotely tracked caribou migration routes in the Lannar Crater and was plotting them on his computer. When he overlaid this spring's routes on those of years past, he saw a sudden, sharp, and unprecedented diversion near the middle of the crater. When Merral flicked on the underlying topographic map, it was with an enormous sense of relief and satisfaction that he saw a blue figure-eight shape with the words *Fallambet Lake Five* printed next to it.

His search area was now down to under a hundred square kilometers, and Merral knew that, if necessary, he could map every boulder and tree of that.

●◆●

On the following evening, Merral found the intruder ship at last.

He felt it was a strange irony that, in the end, the final thing that allowed him to pinpoint the precise site was not the birds or animals, but his own trees. As he scanned the image of the eastern lakeside for what he felt was the fiftieth time, a clump of five firs next to the water's edge arrested his attention. Their tops had snapped off—a common enough result of an ice storm. In this case, though, the broken crests all pointed northward, and Merral knew that no ice storm ever came out of the south.

He then focused on the rock- and boulder-strewn area of the lakeside to the north of the five decapitated trunks. Visually, he could see nothing unnatural, but juggling and merging images of thermal, magnetic, and gravity data at maximum enhancement showed a smooth and regular ellipse, some hundred meters long and forty wide, just to the east of the water's edge and running parallel to it.

Examining the images in visual wavelengths, even with those that had a resolution capable of picking up a boulder the size of a man's head, Merral could see nothing unusual. Rubbing his weary eyes, he peered again at the visual images taken before and after the landing, trying to spot differences. He stared at the earlier of the two images, taken ten weeks before the landing date, trying to register every boulder and shrub in his mind. The features were simple: there was the lake strand, and some hundred meters away, and more or less parallel to it, a steep cliff the height of a three-story house that had been cut in the gravels. Eroded, Merral decided, by the lake at some higher water level. He turned to the subsequent image, taken nine weeks ago, and saw the same cliff. With a sudden thrill he realized it had moved. But his excitement quickly ebbed as he realized that it was probably nothing more than natural erosion.

Discouraged, Merral flicked the image backward and forward on the screen. Then it dawned on him that the cliff had indeed moved, but *toward* the lake and not away from it.

"It can't do that!" he said aloud.

The cliff was now only fifty meters from the shoreline. Somehow, between the taking of the two images, an extension to the cliff had been created. He rapidly superimposed all the other data on the images and found that the new extension to the cliff exactly covered the long ellipse of the anomalies.

"Thank you, Lord," he said aloud.

Merral looked at the time and realized that he had missed the last flight of the day. Deciding that he would travel out on the dawn flight, he called the airport office, booked a seat for the earliest flight, and got them to call Vero and tell him the arrival time. Then he printed off the data, downloaded it onto a datapak, and locked everything else away in the cupboard.

It had taken him almost four weeks, but he had, at last, found the intruder ship. That, however, raised a new and troubling question:

What were they going to do about it?

The next morning the continuing dust storm delayed the flight, and Merral and the other passengers had to stand around in the terminal and talk as the latest meteorological data was checked. As he stood there watching a sun so muted that it was no more than a hazy, coppery glow in the clouds, Merral realized how impatient he was to be at Isterrane and to talk with Vero and the others. He wanted to share what he knew and to talk over his fears.

He also realized that he was particularly looking forward to seeing Anya. Merral found this feeling of anticipation troubling. *Surely,* he thought, *I ought only to feel such an excitement with Isabella?* After all, although Isabella clearly saw their relationship as being further advanced than he did, she and he *were* linked together. Yet Merral sensed that although he was still fond of her, he didn't delight in her presence in the way that perhaps he ought to. In fact, he realized he had been thinking a lot about Anya; indeed, over the past week or so, he had frequently found himself unfavorably comparing Isabella's subtle and roundabout manner with Anya's bluff openness. He found his pleasing thoughts about Anya perturbing. In what he now—rather worryingly— saw as his "old world," feelings and choices had worked in harmony; somehow you both chose whom you loved *and* fell in love with them. The two sides of a personality worked together. Now though, he sensed, a conflict was possible; the feelings of the heart and the choice of the head might not automatically come together.

Merral walked around to the window overlooking the landing strip. Through the heavy air, almost brown with fine dust, he could see the tanker filling the short-haul passenger flier with hydrogen. As he stood there, he was suddenly aware of a conversation from two men seated a few meters away.

"Yes, it's the very weirdest thing," he heard one man say in a tone that made the hairs on the back of his neck prick up. "You know I'm now doing the health certificates for the employment check on the sixty-five-year-olds?"

"Of course," said the other man, whom Merral felt he had seen around the hospital. "I sympathized, remember? It's one of the worst things about being a doctor. People often get unhappy at being told to ease up on work."

"Well, that's the thing. See, in the last six weeks, I have had three—really—*three* people, all thanking me for failing them."

"Seriously?" Merral, held spellbound by the conversation, noted the genuine surprise in the voice.

"Absolutely. The last guy said, 'Well, Doc, truth to tell, I'm glad. It's all been a bit of a strain lately. I reckon I'm glad to go and do part-time work.' The other two said much the same."

"Extraordinary. But I've heard other things too. . . ."

At that point, the navigator came over and called them to the plane, and Merral never found out what other new and ominous novelties had transpired in Ynysmant. He could have asked, but he was already worried about becoming known as the man who was asking too many odd questions. As the plane rumbled up into the dusty air, he knew that there were some very serious decisions to be made in Isterrane.

•◆•

Two hours later Merral landed at Isterrane airport to find the sun shining through an atmosphere swept free of dust by the coastal breezes. The terminal was full, as two flights from the west had just come in, and he could not see Vero. To his surprise, a tall, well-built man came over to him. He was in his early twenties, with short, pale brown hair, a chiseled face, and green eyes.

"Forester D'Avanos? Sentinel Enand sent me for you," the young man said in a musical voice.

Merral stared at the young man and decided that they had never met. "Yes, that's right."

"My name's Lorrin, Lorrin Venn." An open smile broke across the face, and there was an eager and enthusiastic handshake. Lorrin Venn, Merral decided, was another of Vero's team, just out of college.

"This is good," Lorrin announced with enthusiasm. "I am really delighted to meet you, sir. I'm in the FDU, and I'm under instructions to take you to the Library Center to meet Mr. Vero. Straightaway. Do you need a hand with the bag?"

"No, it's light."

The young man, already moving toward the exit, shrugged in an easygoing manner. "Okay, sir."

"But why the Library Center?"

"Sir, I wasn't told and I didn't ask. But over here, please. We have a vehicle."

At a pace so fast that Merral could barely keep up, Lorrin walked through the main doorway and out to where a small, blue four-seat urban machine was parked.

"But can't we find a lift?" Merral asked.

"No need, sir," was the quick and buoyant response. "The FDU has its own vehicles now. Priority."

"I see," Merral answered, wondering exactly what else Vero had acquired for the Farholme Defense Unit. He gestured to the people waiting at the terminal exit. "But shouldn't we offer a lift to someone? We have two spare seats."

Lorrin smiled. "No, sir," he said. "The FDU has priority here too. Orders are to take you straight there and not to wait. Speeds us up no end. It's neat."

"I see," said Merral, noting Lorrin's enthusiasm for the privilege. "I was expecting Zak. What's he up to?"

"Zak Larraine? He's in the contact team. I'm in support."

"What's the difference?"

"Contact's gonna be more exciting." There was a note of regret in his voice.

◦—•—◦

Lorrin whistled softly as he drove; it was a tuneful and happy sound, and Merral found it soothing. Halfway to the Library Center, the young man turned to Merral with a curious, almost awed look. "You know, sir, we've all heard about you."

"About me? What—?"

"That you fought the creatures. On your own. 'Hand to hand' was the old term." His tone was respectful.

"Oh . . . ," Merral said, feeling embarrassed, "you know about that?"

"Well, Mr. Vero told us. See, we don't have much else to go on, really. Your information is hard data. But it sounded well, heroic." He looked encouragingly at Merral. "I'd love to know more. Be neat."

Merral looked out of the window for a moment, turning away from this man who seemed to think he was a hero. "Lorrin, I would give a lot to be able to forget all about it. Forever." Then he realized that his words might sound rude. "But, well, if you need me to talk about it, then I'll do it. But only once. And then under pressure. And, if it's all right with you, not now."

"Mr. Vero said it was nasty," Lorrin said, glancing at him. "But I figured it might just be him. Well, sir, when you tell it, I hope it's not just for the contact team."

"Lorrin, if you don't hear it, you won't miss much. It was nasty. *Very*. Fighting is nasty. Period."

Lorrin seemed to consider the matter and then, moments later, began to whistle again.

◦—•—◦

They parked at the rear entrance to the Library Center, and Lorrin, still whistling, led Merral in through an unlabeled door and hurriedly down a dusty metal spiral staircase that vibrated under their footsteps. From the faint hum from the wall beyond, they were at the back of the data storage units that formed the core of the Library Center. And as he thought it, it occurred to him that what he was hearing was no longer just the sound of one small extension of the Library, the vast information network that spanned the Assembly. As far as Farholme was concerned, it was *the* Library and would be until today's young men and women were elderly.

At the bottom of the ladder, Lorrin turned, pushed open a door, and walked through into darkness. The automatic lighting switched on slowly after him, almost as if it were reluctant to believe that anyone was actually there. Ahead of them lay a narrow, bare, and unpainted brick corridor with a feeling of neglect about it.

"Mind your head," Lorrin called back, gesturing to the sagging cabling festooned along the roof. With energetic strides, he set off down the sloping and curving corridor. Merral followed him as fast as he could, hearing their footsteps echoing all around. After a hundred meters or so, they stopped before a solid dark door in the side of the wall.

The door swung open a fraction to reveal Vero's brown face. His look of caution was suddenly transformed into one of pleased recognition, and he flung the door wide. "Welcome. Do come in!"

Clasping Merral's shoulder in a friendly grip, Vero led him into a tiny, white-painted, brick-walled chamber with a low, curved roof and the air of having been recently cleaned out and painted. It was sparsely furnished with a table, a few chairs, and a wallscreen, and in one corner a number of cables snaked down from an open ceiling duct to the floor.

Vero waved a hand at the young man. "Thanks, Lorrin! Can you find Harrent and tell him our guest is here? Quietly, though. Don't shout it out. Then get the truck ready."

"Right, Mr. Vero," Lorrin replied, in what Merral felt was a strangely formal way, and turned and walked swiftly back up the corridor. As the door closed, they could hear him beginning to whistle.

Vero closed the door firmly behind him and turned to stare at Merral.

"My friend!" Vero said, pleasure stamped across his face. "It's been too long. I have missed you. Especially with Brenito gone. I wanted to be in touch with you, but I thought it best to leave you be."

Then he paused, swelled out his cheeks, and exhaled with a loud sigh. "Oh yes, such a lot has happened since we last met! But take a seat." He gestured to a chair and then bobbed over and sat on the other side of the table behind a pile of datapaks and a battered yellow notebook with a neat 5 inked on its cover.

"And I'm glad to see you, Vero," Merral replied.

He was struck by the odd feeling that Vero seemed at home in this subterranean room.

"But you've found it." Vero stared expectantly at Merral's backpack.

"Yes. On the eastern edge of Fallambet Lake Five; the Fallambet is in the north of the crater. It's a tributary of the Nannalt River."

"Ah. It was off the Nannalt Delta that the *Miriama* found the cockroach-beast."

"Yes. I made that link too."

"Splendid! I can't wait to see it. But I'd better. Anyway, Lorrin looked after you all right?"

"Yes. Happy fellow. Where's Zak?"

"Oh," said Vero rather vaguely, "out with the contact team. But Lorrin was fine?"

"Yes."

"He's a great guy. One hundred and ten percent enthusiasm. The top student last year in Library Science at the College at Baandal. Loves working with the FDU."

"So it seems. I think he's happier than me about it all. But Library Science?"

A sudden look of deep intensity came into Vero's eyes. "Merral, I have realized many things over the last few weeks." He shook his head as if awed by events. "I decided early on that I could create an FDU from first principles, but that it would take about twenty years. And your news from Larrenport and your doctor's alarming report on obstetric problems suggested to me that we might not have twenty months, or even twenty weeks. I realized that the only way of speeding things up was by using the past. So Lorrin—and others—have been working in the Library. And we have found more than we expected." His expression was suddenly pained. "Ah. And also less. But Harrent will explain that."

Then his troubled look lifted and he smiled again. "But it is good to see you."

"I was sorry to hear about Brenito. I'd like to visit the grave."

"I'll try and find the time."

"Do you miss him?"

"Yes. I keep saying, 'What will Brenito counsel?' and then—" Emotion welled up in Vero's voice, and for a few moments he was silent. "But then I tell myself he would have told me to decide for myself."

"Are you living at his house?"

"No. I have been tempted. But it's too far out to run a secure communications link to. And I've been working very odd hours. I have two people staying there, though. Cataloging all that he left behind. It's quite a collection of objects. They have instructions to look for anything that has a bearing on the rebellion." Vero's expression brightened. "But how is Ynysmant? Isabella? your parents?"

"Troubled, Vero. All of them. There are problems in Ynysmant. The mood—whatever we call it—is spreading. I'm sure."

"So quickly?" Alarm flooded Vero's face. "I have heard hints of problems. I don't think we have any time to spare at all." He paused. "Anyway, I've brought you here first because I want you to hear what Harrent the librarian says about a problem. He's not part of us—not really—so don't reveal anything, right? Then we move on to the base."

"The base? I thought this was it."

"This?" Vero seemed amused at the thought. "You don't understand. The base is very much larger. You remember the new water transport project for Isterrane, based up in the Walderand River?"

"Vaguely . . ."

"Well, the project was frozen; the pumps were being brought in through the Gate. So they've given us—that is, the FDU—the pump chambers. It's ideal. But secret." He tilted his head, listening. "Ah, that will be Harrent now. But remember, don't say too much."

There was a knock at the door, and a very tall and elderly gray-haired man in a dark official suit came in, stooping carefully and rather stiffly to avoid hitting his head on the doorframe. Inside the room, he straightened himself up carefully, eyeing the low ceiling with suspicion. He shook hands in a rather ritualistic way, first with Vero and then with Merral.

"Harrent Lammas, Assistant Librarian of Isterrane," he said in polite, formal tones. His air of reserve seemed to Merral to be heightened by the dark eyes and a rather stern expression.

They sat down and Vero turned to Merral. "Let me start by explaining that Lorrin and I wanted to do research in the Library, but I was worried that we might be watched. So I consulted Harrent here and, well, together we found some interesting things. Harrent, please explain."

The tall man rested his long arms on the table, exposing neat white shirt cuffs beyond the dark, precisely turned-up sleeves of the jacket. *This is a man,* Merral thought, *who is everything I would imagine a librarian to be: precise, knowledgeable, retiring.*

"Very well," Harrent said, his expression suggesting that he was far from being at ease in this setting. "Hmm, Merral, I'm not sure how much you know about how the Library works. I take it you have some understanding?"

"I know that the Library is modeled on a fixed geography of rooms, corridors, and stacks which goes back to the days before virtuality when libraries really were repositories of books. So wherever you are in the Assembly and whether you access it by a diary or a computer, you get the same pattern." Harrent nodded encouragingly, and Merral continued. "What else? I also know that there are rules and protocols of Library use, which, to my limited knowledge, have always existed. I suppose they go back to the era of the Technology Protocols?"

"Actually they started to be subscribed to over a hundred years earlier. Anything else?"

"No, not really. It's just there for whatever we want—words, text, images, programs."

Harrent nodded in a rather restrained way. "Hmm, in some ways I am pleased by your ignorance. It is a maxim of Library usage that the system and the librarians should be transparent."

A cautious smile flickered across his face. "Sometimes, in our case, literally."

He tapped his diary and the wallscreen opposite lit up with the familiar picture of a grand vaulted Gothic interior with multiple levels of floors, along which book-lined corridors stretched off on either side as far as the eye could see. As Merral looked at it he remembered the pang of disappointment he had had as a child when he had found out that there had never been a real building as grand and glorious as this.

With a smooth and practiced speed, Harrent slid the viewpoint confidently along the main aisle and then down a side corridor. As he did, he passed gray, stylized human figures, devoid of detail, that were either standing by shelves or moving along purposefully. The librarian nodded at the screen. "The Library at the moment. Very familiar and part of all our lives. Every member of the Assembly has grown up with this exact version since 2170, with only minor software tweaks since. And a billionfold more data." His tone was so dry and formal that Merral wondered how much contact with real human beings his job involved.

"Now for various reasons," Harrent continued, "some practical and some psychological, it has always been found helpful to indicate other users graphically. As we just saw. It's really just a convention."

"But you never know who they are or what they are reading," added Merral.

"Just so. Hmm, privacy. But—and it's a little known fact—the on-duty librarians have a different view. Diary, librarian mode."

The figures on the image were now suddenly marked in multi-colored bands, and as Harrent approached a form standing nearby, Merral saw that superimposed on the color bands were long sequences of letters and numbers.

"See now, this coding allows us librarians to help a little if needed. I can walk down the library, quite invisible to other users, and see all this. Thus I can tell you from the color codes that this, hmm—yes, is a male academic from Qarantia, that he studies language acquisition, and that he is a regular user of text files and familiar with the Library. In this case, he is unlikely to need help. I can even check, if I wanted, from the data displayed on him, what he has ever examined or down-loaded."

"I had no idea," Merral said. "You have more of a supervisory role than I suspected."

A strange, rather awkward smile slid onto Harrent's face. "Hmm, I take that as a compliment, Forester. The ease of Library use is only achieved by a lot of hard work behind the scenes. And anyway, why should you? What we do is only to help users. Though it's also, to a lesser extent, useful for us. It's so much easier to get an idea of what is popular in the Library, and with who. Hmm, actually very usefu—"

"Harrent," interrupted Vero, glancing at his watch, a finger raised in partial admonition, "could you explain the oddities? Please?"

"Hmm, sorry. Ah, I am beginning to fear that in this new era some of the relaxed traditional customs may go. Yes, well when Vero here asked for my help, I realized, after the initial surprise, that he might be able to shed light on some anomalies that had recently occurred. And which were, in my long knowledge of library work, unprecedented."

He delicately tapped a corner of his diary screen. "Now, in order. This is a data record, taken eight days after Nativity Day last year. A remote librarian recorded this view."

There were the multicolored figures again but, in the middle of them, a figure shaded black stood examining a data file on a shelf.

"Harrent," Merral asked, hearing the alarm in his voice, "who is it?"

The librarian gave a little sigh of bewilderment. "Hmm, we really don't know. We at first assumed a data error, or a software glitch. The figure has no code identifiers, no records, no identity. We named him, her, or it, 'the ghost.'"

Vero gestured at the screen. "Please tell Merral what the ghost is downloading."

"It is in the History rooms and it is scanning Lyonel's *Introductory History of the Assembly of Worlds*."

"The basic high school text?"

"Quite."

"Is that all?" Merral asked, remembering having read Lyonel's work when he was around thirteen.

"Odd, eh? But watch, it moves on and we lose it. It was leaving no trail for us to follow. We can't call it up. Very irregular." Merral thought that it was the untidiness of the matter that outraged Harrent. "Not at all the sort of thing one likes to have in a library."

"Was the ghost ever seen again?" Merral asked. As he spoke the word *ghost*, it seemed eerily appropriate.

Harrent nodded stiffly. "Briefly, a day later, which was a Lord's Day."

"But," Merral exclaimed, unable to hold back his surprise, "surely, no one uses the Library then?"

"A few people: doctors, engineers, and, hmm, a surprising number of preachers who need to check some last-minute sermon illustration. Anyway, this happens to be a routine survey frame of the main aisle."

Harrent tapped his diary, and the new image showed the central Library aisle from a high point of view by the main entrance. Apart from two forms heading in the direction of Medicine, there were no figures to be seen. Suddenly the black figure appeared at the entrance, glided along the main aisle, turned down a side corridor, and then stopped and seemed to retrace its steps until it was back in the main aisle. There it appeared to look around.

"Our belief is that it has just realized that it's on its own," said Vero.

The figure rotated again, abruptly headed for the exit, and vanished before it got there.

"After that unhappy incident," Harrent said, "where, incidentally, the ghost seems to have been again heading for Assembly History, it was never seen again."

Merral heard himself speaking, the incredulity thick in his voice. "What sort of being is it that is surprised by the Library being empty on the Lord's Day?"

Harrent looked at him quizzically. "Hmm, I'd like to know too. Very much . . ."

Merral caught a cautioning glance from Vero. Clearly, he felt that it was a question that could be better discussed later. Besides, there was an obvious but disturbing answer: Only a creature from quite outside the Assembly could make that sort of a mistake.

Vero leaned forward toward the librarian. "Now, Harrent, tell Merral why we think it is still there."

"Ah yes. Our guess is that it soon realized how the Library worked and either became invisible or adopted another person's identity. But since then there have been other oddities. It was Vero's idea to set the trap."

"Oh, it was hardly a trap," Vero said, his tone slightly defensive. "It was perhaps a test. It was just that—after I heard this story—I was worried. So, when I went to check some data files, I got Harrent to watch me while there was a virtual camera running." He gestured to the screen and a new image appeared of colored bodies walking and standing in a library corridor.

"There I am," Vero said. "The green hue at the top is because I'm from Ancient Earth, the purple base is for a sentinel. Now watch as I skim through the contents of a file here."

The image focused onto a line of thin, vertical gray files with glowing green lights on their bases. "Now watch as I consult the volume."

On the bottom of one file, the green light turned red.

"The accessing light glows; Anatheon on *The Causes of the Jannafite Rebellion,* for your information. I put it back." The green light came back on. "It's not being accessed. But, on my suggestion, Harrent kept the virtual camera on it. Watch now!"

Abruptly at the base of the file, the light went from green back to red.

"Hey!" Merral cried. "But there's no one there!"

"Exactly—no one we can see. But I was expecting something like it and had Lorrin ready. Watch now as he races across and tries to access the same file. Even in a virtual library our Lorrin is fast."

A figure with yellow and blue bands on its head moved over swiftly and stood by the file with the glowing red light. As the figure representing Lorrin reached for the file, the light instantly changed back to green. A black shape, vaguely human in outline, appeared briefly, flickered, and then vanished.

"Our ghost knew he'd been discovered, panicked, and fled, losing invisibility on the way." Vero's voice was serious. "To use the expression of the ancients, he 'pulled the plug.'"

"'Pulled the plug'?"

Vero shrugged. "As in ending a bath. I suppose." He looked solemnly at Merral. "Well, that's it. So the Library has a ghost."

"A most unhappy state of affairs," said Harrent, his somber expression endorsing his words.

"I agree," Vero said, "but it gets worse."

That, Merral noted with alarm, *is another expression I'm getting used to.*

"Yes, the losses," Harrent muttered in an irritated tone.

"Quite so," Vero agreed. "When I started looking up some works last week, I was surprised to find that they were not there. Not being familiar with library nodes on the Made Worlds, I wondered if they were ones that normally would have been asked for through the Gate. But I checked with Harrent. . . ."

The librarian's face had acquired a look of deep vexation. "Hmm, I checked the index banks and they were not listed. Then, after a suggestion by Vero, I checked an older index that was on an

147

unerasable archive and, well, there they were." He looked at his big hands as if to hide his emotions. "In all my years, I have never heard of titles being erased deliberately. But for them to be erased and then to have the matching records removed too is yet another thing. I have to use the word *wicked*." He paused and repeated to himself softly, "Wicked."

"Can you stop the losses?" Merral asked, suddenly horrified at the prospect of the Library having all its billions of irreplaceable files deleted.

"We are trying to," Harrent said. "Based on what has gone missing we have established a profile of what the ghost is seeking. I have taken the unusual step of having the remaining titles in those areas digitally transcribed to indelible archive format. We think any further erasure impossible." The librarian shook his head in a gesture that conveyed dismay and regret. "But I am appalled. *Most* appalled. Is there anything else?"

"No, my friend. But thank you; now go and watch carefully."

Harrent stood up cautiously, shook hands again with Merral and Vero, and left. As the door closed behind him and the steady footsteps receded into the distance, Vero leaned back in his chair, put his hands behind his neck, and exhaled heavily.

"So, my friend, what do you make of that?"

"Very worrying."

Vero nodded. "But also, in a strange way, encouraging."

"I found no encouragement."

Vero smiled. "Yes. But they made mistakes. *Again*. They are not totally beyond us. Let us be grateful for small things."

He rose. "Let's go. We have a meeting at the base. It's about half an hour's drive, but Lorrin will take us. We can sit at the back of the transporter, and you can tell me about Ynysmant and where this ship is exactly. Corradon and Clemant will be up later, and we need to decide what to do then. But action is urgent. You see we face a double attack: The intruders are getting themselves into the heart of

Farholme, and the evil associated with them is spreading in our society. Time is slipping away faster than we realize."

Merral stepped into the corridor. "It's scary. By the way, what data files were missing?"

"Oh, you can probably guess," Vero said, closing the door behind them.

"No, I can't. Not easily. You tell me."

"Well, a lot of things to do with Jannafy's rebellion; mostly those that talked about how it ended."

"Another common theme."

"Yes, isn't it?" Vero's face bore a knowing look. "And the name of William Jannafy will doubtless arise later on today. Also missing, interestingly enough, were a lot of technical works on late twenty-first century military techniques and weapons."

As he motioned Merral onward he said, in a casual way, "It is almost, my dear Forester, as though they were preparing for us to fight them."

＊＊＊

When they got to the transporter—a big four-wheeled, open-backed LP4 with fading yellow paint and piled high with cases and boxes— Vero led him to the back of the vehicle.

"We can talk here," Vero said, clearing a space to sit. "I want you to tell me all about Ynysmant and the ship as we drive. Lorrin knows a lot, but the fewer that know about this the better. Besides, I think a forester like you may prefer the sun and the fresh air."

Merral sighed. "Indeed, I've had little enough of it lately."

"I find it bright," Vero said. "I spend my life indoors now." He took a blue-peaked cap out of his briefcase and pulled it over his head.

After checking that they were strapped in, Lorrin leapt back into the cab, and they drove steadily westward through Isterrane on the main coastal avenue. As they drove out of Isterrane into the countryside, Vero plied Merral with questions about events in Ynysmant and how he had found the evidence for the ship. For the most part, Vero listened to his account without comment, merely giving encouragement with nods and looks.

Faint snatches of Lorrin's whistling drifted back from the front of the vehicle, causing Merral's spirits to lift. The sky was a brilliant, flawless spring blue, the sun warming, and he could smell the sea salt in the breeze. It was the sort of day that brought to mind thoughts of climbing hills, taking picnics with friends by turbulent and wayward streams, and sitting on new green grass, or lying out, reptilelike, on warm stones. Then it came to him that today he could do none of those things but must talk of darker things, of intruders, sin, and evil. And the contrast saddened him.

Suddenly they turned up from the coast road and climbed northward on a narrow, uneven track along the side of the Walderand River. From the swaying transporter Merral could see the bubbling white waters of the river along the valley bottom. Lorrin, evidently enjoying himself, had shifted to loudly singing a string of folk songs.

Suddenly Vero, who had said nothing for many minutes, looked at Merral. "The landing site; is it accessible?"

"I think so. You are thinking about the expedition?"

"Yes." Vero bit his lip and frowned. "I suppose I need to look at the maps first." Then he gestured back toward Isterrane. "The ghost in the Library . . . Can I guess what you found the most striking thing?"

Merral shook his head. "Too easy; the idea that this thing could be unaware that the Library would be empty on the Lord's Day."

Vero nodded. "Yes. Mind you, reading Lyonel is weird too. It just confirms to me that whoever the intruders are, they are not Assembly."

"Exactly."

"Or if they are of the Assembly—" Vero's face darkened—"then things have gone very badly wrong somewhere." Then he shook his head and fell silent again.

Merral was glad of the break in the conversation, and as Lorrin drove them upward on the winding road, he stared at the scenery, trying to clear his mind from the notion of something unpleasant prowling in the Library. They had gained some height now, and Isterrane was stretched out below them, the white blossom of the orchards and the verdant spring grass breaking up and isolating the red and white patches of buildings. Beyond them and the high gray seawall was the dazzling blue of the sea, where Merral could make out white lines of the waves breaking in the spring breeze.

Now Lorrin turned off onto an even narrower track that showed signs of the recent passage of many vehicles. Ahead Merral could see how the hillsides were closing in as steep cliffs of purple-gray lavas swung across the valley, almost sealing it off. They passed a sign on which the words *Walderand River Project: Site Road Only* were written, and Merral noted that above it had been posted a smaller, newer green sign on which the letters *FDU* had been marked.

As the road became rougher and steeper, the swaying of the transporter became more pronounced, and Merral saw that Vero was starting to look uncomfortable. Then they rode over a crest in the road and Merral was able to see that, a kilometer or so away, the road stopped below the sheer cliff that ended the valley. As he stared at the rocks ahead, Merral was suddenly aware of men and machines working away below them. A small cloud of brown dust drifted slowly upward.

"I thought the water project had been stopped?" Merral asked, gesturing at the construction work.

"It has. That's ours," Vero replied.

"All of it?"

"All of it." Vero sounded almost embarrassed.

"But it's vast." The rumbling of the wheels beneath him was now so loud that Merral almost had to shout.

Vero hesitated for a moment and then exhaled noisily. "Yes—it needs to be." Then he smiled. "But my manners fail me." He made an expansive gesture with his hand. "Welcome, Forester, to the FDU base."

As they drove ever closer to the end of the valley, Merral could see what was being constructed: a semicircular earth wall with a narrow access gap for the road. Nearer still, Merral was surprised to see that the gap was closed off by a moveable metal barrier.

They stopped in front of the barrier, and Vero gestured that they get out. "Let's walk through!" he shouted over the noise of the earth-moving machinery. "It's quicker."

As they walked past the transporter, Lorrin, whistling happily, beamed at them and raised an outstretched hand sharply to the side of his head.

A salute. I've been saluted. The world seemed distorted again. *We only ever salute the emblem of the Lamb and Stars, and that on special occasions.*

Merral tapped Vero on the shoulder. "Lorrin just saluted us," he whispered. "Is that supposed to happen?"

"Ah. Saluting. A problem, that. At the moment, it is voluntary. But we need to make a decision. I should say—perhaps warn you—that while we have made a lot of progress in some technical areas, there are some things we have not resolved. Such as discipline."

"Can't we make it voluntary?"

"A voluntary discipline?" Vero gave a strained smile. "Give that idea some more thought, Forester."

Merral noticed men unrolling metal wire mesh to put up along the top of the earth wall. *A month ago, I would have assumed it was to keep animals in; I can now guess it is to keep things out.*

A young man with a databoard came over, gave Vero an abrupt

but somehow deferential nod of the head, and then, with polite efficiency, took Merral's name and date of birth.

"Sadly necessary," muttered Vero, as if embarrassed by the procedure, and walked on briskly.

Feeling perplexed, Merral followed him to the foot of the towering cliff. There, by the side of two great tunnels, a new wooden building had been erected.

"Excuse me a moment," Vero said. "I just need to check on deliveries."

While he waited outside, a still-bemused Merral watched the noisy activity going on around him. By the perimeter wall there were three earthmovers and a dozen men putting up the wire mesh, while inside the compound two LP4 transporters were being unloaded by another half dozen men and a lift truck. From deep inside the tunnel came noises of further mechanical activity.

Vero returned clutching papers and motioned Merral urgently toward the larger, right-hand tunnel.

"Merral, things are moving fast," Vero said in an impatient tone of voice. "But it's a race and I'm not sure we are winning."

He led Merral past another observant young man with a databoard and a sign that proclaimed "FDU Personnel Only" into the darkness of the tunnel. As they walked carefully along the side of the tunnel, Merral became aware of an increasing volume of noise ahead of them. About eighty meters from the entrance, the tunnel opened out into a vast four-story cavern lit by bright cones of light and the flash of electric and plasma beams.

Merral stopped, gazing around in awe. Ahead of him, in an area the size of a Team-Ball pitch, perhaps fifty or more people were at work at a dozen sites. Some were packing crates and containers, others were working busily on vehicles and machinery, and still others were assembling equipment. The warm and heavy air was filled with sounds: hammering, shouting, clanking, all reverberating off the bare rock walls.

Merral grabbed Vero's arm. "Is all this . . . yours?" he asked, barely able to believe that his friend had been able to organize so much.

Vero stopped suddenly. "It's not mine; it just sort of grew," he said loudly as a new burst of hammering broke out beyond them. "I'll explain how later. Up here." Then, before Merral could ask him any more questions, he was clambering up a metal stairway that led to a walkway along the side of the cavern.

"Just a minute!" called out Merral, catching up with his friend. "Look at those things!" he said, pointing at the two familiar gray vehicles being worked on under spotlights. "Those are gravity-modifying sleds!"

"True," Vero replied in a matter-of-fact way.

"But we were told—in Planning—not to use them. Gravity-modifying engine technology was for urgent and emergency use only. It was a case of priority."

Vero inclined his head in evident agreement. "True, true. But this is why there was that restriction. We needed them. Ours is 'urgent and emergency use.'"

"But—"

Vero, however, had walked on and, opening a door off the walkway, beckoned Merral into a gloomy corridor. He closed the door behind him and the noise of the cavern vanished. They walked a dozen meters along the corridor before Vero stopped in front of another door and turned a handle. The door opened, revealing a room so well lit that Merral found himself blinking.

"Welcome to the office!" Vero announced.

"Greetings, Tree Man!" cried a familiar voice, and Merral found himself being given a disturbingly welcome hug by Anya. Behind her, a smiling Perena rose from a table covered with datapaks and maps.

Vero took a seat at the table and gave a theatrical cough. "Everybody, please! Representative Corradon and Advisor Clemant are on their way. I suggest we get our own business over first."

Still taking in his surroundings, Merral sat at the table, gratefully accepting the coffee and biscuits Anya passed him. As he looked around at the bleak, white-walled room and its harsh artificial lighting, he couldn't help contrasting it with the glorious, open, sunlit countryside that they had driven through. *Is this going to be the pattern for our future meetings? Is the price we pay for security to be that of a permanent existence in windowless rooms underground?*

But his meditations were short-lived.

"Merral," Vero said, "with you here we can start to move forward. This is the base, and it is here that we are preparing for what may lie ahead."

"I'm impressed. Awed. That you have done everything in the time you've had."

"The original team designated projects and appointed leaders for them; then those leaders set up subteams and squads to tackle the projects. For once, the structured and disciplined nature of Assembly society has worked in our favor. And the representatives offering us a free hand was a great help."

Then Vero looked at his watch and shook his head. "But we must move on. I want Perena to speak first. And then Anya. I think that will help put you in the picture and perhaps answer some questions. Captain Lewitz?"

"Merral, I'm glad you are here," Perena began in her quiet, unruffled voice. "We've missed you. Now, on the issue of how the Gate was destroyed, I have made little progress. It seems certain that two things happened. First of all, the various safeguard programs were overridden and then a pulsating gravitational imbalance was established between the Gate segments. No amount of modeling has been able to achieve either phenomenon accidentally."

"So it *was* sabotage?"

"Even the official investigation team is beginning to use that most unfamiliar of words as a hypothesis."

"And the ship?"

"Ah. The ship." Perena paused, as if taking stock of her thoughts. "I organized the checking of all the astronomical data sources we have—every bit of it—to see if I could trace the origin of the ship.

Those results are now coming in. As you know, the Guardian satellites monitor all incoming debris heading for Farholme so they can destroy or divert anything that poses a risk. A check of that data looking at what we now believe was the intruder ship has allowed us to trace it back as far as the orbit of Fenniran. But beyond that is a problem—there is no trace of it. None at all."

"So, what have you concluded?"

"Well, all the data is consistent with it emerging from a Below-Space Gate just beyond the orbit of Fenniran. Not close, of course; you don't put a Gate near a gas giant."

"But there is no Gate there."

"Well observed," she said with gentle irony. "But the data would also fit a ship which had traveled through Below-Space on its own and emerged into Normal-Space there."

"Hence your belief that the intruders can do what we can't. That they have . . . what did Gerry call it? 'autonomous Below-Space travel'?"

"That's right," Perena said. "It increasingly seems like a reasonable supposition."

Vero raised a finger. "A reminder, Merral. The Assembly, it seems, could have done that. Our forefathers were just uneasy about the spiritual side effects of doing it."

"Except General William Jannafy," Merral added.

"Ah," Vero said and gestured for Perena to continue.

"Indeed, Merral, the suggestion Vero made that, during the Rebellion, Jannafy went on to pursue Below-Space exploration also seems entirely reasonable. Anyway, we believe that the intruder ship has a Below-Space drive."

Vero caught Merral's eye. "And that is certainly the hope that Corradon and Clemant have. So before they get here, let's have a look at what you have found."

Merral took the various maps and images out of his holdall and put them on the desk. Together they all peered at the images and carefully marked the identified location on an enormous map of northeastern Menaya that Vero had hung on a wall. Merral watched as Perena carefully measured off the length of the anomalies and copied them down in fine handwriting into a notebook. Another idea of Vero's that was catching on, he noted.

After a minute, Vero looked at her. "So, space expert, is this it?"

"Yes . . . ," Perena said slowly, continuing to stare intently at the image. "I think so. There are aspects about it that I'm unclear about. . . . But it fits." She frowned slightly. "Merral, I need to talk to Gerry on this. Can I have a copy of the data?"

"Of course."

A bell-like tone sounded. Vero picked up from the floor a handset attached to a thin silvery cable and put it to his ear.

"Good, good. Send them up when they come," he said, nodding at Merral, and put the handset down.

"Corradon and Clemant are getting near. We are using an optic-fiber link from the entrance, Merral; we are getting a line laid to Isterrane." He shook his head in wonderment. "Doing that will use 10 percent of the whole annual optic fiber cable production of Farholme. But it's secure." He paused. "*Secure* . . . It's a word I'm getting used to." He sighed. "And I wish I wasn't." Then he turned to Anya. "Anya, tell us what news you have."

"I wish I could skip this," Anya said, sweeping a strand of red hair from her face and looking around. "I think these creatures are the most loathsome things you can imagine. But I suppose I have forced myself to come to terms with them. To distance myself . . . After three weeks plus of DNA work, I suppose you could say that we have made some progress in understanding these creatures. Although actual specimens would, from the scientific point of view, be preferable. But let's deal with the general features first." She pointed her diary to the projector on the table ,and above it a meter-high, three-dimensional ape-creature appeared and slowly rotated.

Merral shuddered and caught a flash of sympathy from Anya.

"The images are from the DNA cross-checked with visual information. The ape-creatures have human and gorilla DNA with some artificial code segments. They have good eyesight, good hearing. They are probably omnivores and are potentially very strong. There is a lot of musculature."

She tapped the screen and a hunched figure of the cockroach-beast hung over the table. As it turned round, Merral felt its reptilelike head seemed to look accusingly at him.

"Despite the superficial arthropod-like appearance, we now know that this is a modified human being: a more or less ordinary skeleton, but with a thickened insectlike cuticle instead of skin and modified hands capable of cutting between the thumb and the fingers; deep-set eyes with, incidentally, extended sensitivity to short wavelengths—they can see in ultraviolet; some ingenious work to adjust for the rigid exoskeleton—they must molt periodically. Another feature—and this may be significant—is that there appear to be modifications to allow for resistance to radiation."

"What about intelligence?" Merral asked.

"It's hard to be specific; *intelligence* is a tricky term. The best guess for both is that they have a patchy intelligence—good in places. There is little evidence of an ability for complex language, but some areas are specialized: hand-eye coordination in them both is probably good. I'd guess that—overall—their intelligence is probably in the lower part of the human range."

"Can you do me a favor, Anya," Merral asked, "and switch the pictures off?"

The image faded.

"That's better. What else?"

"I think the key thing is that these creatures imply something else. They cannot breed, so they must be made in a laboratory as clones. They have limited intelligence; I don't see them making a ship."

"But serving on one?" Vero asked.

"Perhaps," Anya said.

There was an awkward silence, and Vero made a small gesture with his hand. "You'd better tell Merral what you told me. Your speculation . . ."

Anya stared at Vero as if considering defying him and then turned to Merral with a face clouded with unease. "Very well, although you may not like this. These, then, are clearly designed creatures, even if we can only guess what they are designed for. But I am certain that they weren't designed to be predators."

"But they fought—" Merral stopped, struck by the sense of what she said. "No, I see what you're thinking."

"A true predator—a designed animal—would be faster, smarter, have better senses, and have claws or fangs. But having seen what they have done with these, I can imagine what they might produce in that area." She paused. "And it scares me."

Me too. "Let's hope we never meet such a beast."

Vero nodded. "It remains only a speculation. But Anya is right; we need to be aware of the possibility that the enemy may have more creatures than we have met."

As Merral was digesting that uncomfortable news, there was a knock at the door. Representative Corradon and Advisor Clemant entered. They were in casual clothes, and as greetings were made, it occurred to Merral that, unless you knew who they were, you wouldn't have realized their offices. In a disturbing flash of insight it occurred to him that, perhaps, that was the point. *Are we too learning the arts of disguise?* As he framed the question, he knew the answer. *To fight the intruders, we must risk becoming like them. But how dangerous a risk is that?*

"Thank you, Representative, Advisor, for coming," Vero said.

As they sat down, Merral gazed at the new arrivals. He felt that Corradon had subtly changed; the blue eyes seemed tired, the streaked hair now appeared to be more gray than black, and the bronzed complexion seemed paler. Clemant too seemed to have changed: his round, smooth, pale face seemed even more like a mask than ever, and Merral felt that the watchful dark eyes were more deep set than they had been.

"Merral," Vero asked, "I wonder if you would start by outlining what has been happening in Ynysmant?"

"Oh, right. But I thought the location of the ship was the most important thing?"

Vero nodded. "It is, but your story tells us why exactly it is so vital that we find it."

So, as briefly as he could, Merral recounted the various incidents he had observed or heard of within the town, from the disputes at the Team-Ball game, through the emerging irritability and difficulties within Ynysmant, to the incident with Lesley Manalfi and the sparrowhawk. He ended with the conversation overheard at the airport that morning. As he spoke, he was aware of shared, uneasy glances across the table, and it seemed to him that the already heavy atmosphere in the enclosed room became still more oppressive.

There was a long silence when he had finished. He noticed Corradon looking at him as if judging something.

"Thank you, Forester," Corradon said. "Something of what you have said has reached our ears, but not, I feel, the depth or breadth of it. Your firsthand report is helpful, if alarming."

He looked at Clemant. "And there have been other incidents, eh, Lucian?"

"A number," he admitted. "It's very disconcerting."

"For instance," Corradon said slowly, "I have it on good authority that there will be at least one rather odd birth in Larrenport this year. The baby will be born only eight months—or even less—after the wedding."

"I'm sorry, sir," Merral interjected, "that's different from Ynysmant. We have painful births. Not premature ones."

Corradon's face acquired an expression as if he had eaten something that disagreed with him.

Anya nudged Merral in the ribs. "There's another explanation," she hissed quietly. "Think!"

"Oh . . . I see," Merral said, suddenly embarrassed. "You mean that . . . they just didn't wait?"

Corradon merely grunted assent and Clemant shook his head, as if in disbelief.

The representative looked hard at Vero. "So, Sentinel, do you have any comment on all this?"

"I think it just confirms all that we have felt and discussed. With the coming of the intruders, evil has returned to the Assembly, and it is confronting us here on two fronts. We have an external, visible enemy in the ship and in these creatures." The anxious expression on Vero's face gave the lie to his calm statement. "And we also face an internal attack; a subtle spiritual malaise which, it seems, is spreading. That is linked with the intruders, but we do not understand how."

Suddenly, Merral glimpsed Clemant's fingers twisting against each other on the table. *He's afraid. That's why he's supporting Vero. He sees our world slipping away into chaos unless we act.*

"We are addressing the first problem but not the second," Clemant said in his rumbling voice. "Is that wise?"

"Mainly, sir, because we *can* address it. I'm not sure how we can tackle the second problem."

"Surely, Lucian," Corradon said, "the hope is that with the intruder issue—how shall we say?—*resolved,* the second problem may vanish."

"And," Vero quickly added, "their ship or its technology may allow us to seek help."

Clemant stared at him. "This is the hope. Unless there are any other options . . ." He looked around slowly, as if seeking some new suggestion. But there was only silence.

Vero gestured to Merral. "It's time for you to show us what you have found."

Merral slid forward the images on the table and, for the third time in the day, began to talk about what he had discovered. As he spoke and displayed other images, he sensed the total attention of Corradon and Clemant. But as he continued, he was increasingly aware of their disappointment.

Eventually, Corradon turned to Perena. "Captain Lewitz, what do you make of this? I confess I was rather hoping for something more obviously a spacecraft than these rather abstract shapes and lines."

"I agree," said Clemant, his expression leaving no doubt that he too was unimpressed.

Perena stared at the image before answering. "Yes, sir," she said in a voice that, while firm, was barely audible, "I think that this is the ship."

Clemant looked sharply at her. "Captain, we need to be sure. If we go for the wrong location it could be disastrous. I see little hope of a second chance."

"I know, sir. But the data fits. The combination of anomalies is consistent with a craft comparable in size and mass to one of our in-system shuttles."

"Yet, Captain," Clemant said, with a creasing of his forehead, "I thought you had proposed that this vessel goes between stars?"

Perena looked at the advisor carefully. "Sir, there is, as you know, data for that hypothesis. I agree this ship seems smaller than I would have predicted. But we have no idea how a mobile Gate system might look, and this ship might be big enough. It's certainly large enough to carry a ferry craft."

"We are on the point of mounting a risky venture based on scanty data," the advisor said.

Corradon shrugged. "Lucian, we have been through all this. Is this an objection?"

"Sir, it is not an objection. But it is a statement of disquiet."

Corradon said nothing and shifted his gaze to the images. He gestured at the sheets. "Captain Lewitz, Sentinel, can't we get more detailed images?"

Vero scratched his nose. "I-I agree, sir, that they would be nice. But that too is risky; we might alert them."

Perena nodded assent. "Yes, I agree. It might frighten them. And if they were to take off, we might never find them again." She looked around with her keen blue-gray eyes. "There is something else I want to say here. I'm struck by the way that the disguise has been done. After examining all the images, especially comparing the ones taken before and after the landing, I think that all they have done is put a simple metal-frame structure up and drape a polymer fabric cover with reactive paint over it."

"So how else would you do it?" asked Clemant.

"Well, camouflage is not a specialty of the Assembly, but I would imagine that if you had a sufficiently advanced technology you could produce a holographic field or create some deformation of the light around the ship to give it invisibility. This looks far simpler. Even crude. But then—" She hesitated and seemed to be having a debate with herself. When she spoke again, her voice was so quiet that Merral had to strain to hear her. "Yet it doesn't use any energy and it doesn't emit any stray radiation. So it has merits. Indeed, it may not even be that crude, ultimately."

Corradon, who had been gazing at the wall map, turned to Vero. "So, Sentinel, the plan you had suggested to approach the ship . . . now that we have found it, will it work?"

"Yes," Vero answered. "I should say I have not yet discussed it with Merral. But, yes." He gestured to the images on the table. "It needs detailed planning, but I believe it could succeed."

Corradon looked at his advisor. "Lucian?"

Clemant shifted in his seat. "Sir, the decision is a hard one. We are faced with hard choices. . . ."

"Tell me what I don't know!" Corradon said. He was smiling but his voice was empty of humor.

Clemant stared at his hands for a moment and then looked at the representative. "Sir, my decision is that we go with the sentinel's plan."

Corradon closed his eyes for a moment, as if overwhelmed. Then, his face the picture of steady control, he looked around the table. "Thank you. If the rest of you will excuse us—Lucian and I would like to talk with Merral here alone. I realize that this is somewhat unusual. But these are unusual days."

As the door closed and Merral found himself alone with Corradon and Clemant, he felt troubled.

Corradon stared at him with a look of intense scrutiny. "Very well,

Forester D'Avanos, the situation is this: I am—no, we as representatives are—convinced by the analysis of the path of the intruder ship that it is indeed possible that it has some sort of independent Below-Space capability. If it has, we need that technology and we need it badly. There are a number of scenarios for the future we are concerned about."

"More than concerned," grunted the advisor, in a response so rapid that it was almost an interruption. "Each day brings new evidence of problems."

"So, you see, we *have* to approach the intruders." Corradon's tone was confiding. "We will send a negotiating party."

"Remember, Forester, our preference—on every ground—is for dialogue." There was no possibility of mistaking the seriousness in the advisor's voice.

"Agreed," Corradon said. "The negotiating party will approach openly and without weapons. With nothing that could remotely arouse any suspicions. They will approach slowly—with banners, flags—that sort of thing." Clemant nodded as Corradon continued. "Now, hopefully, they will want to talk. But if they don't . . . if there is—what shall we say?—a negative response, then, well, we will have no option but to try and seize the ship."

"You mean, sir, *attack* it?"

There was a pause. "Yes, Forester. Attack it with the intention of taking it in working order. But *only* after diplomacy—if I may use an old word—has failed."

Before Corradon could continue, Clemant had spoken. "We must not underestimate the risks. We do not know what weapons they have."

Corradon waved a hand with a hint of impatience. "Absolutely. And that is why we agree with Vero's suggestion that we need to be in a position where, if diplomacy fails, we can move to a capture strategy instantly. Surprise may be one of the few weapons we have. We can't squander it by summoning a council of the representatives."

Clemant gave a slight and unenthusiastic nod.

"Exactly," Corradon said. "Vero wants to have a second group standing by so that, if negotiation fails, they can disable this ship and prevent it from taking off. And achieve a seizure."

"That raises a lot of issues. . . ." Merral spoke slowly, his mind struggling to cope with ideas of attack and seizure.

"Oh, indeed," Corradon replied, and Merral marveled at how assured he appeared to be. "But we've read twenty-first century law— of course, the matter has not been discussed since—and that suggests that we have a legitimate right to ask for their surrender as they are on our sovereign territory."

"I see, but respectfully, sir, there are practical issues too."

"Oh, we know that. Vero has been working on a plan for the last few weeks. But this is where you come in."

"I see." *Of course,* Merral thought, recognizing with alarm something that had been hinted at all along.

"Yes," said Corradon. His blue eyes seemed weary. "We want *you* to carry it out. To lead. That is the big gap. We have the decision, we have the equipment, to some extent we have the personnel; we even have the inklings of a strategy. But we need a leader to bring these things together."

Merral swallowed, his mouth suddenly and unaccountably dry. "Me?"

"You. Yes, there was a unanimous feeling among the representatives that, in this respect, you are marked out as the man of the hour. That we should appoint you as captain of the FDU."

"I am less sure, sir," Merral replied, oddly aware of his heart beating heavily. "And surely my opinion counts?"

"Well, only to a limited extent," Corradon countered.

"To be blunt," Clemant added sharply, "there are precious few contenders. And we can't risk the luxury of an experiment."

Merral suddenly felt an irresistible urge to stand up. He rose, walked to a corner of the room, then turned and faced the two men.

"Gentlemen, I am not at all positive about this. In fact, I'm very skeptical."

"Forester, there is no one else suitable to lead."

"What about Vero?" Merral gestured at the room. "He has put together an organization in very short time. Remarkable."

Corradon shook his head. "No, not Vero. Not at all. He is a strategist, and I agree a remarkable one, but he is not a leader in battle. It is not his gifting. You and he complement each other."

"Our sentinel is also from outside," said Clemant. He seemed, to Merral, to be ill at ease. "And you, of course, have fought already."

Suddenly, Merral felt a great desire to just say nothing and walk outside, to get out of this room and its claustrophobic, subterranean atmosphere and see the sun. He struggled against his desires.

"That is why I am so reluctant. I will not readily go back to fighting again. Nor would I wish it on others."

As he said it, he wondered if his answer was so frank as to sound disrespectful. Should he try and justify it by talking of the horror he had felt at the fighting? But he felt inadequate to express what he had experienced, and anyway there seemed little point. Their minds were plainly made up.

Corradon's look seemed sympathetic. "Oh, I know, Forester. But we *must* deal with these intruders, whoever they are. If we do, we must prepare for the possibility that we have to attack them, and as Vero has repeatedly pointed out to us, we cannot go halfheartedly into such a matter. We have only one chance, one possibility of surprise. Any attack must be done as efficiently as we possibly can."

"I want to confirm that," said Clemant, looking at Merral with his dark gray eyes. "We may have a single chance. A window of opportunity, perhaps only a few minutes."

There were long seconds of silence. "I see that," Merral answered. "But you must realize that any action like this would carry with it a certainty of death and injury on our side. We had an almost miraculous escape last time. If I was to lead it, I would feel responsible for what happened."

Corradon looked up at him solemnly. "Yes, but if I authorized it,

Forester—if I asked you to do it—why then, *I* would take responsibility."

The silence returned. Eventually Corradon broke it. "But you see, Merral, we have a responsibility whether we like it or not. If we attack, we take risks. If we don't attack we also take risks. I bitterly wish it was not my decision. But what can we do?"

Clemant gave a nod of grudging agreement.

How had this happened? Merral asked himself. How had it come about that he was being asked to lead a battle?

He suddenly knew, with unarguable certainty, that he could not agree there and then.

"Representative Corradon, Advisor Clemant," he said, "I have to think this through. It is without precedent. Yes, I fought before, but it was defensive. I had no choice. This is different. Now we are planning an attack. And . . ."

For a moment, Merral closed his eyes, trying to think of the words; then he opened them and spoke slowly. "There is another factor. The great achievement of the Assembly has been peace. With this we would end that."

"I know," Corradon said, sounding distressed. "But we need a decision. I need you to lead these people."

"I agree," Clemant said. "This is a perilous venture. Your presence increases the chance of success. Your absence . . . " He shrugged.

Suddenly, Merral knew what to say. "My decision is this: I need to think more about it."

Corradon and Clemant exchanged unhappy glances.

"Very well," Corradon said, shaking his head, "but Vero has suggested we act within a week. In fact, he is working to have the contact at dawn a week from tomorrow."

"So soon? We have no more time?"

"No longer than that. We simply cannot afford to have the ship leave, and neither can we risk it heading into Assembly space spreading contamination. Midsummer approaches when the crater will never be in darkness; now, at least, we have some darkness to approach in."

"But only a week? Can it be done?"

Corradon did not immediately answer but rubbed his face between his hands as if weary. Then he looked at Merral, his face showing concern. "Done? I would be lying if I said I had any assurance over the matter. But it has to be attempted. And that is why we need you. Even if we knew what to test for, we do not have the time to test men or women to lead in battle. You are the one man who we know can lead."

"Perhaps."

"*No.*" Corradon's tone was blunt. "Merral, if you do not take this, we appoint someone else. But for all we know, when they are faced by these things, they may run. Only two men have fought for the Assembly in eleven thousand years. You are one; Vero is the other. He is eliminated. The equation is simple."

"Sir, I appreciate that," Merral answered, feeling under an intolerable pressure. "But surely we believe that a man must volunteer for such a position?"

A long, pained sigh came from the representative. "Yes. I cannot order you. We are Assembly still. The Assembly does not force." He looked intently at Merral. "But I can plead," he said, "and I do. But please talk to Vero about the plans. Perhaps advise him. Then let me know before, say, the evening of the day after tomorrow, what you choose to do. On the eve of the Lord's Day. If you will not lead, then we will find someone else. But I would prefer you."

"And I agree," Clemant said.

He and Corradon rose.

"We must return to Isterrane," the representative said. "I wish you peace with your decision. We will pray for you."

◆—◆—◆

As their footsteps faded away, Merral sat down heavily in a chair.

"I do not want to do this!" he whispered, and his voice seemed to echo about him. His memories of the battle at Carson's Sill came flooding back. He even half wished he had not found the ship. *Why am I so reluctant? Is it cowardice or something else?*

Suddenly, the answer came to him abruptly and clearly. It was not cowardice, or not entirely. *I'm reluctant because with this we would lose our innocence. With this action we will put the clock back twelve millennia. At a stroke, we would unleash all the ghosts of the past: the deceitful vocabulary of war, the dreadful concepts we have forgotten, those horrors disguised as "chivalry," "patriotism," or "valor" that lurked in the very oldest books, the laments like that of David over Saul and Jonathan, the grieving of the widows and orphans.*

Then a new and darker thought struck him. If it happened, he could become known to posterity—for however many ages there were yet to run—as Captain Merral Stefan D'Avanos of the Farholme Defense Unit.

The man who brought war back to the human race.

CHAPTER 12

Suddenly anxious to talk to Vero, Merral strode out of the room to the walkway in the cavern. At the railing, he paused and gazed into the space beyond. He stood there, his eyes caught by the angry flashes of yellow and white light and his ears assailed by the cacophony of noises: the conflicting rhythms of hammering and the roar and hum of engines and machinery, all echoing and reechoing off the rock walls. Now all this bustle of activity made sense. Vero was preparing to launch an attack against a vastly superior foe in a week's time.

As Merral stood there, he found that all this activity buried in this vast, half-lit cavern saddened him. *Where is our openness and our innocence? Have we lost it so soon?*

He looked around for Vero and found him standing by one of the gray hulls of the gravity-modifying sleds in insistent conversation with a man in overalls. He clattered down the stairway and walked over to the sled.

As he approached, Vero dismissed the engineer, then came over and took his friend's shoulder in an understanding grasp.

"I'm sorry," Vero said, speaking loudly to make himself heard over the scream of a drill that had just started up.

"Yes, so am I," Merral answered, feeling a strange mixture of emotions. "They want me to lead the fighting."

"I know," Vero said, his face lit by flickers of light. "Have you agreed?"

Merral said nothing for a few moments. "No. I'm thinking about it. There are lots of issues. It's not an easy decision. But you think it will come to fighting, don't you?"

Vero gave an almost imperceptible nod. "I fear so."

Merral looked at the gray sled perched on trestles, noticing the benches that were being welded to the frame.

"Let me ask: what do you plan to do with these?"

"These? The two sleds are the main attack vehicles. Thirty men on each. The hoverer—over there—we will use for the negotiating party. These sleds are quieter and we may be able to get in faster. We are working on them to make them more suitable."

Merral was suddenly aware of his ignorance. "Tell me, Vero, what's supposed to happen. If I am to lead people into this attack, I ought to know."

"Yes," Vero agreed, leaning back cautiously against the polished hull of the sled. "Well, once the order is given—"

"Wait, who gives the order?"

"You . . . or whoever the commander on the ground is. We can't assume that we will be able to keep a link to Isterrane going. They may be able to block it, just as they did with our transmissions."

"So the decision to fight—that may be mine?"

"Yes. But, I mean, there is hardly time for the representatives to debate the matter. Is there? Seconds may count here."

"I see. So if—or when—I say go, what happens?"

Vero's face acquired an unsettled look. "Well, it's still fluid. The idea is to get in quickly and disable the ship somehow. Perena suggests we blow open a hatch or some doorway. All we have to do is stop it from leaving the atmosphere. The intruders can't breathe in a vacuum. Of course, it would help if we knew exactly what the ship looked like, but there must be doorways, landing gear, that sort of thing. . . ." He pointed a thumb over at a nearby pallet where some boxes painted a lurid red lay. "We have had some fast-expanding polymer cut into wedges; when you trigger the reaction, they triple their volume inside a second. They will stop a door from closing. There are also some planar explosives safe down another tunnel. With them we can blast off an entire landing leg."

"I see. You know that they aren't going to stand by while you put these charges down?"

Vero pursed his lips. "No. Of course not."

"So have you weapons?"

"Nothing fancy, but we have some things. Better than just bush knives. Although we will be issuing those—it's a tried-and-tested weapon. But the new weapons . . . do you want to see them?"

Merral suppressed his dislike. "No . . . But I'd better, I suppose."

"Over here," Vero said, motioning him to the corner from where Merral had seen the flashes of light earlier. In the corner, two men and a woman in thick overalls were working on some tubular parts at a bench.

As Vero introduced him, Merral was struck by the look of recognition that his name drew. *They know who I am; my reputation has gone ahead of me.* Was this also why they wanted him to lead? A man who had already fought and won once. Yet the next time might be different.

Cautiously, Vero picked up one of the dull gray tubular objects off the bench. "Recognize this?" he asked. "Careful, the barrel's hot."

"Yes, it's a rock cutter," Merral answered, seeing the handle and the shoulder rest. "I've seen my Uncle Barrand use one in the quarry work."

"Exactly," Vero answered. "The XM2 model. We have been modifying some to give a pulse of energy. We have adjusted the beam focus and put an easy-to-operate switch on. What's the range now, Salla?" Vero asked the woman.

Merral, glancing at her, noticed the beads of sweat on her face, the stains on her hands, the disheveled and dusty blonde hair.

Salla nodded at the rock cutter in a detached way. "Well, with the hundred millisec pulse we have settled on, we can get fifteen meters with a tight beam and fifty meters on the broad focus. Broad focus is lower temperature. Below a thousand Celsius at the center. It's the best compromise at the moment. . . ."

Her tone seemed as clear and precise as if she expected Merral to take notes. He wondered what she had been previously; an engineering lecturer, perhaps?

"I see," Vero said, standing back. "I'd like to show Merral how it works. Give him a demonstration, please."

Salla picked up the weapon. "It's too heavy really, but the XM2s were not designed to be carried about quickly. I wouldn't like to carry one for a long time." She slid a toggle on the side. "Another innovation—a safety switch. Technically, a fascinating compromise." Merral noted her keen gray eyes in his direction. "You have to balance the need to stop it going off accidentally against the need to switch it on fast."

Merral merely nodded, his mounting unease warring against his urge to understand.

She pointed it toward the chamber wall, and Merral noticed for the first time a series of colored concentric rings painted on a plastic screen perhaps twenty meters away.

"With the safety switch off," she said, lifting the gun up and squinting along the barrel, "the power comes on instantly with the first pressure on the trigger." There was a faint hum and a red light on the side glowed. "A further press and you fire. *Thus.*"

There were three soft hisses from the barrel and three small crimson flames flared briefly in the center of the target. As the wisps of smoke faded, three blackened holes appeared in the target, each large enough to put a finger in.

As Salla lowered the gun carefully onto the bench, her smile seemed uneasy, almost guilty. "And then, you put the safety back on. Always."

"Impressive." As he said the word, Merral realized he wasn't sure what he meant by it.

Vero nodded. "Yes, these are the final adjustments being made. We have over a hundred of these ready. What are you working on now?"

"Calibrating the focus switch," one of the men said.

"A focus switch? Why do you need it?" Merral asked.

Salla answered him. "A tight-focus beam will cut through most metals and polymers," she said, "but it's got to be precisely aimed. The broad focus gives a wider burn zone: say a hand's width."

Merral looked at her, suddenly curious whether this woman was married or not, and if she was, whether she had children.

"You'd use that for what?"

Without hesitation came the answer. "For soft targets."

"For soft targets," Merral echoed, trying to conceal his feelings. "I see. Thank you for the demonstration, Salla. You have worked hard. Excuse me."

He turned sharply and walked away a few paces, urgently gesturing for Vero to follow him.

"Let's go back to the room with the maps. We need to talk."

◆—◆

Back in the room, Merral closed the door and sat at the table. Vero sat opposite. "You seem upset," he said.

I am *upset.* Merral tried to contain his emotions. "Vero, let me ask you a single question: What is a soft target?" His voice sounded hard and cold.

"Ah. Yes, well . . . a soft target . . ." Vero seemed to stare at the desk as if an answer was inscribed on it. "Well, it is . . . what shall we say? An objective . . . an opponent perhaps, that is, well, unarmored."

"*Who.*"

"Who?"

"You used the word *opponent*. An opponent is not an *it*, it is a *who.* Opponents are personal."

"Ah yes," Vero replied, intertwining his fingers nervously, "we mustn't lose our grammar."

"The grammar is not the point. As well you know." Vero stared at his interlocked hands in embarrassment, and Merral thought that he was blushing.

"Vero," Merral said, almost horrified at the sharpness of his own

175

voice, "let me suggest that a soft target is unprotected organic tissue. Right?"

"Er, right."

"Do you see what worries me?"

"Yes . . . I'm sorry."

"Vero, that charming woman, Salla, who is, for all I know, a wife and a mother beyond reproach, and the men with her, were happily talking about maximizing the potential for efficiently burning holes in the flesh of living, intelligent creatures. Is this what we have come to?"

Vero rose to his feet and paced the room before stopping, turning, and answering.

"I suppose so," he said, clearly discomfited. "It's just that we have been in a hurry; we've only been going perhaps four weeks here. We have been just too busy to consider some of the issues. Like ethics. And, I suppose, you have to distance yourself. Really."

"But I would prefer not to."

Vero stared at the table, a range of expressions flitting across his face. Then he looked up, his brown eyes wide. "Look, Merral, let me turn it round. You believe that what we face is evil?"

"Yes."

"You believe we are right to be prepared to fight?"

"Yes, I suppose. If negotiation fails."

"Then tell me," Vero said, his voice suddenly hardening, "would you have us use our bare hands or stones?"

Suddenly, Merral was aware that his position was hopelessly undermined. He stood, as much to cover his awkwardness as for any other reason, and faced Vero across the room. As they looked at each other, there was a tense silence.

Unable to avoid the inevitable, Merral blurted out, "I apologize—"

"I apologize too—"

Their words came so close together that they found themselves smiling.

Vero made an apologetic gesture. "You are right; I have been blinded. I should have known better. It was in all the old literature that there was a danger of this."

"Yes," Merral added slowly, "but I see that there is a fault in my thinking too. I have been too idealistic. I accept the idea of fighting, but not the reality of it." He sighed. "Oh, what a horrid, horrid business this is."

"It is so dirty that we must, to some extent, get our own hands dirty," said Vero sadly.

"I suppose so."

Abruptly, Vero sat down.

It's no good. I must now pursue Vero's plan. "So then, the thing I saw is your main weapon?"

"Yes. I'm pleased with what Salla's team has done with the XM2s. . . ."

Merral sensed reservations. "But?"

"I am worried that they are only short-range weapons."

"So you have nothing for a distance?"

"We toyed with projectile weapons. Guns that fire explosive charges, bullets, that sort of thing. But we have nothing to adapt for that. We'd have to start from scratch to make them. It would take months."

"Yes. But doesn't that leave everybody vulnerable?"

"To some extent. We are putting together jackets that may give some sort of protection, a dense, impact-resistant synthetic with a broad spectrum reflective layer under the surface coating, but it is hard to give more than token protection."

"So you will have to get in fast to the target."

"Yes." Vero frowned. "I'd like your thinking on that. Here now . . . pass me those images and I'll show you what I am thinking of."

"Please," Merral said, sliding them over, "if I am to seriously consider leading this party, I have to have all the information I need."

"Yes." Vero flexed his fingers. "I—we—have been envisaging a three-way approach, and your news has helped me clarify that. My working proposal is as follows: We send the diplomatic party up from the south. Up here." On the map, Vero's finger moved along a river toward the lake. "When they come to the lake, I would want them to come up it in the middle, in full view of the ship. They will be using a hoverer and will be fairly slow. It's noisy and I don't think it can be mistaken for anything warlike. We will have the banners on it. But before they move out we will have brought up two assault parties with the sleds. They are silent, so I think that they ought to be undetected until they can be seen. Now with a location to work from, I suggest that we have one that comes from the north." He gestured to the map again. "The other from the west, as close as we can get." He tapped a finger on a stream on the western side of the lake. "Hmm, possibly approach down in this valley here, where they will be out of sight."

Vero measured across the lake with his fingers and checked the scale. "Say two kilometers. So, if the negotiation fails, then both assault parties attack at once. You see the strategy?"

Merral hesitated. "Vero, this is a new area for me and a very unwelcome one. Yes, I think so. Their attention is attracted to the south with the diplomatic party. Then the attack—sudden and unannounced—comes from two other points of the compass. I suppose you might get close enough without being seen. Thirty people in each?"

"Yes. All men, by the way. That's because, as Salla implied just now, the weapons are so heavy. If we had time we could make them lighter."

"But sixty men—is that going to be enough?"

"Probably not. But as soon as the attack starts we bring in reinforcements. A ship flies in and lands an extra sixty or so troops."

Merral shook his head. "And you have the hundred-plus men? And this ship?"

"Actually, yes. A hundred and forty men are being trained. The old texts always said to have extra in reserve. And as for the ship, well, Perena has been given an old subspace freighter that has been unused for over a century: the *Emilia Kay.*"

"A freighter? Your ability astonishes me. But why not just come in with the ship?"

"We discussed this. It's too obvious and too vulnerable. This way, the *Emilia Kay* will bring the sleds and the hoverer up to the crater margin the night before and wait there just over the horizon for whatever happens. If we do have to go for the assault option, then she flies over and lands. It would be easier if we had specialized landing ships: fast, armored machines. But we don't. We can make guns, but not ships. We will have to manage with what we have."

He fell silent as he stared at the images; then he looked at Merral. "So what do you think?"

Merral found himself reluctant to speak. "I have never assessed anything like it. No one living has. It all sounds risky. What if things go wrong?"

"It is risky," Vero said gloomily. "The whole thing is risky."

"I need to think about it."

"Please do, but quickly. We do not have much time."

Suddenly Merral realized that he could make no decision here. "Vero, I am going to go back home and think about all this. For no more than forty-eight hours. I want to stand back from all this. I have to be convinced that what I'm doing is absolutely the only possible way forward. To get a feel for whether the risks are needed."

Vero looked disappointed. "Ah. Well, I can understand that. But be careful not to give anything away. This is not a sports match. If the intruders hear of our plans at all, then we are in trouble. Surprise is almost all we have. That's another reason why I want to move soon. So far we have kept what is happening quiet, but we can't disguise it forever. There are too many people involved."

"Yes, I understand." Merral picked up his bag. "Let me leave you the images. I have copies."

"Thank you; we will study them, I assure you." He stared at the sheets. "I wish that we had better shots of the ship. So much is just guesswork."

"So do I, Vero. Anyway, I want to get out of this underground world and see the sun."

"Very well. But let me come with you to the entrance."

•◆•

On the way out of the cavern, Merral met Anya and Perena. While Vero went ahead to organize transport to the airport, Merral explained to the sisters what he planned to do. After expressions of sympathy and support from both of them and farewell hugs, he walked out to the tunnel's entrance. There, he stepped out of the shadow of the cliff and stood in the afternoon sunshine, enjoying the air and trying to ignore the ceaseless activity all about him.

Vero soon returned. "There is a driver who will take you straight to the airport," he announced.

"Thanks."

"No, thank *you* for coming. But I do hope you agree to lead. We need you."

"If I don't, who does?"

Vero shrugged. "Someone like Zak, I guess. He seems to be doing well in training. But he is unproven."

A young man hurried out of the hut and motioned Merral over to a vehicle.

"Have a safe journey, my friend," said Vero, clapping him on the shoulder.

"Thank you. I will be in touch with you the day after tomorrow."

•◆•

The direct afternoon flights to Ynysmant were full, and Merral could only find a seat on a late and slow circuitous route that took him through Ranapert and Halmacent Cities. He stared out of the window as the purple dusk darkened into night, watching the pinpricks of light underneath him, recognizing towns, tracing roads, and locating vehicles. Each point of light, he reminded himself, represented a person or a family. And within a week, all of them could be affected by his actions or his decisions.

As he thought about it, he acknowledged that Vero's plan seemed reasonable, logical, and necessary. Yet, it was perilous. If the intruders had the power to reach out and destroy a Gate high above them in space, what could they not do on the surface of the planet? Even hundreds of generations ago, mankind had had the power to destroy entire cities and even planets, and had—if the stories of pre-Intervention times were true—come close to destroying Ancient Earth on more than one occasion.

No, planning such an action so quickly, against an unknown enemy, was risky. It was not only an issue of whether he led the forces. Perhaps the operation itself should be stopped. He could probably demand the whole thing be cancelled, and they would probably listen to him; for some reason, people respected him and his views. After all, that was why they wanted him to lead the attack.

Merral stared hard out of the window, watching the lights of a big road vehicle far below, winding its way along a curving trail. He weighed his options. Perhaps he could go to Corradon and Clemant and say that it was too risky and try to persuade them of a less hazardous alternative.

They were starting to descend. Ahead, visible as fine and delicate points of silver in a sea of darkness, lay the lights of Ynysmant. So much seemed to revolve around him and his decisions, and in under forty-eight hours, he had to make his choice.

O Lord, he prayed intently as the pitch of the engines changed, *I must decide. Show me plainly what I must do.*

But there was no answer: no abrupt vision, no sudden certainty, no ringing affirmation. It was just a sort of spiritual silence.

Almost as if communications to high heaven had also been disrupted.

CHAPTER 13

Less than an hour later, Merral reached his house. Only his father was in. His mother had, he was informed, gone to a women's meeting of some sort. Merral helped himself to food and then went and joined his father, who was painstakingly completing a picture puzzle on the table.

His father bent forward over the table, his thin elbows jutting down onto the puzzle, and stared with a pained gaze at the opposite wall.

"I really don't know what things are coming to, Son," he said in a troubled voice, his face somehow strangely aged and forlorn. "People just don't seem as . . . well, *nice* as they used to be. Maybe it's the long winter. Maybe it's the Gate going; some people say that. Maybe I'm just getting older and less tolerant. Why, even your mother now . . . I don't know." He gave a burdened sigh. "It's all 'Move this, Stefan,' 'Tidy that up, Stefan,' 'Oh, comb your hair, Stefan,' 'Those fingernails need cutting.' It just goes on. I don't remember that she was always like this."

He gave a pathetic little moan. "Son," he said, suddenly turning a lined and worried face to Merral, "I'm getting old and I don't like it."

Merral, almost too overcome to say anything, just patted him on the shoulder.

"It's not you, Father," he said finally. "Nor Mother either. There is just something wrong. But we are working on it. We are doing our best."

His eyes watering, his father nodded. "I hope so. Well, I'm tired. Have been for months. I'm going to bed. See you tomorrow."

•◆•

After breakfast, Merral walked over the causeway to the Institute with a heavy heart. There he sat down at his desk to try to plan what he wanted to do in the next day and a half. He decided he had to go to Herrandown. It was there that things had started, and Merral felt that what was happening there now might be some guide to how great the risk to Farholme was. He went to see Henri to ask him whether he could borrow a vehicle to visit Herrandown. Henri shook his head and smiled. "*Ach,* man, I can do better than that," he offered. "There is a rotorcraft due to fly near there tomorrow. It's been delayed by the dust, but the weather's supposed to be clear tomorrow. I can arrange for you to be dropped off and picked up on the return leg. Is a couple of hours long enough?"

After talking briefly about other matters, Merral left Henri and returned to his office, where he called Isabella and arranged to meet her that evening. He felt he needed to see Jorgio and called his brother to find out where he was.

"That's easy," said Daoud Serter. "He's over by you; probably at the stables."

"So he's not up at Wilamall's Farm then?"

"Didn't you know? Not now. But he'll tell you."

Merral walked out of the back of the Institute building, looking for Jorgio. He found the old stable hand stroking one of the horses in the stalls.

"Jorgio!" Merral called out.

"Mister Merral," said the old man, turning awkwardly. They embraced. "Good to see you."

"So you heard about Brenito?"

"I heard." He shook his head slowly. "A nice man. He'll be welcomed up there and missed down here." He made a soft clucking noise. "I hope as I helped him. The Lord told me as we were talking that he had only a few more days. So I felt I'd better tell him."

"I think it allowed him to sort things out."

"See, that was the point. I think *he* was ready; but I've no doubt folks like him have plenty of things to sort out."

"Indeed. But what are *you* doing here?"

Jorgio shook his head. "I've finished at the farm."

"Finished?"

"Yes," Jorgio said, and his distorted face bore a look of deep unhappiness. "Been a change of plan. It's a matter of resources, they say. No Gate now, so new priorities. They don't need people like me there; they need fewer, fitter people."

"I'm shocked," Merral said, genuinely astonished but remembering that Teracy had warned of changes. "I'm very surprised. I knew nothing of it. But then, I'm in the wrong part of forestry."

"It's a new decision," Jorgio added. "So I'm back down in the town with my brother. I'll move my things down soon enough."

Merral felt annoyed with himself. Having promised Brenito he would keep a watch on Jorgio, he now found that the man had been uprooted and he hadn't realized it.

"Of course," Jorgio continued, "I've still my allowance, the same as you. I just don't have anything to do. So I reckoned as I'd come here and see the horses."

"Welcome. But I had no idea," Merral said. *It is worrying. If we are no longer concerned about our weak, then what has happened to us?* Here was yet another small piece of evidence that Farholme was changing for the worse.

"It's the way things is. There's a shadow over us all now, Mister Merral. But what are *you* doing?"

"Me? I work here."

"*Tut.* If you please, Mister Merral, I know better than that. You are struggling over something."

Merral stared hard at Jorgio, wondering if his conflicts were that visible or whether there was some other gift at work. "Truly said, my old friend. I have a hard choice to make. I am hoping that before tomorrow evening I will see and hear enough to make my decision about what to do very plain."

"You're worried what to do about them, aren't you? I don't blame you. Fighting 'em can't be much fun. Not from what I knows about them."

Merral stared at the old man, wondering yet again how he knew so much. "No, it's not fun, Jorgio," he answered. "And do you have any advice?"

"*Tut!* You want me to make your decisions?" he said, raising a rough finger in warning, but there was both warmth and sympathy in his expression. "You must make them yourself."

Then, to Merral's surprise, the old man closed his eyes and fell silent, his big lips moving slightly. After a few moments, he suddenly opened his eyes.

"There. I've done what I can do. I 'ave just prayed as you'll find out very clearly what you have to do."

"Thank you."

"Oh, you may not thank me." There was a curiously distorted smile, revealing his displaced teeth. "You may find out more about the evil than you want."

Jorgio fell into a tight-lipped silence that seemed to discourage further questions.

"Thank you," Merral answered eventually, both gratified and disturbed by the conversation.

"My pleasure," came the response. "I'll continue to pray. And promise—if you decide to fight, let me know. I'll ask that you'll have help."

"Help?"

The look on the broken face became strangely intense. "If you please, you'll need help against them." He muttered to himself, "Knives and guns won't do. Not for *them*." Merral found something oddly dogmatic about his tone. "Not for them all anyway. Not the one in the chamber. And that's the one that matters."

"I see; the one in the chamber, the one that matters," Merral said. "Can you tell me anything more?"

"No." There was a stiff shake of the head. "Don't know any more.

Don't really want to. Nasty. But Mister Merral, don't be surprised at what you find there." He wrinkled his face. "And now, if you'll excuse me, I'm off."

"A moment, Jorgio. Brenito was anxious that I kept an eye on you. Please don't leave Ynysmant. If you have to travel, leave a message with Daoud."

"*Tut*, me travel?" Jorgio smiled. "Hardly. But may the Lord's blessings be with you, Mister Merral."

Then he shook hands roughly with Merral and in his determined, tilted way set off walking toward the town.

Merral watched him go, then, full of bewilderment and foreboding, walked back down to his office.

◆━◆

That evening, Merral met Isabella at her house and, after some discussion, they decided to take a stroll along the town's lake-edge walk. The walk was popular in summer when the nights were shorter and hotter, but this evening it was still too cool for many people to be about, and for much of the way, Merral and Isabella were on their own.

As they walked along, Merral sensed that Isabella was in a strange mood. There was a hint of a carefree, almost reckless frame of mind in the way she bounced down the steps and swung round lampposts. In contrast to her, Merral felt slow, leaden, and preoccupied.

"I was wondering whether you would make time to see me," she said in a light but purposeful tone. "You seem to be so busy." Merral caught a gleam of inquiry on her face.

"Yes," he answered. "I'm sorry. I hardly seem to know whether I'm here or there. I went to Isterrane just for the day yesterday."

"My! It must have been important," Isabella said, peering intently at him. "I wish I could do that. I find Ynysmant just so limiting. So what was it? Intruder business, of course."

Merral looked around, but there was no one who might overhear. "Possibly. But I'd rather not discuss it."

Isabella gave a girlish pout. "A *secret*, eh? We all have secrets now.

Well, I suppose we can live with them. In fact, I quite like the idea. Openness can get dull, can't it?"

"Can it?" Merral countered, sensing that yet another area of difficulty was about to open up. "Well, I suppose a lot of worthwhile things can, in theory, get dull. But it was never something that worried me."

"Well, it did me." She grabbed his hand. "But I suppose I do feel uneasy at the way I am being pushed to the margins of your life. I mean, Vero and this Anya and Perena know *everything*. But I don't."

"I've told you lots. More than I should have."

"But there are limits. And there's lots I ought to know. I'm now heading up the new priorities team. Did I tell you?"

"No. That's new. I thought it was someone else."

"It was, but she didn't realize how much work there was, and she has two children. So I had a chat with her and she has stepped down."

"I see. So you now report directly to Warden Enatus?"

"Exactly. And I think we ought to be told about the intruders. I mean if they came south we'd be on the front line. Is that the term?"

"I think so; Vero would know. But you do make a point. I'll have a chat with Vero—I'm seeing him again soon."

"No doubt. But I'd appreciate it if you could raise the concern. I feel as if I am being cut out of your life. You seem to be so busy." There was recrimination in her eyes.

"I'm sorry," Merral answered, feeling her hurt and the validity of her argument. "Perhaps things will settle down. But what I'm doing is very important. As is what you do."

"Yes, of course," she said, but to Merral her response sounded very automatic.

Then they stopped and together leaned over a stone parapet, peering at the waters of the lake. Isabella was so close to Merral that he could feel her shoulder gently touching his. He was, he decided suddenly, really very fond of her.

"Merral," she asked, "when are you leaving again? And for how long?"

She isn't going to like this. He stared at the ink-dark waters of the lake. "Well, tomorrow evening. And I could be away maybe for a week or more." *Or forever, if I decide to lead an attack and pay the price.*

"Oh—," came the response, full of surprise and even hurt. "But there is a lot we have to discuss, you know."

"Sorry."

"Well, I just feel," she said, her words soft and tentative as if she was expressing something for the very first time, "that, in the light of our understanding, our relationship needs to be bonded more closely. And with you so—well—distracted, it's hard."

"Yes, it is, isn't it?" Merral said, choosing his words carefully. *So,* he thought with a pang of unhappiness, *she has reminded me again that she sees our "understanding" as a private equivalent of a commitment.* He wondered, for the hundredth time, how he could try and retreat from that position.

Suddenly there was a noise to his left and he looked up. A crowd of perhaps a dozen teenage boys, all in the same kind of light gray trousers and jackets, came by in an excited and chaotic circle. They were joking noisily, jostling each other and taking turns to run up and down the sloping wall with squeals and shouts. *Have teenagers always been so rowdy?* Merral wondered. *And why are they trying to dress so much alike? Or am I now seeing shadows that are not there?*

After they went past, he saw Isabella looking at him, her face strangely pale in the light of the streetlamps.

"Oh, Merral," she said in her softest voice, "you know Helga Demaitre, works over in Communications? Lives in Lazent Street by the market?"

"I know her elder brother better. Why?"

"She's just got engaged to some lad from the south side."

"That's nice," he replied, feeling that it was hardly news.

"The thing that's interesting," she said with a quiet insistency, looking at him intensely with her oval eyes, "is that she told her parents *after* they had decided."

"I see," he heard himself say in what seemed a rather distant and feeble voice. Somehow, the night seemed to have grown chillier.

"That's . . . well, I've never heard of that. What did they say? The parents, I mean?"

"Well, after the initial shock, they agreed. Afterward they decided it was a good idea. Interesting, eh?"

"It is," Merral said, realizing as the words came out that what he found interesting was not what Isabella did. The news troubled him. *If we are to honor our parents at all, we must surely not present them with accomplished actions. Not in that area, at least.*

"Let's walk," he said. "I'm feeling cold." He started walking away.

Isabella followed him, putting her hand in his. "I admire her," she said with determination.

Merral, aware that Isabella was scrutinizing his face, felt he should not show any emotion.

"You see," she went on, "*she* took the initiative. Now that's sometimes important."

"Well, yes," Merral replied, forced onto the defensive, "there are times when you have to make a stand. But it's tricky to go against things that are—well—part of tradition."

"Yes, that's what it was, wasn't it?" Isabella said with enthusiastic confidence. "Just *tradition*."

"Well, sometimes . . . ," Merral countered cautiously, "tradition is a good thing." He had a certainty that, whatever he said, he couldn't win.

"And sometimes," she said, her voice filled with something like defiance, "tradition needs to be challenged."

Under the light, he saw Isabella look at him with an oddly hard expression. "You know, Merral, the Gate going may actually be a blessing in disguise."

"It may?" he answered, barely able to keep the horror out of his voice.

"Yes. And it's not just me who says it. There's something of a feeling of release, freedom almost, in the air." She squeezed his hand. "It's subtly exciting. You can feel it with the youth especially. Like that group that just passed us."

So, it wasn't just me. Then the implications of what she was saying sank in, and something seemed to tighten around his heart. He was aware that she was staring at him, waiting for a response.

"As always, Isabella, you are stimulating," he said, in as mild a tone as he could manage, desperately wanting to lower the intensity of the conversation.

She squeezed his hand gently. "Oh, Merral, I hope I'm more than just *stimulating* to you." He saw her frown. "But I do think you, we, need to challenge our preconceptions. I think we are in danger of being trapped in a situation that no longer exists." She paused, and when she spoke again her tone was lighter and happier, as if a light had broken into her mind. "The past is over. There is a new world to think about. The horizons are open. Don't you agree?"

"Oh, I'm thinking about it. . . . Thinking very hard indeed. But I think there's something to be said for waiting. At least for us."

"You are *so* cautious, Merral. You really are." There was now a note of irritation in her voice. "Oh, do loosen up!"

Merral was aware that she was smiling, but somehow it seemed to be a rather artificial expression. He was still wondering how to answer her when they turned a corner and came across a group of his old school friends on their way to a café. To his relief, they insisted that Merral and Isabella join them, and he was spared any more difficult conversations until much later, when he walked back with her through the deserted and echoing streets to her house.

"So what do you think we should do?" she said, holding his hand firmly.

It's no good. I can't prevaricate forever. "Isabella, now you ask me, my decision is this: I wish to do nothing for a couple of weeks. Then, if things have settled and I know better what I am doing, well, you and I will have a long talk."

"And then?" came the rapid reply.

"Then, maybe, just maybe, I will approach my parents to reconsider things."

"Not before?"

"No."

"Oh, Merral," she said, disappointment filling her voice, "I thought we had a commitment."

Feeling peculiarly irritated that she saw their understanding as much more than he did, Merral replied sharply, "Well, Isabella, a starting point would be exactly what you think this wretched commitment means."

As he heard his words, he regretted them. But it was too late.

She dropped his hand and stepped back, staring at him, her mouth half open.

"So it's a *wretched* commitment now, is it, Merral D'Avanos?" she snapped.

"That's not quite—"

"Oh, you! You don't care at all!" Her eyes flashed in anger. "All you care about is your own *wretched* project with that outsider, Vero!"

Then she whirled round and clattered heavily up the stone steps to her house. A moment later there was the sound of a door slamming.

Merral was aware that he was shaking and that his stomach felt as if he was going to be sick. He slowly walked back to his house, his mind preoccupied with a single thought: he had had an argument with Isabella.

•◆•

The next morning, as Merral landed in Herrandown, the matter still loomed over him. As the rotorcraft pilot lifted off and flew her machine eastward, Merral was met by his uncle and aunt who hugged him in turn.

"Good to see you, Nephew," Barrand said. "You just passed through last time. When was it? Yes, over a month ago. Ho, too quick."

"Yes, sorry about that. I've been so busy."

"Not good for you," Zennia said with a smile. "Come up and stay."

"Perhaps one day," Merral answered. "But today it's just a brief visit too."

He looked carefully at them, watching for anything untoward.

Somehow, he felt reassured by the fact that they seemed healthy, if slightly weary.

"So how are things?" asked Merral, looking around the hamlet. Now, with the fresh vegetation, the new grass, and the blossom on the trees, Herrandown looked a tranquil and happy place.

"Better," his aunt replied. "Thankfully. Look, I'll go and put the coffee on. You men go and chat."

As she left, his uncle patted Merral on the shoulder. "Oh, come over to the office."

"So how do you find things, Uncle?" Merral asked.

"Hmm. Well, in some ways, Zennia is right," Barrand said. "They're better. The hounds aren't so nervous for example." As if to make the point, one of the dogs came up and rubbed against Merral's leg.

His uncle continued as they walked along, "So we don't feel as physically threatened as we did. I mean, no one goes into the woods on their own. As you suggested . . . But, oh, I'm wondering if that was an overreaction."

He picked up a stick and threw it for the dog to catch.

"No," he repeated slowly, as if to himself, "not *physically* threatened."

"What about other things. In other ways?"

"Well," his uncle replied, "it's hard to express. Sometimes I think it's as if a dream has ended. I don't know whether it's the Gate going or something else. I only know that when I look back on how we lived before Nativity . . . it now seems it was almost a different world. I mean I used to really enjoy what I was doing here. But now . . ." He shook his head. "Now, it's all changed."

He fell silent as they walked into the office, which seemed to Merral to be more crowded and disorderly than he remembered it. Barrand pulled up a chair and lowered himself heavily onto it.

Merral lifted a stack of maps off another chair and sat down.

"I suppose it's not surprising," his uncle said after a minute's silence. "You see, now that they are cutting back on the expansion program, the whole purpose of being here has changed. I mean, if they do build a new Herrandown now, it looks as though it will not be in my lifetime." He tapped stout fingers thoughtfully on the chair arm. "I suppose you could say that we've really lost our purpose here. Maybe that's the problem."

How disturbing. His uncle and aunt had been carefully selected for this job and must have been assessed as having a resilient psychological makeup. Yet now it looked as though they were having trouble handling the changes that were happening to them.

Merral looked around the office, suddenly feeling that something was missing.

"Uncle, what's happened to the painting you had? The Lymatov? *A Last View of Hesperian.*"

Merral remembered the conversation they had had about it and how Barrand had felt that it symbolized everything the Assembly stood for.

"Oh, *that.*"

His uncle stared in a rather abstracted manner at the pale outline on the wall where the painting had hung. "That. Yes. Well, I took it down. It's safe in the house. I suppose it sort of irritated me in the end."

"But I thought you liked it?"

"Well, I did. But, I suppose, what with the loss of the Gate . . ." Barrand seemed vaguely embarrassed about the matter, and Merral decided not to pursue it.

The conversation turned to the recent departure of the quarry team and then his uncle, suddenly apparently uncomfortable, rose to his feet and suggested that they go back to the house. "The coffee will be ready and the children may be back from school. It's a half day, of course. When did you last see Elana?"

"Well, it would have been, what, a month ago? Then she was still under the weather."

"Oh, she's better now. But changed . . ."

Five minutes later, Merral was forced to agree that Elana had changed. It seemed that she had, at a stroke, crossed the boundary from an attractive girl to a rather pretty young lady. He tried to pin down how it was that she could have altered so much in such a short time. Physically, she seemed to have grown and could now, he thought, have passed for much older than her fourteen years. Perhaps it was the way she now wore her blonde hair, or dressed; certainly the tight blue woolen pullover left no doubt to her newly gained femininity. Yet he felt that it was more than just the physical changes. There was a look of mature self-awareness about her small face, and he felt that her manner and poise was now that of a woman.

When their eyes met, she smiled with a strangely warm, knowing, and oddly adult expression. But the smile disquieted him.

He looked away and concentrated on his aunt and uncle. He tried to distance himself and listen to what was being said and to watch the unspoken body language between his uncle, aunt, and Elana. In some ways, there now seemed to be no tensions just under the surface ready to snap. Yet in other ways, he was not reassured. Merral was disturbed to find that his uncle now played little music and that his aunt had unfinished canvases.

After finishing his coffee, his uncle ambled over to the window. There he rested his elbows on the sill, looking out. "You know," he said in a regretful tone, "I'm no longer sure about the artistic side of me. It's funny." He turned and looked at Merral. "I always used to enjoy being a quarry master *and* being artistic; the two things worked together. Now, it's one or the other." He sighed. "It's very strange. I think it's the long winter. Or the Gate going, of course. That's had repercussions." Then, he turned back and stared out of the window again. Soon after, the rotorcraft pilot sent a message that she would be landing in an hour. Merral, unhappy about the atmosphere in the house, decided to take a walk outside. There was much he wanted to think over.

He strolled behind the house to look over the sunlit hamlet. The air was buzzing with insects, birds were calling from within the woods, and there was a taste of the longed-for summer everywhere. Merral found a smooth grassy bank, lay down on his back, and stared sky-ward, enjoying the warmth of the sun on his face as he tried to relax.

He had barely closed his eyes when there was the sound of soft footsteps nearby. He opened his eyes and saw Elana next to him.

"Hi," he said blinking, rising to a half-seated position.

"May I join you?" she asked quietly, with a careful glance around, as if to see if anyone else was near.

"Of course—," he began, but she had already sat close to him.

He looked at her, catching an odd, fleeting look on her face. She smiled back, but it was a strangely joyless expression.

"Merral," she said in a low, urgent tone, her face close to his, "I want to talk. Privately."

Merral looked around, confirming that they were certainly out of sight and sound of the house. Deep inside him, he was aware of an uncomfortable feeling that he could not pin down. "Surely. How can I help?"

"I need to leave," Elana said abruptly, her blue eyes fixed on his. "I need to leave here." There was a note of desperation in her voice.

"Why, Elana?" he asked, feeling sorry for her.

"It's the atmosphere," she replied. She picked up a blade of grass and began to chew on it, her sky-colored eyes still looking into his. He was vaguely aware that he found her closeness very agreeable. He was also dimly aware that there was something perilous about this prox-imity.

"I want to escape. It's not a good place anymore. It's tiny and bor-ing and the atmosphere gets me down. I want to live somewhere else. I want to *be* someone else. Can you help?"

"Me?"

"Get me out. Anywhere. Herrandown, Isterrane. The Southern Seas, the ends of Farholme. I don't care. Just get me out of here."

He tried to smile. "I'd love to help. How?"

She chewed a little more on the grass stalk, then took it out of her mouth. "There are ways. Get us relocated. Go back to your boss—what's his name?"

"Henri."

"Okay, now, I've been thinking. We've been here eight years. In two years, Mum and Dad's posting is reassessed. So you could, you see, just ask Henri to move us early."

"I can't do that. There are rules. There's a long transfer list."

"Rules can be bent. You could say that Dad's getting weird. Mum's —what's the word?— *unbalanced*. Get us reposted. South. Somewhere with beaches."

"I can't do that," he protested as he tried to think of some other way of helping her. He paused. "I could, I suppose, request a psychological survey of you all. Say you have been through a stressful time."

She gave a firm shake of her head. "No. I've read up on that stuff; it's in the Library. Dad would fight an assessment."

"True."

And you'd never get a verdict in your favor; you are all sane. Or at least as sane as anyone else on this increasingly messed-up planet.

"Merral," she said in a low, soft voice that he found extraordinarily compelling, "Couldn't you go to Henri and ask for us to be moved? Now. As a special favor. A private arrangement."

I could too, he realized with a shock. *Henri trusts me.* "But there's a list." As he said it he felt his protest sounded feeble.

"Please. As a favor. Just get us put on the top of it." There was a gentle, troubling tone of pleading in her voice.

"Elana, I can't do favors," Merral answered, aware that his voice sounded as if it belonged to someone else.

But I can, he thought. *There are vacancies in the new southern colonies.*

"Not even for me?" she implored, flicking her pale hair back and wriggling slightly, as if pressing herself down into the grass.

"Well . . ."

I could do it. Get them put on the top of the transfer list. And why not? She has *had a rough time. And who would be affected by one family moved to the top?*

She stared at him. "For us."

He was silent.

She reached out and stroked his hand gently. *"Please."*

Suddenly, Merral jerked his hand away. He started to his feet, conscious that his face was burning.

"No, Elana!"

She stared at him with a hurt look, as if something precious had been snatched from her.

Merral headed toward the house and then stopped.

He looked behind, relieved to see that she was not following him. He brushed the grass off himself, took a deep breath, and tried to settle his thoughts. He had been tempted and had gone a long way to giving in. In his mind, he began to pray for forgiveness.

A few minutes later, to his enormous relief, he heard the whispering of the approaching rotorcraft.

•◆•

In his urgency to get back to Isterrane, Merral arrived slightly early at the Ynysmant airport terminal. He was walking around the waiting area trying to bring some calmer reflections to bear on what had happened when he saw Ingrida Hallet standing looking out of the window, a travel bag at her feet.

"Hello, Ingrida," he called out, welcoming the possibility of a conversation that would distract him from his guilty thoughts. "I haven't seen you since before Nativity." He remembered again that memorable evening, the night that he had first met Vero, when Ingrida had so warmly wished him well with the new job he was to be given.

"Oh, it's you," Ingrida said in a cold, hushed voice. Her face, framed by her long black hair, showed no trace of welcome.

"Yes . . ." Merral stared at her, alarmed at the lack of welcome in her face. "What's the problem? You don't seem very pleased to see me."

Ingrida bent down, picked up her bag, and then looked at him with a hard, irritated expression. "Frankly," she snapped, "I'm not."

Wounded, Merral shook himself. "Look, what have I done? I don't understand."

"Remember the rain forest job? The one *you* were offered?"

"Yes, you were the first to tell me about it."

"Oh yes. I was, wasn't I?" She snorted, as if furious with herself. "Well, it was a job *I* wanted, the job of a lifetime. And it went to you, didn't it?"

"But—"

She was unstoppable now. "So I had to take something else, didn't I?" she snapped. "And what a second best. They put me on lichens! A millimeter's growth in a hundred years. They are barely alive. Lichens!" For a moment, he thought she was going to spit.

"Well, sorry. But I don't see why you are so mad at *me*." Merral felt overwhelmed by this onslaught that, for all its fury, seemed to have no focus.

Ingrida gave him a look of contempt. "Why? Because I *now* find out you are not taking the job. Mr. Merral pick-and-choose, eh? Henri tells me when I pass through today that you are 'doing something else,' that you are 'no longer really in Planning.' It's wasted!" Her face was pale with anger.

Merral, appalled and sick to his stomach, felt he had never heard anyone be so sarcastic.

"Sorry, I mean—"

"Oh, keep your words!" she snorted. "I can't apply for it now. I'm stuck with my lichens."

"I'm sorry. I had no idea."

"Really?" she grunted, glaring icily at him in a way that no one ever had before. "To change your mind like that . . . it's rotten!"

Suddenly Merral was seized by a sense of how totally and utterly unfair it was. Here he was, prepared to risk his life trying to save Farholme, and this—this senseless woman—was attacking him! The total injustice of her assault irritated him beyond measure. He felt himself getting angry in response and could now no longer be bothered to rein in his feelings. The offence against justice was, he knew, so great that it required an appropriate and just response. He had to tell this stupid woman bluntly, and plainly, how idiotic she was.

Merral was just going to say, "Ingrida Hallet, you are a total fool and you have not the slightest idea what you are talking about," when he saw another passenger staring at them with a look of shocked curiosity. Ingrida followed Merral's glance then, with a toss of her head and a new snort of anger, turned her back on him and walked away.

For a fleeting moment, Merral considered pursuing her to tell her exactly what she ought to hear. Then, suddenly ashamed of his temper, he controlled himself and walked away in the other direction to the men's room. There, instinctively, he washed his face in cold water. When he looked in the mirror, he saw that he was as pale as if he had been sick.

Isabella, Elana, and Ingrida. Jorgio's prayer had been answered in triplicate with an appalling vengeance. One answer alone would have been enough. *Dear God,* he prayed, *have mercy on me.*

Ten minutes later, he got on the plane and made his way to the very back. Ingrida came in later and, without looking at him, sat down at the front. When they landed at Isterrane, she got up and exited as soon as the fuselage door had slid open.

●—◆—●

To Merral's surprise, Vero was waiting for him at the terminal.

"How did you know I was on the flight?"

"It's hardly a stunning feat of intelligence to check the passenger lists." Vero stared at Merral. "You know, you look dreadful."

"I'll tell you about it. But not here."

His friend had a vehicle outside, and once they were inside and had closed the door, Vero turned to Merral. "Have you met them?" he asked.

"No. I found no trace of them. At least not physically."

"But . . . ?"

"I found enough evidence to make me know that I—*we*—have to fight."

"I am glad you now agree. But I am concerned. What did you find?"

"Let me be clinical," Merral said, trying to keep his voice level. "In under two days I found evidence of sin, to my knowledge, unparalleled in Assembly history. I found, among other things, a flagrant and open desire to dishonor parents, a gross outbreak of anger in public, and . . . . something else I will not name."

"In two days?" Vero's eyes opened wide. "The rot is faster than I thought."

Merral stared out of the windscreen at the lights of town. Then he turned to Vero.

"The *rot*? Vero, you have no idea at all how bad it is. You see, I didn't find the rot in others; I found it in myself."

CHAPTER 14

Vero drove Merral to Corradon's residence, an unremarkable single-story building at the edge of the lake that lay at the heart of Isterrane.

As they walked through the garden toward the house, a man standing by the door came over as if to ask a question. Seeing Vero, he nodded respectfully and stepped back.

"Who was that?" Merral whispered as Vero knocked on the door.

"A guard. One of Clemant's ideas. Justified, I suppose."

The representative, dressed casually in an open-necked shirt, answered the door himself. The sounds of family chatter and music drifted past him. "Welcome both," he said, looking unsurprised at their arrival. "Do come in."

Merral was briefly introduced to those members of Corradon's family who were present: his wife, Victoria; one of their three sons; a daughter-in-law; and two grandchildren. They were curiously formal introductions, and any anticipation Merral had had that here, at his home, he might meet a private Anwar Corradon evaporated. Merral had a brief conversation with Victoria, a graceful lady with short white hair, who made some warm comments about Ynysmant, recalling a happy visit there some years earlier. But as she spoke, Merral noticed that her eyes were constantly glancing toward her husband as if she had some deep worry for him.

Within a few minutes, Merral was shown to the representative's study. It was full of books of poetry and theology, family images, and statues, with one wall being devoted to a large map of Menaya, drawn and painted by hand with exquisite engraved scenes scattered across it. Beyond it was another glass door that led to a small conservatory full of plants.

"So, my dear Forester?" the representative said as he sat down behind his desk, his eyes staring at Merral with undisguised anticipation.

"Sir," Merral said, and he found himself swallowing hard, "I am now, very reluctantly, ready to lead the FDU contact party."

Corradon closed his eyes for a moment before looking at Merral. "Thank you. It is about the best news I have heard today. Daily, things get worse. Since I saw you, Lucian and I had a private visit from a senior member of the Farholme Congregations Committee; they are noticing it now. Other events have been reported. There are three focal points: Ynysmant, Larrenport, and Ilakuma."

"Ilakuma? In the Anuzabar Chain? It's at least five thousand kilometers away. Are they sure?"

"It seems the same sort of thing," said Corradon. "A lot of bitterness, but here it's centering on property disputes. They are talking about . . ." He paused. "What was the word? I had to look it up to be sure what they meant. . . . Yes, *lawyers*."

"Lawyers?"

"Anyway," Corradon continued with a shrug, "it's getting messy. They blame the Gate going and I wasn't going to argue otherwise."

"I'm not surprised, sir."

Corradon opened a drawer, pulled out an envelope, and handed it over.

"On the assumption that you would take on the task, I had a formal letter of commissioning drafted for you. Lucian is, as ever, anxious that we do things right."

The envelope was marked "Confidential" and bore the seal of the Council of Representatives. Inside there were three sheets of paper. Merral took the top sheet and, aware that his hand was shaking slightly, began to read it.

Forester Merral Stefan D'Avanos is hereby authorized to take charge of the Farholme Defense Unit as of the above date until such time as he is relieved of his office. He is to take the rank of captain and, under God, is to be answerable only to the Council of Farholme Representatives. His general duties are to carry out, to the best of his ability, the task of countering the intruders. His specific and immediate duties are detailed on the separate sheet. Captain D'Avanos is authorized to use such Farholme facilities and resources as may be required.

At the bottom was a signature and beneath it, *Anwar Corradon, Representative for northeastern Menaya; Chair, Council of Farholme Representatives A.D. 13852.*

Merral flicked to the next sheet, which was headed by "Confrontation Plans: Top Secret." Underneath were four short numbered paragraphs.

1. A body of approximately one hundred and forty soldiers is to be assembled by Sentinel Enand. These are to be divided into four units as follows: a) One six-man squad to accompany the two-person diplomatic team. b) Two thirty-man teams for the possible assault. c) The remaining personnel to be kept in reserve on the Emilia Kay. Each unit is to be under a lieutenant and a sergeant.

2. The diplomatic party will be unarmed and will advance openly without show of force. If, in your judgment, their approaches are rejected by the intruders, you are authorized to attack with all possible speed.

3. If such an attack becomes necessary, your goal—to be achieved at all costs—is to disable the ship. If at all possible, the ship is to be taken intact by the FDU.

4. In the event an attack is undertaken, all reasonable opportunity for the surrender of the intruder forces is to be given. Should there be a failure to surrender, then you are authorized to use whatever force is necessary to ensure the completion of the mission.

At the bottom was Corradon's signature.

The third sheet was simply an acknowledgement form stating *I have read the above two sheets and agree to them.*

Merral paused. "Sir, what's a lieutenant and a sergeant?"

A sad smile crossed Corradon's face. "They are, I'm told, military ranks. The ever-knowledgeable Sentinel Enand will explain."

"I have no doubt."

Merral stared at the paper, struggled with a sea of emotions, took the pen off the desk, and with a silent prayer for help, signed his name.

Corradon took the sheet from him. "I'm sorry. I truly am. You and I are in the same unhappy position of having been given a task that neither of us wants." He rubbed his face before staring at Merral. "A task without precedent, a task that may not even be achievable. To lead a world without a Gate . . ." He stared darkly into the distance. "To lead a world without a Gate that is being infiltrated by evil?"

Merral felt that he had never heard such gloom in the representative's voice.

Corradon put his elbows on the desk, clasped his hands together, and leaned forward so his chin rested on his fingers. It was, Merral thought (and immediately felt ashamed for thinking it), a terribly statuesque pose that made him look rather noble. Yet there was something brooding about the way Corradon appeared that reminded Merral of some troubled king or president from before the Intervention, faced with leading his people through a time of strife or disaster. And then Merral realized such a parallel was all too apt.

"I know you are busy," Corradon said in a quiet voice, "but come through to the conservatory. There are things that need to be said and here is perhaps rather formal. But can I get you a drink?"

"A fruit juice, sir, please."

"I'll be with you in a minute. Go through."

•◆•

The conservatory was full of anemones of many colors, most with their petals closed for the night. Merral was looking around, trying to identify the species when Corradon returned with two glasses of juice.

"Shall we?" he said, pointing to a pair of chairs in a corner.

"A fine collection of plants, sir," Merral said as he sat down and took the juice from the tray.

"Thank you. I have concentrated on the anemones of Menaya." Suddenly the representative's tone of voice changed, and Merral was all too aware of tiredness and strain in it. "But, Merral, let's drop the formality. Here, at least, please call me Anwar."

Merral was surprised to see that any trace of confidence had left the representative's face. The man who sat in front of him now seemed older and troubled.

"As you wish, Anwar," Merral said, feeling both sympathy and alarm.

His host sipped his drink and frowned. "Merral," Anwar said slowly, "I want to explain something. So you understand. Now that you have agreed to help, I can tell you."

He hesitated. "The post of representative—and even more so, that of chairman of the Farholme representatives—is not just functional, it is also public. Indeed, it is perhaps primarily a public role. You know: the opening of schools, the visits to processing plants, the endless speeches and dinners; that sort of thing." Corradon gave a pained smile and stared into the darkness of one corner of the conservatory. "It is harmless enough. A sort of perpetual theatrical performance. You understand?"

"Yes. But I had never thought of it that way."

"No, why should you? But since the loss of the Gate, my role has changed. People now look to me for help, for guidance, for encouragement. I sense them hanging on my every word. They are hungry for me to reassure them that it's all going to be all right. It is almost idolatrous. But do you see the problem?"

"I'm not sure I do, sir—Anwar, I mean—you'd better spell it out."

"It quite simple. I can't show any doubt or concern. I have to deliver what they want."

"I see."

"And increasingly, Merral, I find that my private views are so much at variance with what I have to say in public that I feel a fraud." His face seemed to sag, and Merral felt the blue eyes were close to tears. "I think we are in trouble. I'm worried. But I can't say it. I have to pretend."

"Ah," Merral said, reeling at the situation that the representative had exposed. "I see. I'm sorry; I hadn't realized."

"You weren't meant to. That's the problem. I'm caught every way; I can't even resign. That would be bad for morale. At times, I feel I am putting on an act. As if I am a circus clown, with a fixed smile."

"That must be hard."

"It is." Corradon shook his head bitterly.

"Who else knows?"

"Victoria, of course. And Lucian. He misses very little. He is concerned about it. He wonders how long I can keep up the act. That's another reason why he backs you. I—*we*—need you. And we need a victory. Of some sort. But he has been very helpful."

Merral sipped his juice, aware that the burden on him had just been increased. "I understand. I will do what I can."

The gaunt face that stared at him seemed to brighten slightly as if some burden had been lifted. "Thanks," Corradon said with a long, weary sigh. "Anyway, I just thought you ought to know. I'm the wrong man for this job."

"I think there's at least two of us in that position," Merral told him. "But thank you for your honesty. I will pray for you."

As Merral watched, he felt that somehow Corradon's face regained something of the smooth assurance that it had had before. *He has put back on the public mask,* Merral thought, and the idea appalled him.

"Thank you," Corradon said and sipped his drink. "Incidentally, Merral, it has been agreed that, despite the rush, we and you would all take tomorrow off and keep the Lord's Day."

"Seems sensible."

"Well, we thought not to do so would be a lack of faith. And besides, it would be rather noticeable." The representative shrugged and took another sip. "Anyway, I'll let you go. You'll have a lot to do before you go south."

"*South?*"

There was a pause. "Ah, hasn't he told you? The ever-inventive Sentinel Enand? Well, he will." Corradon rose. "And we'd better not keep him. But let me show you out. I may try and see you before you go, but Vero is anxious that I keep up a normal schedule. Not to alert anyone who is watching."

He ushered Merral to the conservatory door. "Thank you again for listening."

"It's a privilege. I'll keep it confidential. But I have a question. You see, Brenito told me—it was almost the last thing he said to me—that we must all play our parts."

"True."

"And surely to play a part, we have—at least sometimes—to act?"

There was a thin, tired smile. "Ah, how interesting. Yes, I think you are right. We may not like the parts that the Most High has written for us. And sometimes we may not even feel that we can do them. But we must do what we can."

He patted Merral on the back. "Thanks. But do me a favor, Captain? If it comes to a fight, seize the ship! Please?"

•–•–•

As Vero drove him to Narreza Tower, Merral mentioned nothing of his conversation in the conservatory to Vero. But he did mention other things.

"And on Ilakuma," Merral said, "there are disputes; they are talking about lawyers."

"Lawyers!" The vehicle swerved and a red light flashed as the auto-steer circuitry took over and directed it away from the curb. "The people of Ilakuma want lawyers?"

"That's what he said."

"We are in big trouble." Vero shook his head. "Bigger than I thought."

"And he also talked about us going south. Where and why?"

Vero suddenly looked rather sheepish, "I meant to tell you. Do you know Tanaris Island?"

"Tanaris? In the Henelen Chain. A bit lonely, isn't it? Five or six hundred kilometers southeast of Larrenport. There have been various plans for forestry work there, but they never got very far. Why do you mention it?"

"Because Tanaris is our forward base. Zak and many of the men are already there, building a camp, beginning to practice. The rest will be there soon. The day after tomorrow—all being well—you and I will take the *Emilia Kay* to Tanaris."

"But why there?"

"Because the men need to practice and Isterrane is just too public. People will see and maybe talk. If they do that over diary links then the intruders may know. Besides, there are always ships landing, and they get in the way. So Tanaris has become the assembly point; it's uninhabited, isolated, and has a good landing strip."

"Makes sense. You *have* been busy."

Vero sighed. "Yes. Everyone has; that's another reason why we are going to take tomorrow off. Anyway, this is the plan. We have three full days of training at Tanaris. Then the *Emilia Kay* flies due north on the evening of the fourth day, drops the teams off, and lands at the southern edge of the crater overnight. So, all being well, six days from now at dawn, we make contact."

"That's soon."

"I know."

"But what do I need to start work on?"

"I have a folder ready for you."

"Good."

Vero parked at the base of Narreza Tower.

"And, Vero, I also need to talk with Perena urgently. There's a problem with the sleds.

"A serious one?"

"Probably. I was thinking about it as I flew over. It took my mind off things."

• ◆ •

In the apartment, Vero took a thick box file off the shelf. "In this you have three things. We recovered a number of texts from the Library and had them printed out. Some of them are for soldiers and that is a help, as we are using them to start getting the men trained. So you have a military leadership handbook from the 2020s, and it may be a help to you. Mind you, it is in a very peculiar form of Ancient English. There are whole sentences of abbreviations whose meanings are hard to uncover. There is another file of the technical details of the weapons and the *Emilia Kay*. Finally, you have a folder of the men you will give orders to."

"'Give orders to?' That has a strange sound to it."

"Well, the ancient wisdom was—and they had lots of battles—"

"In that context it is questionable how much wisdom the ancients did have."

"Point taken. But their maxim was that if you want to win a battle, you don't stop to take a vote."

"Oh, Vero!" Merral sighed as he accepted the folder. "Are you trying to make me change my mind already?"

"Sorry," Vero said, "but it's the way it must be." He hesitated. "There is one other thing for you. Brenito left you a package."

"For me?"

"Yes. I know a bit about what's in it. And I didn't feel it was right to give it to you before you made your mind up."

Vero went into his bedroom and returned with a small package wrapped in blue paper with an envelope attached.

Merral opened the envelope.

My dear Forester,
If you are reading this then I have indeed—at long last—been called

Home. Although I shall appreciate getting a new body, I feel it is rather a shame leaving things just as they get exciting.

I said most of what I want to say to you at Ynysmant. Basically, guard Jorgio and watch yourself. However, in thinking of you as I arranged to dispose of my considerable effects, a certain something came to mind which you will find in the attached box.

It seems all too likely that it will come to a fight. If, as I expect, you are summoned to lead the attack, I would like you to wear this in my memory. I could wish that it had some magic power, but, of course, it hasn't. But do consider it as an encouragement and a reminder, something like that. If you are tempted to flee, it may encourage you to stand firm.

With every best wish,
In the service of the Lamb,

Brenito Camsar, Sentinel

Merral opened the wrapping paper to find a small, dark wooden box. He looked at it. It was plainly very old; the wood was fine grained, polished smooth, and blackened with age.

"Can I open it?" he asked.

"Of course. The box is recent. Relatively speaking."

Merral opened the lid carefully, wondering how ancient the contents were if a box so old was "recent." Inside, nestled on a soft black fabric, was a dull gray-brown titanium disc just big enough to sit in the curve between joined forefinger and thumb, attached to a fine but plain neck chain of identical metal. *It is jewelry,* he thought, then realized there was a functional air about the chain that proclaimed that it was never meant for display.

Merral lifted the chain and, as the disc spun before him, saw there was writing on it. He stopped it spinning and peered at the words. The script was Early Assembly Communal, slightly scratched and hard to make out. He read some words, then, as they made sense, found his hand shaking so much he could not read the remainder.

"Is it . . . is it the real thing?" he asked, finding himself almost overwhelmed at what he apparently held.

"Oh yes. May I see it?"

Vero came over, took the disc, and read aloud, "'Lucas Hannun Ringell, Space Frigate *Clearstar,* Assembly Assault Fleet. Date of Birth: 3-3-2082.'"

"His identification disc. Really?"

Very gently, Vero lowered the disc back into Merral's hand.

"He told me it had been kept in the family. Ultimately given to some distant ancestor by Moshe Adlen, to whom General Ringell gave it in his old age."

"But," Merral protested, "we must be talking, what—five hundred generations? This is older than almost anything else on this planet."

"Probably, but put it on."

Merral lowered the chain over his head and let the disc, oddly cool, slip down inside his shirt. *I could not feel stranger if they had put some crown on me.* "If I understand this correctly, I am now wearing the identification disc that was hanging around the neck of the man who, in killing William Jannafy, ended the Rebellion and the Last War."

Vero nodded. "He thought it would be appropriate. A symbol of our last war goes into the next. A continuity."

"Yes . . . ," Merral sighed. "And by giving it to me, he also placed a high burden on me: the burden of history."

Vero gave him a sympathetic look. "Yes, he did. And that was doubtless what he meant to do."

"Ah," Merral said, feeling unable to say anything more profound.

"Anyway," Vero said, "let me go and get Perena."

• ◆ •

Ten minutes later, Merral's attempt to understand the manual's alien concepts of imposing discipline were interrupted by Vero's return with Perena.

"Sorry for the delay," she said, amid a gentle hug. "I was showering. I've been busy all day supervising the work on the *Emilia Kay*. It's the only flying craft I have ever had where you've had to hose bat droppings out of the turbine scoops."

"That bad? Is it going to work?" asked Merral, abruptly realizing that the whole strategy hung on an ancient ship.

"Yes, it will be fine." She frowned slightly. "Probably. It's just that they never really expected to use it again, so for ten years or so the protective storage coat was breached on the port side. Anya reckons we could have done an ecological study on the wildlife inside. We have removed rats, mice, a dozen scorpions, and a couple of snakes. And the bats." She ran a hand through her short hair.

"I thought it was an operating ship."

"No, it had been put in mothballs," Vero said, sitting down at the table.

"What?" Perena asked.

"Ignore him," Merral said. "It will be some sort of Ancient English phrase."

"Okay, but what does it mean?"

"Well," Vero answered rather defensively, "it means . . ." He frowned. "Hmm. I don't actually know. A mothball was a small ball of naphthalene." His frown deepened. "How could you put a ship in them? You'd need tons of the things. Very odd."

Merral interrupted him by asking for the images of Fallambet Lake Five. The three of them gathered round the largest image. Silently, Merral measured distances on the sheets and then looked up at the others. "As I thought, we have a problem."

A new frown crossed Vero's face. "You'd better explain."

"It's the sleds. When you first envisaged using them, you were planning to do it over land. Right?"

"Pretty much so."

"Sneak up close and then race in. Right?"

"Again. Yes."

"But how fast are they?"

"Say, eighty kilometers an hour."

Perena muttered something under her breath, but it was Merral who answered. "Vero, that's a maximum. Try sixty when laden. So how long to cover two kilometers?"

"Two minutes. Ah."

"It's too long. There is no cover. They will have a clear shot in that time. The last kilometer is open water. And we know that they have beam weapons of some sort."

Perena nodded. "I should have thought of that," she said.

"No, it's my mistake," Vero added. "You've been busy on the *Emilia Kay*. And this is new territory for us all. Merral, I hadn't realized that the lake position is far more open than I had hoped."

Merral looked at Perena. "So, Captain, a technical question. How can we increase the speed of the sleds?"

She returned his gaze, and he felt he could almost hear her mind calculating. "How fast do you want them to go?"

"Oh, so fast they can't be hit. See this lake stretch? I would want them to cover that last kilometer in well under thirty seconds. So, say about one hundred and fifty kilometers an hour. Oh, and as close to the water as you can get. Under a meter?"

Perena shook her head. "Tricky. And you want it within two to three days, eh? Well, the simplest solution is the oldest: bolt a rocket booster propulsion unit onto the back and strap everybody in. Glide down the valley silently under normal GM power, then when you hit open ground, just fire the motors. A small motor will give you that acceleration. Of course, at that speed, handling will be a problem. And then you have to decelerate on the other side. Hmm." She paused, evidently doing mental calculations, then looked hard at Merral. "And you want it close to the water too? Well, you'll have to have the controls automatic. Human reflexes can't handle those speeds. Still, you know where you are going, so it's a simple program. And the surface, apart from waves, is fairly flat. I'd say it's possible to modify the circuits that control the altitude and course."

"So," Merral asked, "it could be done?"

"Yes . . ." Perena dragged the word out slowly. "But you'd have to calculate how many g's you'd pull though."

"Is a straight-line course the best thing?"

She thought for a moment. "Probably not. You could write some swerves into the control program. But then it could be a wild ride. Lots of strains."

Perena looked at Merral, "So you want me to try and get it organized? I have enough work to do with the *Emilia Kay,* but I can find engineers who would like the challenge. They will have to work very hard, though. And there're no guarantees."

Vero nodded assent.

"Okay, Perena," Merral said, "can you try and see if you can get someone to do it? Please?"

Vero tapped him on the shoulder. "You could order it."

"Order it?"

"You're the Captain of the FDU. You could say, 'Captain Lewitz, I hereby order you to get it done.' Only snappier. And no tentative 'please' is needed. It's the sort of thing you ought to practice."

"Are you serious?" Merral asked, staring at Vero. "She's a friend. I can't order her."

Perena gave him an intense look. "He's right, Merral. Sadly. You have to give orders. In this context, I'm your obedient pilot."

"But this is horrible."

"Oh, just do it!" Vero snapped.

"Now who's ordering who? Oh, very well . . . Perena . . . . No, *Captain Lewitz,* I hereby order you to get it done."

"Yes, sir." There was a nod, a smile, and she left.

After the door closed behind her, Merral turned to Vero. "This is hopeless," he said. "I'm not up to it."

Vero smiled and clapped him on the back. "The orders thing is— I think—easy enough to pick up. The more important thing is that you have identified a tactical problem that I had overlooked. You've just shown why we need you. You have a flair for this sort of thing."

"Perhaps . . ."

"No, definitely. Now let's get to work."

• ◆ •

The next day Merral rose early. Normally on a Lord's Day he would have lain in bed until later. Now though, he felt that he had no mandate for any such luxury. Instead, he spent time praying and reading his Bible.

Then he sat on the bed and called Isabella on his diary. She seemed to stare at him for a few moments before answering. Slowly and painfully, Merral made an apology for what had happened when they last met. Isabella seemed only reluctantly to accept his apologies. "The trouble is," she said rather sourly, "you're never around for long enough to talk to properly. And when are you back next?"

"I really can't say, Isabella, I'm afraid, but that is the way it is. I may be out of touch for a few days."

"There we are again," came the sharp response, accompanied by an exasperated shake of her head. "As I said, you're never around. Look, I have to go. Good-bye."

Then, before he could say anything more, the screen went blank. He stared at it for a moment or two, then, in exasperation, slammed his fist onto the bed.

Early the following morning Merral and Vero drove to the airport but went on past the main terminal to the western extremity of the complex.

Merral soon spotted the *Emilia Kay*. She was a large vessel, the gray of a winter's sky, hanging low to the ground, with a swollen belly and stubby wings. The ship might have reminded him of some animal—perhaps a whale—but it lacked any sense of the harmonious unity of an organism. It was too easy to see that it was made of individual components: wings, fin, four engines, fuselage, and load module. As they approached, Merral decided that the intention had been to conceal the ship by parking it at the extreme end of the western runway system. But to him, particularly in the absence of the regular Gate shuttle traffic, it still seemed glaringly prominent, and the dozen or so vehicles in attendance around it seemed to highlight the fact that something unusual was going on.

Vero drove onto the service track outside the earth ramparts that marked the runway edges. As they turned a corner and went out of sight of the terminal, he slowed the vehicle and brought it to a stop in front of what was clearly a brand-new barrier of sand-filled containers and wire mesh.

Two men in matching blue overalls stood by a gate in the barrier. They nodded in recognition at Vero and walked round to Merral.

Vero leaned over. "Show them your letter," he whispered.

Merral pulled it out and let the men examine it. They glanced at each other, stared at Merral again, and then turned quizzical looks to Vero before raising their hands in tentative salutes.

"Welcome, sir," the taller said. He glanced at Merral's belt.

"Oh yes," Vero said, "can you let him have your diary?"

"What is this?"

"A new program that restricts use of the diary. No location of position, no signals out except emergency ones or ones on a coded FDU band. You'd best get it done. A temporary measure."

Noting that Vero had taken action on a problem that had emerged in their last dealings with the intruders, Merral handed his diary over. The man slid it into a downloading interface slot, pressed a button, and passed it back.

"Thank you, Captain D'Avanos," he said with a salute. He lifted the barrier and Vero accelerated through toward the *Emilia Kay*.

"So this is how it is to be," Merral said, as much to himself as to Vero as he put the diary back on his belt. "*Sir* this, *sir* that, *Captain D'Avanos, sir* . . . And the salutes."

Vero looked at him out of the corner of his eye. "Merral, in the past no one invented a better way, and there's no time to try and find it now." He seemed to consider something. "My friend, if I may suggest something?" Vero's tone seemed guarded. "You have to play the part whether you like it or not. Among the men and the few women you will command, everyone is confused, and some are scared. All will be both at some point. They will look to you to hold them firm. I know it's hard because you have no models to base yourself on. But then neither have they. In Tanaris you will have to work hard. But I think you will do it."

"And supposing I can't?"

Vero slowed the vehicle to a crawl and looked sternly across at him. "Don't ever even think that!" There was rebuke in his voice. "I believe—*we* believe—that God has called you to lead us. If he has called you to play the part, then he will equip you for that. You mustn't doubt that!"

Then, as if to soften the rebuke, he punched Merral on the arm. "Come on Captain D'Avanos," he said as the vehicle sped up toward the confusion of activity around the ship. "You'll do it."

They parked a hundred meters from the ship. Given that so much was going on around, in, and on top of the vessel, Merral decided any closer would have been risky. A quick glance suggested that there must be at least a hundred people and fifteen vehicles clustered about the ship. He counted six LP4 transporters alone, each in various stages of being unloaded, their contents of boxes, bags, and drums lying next to them and being checked off. There were other vehicles too: a hydrogen tanker parked at a safe distance, numerous smaller four-seater vehicles, and even the odd bike. Everywhere there were businesslike noises— hammering, the whine of lifters, the hum of motors, the shouting out of requests—all merging into a continuous hectic buzz of activity.

While Vero was detained by a man with an inquiry, Merral walked on, a robotic lifter pausing to let him pass with a bow of its head, and threaded his way past two men earnestly comparing databoard lists. Near a wingtip, he stopped and stared at the ship. The vessel was larger than Merral had imagined; he could easily believe that it would swallow the sleds, the hoverer, and a hundred or more men with room to spare. Merral cautiously identified it, from a memory of a model he had once made as a child, as a Series D Freighter. The phrase *the flexible workhorse of the Assembly* came to mind but, he decided, if it was after all to be compared with an animal, it was not a horse. Particularly not in this mode, where the massive landing legs were bowed so that the flat bottom of the cargo module that made up half the fuselage was now within centimeters of the ground, making the whole ship look squat and low slung. It was as if someone had started by modeling the ship on a toad and then, at the last minute, had decided that it had to fly.

As he approached he saw that the long, curved, slablike doors that ran along most of the length of the cargo module were open, allowing him to see inside. On the floor of the module, the two sleds were already in and the hoverer was being winched aboard. Trying not to trip over piles of equipment or get in the way of the numerous workers, Merral walked into the shadow of the wings of the *Emilia Kay* and looked up at the gray bulk hanging above him. There were scratches and dents on the body, and the paintwork was dulled and locally peeling. Two high gantries had been erected under each rear engine, and on them people were standing, peering into panels, and inserting cables and tubes.

"Awesome, isn't it?" Vero's voice sang out behind him.

Merral glanced at him, then looked around at all the activity. On the high single tail fin with the faded Lamb and Stars emblem, the rudder was swinging backward and forward in some mysterious test procedure.

"Yes, it is. How did you get all this organized?"

"I just set it in motion, my friend."

"What am I supposed to do here?"

"Nothing much. Most of the men are already at Tanaris; there was another flight this morning. But you may want to familiarize yourself with the ship. I suggest you go and see Perena. Here, as captain of the *Emilia Kay*, she is almost more important than you."

Careful to avoid getting in the way of either people or machinery, Merral made his way into the ship and, after asking directions, found Perena in the spacious three-seat cockpit high at the front end of the ship. At least, Merral concluded, it would have been spacious had it not been filled with six people wrestling with cabling in access panels, squinting at flashing screens, and calling out incomprehensible codes to each other.

Perena, in T-shirt, baggy jeans, and worn running shoes, was leaning with apparent nonchalance by the cockpit door, looking at a databoard in her hands and ticking off lists on it. It occurred to Merral that with her relaxed air, casual clothes, and slight build she looked insignificant—the very last person in the room who one would expect was the captain.

Perena glanced up and winked at Merral. "So, Captain, stealing aboard without ceremony?"

"I'm afraid so, Captain Lewitz. I'm enjoying the anonymity while it lasts. How's it going?"

"Not bad; I think it will be late afternoon before we take off. Come back here; there's more room and it's quieter."

She led him to the bare and shabby passenger compartment just behind the cockpit that had twenty or so rather austere seats. There was no one else there. Merral noticed the faintest remains of a spider's web in a corner.

Perena looked around and nodded. "Scruffy, eh? For an Assembly ship. But it will do."

"Are we on schedule?"

"No. We will be two hours later than planned, but as the camp is already set up for us at Tanaris, arriving in the dark isn't a problem. We still have to repaint the ship's exterior. That's the last task. That and fueling."

"A nice color scheme?"

She grinned. "I've ordered a nice, pale, eggshell blue."

"You're not serious?"

"Yes. But only for the underside—matches the sky. On a good day. The top is a disrupted green-and-brown camouflage."

"Camouflage! No, I suppose it makes sense. I hope they can't see us now."

"We don't think so. We have monitored Farholme local space for satellites and found none. And just in case they are planning to use our own, one of Vero's people arranged a widespread satellite communications malfunction for today. All signals are being lost."

Merral found himself marveling again at his friend's inventiveness. "Smart move. I'm glad he's on our side."

"He is very ingenious. I have played him at chess."

"Is he any good?"

A smile with a hint of disquiet crossed her face. "Ingenuity, Merral, is fine, but it has its limits. Vero's strategies are cunning, but they can be overambitious."

"Ah," Merral said, suddenly alarmed at the thought that such a weakness might extend beyond the chessboard.

As he saw the expression of tender unease cross Perena's face, Merral realized something.

"You care for him, don't you?" he said, wondering if he was intruding into private matters.

Perena seemed to think hard. "Yes. But is there anything more? Any possibility of a deeper relationship?" She gave a slight shrug. "There could be, perhaps. But, for the moment, I have put it to one side." She stared into an infinite distance and her voice became even quieter. "By temperament, Merral, I am a dreamer. And for someone who plays chess—and flies ships—that can be dangerous. I handle it by being focused, by pushing everything to one side. So might there be anything with Vero? Maybe, when this is all over. 'For everything there is a season,' and I'm afraid our season is war. Or at least we must be prepared for that." Perena's eyes seemed to stare at Merral with a new intensity. "So 'anything more' assumes a lot."

"That we survive, for a start."

"There is more than that."

"What do you mean?"

A strange tautness seemed to come over Perena's face. "You have recognized that our world is changing, Merral?" At his nod, she said, "Where there was sunlight, there are now shadows. Where our paths were once straight and smooth, they are now winding and rough. And as our world changes, so do we."

Perena's voice had become hushed and distant, and Merral felt he was being given access to her most private thoughts. He said nothing as she continued. "Some people are adapting to the new world. Clemant, for instance, has realized the way the wind is blowing and, although he hates it, is trimming his sails to suit. Corradon? I think he senses the changes but can only hope and pray that they will go away. But we are all reacting to it." She gave Merral a smile whose meaning he found impossible to fathom. "But will any of us be the same when the storm passes?"

"A good question," Merral replied, feeling troubled.

Perena fell silent.

A heavy knocking reverberated through the hull. Perena winced.

"And are you happy with this ship?" asked Merral, feeling a pressing need to talk about practical matters. "I mean, I gather it's not been used for years."

Perena looked around as if anxious not to be overheard. "Only partially," she said in a confidential tone, "but I'm not shouting about it. It's not the age either—that can be fixed. And the test flights showed she was fine. No, I've read up on ships of war, and this is a long way away from being one."

"I can imagine. What's the problem?"

She smiled, but it was a severe and joyless smile. "*Problems*, plural. Too slow, too unmaneuverable. There is no armor whatsoever; the hydrogen tanks in the hull are very vulnerable. Ironically, my general survey craft is better equipped: that at least has thermal plates and an ability to take some impacts. But *Emilia* was designed as an atmosphere-only ship, so the hull is barely two mills thick. There is little that counts as defensive sensors, nothing that acts as electronic countermeasures. The ability to accept different modules in the load bay is a great feature for a freighter but it weakens the structure; it can't take severe stresses. And the doors cannot be opened quickly. Do you want me to go on?"

"Definitely not. But practically, what does it mean?"

"Good question. What, as Vero would now say, is 'the bottom line'? Well, it means I can't take risks. There will be no dramatic rescues for you under fire with this old lady." She tapped a girder near her.

"Thanks for the warning."

"But I like her all the same. The test flights yesterday were encouraging. Typical Series D. Slow, steady, stable."

"Good. And this is all the equipment?"

"Not at all." She shook her head. "There is much already at Tanaris, and there will be a series of supply flights almost every day. There's a lot of gear outstanding: uniforms, medical gear, that sort of thing. The booster jets for the sleds and their controllers. All being well."

"I see."

A figure appeared at the door and beckoned Perena. "Sorry," she said. "Nathan, my chief electrics man. Have a look round but watch your step. To have your captain break a leg tripping over a wire might be seen as, well . . . inauspicious."

Then, with a light pat on his arm, she was gone.

Merral wandered back along the upper hull of the *Emilia Kay,* in a corridor that he found hard not to think of as the spinal column of the great misshapen toad. He was trying to get a feeling for how the ship functioned, but not being an expert, found the various labels on the hatches and doors confusing and felt disinclined to ask explanations from the men and women who were preoccupied with cabling and circuits.

Halfway down the corridor, he heard footsteps behind him, and a familiar voice called out, "Tree Man! Or should I say *Captain* Tree Man?" Then an arm was linked playfully into his.

He turned. "Anya!" he said, pleased more than ever to see her freckled face. "I thought you would be elsewhere. . . ."

"No," she said wrinkling her nose, "I played my part in this affair starting and I will see it through. But come and see what I've been working on."

Anya led him down to the very end of the corridor, where there was a door with a small window in the middle. There were bolts at the top and bottom and a complex box with a keypad in the middle. All the features had the air of being recently fitted. Merral peered in through the thick glass to see a sizeable room with padding on every wall. Puzzled, he looked at Anya. "What's this for?"

"Prisoners," she murmured, with a strange note in her voice. "I am preparing to be a zookeeper."

"And if they aren't alive? What then?"

She gestured below. "We are fitting a freezer unit down there. And we have bags and disinfecting agents. We have to be prepared."

"I'm glad *you* are! So you are coming?"

Her blue eyes seemed to flash. "Why not? You may need a biologist. And I'm hardly going to miss the biggest bug hunt in history, am I?"

"No," Merral said.

Anya looked cautiously at him, as if concerned that he would veto her accompanying the ship. "Besides," she declared firmly, "my first aid isn't bad, and I can act as a medical orderly if needed."

"And we have those facilities?" Merral asked, suddenly realizing that this was yet another thing that he had overlooked. The gloomy thought struck him that there were probably many other oversights that he might make.

"Two doctors, six orderlies. A lot of equipment. Enough synplasma to replace everybody's blood. On our side anyway. The moment there is any contact, a hospital vessel will be mobilized. It will be there in an hour or less."

"Let's hope it's not needed," he said and then added, "But welcome on board, Doctor." And as he said it, he realized he felt both pleased that she was coming with him and also slightly guilty that he felt so pleased.

They walked back down the corridor and into the cargo module, where at least a dozen people were either hoisting things on board or fastening them down with straps and cabling. Merral was conscious that a number of those in the hold were staring at him and that whispered comments were being passed around. *They know who I am.* He looked at the growing piles of equipment being assembled.

Outside the cargo unit he could see more activity. By a wing, the complex structure of a robot painter with its multiple tubular limbs, flexible pipes, and nozzles rose like some strange insect emerging from a chrysalis.

"You look worried," Anya said to him.

"The scale and complexity of all this intimidates me. Vero has done a superb job. But I'm worried we will get there and find something missing."

"That's why there is the time in Tanaris to—"

There was the clatter of footsteps on the metal floor behind him. A voice shouted, "Captain D'Avanos here?"

For a fraction of a second, Merral thought that the reference was to someone else. Then he turned to see a young man dressed in blue.

"Yes, I'm Merral D'Avanos. Can I help?" As he said it, Merral realized that a decisive "What do you want?" would have been more in keeping with his rank. Oh well, he would learn.

"Sir!" The young man saluted again. "Sentinel Enand wants to see you, promptlike. There's a problem. This way."

With a nod and a shrug to Anya, Merral followed.

An evidently agitated Vero was waiting by a four-seater. "We have a difficulty at the entrance. It can be handled, but I'll need your help. Get in. I'll explain as we go."

Carefully, Vero turned the vehicle through the equipment and set off toward the line of wire they had come through earlier.

"The problem is," Vero said, "that two people from the Menaya news team have turned up. They have seen the *Emilia Kay* and the activity and—quite naturally—want to see what is going on."

"Vero, that could be disastrous! I mean, everybody on the planet will know." Merral looked at the activity behind him. "We can't disguise this. What can we do? Can we make them promise not to tell?"

Vero frowned and shook his head, "They would still know and it might get out. We could get it banned temporarily through Corradon. But that raises monumental constitutional issues. There is another way."

"How?"

A look of cunning flickered over Vero's face and then disappeared beneath a bland gaze of innocence. "Ah, *secret*. No, you introduce yourself as the 'head of what is going on here'—now use that exact phrase—and then designate me as the person who will talk to them. With my accent they may be uneasy about me, but if you back me that will be acceptable. Then get back to the vehicle and stay out of earshot."

"Why?"

Vero winked. "I just don't want you standing by when I talk. Trust me."

Merral had seen enough reporters at sports matches, weddings, and festivals to recognize the type, especially when they carried the trademark recording gear on their belts as this young man and woman did. The way they were sitting cross-legged on the ground suggested the sort of dedication associated with reporters who refused to leave the stadium without interviewing the losing captain.

Merral walked over, shook hands, and introduced himself by name, but without mentioning his rank, and then introduced Vero to them. As he walked back to the four-seater, he saw that Vero had gotten the reporters into a huddle with him as if they were discussing something confidential. A few minutes later, the group broke up with the shaking of hands, and Vero walked back with an awkward smile on his face.

"Back to work," Vero said and then, whistling tunelessly, lowered himself into the driving seat and switched on the engine.

"So what did you say?"

Still whistling, Vero set the vehicle rolling back toward the freighter where the painting machine had now risen above the wings. Only when the four-seater had sped up did he speak. "Promise you won't be angry?"

"No," Merral replied suspiciously. "I will probably be furious. What did you say?"

"Ah . . . I told them the truth. In a, well . . . modified form. I told them that there was a group being set up to carry out rescue operations within Farholme, in the event of forest fires, earthquakes, volcanoes, and other perils. To do the sort of things that the Assembly would normally send ships for."

"Good grief—"

Vero continued as if he hadn't heard Merral's expostulation. "But, I said, we were keeping it secret because we didn't want to alarm everybody. As everybody was already concerned about the Gate loss, we didn't want to make it worse. So I asked them not talk about it. Not yet. And they were persuaded."

Merral could barely believe what he was hearing. "Vero! You *lied* to them!" he shouted. "Completely and utterly!"

The response, when it eventually came, was thoughtful and

restrained. "Hmm, that's open to debate. You see my definition of 'perils' was sufficiently broad that it would allow for the invasion of hostile aliens. Or similar. And my definition of 'rescue' was, likewise, broad."

"But, Vero, you fell well below the standards of openness and truth that we have always held to. Far below."

"Yes, well, remember Rahab the whore in Joshua, chapter 2—one of those Old Covenant stories we pass over quickly with children?"

"That? . . . That was in the bad old days."

"Merral," Vero replied, with a tone of exaggerated weariness, "wake up! See those robot arms climbing over the top of the dear old *Emilia Kay?* It's painting her in camouflage. We are loading her now with explosive charges and guns. These are the preparations for war. As captain of operations it would be a help if you acknowledged this." Vero threw Merral a look that was somehow both critical and sympathetic. "See, my friend, the bad old days are back."

•—◆—•

Back at the *Emilia Kay,* Merral decided the best thing he could do was stay out of the way and try and master what he was going to be responsible for. So he made himself comfortable in a patch of shade in the back of an empty LP4 and spent some hours alternatively reading the leader's handbook and then flicking through the folder with its details of the men he was commanding. Some things, he was glad to see, had already been done. The assignment of seven lieutenants and sergeants and the heads of medical, logistics, and communication teams had also been made. Vero, he saw, had even made a choice of someone as chaplain. As a starter, Merral decided to memorize those names, faces, and details.

So, as the afternoon passed, he tried to get his mind around the immensity of what he was shortly going to have to undertake. The only relief he took was that, every so often, he emerged from his shaded seat to walk up to the ship and see how progress was being made. On one visit, Vero came over to him accompanied by a man with a familiar open face, carrying a holdall.

"Lorrin Venn," Merral said, extending his hand to the tall man with the pale brown hair and green eyes. "Nice to see you. Still working in support?"

Lorrin smiled, as if anxious to please. "Sir, that was what I've come about. I was wondering if I could be released from that, just for a week, and come and join a team. It was my first choice. I know it's late. But I have my gear with me." He looked plaintively at Vero, as if for support.

"He meets the physical requirements," Vero said. "And we could use some spare men. But it's up to you."

"So, Lorrin, you know that it may be unpleasant. Even dangerous?"

Lorrin nodded urgently. "It's really what I want, sir. It'd be neat. I know Zak. Maybe I could be on his team?"

Merral stared at Vero, hoping for assistance, but found that his friend was looking away. *He wants me to make the decision myself.*

"Very well, Lorrin. I would imagine we can use you. Get Sentinel Vero here to assign you to a squad when we get to Tanaris. See you on the flight."

"*Yeah!* Thank you, sir!" the man said, eagerness written across his face. Then he gave a sharp salute, turned, and beginning to whistle happily, left the ship.

Merral, watching him depart, shook his head in amusement, and turned to Vero. "Was that okay?"

"Yes. I suppose so."

"You don't sound convinced. Why wasn't he put on one of the contact teams first? He's a nice guy. There's a contagious happiness about that man."

"Yes, isn't there? I refused because he's an only child. We have made no ruling on it. But I thought . . ."

"I see . . . ," Merral responded slowly, realizing that Vero expected not just fighting but also loss of life. Chastened, he returned to his seat in the back of the transporter and, preoccupied with unhappy thoughts, stared blankly at his notes for some time.

•-•-•

Late in the afternoon, Merral looked up to see Dr. Clemant, his neat dark suit and carefully parted hair making him conspicuous among the sweaty, dirty, and increasingly disheveled men and women laboring around the *Emilia Kay*. The advisor stared at the ship in a thoughtful manner for some time before coming over to Merral.

"Good afternoon, Captain," he said.

"Advisor, good afternoon." Merral said, leaping down from the transporter. "How are you?"

"Well, thank you. I thought I'd come and have a look at the preparations. I have followed the planning closely."

"I'm sure," Merral said. "I don't know about you, but I'm awed by everything that has been done."

Clemant's eyes scanned the busy scene ahead carefully before answering. "Yes, it is a remarkable achievement. But—alas—it is not here that the plans will be tested."

"True."

There was a long silence. "I came to see you, Captain. I thought it right to do so." Merral felt there was a stiffness in the way Clemant spoke that hinted he wanted to say something.

"Thank you."

"I am truly delighted that you have accepted the task of leading the approach."

"I am less enthusiastic."

"I understand." Clemant continued to stare at the *Emilia Kay*. "Captain, let me say that no one is more anxious than me that this operation succeed."

"Thank you again," Merral said.

"You see . . . I know this planet well. It is my business; my life. I have my finger on its pulse and . . . " The advisor paused, stared stiffly at the ground, and when he looked up, Merral could see the fear in his eyes. "And frankly, I am scared."

"By what?" Merral asked, surprised by Clemant's candor.

"By the sense that it is all unraveling."

"I see. . . ."

"Do you?" Clemant said, and Merral was struck by the bluntness of the question. The advisor's pale face colored slightly. "I'm sorry," he said awkwardly. "I find it hard to express myself properly these days; it seems to come out wrong. No offense meant. What I mean is . . ." His words faltered for a second. "What I mean is this: as a world we have been bound together by grace and goodwill. But faced with a return of evil, that may not be enough. In the last month, I have been reading about the past." His eyes closed briefly as if he was in pain. "I have read and watched horrors. The Plague Wars, the destructions, the burning cities, the victims . . ." The advisor shook his head and fell silent. As he continued, his eyes bore a strangely intense expression. "And each new incident here is another point on a graph that marks out a trajectory. And, Captain, I have seen where it is heading."

Somewhat shaken by the analysis, Merral found himself denying it. "It may not be that bad. There is an enormous resilience here."

Clemant gave him a cold shrewd look as if to say, *I know you don't believe that.* "Perhaps. I hope you are right. But you do see that we have no barriers? no defenses? no structures to protect us?"

Merral struggled with the concepts. "I suppose so. We don't have such things."

Clemant's dark eyes stared at him. "I am from Kelendara. In your former profession you will have heard of our town."

"Indeed, the big forest fires of '22."

"I was a teenager then and I watched the hillsides burn for weeks. You know the verdict of the investigation?"

"I read it at college. The firebreaks weren't wide enough; the first fires weren't tackled fast enough."

"Yes." The advisor's expression suddenly showed a deep concern. "Farholme is like those forests, only worse—there are no firebreaks.

We have seen sparks: Larrenport, Ynysmant, Ilakuma, and who knows where else? If they catch . . . " His eyes seem to stare into an infinite void. "We will lose everything. Everything."

Merral, troubled by the vision, said nothing.

"You talked to Anwar last night, I gather?" Clemant said, and Merral knew he referred to something more than an ordinary conversation.

"I did."

"I worry about him. I think he's close to the limit of what he can take. In a storm, some trees bend and recover while others snap, do they not, Captain? And which is our representative?"

"I've never applied the analogy to human beings, Dr. Clemant."

"Perhaps wisely so. But if this tree breaks, we are in trouble." Clemant shook his head, and the expression on his face returned to one of inscrutability. He looked at the ship.

"So," he said, and his voice was less intense, "I came to encourage you. To urge you on. We need that ship. More than you can imagine. We need to be reconnected to the Assembly, and fast."

"I will do what I can," Merral said. "Everyone I have met here is totally committed to doing their task."

"Good." Clemant stared at the ground, and Merral felt there was something else he wanted to say. "There is one other thing," Clemant said finally, looking up at him, a new expression in his dark gray eyes.

"Please."

"I don't know how to say this, but I have a concern."

"Go ahead."

"I hope—as we all do—that diplomacy will work. That they, whoever they are, will say, 'Sorry, it was all a misunderstanding.'" He paused, and Merral knew that he didn't have the slightest faith that this would be the case. "But, Captain," Clemant continued, "if you do have to attack, I want you to be firm."

"I see. In what way?"

He shrugged. "I cannot say exactly; I do not know what will happen. But I don't want you to be overly cautious. Increasingly, I see this evil as a cancer in our world. It needs to be dealt with." He hesitated. "You may need to be a surgeon, Captain."

"Another interesting image, Advisor," Merral said, thinking that, in fact, he found it a very disturbing one.

Then, apparently embarrassed by what he had said, Clemant opened his hands wide in a dismissive gesture. "Well, that's just my view. But I do apologize for taking up your time."

"Advisor, it was very helpful to hear your concerns."

Clemant seemed slightly embarrassed. "Thank you. I felt I needed to express them." He looked around. "Oh, I was also looking for Zachary Larraine. You know him?"

"Zak? He's on Tanaris."

"Ah, I should have checked."

"But how do you know him? Oh, wait, he's from Kelendara too."

"That's right. I know his parents slightly. That's all. Incidentally, Professor Habbentz is at the ship and mentioned she would like to see you."

"Gerry? I'll go and find her."

"Do so. Well, I must go." Clemant's smile as he extended a hand seemed weak. "I will be praying for your success."

They shook hands and the advisor walked away. Merral found himself watching the neat departing figure with a great deal of unease. He sighed and then turned and made his way to the ship.

—•—

Gerry Habbentz's tall frame and long flowing black hair made her easy to find.

"Hi, Merral," she said with enthusiasm as he walked over to where she stood staring at the ship. "Good to see you again. I hear you are a captain now."

Merral shrugged. "I am still working out what that means."

"You'll learn." She grinned, and Merral felt that some of the strain she had borne when they had last met had lifted.

"What are you doing here?" he asked.

"I was at the airport and I came to say farewell to Perena. She flew us to the lab last time. And we've talked about this intruder ship. If you seize it, I'm down to view the engines."

"I'm hoping we are going to have a guided tour from the crew."

"Yeah. Really. You don't believe that, do you?" Her dark eyes glinted.

"I try to, Gerry. But it's hard. How's the physics?"

"Well, your message went. As you know. Whether it was received is another matter." Her face clouded. "Like a lot of other people, I am coming to terms with isolation." She wrinkled her face in an expression of dislike. "And separation."

"Sorry. And the research?"

Her face brightened. "The research is, well, promising. Yeah, *promising* will do."

"Good. Any progress to understanding how the intruders got here?"

"Perhaps. We have been working on the math of the Normal-Space to Below-Space boundary. It is very technical, but we have been trying to see how you could make a ship that could enter and leave Below-Space without using a Gate. We have some ideas. Let's say no more at the moment."

"Just be careful about exploring Below-Space. Please?"

"The *Argo* business, right? Perena told me." Her hair flew about as she shook her head. "No problem. We are a long way from creating any physical model. But anyway, this is a fine place and time to talk about risk, right? Look at that!" She gestured to a box marked *Explosives!* in big red letters being wheeled carefully past them.

"Point taken."

Gerry looked longingly at the *Emilia Kay*. "Oh, I wish I was going with you guys. Incidentally, did Lucian Clemant find you?"

"Yes. How do you know him?"

"Easy; our research has to go through him. He approves most things. But he keeps an eagle eye on what is going on. He's been very encouraging."

"I can imagine."

"Hey, look who's here." She pointed to Vero, picking his way between the few remaining boxes.

Vero came over and hugged Gerry.

"Good to see you, Prof. But it's a brief meeting. Merral, it's soon going to be time to get on board."

"Okay, guys, I must go. I find my hair responds badly to rocket exhaust. But do me a favor, Captain."

"What?"

"I hope, like you, it's a peaceful encounter, but I kinda doubt it." Her brown eyes seemed to become frosty. "But you take that ship. I want to see it. I want to know how they do it, and I want to ride that ship back out of here. Please."

"It seems a popular request," Merral murmured.

Gerry's fingers clenched tight. "And if these animals get in the way, don't be too squeamish. You give it to them from me. Okay?"

As she walked away, Vero and Merral looked at each other.

Vero shrugged. "That is one mean lady."

"Mean?"

"Just an expression. But I wouldn't like to be the cockroach-beast that walked into *her* lab."

◆—◆—◆

In the event, there was a further delay, and Merral walked back to the LP4 and resumed his studies. Finally, around five o'clock, the robot painter finished. The *Emilia Kay* now looked very different, but Merral decided he felt ambivalent about the effect. It was splendid to see Perena's "old lady" now dressed up in new paint, and the color scheme of blues and greens gave her a real sense of purpose, but seeing a ship in camouflage was too evocative for him of the ancient wars. He found a slight assurance in the fresh gleam of the Lamb and Stars emblem on the nose and tail.

The fueling was completed, and Perena and an engineer walked around making last-minute external checks.

Merral looked up at the sky, sensing a slight breeze. Sure enough, high above them, fine wispy clouds were sweeping in from the southeast. They would be on their way before any rain came in.

Vero, whom Merral had seen busy consulting with people and checking lists, strode over with a sense of purpose. He scrambled on board the LP4 and sat next to Merral. "Everything all right?" he asked.

"Pretty much. I feel nervous," Merral confided.

"Yes. Me too. Anyway, I have some good news. Possibly."

"Go on. I need it."

"You know how we have been worried about the poor data on the intruder ship?"

"Of course." One of many vague and dreadful scenarios Merral had considered had been that they would land at Fallambet Lake Five and find a perfectly elliptical—and perfectly natural—lump of iron ore.

"Well, I think we may have images in two days."

"Really! How?"

"Well, I was much struck by the dreadful business with that surveillance buzzard, the thing that was a machine but with the dead bits." There was a look of disgust on his face. "And I felt that something like that was what we needed. Only not exactly like that, if you follow. So I wondered if we could train a living bird to fly over and image the ship; like you can steer a horse."

"With a micronic camera and transmitter system? Interesting idea. Possible, but not in the time."

"Exactly what the two people I put to work on the idea said. But not impossible with a horse. So a day ago they landed a horse equipped for signals on the southern edge of the Lannar Crater and are now nudging it slowly northward. I've just heard from them on the secure link; it seems to be working, and the horse should be going along the other side of the lake the day after tomorrow."

"*Whose* horse?" Merral asked urgently, suddenly concerned that Vero might have enlisted Graceful.

"A small, wiry, and shaggy gray mare called Felicity. From

Isterrane stables, but originally from high along the rift flanks. Sure-footed and looks wild, so she shouldn't be suspicious. The transmission is a low-energy directional burst signal southward. That should be undetectable."

"And you are looking after her?"

Vero gave him a cautious smile. "Merral, try not to be too suspicious. The guys are taking it very slowly and have a metabolic monitor on her to check stress levels. She's doing fine."

"Good. I wish you'd told me, though."

"I started it off when you were in Ynysmant, and anyway, I wasn't sure it was going to work. It may not."

"I don't mind it failing. It's a good idea, typical of you. But I'm worried it will alert the intruders. It may be risky to Felicity and maybe to us. But look, just keep me in touch on it."

"Yes, I will do."

Another vehicle drew away from the ship. "Oh, Vero," Merral said, "I've been thinking. About what to do when we get to Tanaris. My feeling is that the best thing I can do is to start off with a meeting of all the leaders you have set up. The lieutenants, the chief of logistics, communications, etc. Perena, of course, as ship's captain, Anya as chief of intruder studies. Get them to introduce themselves and give me status reports. You agree?"

"Yes, that would be a good idea."

"Good. But, by the way, what are you?"

Vero chewed his lip and turned his brown eyes toward the ship. "A title for me? I have thought about it. . . . There's an old term, but it describes what I want to do. Intelligence."

"So you will be chief of intelligence?"

"Yes, why not? Chief of intelligence—" he made a slight bow—"at your service."

"Very well, but I will expect you to define exactly what you do."

"Terms of reference, *et cetera*. Yes, you will have it."

"And so, Chief, at this meeting, what else do you propose I do?"

"Oh, announce a provisional timetable for the next few days. Show them you are decisive."

Merral sighed. "But I gather the trick is to be sure that your decisions are right."

"True. That as well. But to be indecisive is to be wrong before you start. You must be decisive and decisively right."

"Help! And I suppose also at some point I must address the men? As soon as possible?"

"That would be wise. They are expecting their leader."

While he was considering an answer, Merral caught a glimpse of Perena waving at them from the side of the *Emilia Kay*.

"Well, time to fly, Vero. Tanaris beckons."

Vero left to get his bags while Merral started walking to the bulk of the *Emilia Kay* with his holdall. As he paused on the runway, waiting for Vero to catch up, he felt suddenly daunted by all that lay before him. He was strangely reminded of the Lymatov painting that, until recently, had been in Barrand's office; he could imagine a similar painting of him, now in that same genre of historical realism. He would be a small, vulnerable figure with a large bag walking across the empty black runway to the looming, freshly painted bulk of the ship. And the *Emilia Kay* would be so depicted that the name and the emblem of the Lamb and Stars would be clearly visible, as would be the late-afternoon sky in which clouds were ominously gathering. What would the title be? *Captain D'Avanos leaves Isterrane? On the way to Tanaris?* or even *The War Begins?*

Then Vero caught up with him, and Merral curtailed his imagination. The present reality was more critical than any fantasy of the future.

Besides, he reminded himself, if he failed, there might be no one to paint pictures.

CHAPTER 16

Inside the *Emilia Kay*, gently throbbing and humming with new life, Merral and Vero found seats in the passenger compartment behind the cockpit. There were eleven other people there; most appeared to be technicians and engineers. Merral realized that all of them seemed to know who he was. *This will be the way now; the title "Captain" hangs round my neck like Lucas Ringell's identity disc.*

As if sensing his unease, Anya smiled warmly at him. "Preflight nerves, eh?"

"The flying, Anya, is probably the easy bit."

Then the engines coughed and rumbled to life, the airframe began to vibrate softly, and they rolled forward onto the main runaway.

There was a long pause and then, without warning, came a sudden ear-jarring blast of thrusters and the ship began accelerating forward until, after what seemed an uncomfortably long time, it juddered free of the ground.

Ten minutes later Merral slipped forward into the cockpit and stood quietly at the back. The view ahead out of the expansive windscreen caught his attention immediately; whatever vices the Series D might have had, poor pilot visibility was not one of them. Through the broad, bronze-tinted screen Merral could see a mosaic of small, white, fluffy clouds hanging over the brilliant blue-green sea, the golden rays of the late-afternoon sun illuminating the clouds and casting vast black shadows on the ruffled waters below. The effect was one of great beauty and charm, and Merral felt uplifted and somehow soothed. *It is a view I could watch for ages.* Then he reminded himself that today—and for the foreseeable future—preoccupying himself with the admiration of creation was something for which he and others might pay a high price. It was yet another disturbing thought.

He dragged his eyes down to look around the spacious cockpit. Only once or twice had he been in a similar position in any atmosphere craft when it was flying, and he didn't know what to expect. But he saw nothing in either the many screens and lights or the language or attitudes of Perena, the copilot, and the flight engineer to raise any alarm. All seemed ordered and calm.

Perena glanced back and motioned him to her side.

"Everything okay back there?" she asked, keeping her eyes on a multicolored display of daunting complexity.

"Fine. Noisy though."

"Yes. Ideally we would have replaced the acoustic insulation, but there were other priorities."

"And everything is all right here, Captain?"

"So far fine, Captain," she answered, an amused irony in her tone. "Barely two hours' flying time. But she's doing okay. Some fine tuning needs to be done."

He watched her eyes flick carefully across the screen. "But no, *Emilia Kay* is one nice old lady. I have a good feeling for her."

Perena gestured forward with her head. "We are flying due south for another few minutes. Mainly to mislead anyone watching by giving the impression that we are going to one of the Farakethan Islands."

"Deception again . . . ," Merral remarked, as much to himself as to her.

"Yes, sorry. I think we shall all be forced to retake Basic Ethics when this is over." As she said it, she gazed up at him with a troubled expression. *I too am worried,* it seemed to say.

She looked back at a screen. "But, more immediately, I'm concerned by the weather. There's the tail of a storm belt coming in, and we will probably intercept it in forty minutes."

"How bad?"

"I don't know." She shrugged. "That's the fun. Vero's ensuring that all the observation satellites, including the weather monitors, were down today was clever, but it has left us blind too."

"You can't fly above it?"

"No. We are staying pretty low to keep well over the horizon from anything watching in northern Menaya."

There was a gesture from the copilot.

"The turn coming up. Watch out ahead." Perena's voice was flat.

The ship banked left gently, and as it turned, the vista ahead changed. The isolated clouds seemed to suddenly cluster, thicken, and darken, and as they did, they lost their innocence and became threatening. As if to add emphasis, the ship was buffeted slightly, and Merral reached out to hold a strut.

When he looked forward again, there was just a wall of black dense cloud ahead stretching from the sea below to a level high above them. Staring at it, Merral could make out swirling and boiling billows within the cloud barrier. A flicker of lightning illuminated the interior of a cloud column.

Although he could hear the quiet but urgent discussion occurring among the three crew members, Merral felt unable to take his eyes off the scene before him. The view seemed somehow symbolic of all that had happened over the last few months—how his life and that of Farholme had gone from an infinitely open and benevolent landscape to one over which a turbulent darkness loomed.

Perena, her voice cool and tense, interrupted his thoughts. "Merral, we are going to risk flying through between the cells of the front. Sensors say it's a thin but violent weather unit. As you can see. We have about ten minutes before it gets really rough. Better make sure everybody is strapped in back there."

With a final glance at the impending cloud mass, Merral slipped back into the passenger cabin as another judder struck the ship.

"Captain's warning," he announced as he took his seat. "Storm ahead. Fasten belts."

Merral caught a shudder of expectation from Vero and remembered that he was a bad traveler.

"You're serious?" he said, peering nervously at him.

"'Fraid so. She's says it's all your fault, switching off the weather sats."

"Ah. It seemed a good idea at the time. I have antinauseants. Oh no, they're in my bag."

"Where's that?"

"In the hold. Oh, the moment you get a new Gate here I'm back to Earth. The weather on the Made Worlds isn't for me. Not—"

"Alert! Imminent turbulence!" proclaimed a mechanical voice from above their heads.

The ship suddenly dropped as if the air had been removed from underneath it.

For a second it seemed to Merral as if his stomach had been punched skyward, then he was crushed down in his seat.

All around a great rattling and slithering erupted as unsecured objects flew around the cabin and crashed against the floor and walls. Someone's diary flew past Merral and struck the side with a crash. There were exclamations and groans around him. The *Emilia Kay* banked and then nosed slightly upward. There was more juddering and creaking.

Above the noise, coming vaguely from somewhere below and behind the cabin, Merral was aware of a strangely ominous rumble. Perena's voice, now insistent and tense, sounded through the speaker. "Captain, Anya, can you come forward, please?"

Merral released his belt and made his way forward carefully as the ship jolted again. The worrying rumbling below them continued. As Anya joined him, he caught a glimpse of Vero reaching for a sick bag.

The strained and tense atmosphere in the cockpit and the flashing red light on Perena's screen confirmed Merral's unease. She didn't look up but gestured to an ancillary monitor.

The image on it was a wide-angle view of the hull interior and, as Merral watched, he saw a large yellow drum roll along the floor and strike a crate. He now knew the source of the rumbling.

"We have something loose among the cargo," Perena announced

in a coolly precise tone. "It shouldn't have happened, but it has. Anya, is it one of yours?"

There was a cluck of distress from her sister. "Yes. It's the fifty-liter drum of disinfecting agent. Thyrol 56."

"Full strength?" Merral asked, remembering the care enforced when they used it in the lab for sterilizing equipment. There was a new, violent juddering, and he clutched the seat back. Out of the window, he could only see a swirling blackness ahead now. Raindrops were splattering on the windscreen.

"Yes," answered Anya. "The concentrate. We assumed a potential major biohazard risk. But it should have been secured properly."

"Results if it breaks open, Sister?" The anxiety underlying Perena's level and controlled tone was all too obvious.

"Not good. It's horribly oxidizing; it will dissolve strapping and maybe insulation."

Perena didn't look up. "And if it meets explosives?"

There was the briefest of pauses. "Guess . . ."

A new jolting began. Ahead, a flash of lightning sliced through the darkness.

Perena flicked an urgent finger at the engineer next to her. "Pierre, start rehearsing the routine for ejecting the cargo module."

Merral caught the engineer's eyes widen. "Ejecting? Yes, Captain."

Perena glanced at the hold image, where the yellow barrel was still careering around.

"Merral, if I feel it's leaking I have no option but to shed the whole cargo module. It won't do the aerodynamics or the mission any good, but we may land in one piece. Better get a couple of men to try to secure it. Fast."

She flicked a switch. "The hold microphone is on for anybody to communicate with me. I'll give you warning once we start the ejection sequence. Sister, get back to your seat; there's more turbulence to come."

The ship bounced around again as Merral made his way back to the passenger compartment. Ten faces with various degrees of anxiety on them looked up at him; an eleventh was too busy burying itself in a large brown bag. For a brief moment, Merral paused, realizing that, as captain, he could just order them to do it while he stayed up with the others. Somehow, though, he felt that wouldn't be right.

"Lorrin! You!" he yelled at the two men at the end of the row of seats. "Follow me!"

As the men unbuckled themselves, Merral made his way down to the hold. As he went down the spiral staircase, further jolts bounced him off his feet, throwing him against the walls.

The rumbling noise was louder at the bottom of the stairs. As he triggered the hatch switch, he saw for the first time the multiple seals around the door to the cargo module. It came back to him that on the model he had made in his childhood, part of the fun had been sliding the specialist load components in and out.

As the hatch door slid open, a pungent chemical aroma struck Merral. *We have some leakage already.* He paused, peering across the darkened cavern of the hold as he tried to evaluate the scene. The ship was buffeted again. Ahead the yellow drum rolled angrily backward and forward.

Perena's voice spoke from above him. "Okay, Merral, I have you on camera. Is it leaking?"

"Well . . . there's a smell."

"Okay. It's leaking. We'd better start preparations for ejection."

There was a jolt. Everything in the hold seemed to lurch and creak. The drum struck a crate with a loud crack.

"Perena, wait. I think it's a minor leak so far."

"Negative, Merral. Pierre has pointed out that we can only safely eject on the straight and level. We have to do it before we hit the main belt of turbulence."

Merral looked at the hold. "Give me five minutes. Please."

"Three." There was a note in her voice that forbade further negotiation. Through a porthole a flash of lightning flickered.

"Okay. Perena, can you put her into a smooth climb? Say, five degrees. I want the barrel to slowly, *slowly* roll to the rear."

"Okay."

Merral turned to the men behind him. "We have to get that barrel upright and secure it. And quickly. Try not to get any fluid on your hands."

The ship began to tilt gently nose upward. After a moment's hesitation, the barrel began to roll backward. Then it accelerated and for a horrible moment, Merral thought it was going to smash against the far wall, but the tilt eased off and it thudded to a stop.

"Now!" Merral shouted. He ran across the hold, winding his way past the boxes and the edge of the hoverer. The hold seemed full of bouncing and clattering objects. Under the lights, he could see glistening smears of fluid on the barrel. On the floor, though, there were only a few small drops. So far, at least, any leakage had been minor.

Handling the barrel, he realized, was going to be difficult, and he wished he had gloves. Trying to ignore the now persistent shuddering, he steadied himself against a sled, looking around for something to handle the barrel with. There was another flash outside, and he glimpsed the window smeared with rain.

To his right Merral saw a pile of familiar gray fabric cylinders in a box labeled "Tents." He jerked one of them out and threw it to Lorrin, who caught it.

"Open it!" he shouted. The shaking was almost regular now, as if the ship were bouncing over a corrugated surface.

Lorrin tore it open and folds of green fabric spilled out. "Use it to push the drum upright!" Merral yelled, trying to make himself heard over the noises of the lurching ship.

As the two moved to the bouncing drum, Merral moved back, searching for something to lash it against the wall. Spotting the end of some line protruding from a holdall, he pulled out a coil of rope. He ran back with it to where the men had managed to get the barrel upright, smelling the chemical again and noticing that the floor around them was slippery. The hold was humid, and Merral was aware that he was sweating profusely.

Perena's voice echoed about them. "Merral! We have to initiate separation shortly. Is it secured yet?"

Merral looked at the barrel, aware that the rope was still in his hands.

"Almost. Can't you wait?"

"No. I need a decision. Can you guarantee it's safe?"

Lightning flashed, so close that even through the portholes it illuminated the hold. An instant later, a peal of thunder rang through the hull and the lights above them flickered briefly.

Merral glanced at the men by him, aware of their pale, sweat-beaded faces watching him. *Lord,* he prayed, *give me wisdom.* He was aware that his options were few. If he told Perena to stop the ejection sequence and he couldn't tie the Thyrol 56 safely in place, they might well blow up and perish. Yet if he let the cargo be ejected, they might never get another chance against the intruders. Merral wanted to shout, *I've been captain for less than twelve hours and already I have to make an appalling decision!*

"Perena, cancel the ejection procedure," he said. "Repeat, cancel the ejection procedure. On my orders. If we blow up, I'll take responsibility."

"Cancelled on your orders," came back the quiet voice. There was a further jolt. "So if we blow up, you'll apologize as we wait to enter heaven, eh?"

For once she sounds like her sister.

With the two men pushing the barrel against the wall through the fabric, Merral looped the rope round a strut. Trying to ride with the bucking of the ship, he thrust the other end round a hole in a girder on the other side. With each jolt, Merral half expected to be thrown free. Somehow he managed to wrap the cord outside the tent fabric and pull it as tight as he could.

The barrel stiffened upright and Lorrin, his face running with sweat, gave a cracked cheer.

"See if you can find the leak," Merral snapped as he tightened the knot, desperately hoping that the barrel was not irreparably cracked. He tied off the rope awkwardly and started another loop across the barrel.

"Sensors say severe turbulence coming up in less than a minute," Perena's insistent tone sounded from above them. "We can't turn back."

"The cap has been loosened, sir," Lorrin shouted as the second loop was tied.

The ship lurched again and Merral could hear the Thyrol sloshing about in the drum tank. As he caught a fresh waft of its acrid fumes, his eyes watered. Now he grabbed a corner of the tent, found the cap, and twisted tight. For a desperate moment the fabric, greasy with liquid, would not grip the cap. Then it caught and Merral felt the lid tighten under his grip.

"You guys—get back! I'll finish this off."

They looked at each other, hesitating.

"Let me do it, sir!" Lorrin shouted.

"No! Get back! That's an order!"

The ship seemed to fall again. Merral held on, and when he had stopped being jolted about, he screwed the cap further, until it would go no tighter.

Gasping, he stood back, bracing himself against a strut and another crate. Out of the corner of his eye, he could see the others now exiting the hold.

Without warning the ship dropped.

The force was such that, for a moment, Merral realized that every part of him was off the ground. Then he crashed down, his shoulder jarring painfully against a crate. Yet, although the barrel had bounced up and down, it had stayed lashed against the wall.

Ignoring the pain in his shoulder, Merral stepped back and braced himself against a crate as further jolts struck the ship. It would have to do.

He wiped his forehead with the back of his hand and carefully, mindful of his throbbing shoulder, he turned and made his way back to the hatch.

Back in the passenger compartment, aware that he smelt of disinfecting agent, Merral lurched back into his seat and strapped himself in. There was the sound of clapping, and he looked up to see everyone applauding him. Embarrassed, Merral shrugged and gestured to the beaming Lorrin and the other man.

"Very nice, Captain. And you two—many thanks," Perena commented.

"So we may survive, eh, Vero?" Merral said, turning to his friend.

But Vero, his head deep inside the bag, was preoccupied with being violently sick.

•◆•

An hour or so later, the appalling bouncing and shuddering began to wane and, shortly afterward, Merral felt the ship descending in a slow, low-angle flight path. Despite the limited illumination on the landing strip, Perena brought the *Emilia Kay* in smoothly to land on the wet surface. Or maybe, thought Merral, it just seemed smooth after what he had passed through.

"Welcome to Tanaris," announced Perena. "Sorry about the flight."

One by one, Merral and the other passengers filed down the stairs, picked up their bags, walked out of the ship, and stood on the gritty basalt runway. Under the thick purple-black clouds that hung overhead, a premature night was setting in. Here at least, though, the storm seemed to have already passed over, and there was only an occasional flurry of heavy raindrops. Far away, westward over the seething sea, the lightning and thunder still erupted spasmodically.

Merral, rejoicing to have his feet on the ground, said a silent but heartfelt prayer of thanks. He looked around in the humid gloom, aware that, by his side, Vero was feebly propping himself up against the fuselage. Beyond the strip, the lights of the runway showed a somber landscape of bare and jagged black rocks broken only by the occasional low tree. From the other end of the runway, a line of paired lights revealed a column of approaching vehicles.

Merral saw that Perena was next to him. "Is Vero all right?" she asked in a voice of quiet concern.

"Yes," Merral said, "but it's the last time he will switch the weather sats off when there is a risk of him flying. Nice landing, though."

"It wasn't hard, really. The Tanaris strip was made originally for emergency landings for in-system shuttles if Isterrane was closed with bad weather. I think it's the longest on the planet. I could have come down vertically, but you need to be absolutely certain of your equipment to do that." Then she lowered her voice and whispered to Merral. "Look—while the vehicles are arriving—come into the hold with me."

Inside the ship, the smell of the disinfecting agent was still powerful and Perena sniffed dubiously. "Nasty stuff. Anyway, full marks. We survived. So you made a bold and decisive decision."

"Thanks. And if we hadn't survived?"

"It wouldn't have been bold and decisive; it would have been rash, foolhardy, and badly judged. We won this one. But you got a lot of credit for your action, and you made the right decision."

"It wasn't easy." Merral was surprised at the emotion in his voice. "Would you really have ejected the module?"

Perena shrugged unhappily. "Under the old rules, yes. By letting you do this I broke with Standard Operating Procedures. But do those old rules apply in what is, effectively, a time of war?" She sighed. "You see, Merral, we are all having to learn new things and new attitudes."

Making no further comment, Perena walked over to the barrel and peered around it.

"What are you looking for?" Merral asked.

"I want to find out why it broke loose," she said, squatting and staring to one side of the drum. "Under normal conditions we'd have a full inquiry. There's no time here. But I'd still like to know. It's very odd—almost unprecedented—for a load to break free. But see, here's where it was attached." She leaned forward and lifted up a broken strand of silvery webbing. "Okay, so it snapped. But why, eh, Merral?" She looked at him, her face angular in the hold lighting.

Merral shrugged.

"Well," she said, "we have an imaging record of the loading, so we will find who was responsible. And I'll get this looked at in daylight." She peered closely at it and muttered, "You know I think this is old. It's got an orange safety thread in it."

Merral bent down and looked at it, noting that he, too, could make out a fine orange line along it. Safety threads occurred in most critical rope or straps, whether for climbing or for lashing down equipment. Green indicated pristine condition with full strength, but over time and use that shifted to yellow, orange, and then red to indicate a progressive weakening. It was a well-known ruling that, for critical tasks, you never used less than green. He turned to Perena. "Okay. Let me have a full report. We nearly lost the mission before we started."

"We could have lost us."

There were noises at the hold door. A tall, green-clad man with a long face dominated by a hooked nose climbed into the hold. "Captain D'Avanos? Captain Lewitz?"

"Indeed," said Merral, struck by the way the man's wide smile was accentuated by his thin dark moustache. There was an awkward salute and smile on the broad face.

"Lieutenant Ferenc Thuron, sir. Welcome to Tanaris."

"Thank you." *Thuron,* Merral thought, going through the list of names in his mind. "Ah yes. You're a team leader?"

"Yes, sir."

"Your team will come in from the west. Right, Ferenc?"

"Yes, sir, but I am afraid everyone calls me Frankie." The gentle brown eyes were apologetic. "The Ferenc was because my dad was into the Old Hungarian at the time I was born, but it's confusing to spell. So it's Frankie. But only if it's no trouble. You're the boss."

Merral found it hard not to smile back. "Trouble, Lieutenant, is a relative thing, and you going from Ferenc to Frankie does not really rate in the scheme of things. Not now. Does it, Captain Lewitz?"

She grinned. "Hardly. Not now."

Frankie looked around and sniffed. "If you don't mind me saying, sir, you haven't half had the ship cleaned out, have you?"

"A leak, Frankie."

"Yeah. I guess that explains it. I'm ready to take you to the base. Any immediate instructions, sir?"

"Only that I want to have a meeting with you, the experts, and the other team leaders later. We need to get started here fast."

"Sounds okay, sir."

As he exited the hold, Merral saw, by vehicles, other men wearing green. With a shock of recognition, Merral realized they were in uniform, and suddenly the significance of what he was about struck him. *We have made soldiers, and I must lead them.* It was all he could do to stop himself from trembling.

•◆•

Zak, smartly dressed in a green uniform, was waiting for Merral at the main tent.

"Sir," he said, with a smart salute, "good to see you here. Welcome to Camp Alpha."

"'Camp Alpha'? I thought this was Tanaris?"

Zak looked nonplussed. "We figured, sir, we ought to give it a name that wasn't on maps. So if anyone overheard they wouldn't know the address. That's what they did."

"I see," Merral said, trying to ignore feelings that he was utterly out of his depth. "Camp Alpha, it is. Everything okay, er . . . Lieutenant?"

"Good, sir. Do you want me to brief you now?"

"I need to change my clothes."

"Yes, sir, your uniform's in the tent there. There are a couple of tunics and trousers; we weren't sure of your size. You'll want to put them on straightaway."

"Thank you, Zak." Merral forced himself to smile. "Let's have the briefing later. I want to meet all the lieutenants, in half an hour, say, at seven-thirty."

"That's 1930 hours, sir?"

"Nineteen—? Yes, of course, Lieutenant, that's what I meant to say. Pass the word around."

"I'll give the order, sir."

Merral hesitated. "Yes, well, whatever. Go on and do it, Lieutenant."

"Yes, sir!" Zak said with a snap in his voice, saluted, turned, and left.

Merral walked into the tent, closed the flap, and stared at the uniforms on his bed. He sat on the folding chair and put his head in his hands.

"Oh, Lord, they've picked the wrong man," he said in quiet prayer.

•—•

Less than an hour later, the last few of the ten men and women Merral had summoned came into the office tent and took their seats around a long collapsible table. As the chattering and introductions slowly died away, Merral, feeling a little more sure of himself, gazed around again.

On his immediate left were five men in the same uniform that he now wore. All were in their mid- or late twenties, and Merral, whose twenty-seventh birthday was still six months away, felt slightly encouraged that he would not have to order men about who were much older than him. He reviewed again who they were and what their responsibilities would be if it came to fighting. Closest to him was Zak, sitting bolt upright in his chair as if he found it perfectly natural to be on a remote island wearing a military uniform and preparing to do battle. It wasn't just pretense either, Merral reminded himself. By all accounts, Zak had excelled in organizing the setting up of the camp and had been designated as the leader of the team that was to approach the ship from the north.

Next to him was the lean, tall figure of gentle, apologetic Frankie Thuron, who, it turned out, was a chemistry research student and a long-distance runner. Beyond Frankie sat Fred Huang, a large, long-limbed man who wore his thick and lengthy dark hair tied back and who seemed to have a permanently fixed grin and loud, cheery voice. Fred, Merral knew, was a marine biologist and an accomplished diver from one of the smaller islands of the Mazarma Chain. It was Fred, Merral reminded himself, who would go with the diplomatic team and attempt first contact.

Forcing himself not to think about whether Fred's mission could succeed, Merral moved his gaze to the tall figure of Barry Narandel slouched in a chair beyond him. Barry, down to lead the reserves, had his hair cut so close that it was almost stubble and thoughtful blue eyes that seemed to drift around in a lazy scrutiny. The fifth of the line of uniformed men was Lucas "Luke" Tenerelt, who had been designated chaplain, his green uniform marked with improvised bronze clerical flashings. Merral knew from his folder that Luke, whose almost gaunt face and piercing dark eyes were accentuated by the basic lighting in the tent, was in his late thirties and had, after an outstanding dual-track theology and engineering degree, become a leader in his home congregation in Maraplant.

As the silence deepened, Merral turned his gaze to those on his right. There was Perena, the still-gray-faced Vero, and next to him, looking unusually solemn, Anya. Beyond her was the head of communications, the short but strikingly blonde Maria Dalphey, and next to her, Lucia "Lucy" Dmitri. Lucy had been seconded from the Farholme Atmosphere Transport Board and made responsible for the logistics; she was a willowy brunette with green eyes, and Merral was struck by her look of quiet competence.

So, the solemn thought came to Merral, *this is my team.* Well, his first impressions suggested that Vero, Corradon, and Clemant had chosen well. Merral opened his folder to a blank piece of paper. "Gentlemen and ladies," he began, wondering even as he said it whether it was the right mode of address, "I just have a few things to say, and then in half an hour we shall adjourn for the evening meal."

He caught the grimace on Vero's pallid face. "For those who feel like eating, that is. But I thought it would be good if Luke, as our chaplain, would pray for us."

Luke nodded, got firmly to his feet, and as everybody bowed their heads, prayed clearly in a loud, confident, and booming voice. "Lord of the Assembly, we pray that You go with us in our planning and preparations. We pray too that we do not forget You in the urgency of the hour and that You protect us all through the blood of Jesus, the Lamb of God, from all the powers and principalities of evil that we face. In the name of the Father, the Son, and the Holy Spirit. *Amen.*"

Merral felt that if Luke had any doubts about the task ahead, he kept them well hidden.

As Luke sat down, Merral looked around. "By any reckoning," he said, "the last meeting like this happened in the Rebellion. So I suppose this is, very sadly, a historic occasion." He watched heads shake in agreement, then went on. "The schedule is this: After the meal, I want to address everybody briefly. Then we have three days of training ahead. Tomorrow I want an early morning meeting of us all for a progress report. At eight." He caught a glance from Zak. "That is, 0800 hours. I would like to see you individually during the rest of the day. Is that okay?"

There were glances and nods of agreement. "Fine then. I want us now to go around. Briefly say who you are, what you see your job as being, and what stage you think your work is at now. Then we shall go and eat after that."

There were more nods.

"So then, let's start with Zak here. . . ."

• ◆ •

When they all went to eat, Merral felt so preoccupied about his forthcoming speech that he found he had lost his appetite. After picking at the first course, he made an apology and went and stood outside the mess tent. His shoulder still ached.

In the darkness above him he could glimpse patches of fierce stars where the clouds had been ripped open. The air was still moist from the rain. Just beyond him, in a dip in the ground illuminated by a delicate spiderweb of silver lights, stretched the accommodation tents. Seventy tents, Merral reflected, perhaps two hundred people in total. Over half preparing to fight, the rest to support. All puzzled, all uncertain, and all looking to him for decisions and wisdom.

Merral watched the scene as he tried to rehearse his words, noting the tents with their eerie internal glow, the reflected glitter of the lights off the muddy pathways, and the shadowy figures padding to and fro. The sight in itself was not novel to him; he had camped a lot, but those campsites had never sounded like this. There were sounds aplenty here tonight, but there was no laughter and no noise of children, and all the voices he could make out were serious. Slowly, one by one, the men and women drifted toward a broad, level square that must once have been an extension of the runway.

A tall figure came over to him from the tent; it was Frankie. "Sir, sorry to disturb you. But it'll soon be time for you to say something. There's a few guys we've posted as what they call perimeter guards and a couple of guys in the Comms center, but otherwise everyone will be here soon and waiting to hear you. And we are recording it for posterity. If that's all right?"

Merral shook his head. "Why not, Frankie? Okay. Let's go."

They had made him a low platform out of stacked containers and turned lights onto it. Merral went and stood silently to one side, just out of the arc of illumination, watching the company as it gathered and half wondering whether he should have arranged for amplification. The dazzle of the lighting was such that he knew he would be unable to make out more than silhouettes facing him. Perhaps it was best he could not see their faces; he was nervous enough already. He had spoken regularly at conferences and meetings, but never at anything like this. Indeed, it occurred to him with a tingle of strange excitement, the last person to do anything exactly like this was the man whose identity disc hung cold and light against his chest. And he had been dead for a hundred and twenty centuries. Perhaps, Merral suddenly thought, he should have found the famous clip of Lucas Ringell briefing his men before the attack on the Centauri station.

Frankie nodded to him, teeth shining in the glare. "I'd say that they are about all here, sir. So whenever you are ready."

Merral clapped him on the back and walked up slowly onto the platform. There he paused briefly, tensing involuntarily, as an expectant silence fell on the crowd before him. He was uncomfortably aware that they were all staring at him. He paused. *So, help me, God.*

"Ladies and gentlemen; troops and technicians; colleagues and comrades; above all, brothers and sisters in the Lord." Merral paused, listening to his words die away in the silence, reassured that he was loud enough, that the words had come out at all. "I am unclear which of these titles I ought to address you with. So I address you with them all. I am Merral Stefan D'Avanos. Of Ynysmant, Menaya, Farholme."

Take your time. Don't fumble it out of nerves, keep making pauses. "Until yesterday I was Forester D'Avanos. My present title, given to me by our representatives, is that of captain of the Farholme Defense Unit. It is my hope to return shortly to my former title."

Merral paused again, weighing his next words, relieved that nerves had not caused him to dry up. The stress was lifting; he felt more at ease. "Indeed, it is my real hope and prayer that all of us will shortly be able to return to our old professions. I would wish nothing more than that this extraordinary episode we have become drawn into be ended. I look forward to it being a footnote on one of the many pages of the history of the Assembly. However, our wishes are one thing and our duty is another."

He stopped, let the words register, and continued. "I want to say to you that I have not taken up this task lightly. Indeed, I refused the commission for two days while I returned to my hometown to think it over. But what I found there convinced me that, however great the many risks of this operation are, the risks of *not* confronting the intruders are greater. They must be faced. If they are not, then all that we are may perish."

The electric silence continued. "We do not know entirely what we face; all we know is that the intruders are from beyond the Assembly and are hostile to us. As some of you have apparently heard, Sentinel Enand and I have encountered them and were forced, reluctantly, to fight them for our lives. I plan to have a full briefing with the leaders on everything we know about them tomorrow. Now I will only say that they are strange and frightening and hostile, but also vulnerable. By the grace of God, our first contact resulted in substantial losses to them. I should warn you, though, that this may simply have been because they were caught unawares. They demonstrated the posses-sion of weapons that we do not have. I have since learned that they have tried, and to some extent succeeded, in entering our data files in the Library at Isterrane. It is also almost certain that it was they who caused the destruction of the Gate."

He heard someone say, "Told you so," and a ripple of angry whis-pering ran through the crowd. Merral paused, letting everyone quiet down. An almost tangible silence returned. "Above all, I should warn you that there is a good deal of evidence that they are evil . . . and that they can transmit evil." Merral felt hundreds of eyes staring at him. "If I may speak of something which is almost beyond my understanding, I want to warn you all that we may be moving into a spiritual atmo-sphere that is like nothing any of us has ever known. Or that anyone in the entire history of the Assembly has known since the Rebellion was ended."

There were mutterings of agreement here and there, and Merral wondered if others had felt it. "All I can say," he said, "is that of late I have been reading those parts of the Old and New Covenant writings that deal with the struggles against evil with a greater interest and a greater sense of reality and relevance than ever before. In the past when I read them, I, like you, always saw them largely as a sobering history. They recorded a time that we could rejoice was behind us. I have now come to realize that they may not represent just our past, but

259

also our future. To every one of you I say this: watch; be mindful of your thoughts and words."

He stopped for a moment. There was total silence. In the western distance, where a faint purple glow marked the remains of sunset, a fork of lightning flashed. He had planned to end here, but for some reason, he found himself continuing.

"In this present conflict, we have all been given a part to play. Some of us may find we dislike the part we have been given. Yet that is irrelevant. I, and you, must play the part we have been given as best we can."

Merral caught his breath, aware of the tension all around him, and continued. "According to the present plan, we have just under eighty hours before contact. We need to make the most of every minute between now and then. I'll take no questions now. I'm going to hand over to the chaplain to lead us now in prayer and a hymn." He hesitated, suddenly overawed almost beyond bearing by the situation. "God be with you. With us. With the Assembly," he said, his voice suddenly thickening with emotion.

As his words died away, Merral had no idea what reaction he would get: neither clapping nor prayers would have surprised him. Then a voice sang out, shaky at first but growing in strength:

"Lord of all worlds, whose mighty power,

"Sustains your people hour by hour . . ."

One by one, others joined the voice until everybody was singing the great anthem, and the air seemed to vibrate with the words as if they were a challenge flung at the darkness.

Along the horizon, silver lightning flickered again. In support or in defiance? wondered Merral.

CHAPTER 17

Over the next two days, Merral found that he had very little time to reflect on how things were going. It was not for want of trying. As a matter of the highest priority, he endeavored to make time to be alone and to evaluate progress. Yet, no matter how carefully he scheduled events, he found it impossible to make the space. Something else always seemed to seize any time slot he left vacant.

Although he delegated as much as he dared, he felt obliged to keep something of a personal eye on what was happening. Everything was so new that he felt it essential to participate to some extent in order to learn what the tasks involved. So he took part on the firing range with the modified XM2s, or "cutter guns" as the soldiers now called them. He strapped himself into the sleds with their newly added boosters and was buffeted with the teams over the waves of the nearby lagoon that they used to simulate Fallambet Lake Five. If he wasn't the fastest out and up the beach from the sled, he was up there with the leaders. He flew with the reserve team in the hold of the *Emilia Kay* and rappelled with them out of the open doors and down the swaying thirty-meter-long ropes to the ground while the hot engine thrust bellowed and roared just meters away from his kicking legs.

As a point of principle, he took part in the training drills with the explosive charges and the expanding wedges and, amid cheers, personally felled an isolated and ailing palm tree—standing in for a landing leg—with a circlet of planar explosives. He even took part on one of the cross-country runs carrying gear after a hint that some people were finding it tough. In the course of all these activities, which had left him bruised and tired, he had become better acquainted with the men. Now, after two days, he knew most of them by name, and they all knew him and seemed to respect him. And, as far as he could tell from his reading of that long-dead world where war had been a way of life, these were all good things for a military leader.

Yet Merral's time was not just eaten away in activities; it was also taken up by the need for discussions and decisions. There was also a lot of debate over strategy, and the plans for the assault were slowly refined. After consultation with Vero, it was decided that Merral would go with Frankie's team, which was approaching from the west. From the western side of the lake, he ought to have a good view of the intruder ship and—critically—be able to observe firsthand the response that the diplomatic team received.

The decisions Merral had to make seemed endless. Everything was so new that the team leaders were always coming to him to clarify some point of protocol, a safety ruling, or an issue of discipline. Strangely, the one leader who bothered him least was Vero. He was now almost permanently surrounded by three young men of his "intelligence group," and the four of them were often closeted together in an isolated tent where animated discussions could frequently be heard.

One of Vero's contributions was, however, a disappointment. On the afternoon of the second day, the sentinel had announced that the progress of Felicity had been slower than expected and that the horse was still ten kilometers away from the lake. Privately, Merral wondered whether they would be at the lake before she was.

Urgent and unpredictable incidents took up time. Despite a reduction of the battery power on the cutter guns to 5 percent strength, a persisting habit of firing before aiming had resulted in an unacceptable level of minor burns. More seriously, two men broke limbs because of overzealous assaults out of the *Emilia Kay*. Following consultation with Dr. Felix Azhadi, the grizzled veteran trauma-care surgeon who had been persuaded to be the medical officer, they reviewed procedures and sent a message to Isterrane, asking for a dozen extra men to be sent. In one of the personnel shifts that resulted, Lorrin Venn found himself shifted from the reserves to Frankie's team. When Merral saw him hours later, he was whistling through a broad grin.

•◆•

In the end, after two days of hectic busyness, Merral decided that he had to make time to think. Noting that he was exactly forty-eight hours away from the planned contact, he set his alarm for just before dawn and, after quarter of an hour in prayer and Bible reading, put on running gear. He briefed a bleary-eyed Frankie, yawning apologetically over his cup of coffee, and then, as the first rays of the sun struck the craggy rocks, set off jogging up to the rocky crest of the ridge that dominated Tanaris. He ran slowly, aware that, even by Farholme's low standards, the island's bare and rocky landscape was unforgiving.

Twenty minutes later, Merral gasped his way past a sentry onto the summit ridge.

Regaining his breath, he slowed to a labored walk and strolled out onto an overhanging rock slab that formed a viewing point. Here, with the emphasis granted by the low-angle sun, he could see the *Emilia Kay* at the southern end of the runway, the tents where lines of people were assembling for breakfast, and the lagoon where they practiced to the north. *So, tomorrow evening we fly, and this make-believe practice world of Tanaris gets replaced by the reality of Fallambet Lake Five. Are we prepared?*

It was, he realized, an unanswerable question. Prepared for what? How could anyone make any prediction when faced with something as totally unknown as this? Warfare, he knew, had always been a reckless and uncertain business. Yet even in the endless wars of the far past, men had always known that they faced other men or the machines of men. *Now, though, we do not even know what we face.*

Merral sighed. Realistically, he knew, all they could aim to do was the best possible. With regard to the men of the assault teams, he sensed everywhere a rising confidence coupled with a growing discipline and skill. But were any—or all of them together—enough to outweigh the total lack of experience?

As Merral thought about the probable conflict, he was aware of something that tugged at a corner of his mind, something outstanding that he had to do. While he was attempting to pursue the thought, he heard a call of "Sir!"

The sentry approached, clutching a low-power short-range communicator.

"Yes, Lennis. What is it?"

"A message, sir. The freighter *Henrietta Pollard* is coming in to land. In fact, I reckon you can see it." He pointed at a small black dot low above the western skyline.

In addition to bearing the remaining supplies, the flight carried the dozen replacement men as well as the pair who were to try diplomacy with the intruders. Was there to be no chance of escaping his responsibilities?

"Thanks, Lennis," he sighed. "I'd better go on down."

◆—◆—◆

Merral had barely had time to shower and change before two visitors were shown into his office and the fabric flap lowered behind them. They were a man and woman, both of late middle age, and the first thing that struck Merral was how elegant they looked. Perhaps, he thought as they shook hands, the smartness was especially marked because of the new world of sweating, uniformed men that he seemed to now dwell in.

"I'm Erika Nateen," the lady said with a polite, tired smile. Her accent was not quite that of Farholme.

"Van Denern. Louis Van Denern," the man added in a rather precise way as he looked around the tent with cool, evaluative gray eyes. He had a rather pale complexion, and Merral wondered if, like Vero, he was a bad flyer.

"Welcome," Merral answered, uncomfortably aware that, despite the shower, he was still sweating from his run. "Merral D'Avanos, recently forester, now—by an act of Providence—captain. And yet hoping to be forester again very shortly. Please take a seat. You had a good flight?"

As they sat on the chairs, they looked at each other as if for reassurance. "Yes," Erika answered. "An early start but otherwise fine. Representative Corradon—who sends you his greetings—was anxious not to obviously disrupt the scheduled flying schedule. The best way of doing that was to squeeze in the early morning flight for us on the—whatever it was called."

"*Henrietta Pollard*," Louis added in a tone that suggested he liked accuracy.

Merral realized he was overlooking hospitality. "Can I order you a drink? or breakfast?"

"Just a coffee, please," Erika said with a formal smile that reminded Merral of one of the teachers at his junior school.

"Water," Louis said firmly. "Just water. I presume it is sterile?"

"Oh yes."

Merral gave an order to one of the guards and then sat back down in his chair. "So," he said, looking at his guests, "you are our diplomatic team?"

The visitors looked at each other and Erika seemed to sigh slightly.

"Yes," she answered with what Merral felt was a lack of enthusiasm. He stared at both of the newcomers again, feeling slightly puzzled. Somehow, they were not what he had expected.

"Can I ask something?" Merral said. "Why did you volunteer for this? You do realize that this is likely to be risky?"

Again, he caught a shared, confiding look passing between them. It was almost as if they were married to each other, something that he knew wasn't the case. Erika gestured for Louis to speak.

"I am a language teacher," he replied in his rather stiff way. "Isterrane University. Grammar is my specialty. I have five historic languages, plus Communal and Farholmen, of course. And I am an old friend of Anwar Corradon."

"I see," answered Merral, wondering whether he would answer the second question. Louis put his head slightly on one side for a moment. "Now, as for the risk . . . I am sixty-five, a widower, and I am—I suppose—one of the few medical casualties of the loss of the Gate. Other than those on the *Schütz*."

"I was not aware there were any."

Louis nodded in a slight but precise way. "Oh yes. I have a degenerative liver disease coupled with an oversensitive immune system. A tailored prosthetic liver was on order. My hepatic specialist assures me that if we have a new Gate in fifty years, it will be around forty-eight too late. More or less."

That, thought Merral, *is as elegant a circumlocution as I have ever heard for saying "I have two years to live."*

"We are honored to have you with us," he said.

"Thank you, Captain," responded Louis with a little bow of the head.

"And, Erika, what about you?"

She gave him a pained look. "I'm not from Farholme; I'm from Bannermene."

"Our next-door neighbor. We say here that it's the next best thing."

"And we say the same about you. Well, I work on Assembly government protocols for our sector. I was caught here by the Gate's loss—*destruction*. Call it what you will."

"Ah, I see."

"Yes, all my family are—" she glanced skyward—"over there. I too know Anwar Corradon, of course. He asked if I would volunteer for something difficult. If these intruders do have the technology to go through Below-Space, then I would certainly like us to get it."

"So you can go home?"

"Of course. But equally, if they are evil, which I gather we suspect, then I don't want them going on to the next system and wiping out their Gate. I don't want what happened here to happen there."

"A fair point."

Merral was thinking what to say next when the drinks arrived.

As Erika drank her coffee and Louis cautiously sipped his water, Merral outlined the plan for them to approach openly. He watched them carefully for their response.

Louis just shrugged in a polite way. "What you've said is about what we were told. How many people are there with us on this hoverer?"

"Fred Huang—your lieutenant—suggested four. The only arms I can offer are bush knives, which are now slightly modified and probably more effective."

"Do they work?" asked Erika.

"Oh yes," Merral replied, rather reluctantly. "They work. At close range." He tried not to think about his own experiences. "And we are also giving you smoke canisters. If there is trouble, Fred will tip them overboard. They float, and they may give you a screen to escape behind." The smoke canisters had been Vero's idea.

Erika bent over to whisper something in Louis's ear. Whatever it was, Merral decided it was well received, because he nodded agreement.

"Captain," Louis said, leaning forward, "Erika is suggesting that we reduce the crew going with us. To the minimum. Two, I would think. A pilot and this Lieutenant Huang. As you gather, we are not particularly concerned about our own lives. But I am—no, *we* are—about those of others."

Merral evaluated the request for a moment before answering. "Very well, I accept that suggestion. I will talk to Lieutenant Huang about that. So you are not very optimistic about a negotiated settlement?"

"No," Louis said firmly, and he put down his glass with a look of slight distaste. "I've talked with Anwar, and I can make my own deductions. If they wanted to talk they would have done so earlier."

He peered into the empty glass and then looked up with sad eyes. "If I were you, Captain, I would prepare for the worst."

•—◆—•

After Erika and Louis had gone to the tents assigned to them, Merral sat down to check the manifest from the *Henrietta Pollard* and was encouraged to see that it had brought the dozen men needed and the outstanding equipment. As he put the manifest down on the table, he heard the sound of the freighter taking off on its way back to Isterrane. *The next time engines like that roar over this island, it will be us on our way north.*

A few minutes later, his guard admitted Perena, accompanied by a pale-faced young man in civilian clothes whom he did not recognize.

"Sorry to interrupt you, Captain," she said as she saluted, her face stiff.

"You are always welcome, Per—Captain Lewitz," Merral said, rising and saluting back. He was wondering at her formality when he noticed the worried look of her companion.

"Have we met before?" he asked, extending his hand.

There was a look of hesitation in the man's face as he shook hands. "No . . . sir. Not so as you'd remember. I was loading the *Emilia Kay* the other day when you came through. I'm Leonas Vorranet."

"Loading, eh, Leonas?" There was something about both his and Perena's manner that allowed Merral to guess at what was to come. "Take a seat, both of you."

The young man sat down and stared at the floor as Perena began to speak. "After our problems with the barrel I made inquiries. Leonas very kindly volunteered to come over from Isterrane in the *Henrietta Pollard* and tell us what happened. Exactly."

Leonas tilted his head up enough that Merral could see his eyes, deep blue and tinged by guilt.

"Sir, I've come to apologize," he said, his voice faint and strained. "It's my fault. Somehow, I used old strapping. Stuff that was already on the ship. Not the new stuff."

Perena looked hard at Merral. "That's what tests confirm," she said. "The strapping was decades old and decaying inside. We thought we had removed it all, but there must have been bits lying around."

"I see, Leonas," Merral said, already wondering whether he was supposed to discipline this man and, if so, how. "But wasn't it obvious that it was outdated? It's color coded."

There was a long pause and the blue eyes looked down at the floor. "Well, it was really, sir. But I was . . . careless, I suppose. I didn't think it mattered. There was the hurry. I suppose I thought that Assembly standards are always overcautious." There was a pitiable tone in his voice. "I'm sorry."

Merral walked round to the front of his desk and sat on it. *What do I do with this fellow?* He saw that Perena was frowning.

"And, Leonas," Merral asked, "I take it Captain Lewitz has told you how she nearly had to eject the cargo module because of your stupidity?"

"Sir," interrupted Perena, her diffident tone suggesting how unhappy she was about intruding, "if I may make a distinction; I have had a longer time to think about this. It was *not* stupidity. Leonas is not stupid. It was *negligence*. In some ways that is more worrying."

"I see. . . . Negligence, eh?" Merral wished he'd had a chance to look that term up in the dictionary and also in the section on military discipline in the handbook. "As in carelessness? Perena, I suggest we send this fellow off to Luke while we have a talk together."

"I think that would be very wise," she said. "Very wise indeed."

Merral turned to Leonas. "I accept your apologies; I will decide what to do with you later. In the meantime go and find the chaplain and tell him why you are here."

Leonas bowed his head in a way that Merral thought was possibly indicative of gratitude. "Thank you, sir," he said and rose to his feet.

As he went to the tent door, Perena called out, "Oh, Mr. Vorranet. One last thing. Would you just tell Captain D'Avanos where you are from?"

"I don't see as—," Leonas began, but Merral saw Perena's thin eyebrows rise in irritation and he seemed to change his manner. "Yes, sir. Larrenport . . . sir."

"Larrenport?" Merral said loudly as the significance sank in. It had to be coincidence. "I don't suppose you know the crew of the vessel *Miriama?*"

Leonas gave a weary grunt. "*That* again. Yes, one of the crew stays with us. Lawrence Trest. But I fail to see . . ."

Lawrence Trest, Merral remembered: one of the men who, with Daniel Sterknem, had met the cockroach-beast on the floating tree trunk.

"You fail to see, do you?" Merral replied, rather more sharply than he had intended. "There's a lot we fail to see too. But I suggest you go to the chaplain."

When Leonas had gone out of earshot, Merral stared at Perena. "So what do you make of it?"

Perena ran slender fingers through her cropped hair and shook her head sadly. "Merral, I'll be honest; as a pilot it scares me rigid. Of everything that has happened here, including those holes burned in my ship, this is the worst."

"I think I see why, but go on. Explain."

"Certainly. Negligence of the type perpetuated by Leonas is almost unknown. There have been odd instances in Assembly history of accidents caused by the coming together of minor acts of forgetfulness. You know, X forgets to put in the right computer code, Y is away, and Z forgets to check it, that sort of thing. But that is basically it. Nothing like this. Ever. And we are very vulnerable to negligence. If it breaks out on a large scale, we could be in a lot of trouble. We may have accepted the Technology Protocols, but an awful lot of our technology—diaries, ships, Gates and so on—are very complex machines. And we have very few defenses against negligence."

"Forgive my stupidity, Perena, but how *can* you defend against it?"

"Oh, ask Vero. The ancients did in the old days. Before the Intervention and the Assembly. They double-checked things for a start. They trusted nobody—least of all themselves. So in this case there would have been a loading supervisor in the module who checked Leonas's work, and there would have been a specific list to check it off against. There would have been rules and instructions and discipline for any breaches."

"I see." Merral felt his mind reeling. "So is this another manifestation of evil?"

"Yes. And one we had not expected. Evil is proving more complex and subtle than we had anticipated." She stared into the distance, rubbing her face with her hands. "You see, Merral, think of evil and you think of murder, rape, and war. Yet there are lesser manifestations, and they may be just as dangerous. Fear, grumbling, pride, and yes, negligence. All could be our undoing."

"A depressing but valuable thought. But the Larrenport link again? I wonder how many—"

"*Three.*" She gave him her severe introspective smile. "You have three men from Larrenport in the existing teams."

"You guessed my question. What do I do? Pull them all out?"

Perena gave him an odd look. "Aren't you forgetting something?"

"What?"

"There is another center of infection. If you pull out the Larrenport men, then you'd better be consistent and remove the Ynysmant men too. You'd lose a man from the reserve unit—"

"Jonas Trinder . . ." Merral snorted as the implication sank home. "And also the captain himself. I can hardly discriminate against them except by discriminating against myself."

Perena looked at him in knowing sadness. "Just so. You must be fair. But the implications are, Merral, that we all need to be on our guard. To check and double-check."

"So what do I do with Leonas, then?"

"Your decision. But seeing as he resulted in a tent being ruined, why not have him sleep out in the open?"

• ◆ •

Just after lunch, as Merral was reviewing the plans for the following evening's deployment of forces, one of the young men who worked with Vero came into the tent with an air of urgency and handed him a piece of paper. He unfolded it to see Vero's fine neat handwriting.

Felicity is approaching the ship!!! We are getting images! Can you assemble the team leaders? I will bring the printouts over. Get a screen fixed.

It took twenty minutes for Merral to find and assemble the leaders in the humid meeting tent and get a wallscreen hung up at the end. No sooner had everybody sat down than a sweating Vero pushed his way in through the flap, clutching a datapak and a roll of large prints. The sentinel's face bore such an intensity of consternation and unease on it that, for a moment, Merral thought he had failed. Vero nodded clumsily to everybody, pulled up a chair, and sat down.

"H-here it is," he said, with a hint of a stammer, and let the sheets unroll on the table. "Th-there's a copy each."

Perena leaned forward and, in her enthusiasm, almost snatched a sheet. The others followed. Merral pulled off a copy and stared at the image, barely conscious of the hum of excited chatter developing around the table.

They were large, grainy color prints. At the limit of resolution for a micronic camera, thought Merral, trying to assimilate what he was seeing. At the bottom of the image lay the blue lake waters, and in the upper part, above a rugged slope, were the hazy gray hues of the sky. In between the two, not quite horizontal, lay the shoreline on the other side of the lake, and on that rocky shore was the ship.

Merral's first impression was of a giant matte black slipper stretched out under some sort of extended awning.

"Brilliant!" cried someone in the room. "Just brilliant!"

"Marvelous, Vero! Well done!" called another.

Merral did not look up but stared at the image, trying to pull out as much information from it as he could. There was a sharp rear end and smoothly rounded front. The rear section was supported by two massive legs, apparently paired, while the front was held up off the ground by a high, single column. The only other features appeared to be long, lateral, finlike protrusions on the sides and top and, three-quarters of the way along, a ramp that sloped forward onto the ground. Below the ship, and dwarfed by it, were four small bipedal creatures and three taller creatures of a broadly anthropoid form. Neither was human, and the sight of them gave Merral a sick and fearful feeling in the pit of his stomach. He realized how much he had hoped not to see them again.

Merral looked up to see that Vero was leaning forward on the table, his head supported on his clasped hands, staring darkly into the distance. *Funny. I would have expected him to be excited about these images. But perhaps he feels the same as I do on seeing these creatures again.*

Merral saw that Perena was measuring off the size of the ship with her fingers.

"Perena, your initial thoughts?" he asked. "Please."

She looked up, her face thoughtful and wary. He saw the others look at her.

"Only very initial. Size—bigger than predicted. The shape is less ovoid—your computer smoothed it too much, Merral. From the tactical point of view, my guess would be for the teams to go for severing the nose leg and blocking closure of the gangway ramp. The rear legs look too solid."

Frankie and Zak nodded agreement.

"Seen anything like it before?" asked Maria Dalphey.

"No." Perena's voice was sharp. "I'm fairly certain no production Assembly craft has been designed like that. If we had the time, I'd compare it against any of the prototypes. But it's not like anything I recollect seeing. And it looks all wrong. It's *ugly*."

That's right, thought Merral. *No Assembly ship looks this unattractive.*

"But you reckon as there's any evidence of Below-Space technology?" It was Zak's voice.

Perena looked at the image again, pursed her lips, and shook her head. "No . . . not that I can see. Looks like a chemical or ion engine at the rear. I think I can see evidence of where a hatch for a ferry craft hold may be. On the top. The closest thing would be, oh, one of our inter-system liners. Say the current 20D series."

Anya caught Merral's attention with a gesture of her hand. "The creatures we can see. Cockroach-beasts and ape-creatures?"

"Yes. I'm afraid so."

There was a moment of silence as everybody looked at the images again.

"Funny thing there," Luke said. "The dark object. On the water . . . Or above it? Just to the right of the ship. Debris?"

Merral looked at the image again, seeing, not far from the ship, a black object that eluded immediate identification. *A bird,* he thought, before he remembered that birds shunned the ship. He stared at it, wondering how big it actually was.

"It's n-not debris," Vero said with such a tone of numbed assertion that everybody turned to look at him. Seeing his strained face, Merral wondered whether he was ill.

"So what is it?" Merral asked, somehow unable to restrain a shiver of unease.

"I-I don't know," Vero said in a distracted tone. "It's in other frames. . . . It is s-something new."

Suddenly a thought came to Merral. "Vero, the horse—Felicity? Is she all right?"

The brown eyes blinked. "No," Vero said eventually, and his expression told of some awful fate. Then he breathed in deeply and seemed to regain some measure of control.

"I'm sorry, Merral, ev-everyone. We'd better watch the whole clip. I should warn you that it is not . . . not easy watching."

People looked at each other, their faces openly expressing alarm and bewilderment.

Vero started speaking. "This morning Felicity reached the southern end of Fallambet Lake Five." His voice was now controlled, but under its flat tone Merral was aware of a real anxiety. Vero tapped his diary and the wallscreen flashed on with a tilted and grainy image of the lakeside.

"Part of the problem was that increasingly we had been having problems motivating her. She seemed reluctant to go north. Anyway, this morning she did. F-frame rate here was once every ten seconds, so we can fast forward."

A flickering and juddering succession of images filled the screen. The pointed end of the lake got progressively nearer and nearer as the mare moved slowly and hesitantly northward. She seemed to stop every so often. *Presumably*, Merral thought, *to eat*. Now the images looked across the lake waters toward the other side.

"It was about at this point that the metabolic indices of stress started to rise," Vero said, his voice drenched with unhappiness. "Heart rate, adrenaline or its equivalents."

The images jerked onward, and for the first time they caught a glimpse of the ship. Vero paused the display, freezing on a tilted image with the lake leaning strongly to the right.

"We haven't printed these yet, but I don't think they will show too much more than you have seen already."

He unfroze the screen, and as the new images flickered past, Merral decided that the horse was no longer stopping to eat.

As the imagery became increasingly like the printout they had studied, Vero spoke again. "The idea," he said, "was to get Felicity opposite the ship and then get her to veer away westward. Then she could make her own way back south. Or we could have picked her up in a couple of days' time. That was the idea. . . ." He tailed off into silence and more images flashed up. "By the time we got to this point she was under severe stress. The control team was very worried."

"Why?" asked the dry, worn voice of Dr. Azhadi. "Why was she scared?"

It was, Merral thought, a question a doctor would ask.

Vero looked at him. "We . . ." He paused, looking at the table. "Doctor, we have noticed that animals seem sensitive to the intruders.

We think she was afraid. But she was so disciplined that she kept going northward as she was trained to do on the appropriate sound stimulus."

With a look of guilt on his face, Vero turned to the screen. "Anyway, the new frame rate is now one every second."

The images still jumped, but the transitions were smoother. Finally they got to the one they had all examined, and Vero paused on it.

"By now the control team was very concerned about her. I gather they were on the point of switching off all commands. They had the images they w-wanted. But then—No, you watch. See the black mark? Let me go back a bit."

There was a flicker, and as Merral watched, he saw the black object move back to the landing ramp.

"Now forward."

The thing seemed to bound and jump through the air. Merral decided that, even allowing for the time lapse between the images, it still flew in a very strange manner. Aware of gasps around him, Merral tried to focus on the object, trying to interpret what he was seeing but struggling because it was so totally unfamiliar to him.

His first impressions were of some kind of black sheet that undulated through the air as if it were a rug or a blanket carried by the wind. But the lake was calm, and there was a purposefulness to the thing's motion that told of it moving under its own power.

After a few more frames, Merral decided that it was an animal, but like nothing he had ever seen. It seemed to change course, and as it turned, it tilted and he glimpsed that its profile was kite shaped. There was even—and suddenly he was sure of it—a long tail.

Merral was aware of Anya beside him, shaking her head in disbelief. "How's it doing that?"

There was no answer.

Vero let the frame jump forward and froze the image. "Now," he said in a strained voice, "we get a better view."

Merral noted new details. Unlike a bird or a bat—and it was

surely much larger than either—there was no separation between body and wings; there was just a single smooth unit, thicker at the middle and thinner at the edges. Equally, there was no distinct head.

"A flying wing," someone said, horror in his voice.

"It's like a ray; you know, the sea fish." It was Fred Huang's voice, and Merral was reminded he was a diver.

"A manta ray," said someone else.

"Yes, but this thing's flying, like a sheet," said another voice, full of incredulity and fear.

Vero pressed a button and more images flickered by. Merral could now see that the creature moved by slow but steady wing beats. There was something unnervingly determined in the way it moved.

It was getting closer, Merral realized, and he was able to see the black shadow of the creature on the water. Then it came to him with a spasm of horror that this thing was speeding toward the horse.

"Yow, it's big," said an apprehensive voice.

Suddenly the creature went off the screen, and the scene became an angled one of rocks and scrub with little patches of grass.

Vero paused the images. "Th-the controllers released her here. H-heart rate was far too high. She was panicking. Image quality goes here too. There was s-signal loss; she was moving too rapidly."

The images shifted again. There was another frame, also at a bizarre angle, of a stream valley and white flowing water. *She's running away,* Merral thought. *She has seen the creature and she's fleeing it. And I don't blame her.*

There were disconnected images of sky and distant ranges. Now there was a new image, and a gasp of horror came from someone. Was it from Anya?

Most of the image was sky, with just a patch of ground in a corner. But protruding into the right side of the image and tilted as if it was banking to swing parallel to the horse was the front half of the creature. On the underside of the black sheet, running lengthwise as if below some spine, was a long pale slit with strange appendages hanging down on either side. *A mouth,* Merral thought. The next frame showed it more clearly. It was a mouth and the appendages either side of the long jaws were now eight or so pairs of tiny clawlike limbs.

Merral, suddenly holding the table edge tight, was aware of a smell of fear in the sweaty and sticky air of the tent.

"Oh, Lord," someone said quietly in a horrified prayer.

Vero froze the screen. "At th-this point the decision was taken to jettison the equipment," he said in a voice that was unnaturally calm. For a fraction of a second, Merral tore his eyes off the image to look around the table. Every face bore an expression of utter horror.

The image changed. The shot was now clearly from a lower angle; the creature had gone, and all that could be seen was a pile of rocks.

"Any more?" asked a voice, heavy with distaste.

"Just one that is relevant . . . ," Vero answered. "A few minutes later."

The new image screen showed the rocks again but now there was the thing flying above them, tilted again, allowing a glimpse of the underside. But this time the pale slit of the mouth was a different color: the wet bright red of fresh blood.

Merral was aware of voices all around him, of cries of horror, of a chair leg being scraped as someone got to their feet and moved unsteadily to the tent door.

"Switch it off!" someone ordered angrily. Merral realized that it was his own voice, but who he was angry with, he could not say.

The image vanished.

Merral swallowed, his mind awhirl with fears and worries. He was aware that outside the tent, someone was sobbing.

"One question, Vero," he said.

The sentinel looked guiltily at him, as if bracing himself for a rebuke. "Yes?"

"Can you guarantee, *absolutely guarantee,* that the equipment—the micronic camera, the transmitter, the biosensors—have not been picked up by the intruders?"

There was silence for a moment. "N-No . . . ," Vero replied after a pause, the words seemingly dragged out of him. "The camera failed shortly afterward."

"In other words," Merral said, aware that everyone was looking at him, "there is the possibility that these . . . that they now know we have found them?"

Vero interlocked his hands and stared blankly at Merral. When he spoke his voice was barely audible. "I-I think . . . Well, there is no evidence for that. But I must say—I suppose—that it is conceivable. . . . A possibility."

Suddenly Merral realized there was a decision that needed to be made. He closed his eyes, partly trying to focus on the issues, partly praying. The answer came easily and he opened them. He looked around, seeing ashen faces, noting people dabbing their eyes.

They were all watching him. He was strangely conscious that his lips were dry and that there was sweat dripping down his back.

"*Everybody,*" he said, thinking as he said it that he sounded more confident than he felt, "we must now bear in mind the possibility that we have been discovered. We are at approximately forty hours before contact. Unless, in the next minute, anyone of you can give me an absolutely unassailable reason why we shouldn't, I want to change that to put us at sixteen hours before contact."

"Huh?" grunted someone in surprise.

"Yes, I want to bring the mission forward a full twenty-four hours."

There were gasps from around the table, but Merral continued. "I want us to fly in six hours' time. Tonight. And I want to make contact at dawn tomorrow."

There was silence.

"Very well, the decision is made." Merral glanced at his watch. "So everyone bring forward all times by twenty-four hours. We will shortly be at contact minus sixteen hours."

In the silence that followed, Merral spoke again, slowly. "And Luke, I want you to make sure that every man and woman among the contact teams has recorded a final message for his or her family. And that we have a copy on file."

The chaplain closed his eyes and nodded.

Merral got to his feet and leaned forward, his hands pressed down on the desk. Again, he scanned the faces.

"Maybe God will grant us a diplomatic miracle. . . . I think not." He saw pale, taut faces staring blankly back at him. "On the basis of what we have just seen, I think we will have combat tomorrow. And we must expect casualties."

CHAPTER 18

Five hours later Merral sat wearily back in his seat in the passenger cabin of the *Emilia Kay* as they prepared for takeoff. He wanted to relax, but he knew the effort was futile. Since the decision to move the mission forward a day, the afternoon had been a frenzied whirlwind of activity. He had barely had time to record two brief messages: one for his parents, the other—full of apologies—for Isabella.

Outside the window, the sun was sinking into the sea and casting an orange glow on Anya as she leaned back in her seat at the very end of the row. She smiled at Merral. "Tired?" she asked sympathetically.

"Yes, but I don't mind being tired. It's just not the right sort of tiredness."

Anya nodded and gazed at him with a soft and caring look. *What is going on between us? Does she care for me beyond an ordinary friendship? Or am I simply imagining this because that's what I would like to believe?* On and off through the chaotic afternoon, he had caught her watching him. Or had he been watching her, and had she just caught his glances? He wondered whether she had a special friendship with any other man. He would have known if there had been any commitment, everyone did, but was there, perhaps, something less formal? At the memorable meal at her apartment the night before Vero and he had left for their trip up the Lannar River, she had seemed to be very friendly with Theodore, the extroverted oceanographer. However he realized that he hadn't heard anything of him since. As he thought about it, his troubled relationship with Isabella prodded his mind, and he suddenly felt guilty.

Perena's voice from the loudspeaker overhead announced an imminent takeoff, and Merral put Anya out of his mind.

Here in the passenger cabin, we can at least belt ourselves in. Down in the cramped hold, the men could only brace themselves as best they could, but at least there was so little space that they were unlikely to be thrown about.

He surveyed the others around him. Vero, sitting on his own, was trying to stretch out, but his expression and movements proclaimed an inner agitation. Merral felt sure that it was not just the prospect of more flying. Ever since the images from the doomed Felicity had come in, Vero had been withdrawn and pensive. Merral felt that he must find time to talk with him before the flight was over, but now was not the time. Louis and Erika were also silent, both staring ahead. Among so many uniforms, they seemed strangely incongruous with their smart, pale fawn jackets with the Lamb and Stars emblem neatly affixed to the breast pockets and their matching trousers and polished shoes. Maria Dalphey, with a bag full of communications gear at her feet, was absorbed in studying sheets of paper. "Logistics Lucy," as Lucy Dmitri had become known, was slumped back in her seat with her eyes closed. Merral felt certain that not only was she not sleeping, but that she would not sleep.

Could anybody?

As the noise of the engines began to build up behind him, Merral reviewed the planned flight path of the *Emilia Kay*. The first part, keeping low over the sea, would be a wide arc southeastward to clear the rest of the Henelen Archipelago. Then, having swung wide around Cape Menerelm, they would fly out into the Mazurbine Ocean before flying northwestward at as low an altitude as possible, to make landfall on Menaya just east of the Lannar Crater margin. From there, the three teams would be progressively dropped off clockwise around the margins of the crater.

With a frame-rattling engine roar, the *Emilia Kay* lifted off heavily from the runway. Perena, anxious to stay low, leveled off quickly and then banked gently southeastward. *Fortunately,* Merral thought, *the forecast is for fine weather.* With a maximum flying altitude of under two thousand meters, there wasn't going to be much space for sudden drops in altitude.

As soon as the *Emilia Kay* had become horizontal, Merral left his seat in the passenger cabin and went down to the cargo module. As he slid open the door, the smell of sweat and anxiety greeted him. He paused in the shadow of the doorway, surveying the scene. Even after having left everyone—and everything—that wasn't essential behind at Tanaris, the hold was still almost completely filled. There were people everywhere: squeezed together on the floor, sitting in the seats inside the sleds and the hoverer, and standing, braced against the equipment or the walls. All were uniformed in the new green armored jackets with their embossed Lamb and Stars emblems, but only a few were wearing helmets. The hold was too warm for that. Beneath and behind the soldiers, Merral could make out the two camouflaged sleds on their handling trolleys, the hoverer painted an innocent white, and various stacks of equipment.

There was surprisingly little noise for well over a hundred people, but a lot of them were silent, seemingly engrossed in their own thoughts and prayers. The few that were talking were doing so quietly. Merral, trying to understand the unfamiliar atmosphere in the hold, sensed expectancy, uncertainty, and fear.

As he surveyed his men, the *Emilia Kay* made a small course adjustment, and the rays of the setting sun shone into the packed compartment, throwing a weird, ruddy light on the men and machines. *Like blood,* Merral thought unhappily.

The soldier nearest the door looked up, saw Merral, and with a tense smile on his face, tried to salute. *Philip Matakala,* Merral thought, remembering his name.

"Oh, forget it, Philip," Merral said more strongly than he had intended as he squatted down next to him, feeling a sudden revulsion for the whole business of orders and rank. *What do I really know of this man?* Philip was the sergeant and sled pilot with Frankie's team, so Merral had had more contact with him than with many of the other men. But even so, all he really knew was that Philip was an agriculture graduate, a sailor, and a single man from Caranat, one of the smaller coastal settlements. And the thought came to Merral with no pleasure that he was in some way accountable for this amiable but retiring man's safety.

"You're ready?" he asked him, trying to say something to cover his feelings.

"I suppose so, sir," Philip replied, then looked up inquiringly with thoughtful eyes. "Are you?" He paused. "Sorry, am I supposed to ask that?"

Merral, bracing himself against the doorway, thought hard. He realized that he faced Corradon's dilemma.

"Why not? Am I ready? A good question. I vaguely feel—from the depressing ancient stuff I've read—that I should be confident and so fill you with confidence."

"And you aren't?" Philip asked, his words tinged with sympathy.

Merral hesitated. "I don't feel confident. I simply don't know enough to know whether we are good enough. I think we—especially the teams—have worked wonders to get so far, but how good we really are is something hard to determine. Especially when we don't know what the opposition is like. I wish we had some old soldiers here."

"Old soldiers?"

Merral laughed. "I'm getting like Vero. It's an expression. Veterans. In the Dark Times, wars were so frequent that when an old one ended they seemed to start a new one. So there were generally soldiers in the ranks who had fought in the last one. It gave continuity."

"Yes. I remember. But it sounds like a crazy way to run a civilization."

"Well, it was. But we don't have any veterans. I'm the nearest we've got. So we just hope and pray and stay prepared for anything."

Philip winked reassuringly at him. "We'll do our best, sir."

"Yes. I have no doubt about it."

Merral patted him on the back and rose to his feet. The hold was too full for him to walk around in, and he knew he ought to get back to the passenger cabin. He looked around, catching thumbs-up gestures from the men and noticing Lorrin Venn grinning at him. He forced a smile back in response. *I suspect he's going to see his action. I only hope he likes it.*

He saw Chaplain Luke and Dr. Azhadi squeezing their way through the press of men as they did their rounds. They had more defined and easier tasks, and for a brief moment, he felt utterly overwhelmed by what he faced. He was aware of Lucas Ringell's identity disc around his neck, and he felt that somehow it mocked him. He found himself wondering why he had accepted this whole monstrous task. *It's too late to argue. I'm here, I have been called to be here, and I must do my very best.*

Full of thought, Merral returned to the cabin, which seemed surprisingly roomy after the hold. Anya, who seemed to have been watching for his return, gestured him over to a seat next to her.

"Merral," she said in a soft tone as she leaned over toward him, "I need to talk to you." Her eyes were wide and bright.

"Go ahead," he answered, realizing again that the urgency of the hour could not suppress his feelings of a growing attraction for her. In fact, he realized that, in some bizarre way, the impending action seemed to heighten his feelings for her.

Anya put her diary on her knees, bending closer to him so that her words would not carry beyond the two of them. "I suppose I really need to talk to you about that creature. Whatever we call it." She looked up at him with a strange concentration as if trying to read his mind.

"I have no name for it. A flying sheet? A two-dimensional dragon?" Merral said, tearing his mind away from other, more pleasant things.

"A two-dimensional dragon? A sheet-dragon? " She seemed to weigh the words. She tapped her diary and a still image of the creature came on the screen. She looked at it and seemed to shudder.

"Anya," Merral suggested, "you don't have to talk about it if you don't want to."

She gave him a stern smile. "I was shaken when I saw it. And I don't want to talk or think about it, but I have to. It's my job. I'm a biologist, and I am supposed to be your expert. So I've looked at the images and cleaned them up."

"So what is it?"

"I don't know. This 'sheet-dragon' is, I presume, a vertebrate; there's got to be a skeleton under that. But what sort of a skeleton . . . ? Ah," she sighed, "I think it's very lightly built. The feature on the underside is, of course, a mouth—there are teeth visible on the enhanced images—and it has these members around it, feeding palps, claws, limbs, mandibles; whatever you want to call them. Two small eyes inset on what my sister would call the leading edge. It's like no creature that we know of."

"Is it made of other things? Like the other creatures? A bit of bird, a bit of lizard?"

"I can't see it." She shook her head. "I just think it has a sort of elemental quality."

"By which you mean . . . what?"

She grimaced. "It seems quantitatively different to the cockroach-beasts and ape-creatures. They can be considered as bits and pieces of different organisms put together. This is something else."

"Could this sheet-dragon be a genuinely alien creature?"

"Maybe . . ." She stared at him, her eyes wide in the darkness of the cabin.

"Any advice if we meet it?"

"Fire first. No, I have a few thoughts. Size, first: We think the wingspan is just below two meters; say the width of your outstretched arms. And the way the mouth is structured, it's not going to be a great biter. The gape isn't that wide. But if it got a chance at exposed flesh . . ." She shivered.

Like the back of a horse or a human face.

Anya stared at the images again. "What else? Oh, and the tail could be nasty; it might be able to use it as a whip."

"Ah . . . In other words, keep your distance."

They exchanged glances, and Merral felt that there was more being transmitted between them than just thoughts about this strange and dreadful creature. Silently, she tapped the screen off.

"I see," he said after a while. "But you are worried, aren't you?"

Merral received a confiding glance. "Yes, yes I am. I have no idea what is in that ship. I hope we can immobilize it, seal it up, and deal with what's in it at our leisure." She glanced around the cabin, and Merral, following her gaze, saw that no one was looking at them. She reached out, touched his hand briefly and shyly, then withdrew it.

"And, my Tree Man," she said, with an affection that was no longer concealed, "I'm concerned that something may happen to you."

"I see," Merral answered, his mind already clouded with all sorts of strange thoughts. Suddenly, finding Anya's unmistakable expression of affection too overwhelming, he realized that he needed to focus on other things. He could not afford to be distracted, and anyway, the unresolved matter of Isabella still hung over him. With a flustered apology, he got up and went forward into the cockpit.

There the lighting had been turned down so low that it was hard to see anything at first other than silhouettes of the three people in the cockpit outlined against the multicolored lights of their screens. Merral was trying to regain his composure when he saw Perena's head turned toward him.

"Okay, Captain?" he inquired.

"Yes . . . ," she said, turning back to look ahead. "The ship's fine. Fully laden and we are flying too low for comfort, but we are in good shape."

"Where are we?"

She gestured to a glowing map nearby. "Still going north, well over the horizon from the most northern coastal settlements. In fifteen minutes, we cut due west toward the coast and come in just north of the Nannalt Delta. So we will have the first landing in about an hour."

There was a catch in her voice. He bent his head forward so that he could talk to her without the others hearing. "Are you all right?" he whispered.

"Yes," she murmured back. "I suppose so. . . . I'm just in a strange mood. Am I worried? Is that it?"

"Understandable. I mean—"

"No," she interrupted, apparently realizing something. "It's not worry. Or not entirely. It's a feeling—I suppose—of awe. That we are, somehow, on the edge of something immense. Something momentous? Is that the word?" She paused. "Sorry, I guess I'd better focus. This is not the time for reflection."

She fell silent, and Merral decided to take the small spare seat at the extreme back of the cockpit. He tried to run through everything in his mind to be sure that he hadn't overlooked anything. Had he done everything that he had to? There was so much to manage. The idea nagged him again that he had forgotten something, that there was something that he should have done but hadn't. But what was it?

His thoughts were interrupted a few minutes later when a low bell tone chimed, and then he heard Perena's voice on the speakers. "Captain Lewitz here. Just to say that we are nearly as far north as we get and very shortly I'm going to start flying due west to put us toward the northeastern edge of the crater. From now on, we will be at a very low altitude, and I want to reduce the possibility of us being seen by dimming the interior lights even further. I should warn you that as we go overland, the ship is going to bounce around. So be prepared. Fifty minutes to Landing Site One. All being well, my next message will be just before the landing maneuvers."

Behind him, Merral saw the corridor lights fade out, and a moment later the ship started to drop in height and began a leisurely turn. Out of the small window to his side, Merral peered into darkness. *I should go back to the passenger cabin.* But if he went there, he had to choose to sit next to Anya or not. Part of him badly wanted to sit next to her, but he was somehow uneasy about what might happen between them. *There seems to be the potential for things to happen between us that I ought to think hard about. There are matters too that I must sort out with Isabella first.*

There were footsteps beside him, and he looked up to see Vero, bracing himself unsteadily against the wall. Vero bent down so that he could speak to Merral and not be heard by anyone else.

"Merral," he whispered in a strained, hesitant voice, "I just want to say that I am sorry about the business with Felicity. I really am." His unsteady tone suggested an intense unhappiness. "I am very worried that I may have jeopardized things. At the time, it seemed a good idea. . . ."

"Oh, Vero, stop it!" Merral whispered back, clapping him on the shoulder. "Have I blamed you?"

"No, but I blame myself," he murmured.

"Well, better not to," Merral answered. "I need you with your mind alert here. We are entering unknown territory. All our actions have a risk."

"Yes, you are right," he said a few moments later, a renewed resolve apparent in his voice. "Sorry . . . But I was just shaken by what we saw earlier."

"Me too. But it may have done us a service. We have learned a lot more about the intruders. We know there is another type."

"Yes. And it is carnivorous. Each new thing unsettles me more," Vero responded. "I can only hope and pray that we have not got involved in something too big for us to manage."

"That's out of our control now. We must just do what we have to do."

"I guess so."

Perena turned her head toward them. "Coastline coming up," she called out in a low voice.

Vero tapped Merral on the shoulder. "Many thanks. I'm going to get strapped in. See you when we land."

Merral stared out of the window into the darkness, and a few minutes later, he was rewarded by seeing a faint line of starlit white breakers and then a pale ghostly strip of the seastrand. Then they were flying over ground, low enough for him to sense the rough fabric of the forests racing away underneath and to distinguish the raw, ash-colored rocks around. They were so low—perhaps barely five hundred meters above the ground—that although he knew Perena had slowed the speed down, they still seemed to be going appallingly fast.

As Merral peered down, seeing starlight glimmering on dark lakes, the ship began to sway laterally and vertically in a sickening motion. *It's the computer, nudging us over and around the oncoming landscape.* In the cabin ahead, he could make out the crew scanning their sensor screens, trying to detect anything unusual. This far north there would be no one to see them. At least, he thought ruefully, that was what he had once believed as a certainty. Now though, that—as so much else—was in doubt.

Time passed as the *Emilia Kay* swayed this way and that and the shadowy landscape slipped by underneath. Suddenly Perena was talking to him, her voice terse. "Captain D'Avanos, no anomalies ahead at Site One. Do we go for landing?"

"Yes," he said, "or rather, affirmative."

Seconds later Perena's voice came over the speakers. "Landing maneuvers starting in thirty seconds. Brace yourselves. On my command, Lieutenant Larraine's team begin to disembark."

The *Emilia Kay* started to reduce speed even more, and a new whispering whine indicated the vertical thrusters were firing. As Merral watched out of the window, they sank down into a river valley and then in a series of fierce turns began to veer from side to side as they followed the meanders. Outside in the darkness, he could now see silhouettes of crags above him. There was a hissing and a soft clanking noise as the landing gear was extruded, and the speed dropped to what he judged was little more than walking speed.

A moment later, the ship slowed to a dead stop, dropped slightly, and then, with a thud and a gentle bounce, settled slowly down to a horizontal angle.

"Stable," Perena pronounced over the speakers. "Location correct. Team, you are clear to leave. God be with you."

Even before she had finished speaking, Merral was already heading for the hold. By the time he arrived, the port side door was raised, a ramp had been lowered, and in the dim lighting, men were already working on unloading the sled.

Carefully, Merral clambered down the ramp and stood on the ground. Here there was a cool, fresh breeze on his cheek. The smell of pinewoods wafted past him, clearing away the stale and all-too-human air from the hold. The night air seemed to speak to him of the past, of the unsullied days before the intruders arrived, and for a moment, Merral felt he could almost weep. He was aware of Zak giving low, curt orders to his men as they manhandled the sled out on its trolley and then the whispers and grunts as the men pushed and rolled it down the ramp.

Merral looked at the stars above the ragged tips of the firs. *I would give a lot to see the hexagon of the Gate again. And a lot more still to be camping out here with no cares except that of filling in my trip report.* As if to deepen his mood, there came the call of an owl from within the woods.

A few minutes later there was the faintest of whines as, safely distant from the ship's electronics, the gravity-modifying engine came on and the sled floated up and free. As they loaded the trolley back into the hold, Merral saw someone come over and stand by him. In the starlight he recognized Zak.

"Sir," Zak said in clipped tones, and it came to Merral that no one had acquired the trappings of soldiering better than Zachary Larraine, "my team is clear and the sled is operational."

"Good work so far, Zak," Merral said. Then he realized that he didn't know what else to say to a man who, in all probability, he would next meet at the scene of a battle.

Merral hugged him.

"For the Assembly, sir," said Zak, returning the hug.

"For the Assembly, amen and amen," Merral answered, feeling surprisingly moved.

Zak stood back, and in the darkness, Merral made out a salute. Merral returned it and clambered back on board. "Perena," he announced, looking toward the wall microphone, "Zak's team is clear. Ready to go."

"Okay," came the response, and even as the hatch door slid down, the faint hull vibration trebled its force. Within seconds, the *Emilia Kay* was airborne and turning on her axis.

Merral climbed up out of the hold, which now looked much less crowded, and returned to the cabin. Exchanging smiles with Anya, he went over and squatted by Louis and Erika who were making desultory conversation.

"Twenty minutes or so going south and then we drop you off," Merral said. "You're ready?"

The diplomatic team had seen some of the images from Felicity, but only Fred Huang, the team leader, had seen the awful final frame. Louis looked at him. "Yes. I'm trying to maintain my faith that negotiation may work. But now, after those images, I expect otherwise." His voice was calm and resolute, and Merral found himself with a new respect for this man.

"I also," returned Merral after a pause.

Erika just nodded an obviously reluctant assent. Then, after a short silence, she turned to Merral and spoke in a confiding tone. "Captain, I just want to say that if our mission gets in trouble, I expect you to put gaining the intruder ship as a priority."

"Thank you," Merral answered slowly. "I know that, but I am grateful for you saying it. Fred and Nate will do their best. They are under orders to get out as soon as there are any hostilities."

Louis merely nodded with an air of resignation.

"Not long now then," was all he said.

•-•-•

Shortly after, Perena set down the ship on a bank of rough sand on the side of another river valley, and as they manhandled the cumbersome hoverer onto the ground, Merral clambered out again. Unlike the sleds, the hoverer had conventional hydrogen turbines and could have been switched on in the hold, but it was still too crowded and there was too much sand and dust about. As they heaved and slid it out down the ramp, Merral walked some paces clear from the ship and peered around in the darkness.

At first, all he could see was the dull sparkling silver water of the river as it tumbled down out of the crater on its way to the sea. Then, his eyes adjusting to the gloom, he began to make out towering cliff walls on either side, with dark gray forests draping their flanks. Behind him stood the great mass of the *Emilia Kay,* with little figures moving below it holding shielded flashlights as the pale hull of the hoverer emerged on the sandbank. They were a hundred and fifty kilometers away from the intruder ship here, but it had been estimated that it would take most of the rest of the night for the sluggish machine to make its way up the river and across the rough ground to the southern part of Fallambet Lake Five.

As a cool gust of air blew past him, Merral shivered slightly. Even with the start of summer only a few weeks away, here in this windy valley it was still barely warm. Merral looked up at the thousands of perfect twinkling diamonds of the stars and was strangely reminded of that fateful night before Nativity when he had first met Vero and had seen the stars on the journey south from Wilamall's Farm. As he thought about it, Merral was reminded that it had been that night that he had had the first strange conversation with Jorgio Serter.

Jorgio!

With a start, Merral realized what it was that he had forgotten to do. He had made a promise to contact Jorgio before there was any fighting. He was halfway to switching on his diary before he realized that it was disabled. He jogged back across the coarse, gritty sand to the *Emilia Kay,* where Vero was standing quietly in the hold doorway.

"Vero!" Merral said. "I've just remembered. I've got to call Jorgio. Can I use your diary?"

Vero, his dark face lit only by the dull gleam of the dimmed interior lights, appeared to hesitate. "Is it really needed?" he said. "I'm trying to keep communications to the minimum."

"He said that he would pray for us if it came to a fight."

"Ah." Vero nodded in the darkness. "I suppose you'd better tell him. After what I have seen today, I feel unsettled. I think we will need all the help we can get. But—please—say as little as you can. Be brief."

Fortunately, Jorgio turned out to be with his brother Daoud and had not yet gone to bed. "Jorgio! It's Merral."

"Why now, Mister Merral!" said the old man, staring at the diary from such an odd angle that Merral wondered whether he had ever used one. "And where might you be with so little light eh?"

"About the King's business. On a task we discussed."

"Oh, *war*. So it has come to that, has it?" The old man scratched his crooked nose leisurely. "About time really. Well, I suppose I'm glad of it. Hmm . . ." He seemed to drift off into his own thoughts.

"You asked me to tell you. I—*we*—need your prayers."

"I thank you. I knew it would happen, but I appreciate not being forgotten. And I will pray."

"Thank you," Merral replied.

Jorgio looked at him with his thick eyebrows raised. He smiled strangely. "Off to war! Just like Lucas Ringell in the old days. You remember him?"

Merral shivered, and as he did, the cold metal disc tingled against his chest. "Yes, Jorgio. I know of him. But that was a long time ago."

"Quite so. And things change. . . . Or do they?" There was now a strange, wild look on the old man's face. Out of the corner of his eye, Merral saw Vero watching him and gesturing urgently with his hand.

"I must go, my friend. But do you have any counsel?"

"Me?" There was a tilted grin. "Oh, hardly. Only I'll pray. But I think you'll have some help."

"From who?"

"Well, I'd say as the King will send whoever he sees fit. And who it is will depend on who *they* are. But I hardly think he'll let you be outmatched. Mind you, he sets his own terms."

"I see," Merral answered, trying to memorize the words so that he could puzzle over them later. "Well, thank you."

"Fight well, Mister Merral. And remember there are many enemies. Fight well."

Merral ended the transmission and handed the diary back to Vero.

"So was he helpful?" his friend asked.

"In a way, yes. He thought there would be help."

"I hope so," Vero said in a low, self-pitying voice. "The nearer we get, the worse I feel about it."

There were the sounds of the hoverer being pulled and pushed free of the landing gear.

"Ah, we're ready," Vero said, pointing to where, by the faint bleached shape of the hoverer, a man was gesturing. They walked carefully over in the darkness to where Merral could hear the flags on the hoverer making weak fluttering noises in the breeze.

Merral shook hands solemnly with Fred Huang, Nate the pilot, and Louis. There was a lot that he wanted to say to each of them but he felt he couldn't. Then he turned to Erika, and by the metal hull of the hoverer they faced each other in the near total darkness.

"I hope," he said, "that we shall meet by the lake tomorrow."

"Perhaps," she replied in a solemn way. "But I am less sure. I fear our diplomatic efforts are doomed. But they must be done. If we perish . . ." She faded away into uncertainty. Then when, moments later, she spoke again, Merral was heartened to hear that her tone had acquired a new, thoughtful confidence. "And so, if we do perish? What better way than in the pursuit of peace? After all, we would follow a good example."

In the darkness, Merral could vaguely see her reach out and trace something on the fluttering flag by her side. Then a gleam of starlight caught the fabric, and he was able to discern that, in the symbol of the Assembly, she was touching the Lamb.

·•·

A few minutes later the *Emilia Kay* lifted off and, keeping as low as possible, made its way southwest round the crater rim to the third and final site. Merral stood at the back of the cockpit for the approach to this last landing zone where Frankie's team would be unloaded and the ship and the reserve team would wait until dawn. As slowly as she could, Perena flew in a winding path up a rugged river valley broken by waterfalls, rapids, and vast boulders.

When the scan of the area revealed nothing untoward, Merral approved a landing. From the images he had seen in the planning stages, he knew it was a difficult landing zone, a deep hollow set amid high cliffs. He held his breath as Perena took the ship down vertically, nudging it gently sideways in a series of little taps until it came to rest.

After long seconds of scanning screens and readouts, Perena stroked switches and the ship's engines became suddenly silent. Amid a flurry of orders to the engineer, she got up from her seat and, stretching her arms wearily, came over to Merral. "We can still take off within five minutes if we need to," she said. "But I want to check our site. Let us survey it together."

Merral found his armored jacket under his seat and put it on. It was an action he had left to the last moment not just to give him more comfort—it was hard and inflexible—but because he felt that putting it on was symbolic: it was an admission that fighting now seemed inescapable. *And when will I get to take it off?*

Leaving Frankie and his men to get the sled out, Merral climbed out of the ship with Perena and peered around in the intense darkness. This was by far and away the darkest site so far, and it was only with difficulty that Merral could make out anything at all. Here they were so deep down into the dry gorge that the sky above them was just a torn, star-filled strip between sheer black walls of rock.

Perena switched on a powerful flashlight and pointed it around the cliff sides.

"It will do," she said, her voice seeming to echo around the gorge.

"There are bits of loose rock above, but the ground is stable and the night is dry. I think we are safe here. We'll await your signal. I'll have the engines ready to fire up from six. All being well, I will be with you within fifteen minutes."

"I hope that's fast enough," Merral said, feeling that down there the air was as still and heavy as if it hadn't moved since the Seeding.

"The old lady will do her best," Perena said. "But there are limits. I can't just pull up straight out of here. I need to check all systems are working acceptably. And I will have to approach you carefully."

"Well, take no more risks than needed. You know the rules we agreed to."

"Yes. And as soon as I know it has gone to a fight, I'll summon the medical support."

"Thanks."

Through the still darkness, Merral heard Anya call out his name lightly.

"Over here!" he answered.

"Well, I'd better go back to the ship," Perena said, reaching out for his hand and squeezing it.

In the darkness, Anya came over and stretched out an arm to touch him softly.

"A strange night," she murmured.

"One of the strangest in the history of the Assembly," Merral replied, feeling strangely tense and excited.

"Indeed so, but I was—I suppose—thinking more personally."

"I see," he said, trying to sound matter-of-fact but suddenly aware that all his feelings were in total confusion. Here in this dark, still cleft with the stars so high above, it seemed that he was in another world from the rest of Farholme.

Anya grasped his arm tightly. "Look, I'm worried about you, Merral. I've come to care about you." She paused, and he could hear her breathing. "Of course, now is the wrong time to say this. And you probably don't want me to say it."

I do. But he didn't say anything.

"But it's just now," she said, "facing what you face, I, well, just wanted you to know. . . ."

If only I could freeze this conversation until after everything is over. Then another voice within him said that she was right, and that when you were faced with the prospect of death, there were things that it was appropriate to discuss.

Merral was suddenly reminded of his meeting with Theodore, the man from Maritime Affairs. It had been that odd evening, the night before Vero and he had left for their trip up the Lannar River. The night before his world changed.

"I thought . . . ," he answered, "that, er, you and Theodore were . . ."

"Him?" In the darkness, he knew she was smiling. "No, he's not my sort really. Or so I've decided. *Now.*"

His heart seemed to bound, but with the surge of excitement came a cloud of unease about his relationship with Isabella back in distant Ynysmant. Anya—and suddenly Merral realized he was thinking of her as *his* Anya—was talking to him. "And you? I thought there was something with this Isabella?"

Merral felt a stab of awkwardness at hearing Isabella's name mentioned. She seemed so far away now, so remote from this present, very private moment. She and Ynysmant might have been on the other side of the galaxy from this dark, secret cleft. She was, he felt, so much a part of the past. And surely, he told himself, that past, like his title of Forester, was gone.

"Once . . . there might have been," he whispered. "But not now. There is nothing special between us."

As he said the words, Merral reassured himself that what had happened there had a been a lifetime ago, before the world went to bits. Besides, he told himself, it had never been with parental approval. And it only remained for him—for them both—to sort out the final details of their return to being merely good friends. And with that, he pushed Isabella out of his mind.

Merral looked at Anya's dim outline. Suddenly he snatched her into his arms, his armored jacket strange and stiff against her yielding softness. He ran his fingers through her wild hair, sighing at the touch of her arms around his neck. He wanted to hold on to her and be with her. There was nothing sweeter he could think of than Anya. And this night, with its threats and tensions and its brevity of time, seemed to make it all much more precious, just as darkness heightens the smallest light.

For an immeasurable time, he stood there holding her, until a low voice called out his name from somewhere by the *Emilia Kay*.

"Look, it's nearly time," he said quietly, wondering why everything had to happen at once.

Their lips gently kissed.

With an extraordinary reluctance, he forced himself away from her, telling himself that there was much to be done. Then, his mind in turmoil, Merral walked carefully back over to where the sled was now hovering just above the ground with a gentle whisper. In the darkness he could make out the men moving against each other as, weighed down by equipment, they settled clumsily into their seats. Between the sled and the *Emilia Kay*, he could vaguely make out the men of the reserves spilling out of the ship and stretching themselves.

From the front of the sled, Frankie called out in a muted voice, "Captain, if it's all right with you, I think we ought to leave."

Suddenly Vero quickly embraced Merral. "Come back safe," he said.

"I'll do my best," Merral replied, feeling that he sounded utterly feeble.

Then after Maria, Lucy, and Perena hugged him, there was a longer and more meaningful hug from Anya.

"See you at the lake," she whispered.

"Maybe it will all work out," he muttered. "Perhaps we will be invited to breakfast."

He felt, rather than saw, her wrinkle her face in amusement. "Given what we know of their eating habits, I'd say it'd be a good time to fast."

Then, after a brief but precious grasp of her fingers, he clambered on board and was tugged toward a bench seat near the front, just behind Philip and Frankie. With a chuckle, someone that Merral decided could only be Lorrin Venn passed him a helmet, and he put it on. He tightened the strap and fastened the security belt around his waist, took the offered weapon, and put its cold metallic mass carefully down between his feet.

Then the chaplain was praying over them.

"Amen," came a low chorus of voices from the sled's occupants and the bystanders.

Then switches were flicked and the whispering of the sled's engine grew to a slight hum. There was a soft tug underneath him as the vehicle began to move at little more than a fast running pace over the ground.

His heart torn by a dozen emotions, Merral looked back as they slid northward out of the gully, and one by one, the faint lights of the *Emilia Kay* vanished behind him. Then he swiveled round on his bench seat and faced forward.

Ahead of us, in less than seven hours, lies a confrontation about whose outcome not one of us has any certainty. We face unknown foes of unknown powers with unproven weapons and untrained men.

It was not a comforting thought.

CHAPTER 19

The sled moved steadily northward toward the Lannar Crater in almost total silence. It was so dark that Merral could make out very little clearly. There was a constant sense of trees and bushes racing past, and occasionally branches and leaves would whip against the sled and rattle off helmets or hands. Almost the only noises were the soft whistle of the air, the low hum of the engine, and the gentle rustle of grass and small shrubs against the sled's underside. Their passage was so quiet that more than once they startled animals. Once, a herd of deer bounded away as leaping shadows. Another time they stopped abruptly, and ahead of them Merral made out the shape of a large bear lumbering irritably out of the way.

Normally Merral would have found the journey invigorating, particularly after being enclosed inside a ship. He had always loved being out in the open, and this journey with the stars above and the fresh clean air with its scents of pine and heather all around should have been enjoyable. Tonight, though, everything seemed to conspire against any enjoyment. He had to keep his head down to avoid being lashed by branches, it was impossible to find a decent position for his legs in the cramped space, the armor made his spine ache, and soon, as they climbed higher, he was very cold. Repeatedly, memories of his fight with the intruders at Carson's Sill came back to him, and he found himself quailing at the prospect of battling against those terrible creatures. And what he fought against then had now been supplemented by this new flying monstrosity. Unease also nagged at his mind about what had happened between him and Anya. The memory of her embrace left a warm glow. Nevertheless, in another part of his mind, he told himself that he could perhaps have handled it in a better way. He had somehow allowed himself to be caught unawares by events. It would have surely been better to have resolved matters with Isabella first.

After ninety minutes, his troubled reflections were broken when they stopped in the midst of a pile of gravelly dunes overlooked by a high, saw-edged line of summits. With groans of relief, everybody clambered out and stretched to restore circulation.

Merral checked the dimmed digital map with Frankie and Philip. He saw that they had slowly climbed up from the landing site but still had the main part of the southern Rim Ranges to negotiate.

After ten minutes they set off again. Over the next hour, they wound their way through the mountains, climbing ever higher and going round great fragments of rock beside which patches of snow still persisted. Above them the stars seemed to burn ever more brightly, and in the deep cold everybody huddled next to each other, grateful for even the slight warmth transmitted from the man on either side. They slowly descended into the crater proper. The high, sharp-edged blackness of the bladed peaks was now behind them. They descended gulches and ragged screes to the crater floor, and as they did, Merral found himself ever more troubled. He tried praying, but that gave him no peace, a fact that unsettled him still more. He sat there shivering, trying to keep warm and wishing that, one way or another, it was all over. Slowly, the bare angular rocks gave way to a flatter and more swampy area, and for some time the sled pushed through tall reeds, while in the waters below, unseen creatures plopped and jumped as the sled glided over them.

On the other side of the marsh, they stopped again amid clumps of dwarf willows and, on a bank covered with thin sparse grass and moss, stretched out trying to massage cramped muscles. Frankie sent a brief coded message, compressed into a fraction of a second's tight directional transmission, southward to the *Emilia Kay*. A few moments later, the terse acknowledgement came back from Maria Dalphey. All parties, the message said, were on schedule.

They continued on, and as the ground rose again, Philip was forced to steer the sled in an increasingly circuitous route in order to keep them low in valleys. Merral tried to doze but found that he could not.

An hour later, there was a final stop in a barren, gravel-strewn depression. Everyone dismounted, did more stretching exercises, drank water, and ate biscuits. Here, Merral noted, all the men seemed subdued, and an air of unease hung over everyone. At least two of the party kept their guns with them, and in the darkness he could sense people looking around warily.

Merral was lying down, trying to bring life to stiff legs, when one of the men came over to him.

"Sir, a question: You were a forester, right?" Merral recognized Lee Rodwen from his southern Varrend Tablelands accent.

"Yes, Lee," Merral sighed, "and at this moment I would like to be one again. As you would want to go back to your farming studies."

"Aye, true enough. But is it always this quiet up 'ere?"

Merral listened beyond the low whispers of the men and realized that he had heard no sign of either bird or animal for a long time. *I have been too preoccupied. I must concentrate more on this undertaking.*

"You feel something is missing?" he asked.

He sensed Lee looking around, sniffing the air. "*Life*, sir, is what's missing. Birds, rabbits, foxes—anything. I'm no forester, but I am a countryman, and this is a funny place 'ere. *Bleak*. As if round 'ere, the Seeding went wrong."

Merral listened again, hearing only the tense silence, as heavy as the air before a summer storm.

"No, Lee, the Seeding went right. But, if I can make up a word, perhaps it's been unseeded."

"Unseeded?" There was a pause and then the man spoke again. "Aye, that about feels like it. But sir, who—or what—unseeds what the Assembly seeds?"

"A good question, Lee."

Then behind them there was a murmur of activity, and Merral was aware that people were starting to climb back into the sled. It was time for the final lap.

• ◆ •

Forty minutes later, the sled glided to a halt in a shallow but steep-sided river valley. It was still dark; indeed, the night was now thicker and more impenetrable than ever before.

There were whispered commands from Frankie; the sled sank slowly to the ground, and the faint hum of the engine died away. Stiffly, but with great care, the men dismounted from the sled and, trying not to make the slightest noise, began taking out their weapons and their packs.

In low whispers, Frankie assigned duties. "Three hours sleep, one hour on guard. If you're not on guard now, go and sleep. Everyone keep your weapons next to you." Then he turned and touched Merral on the arm. "If it's all right with you, Captain, shall we go and take a look?"

Putting on light-enhancing goggles that, in happier days, Merral had used for monitoring wildlife, he and Frankie grabbed their guns and picked their way down the stony valley bottom. There was little vegetation, just straggly thistles and wiry grass clumps around the flanks of the sluggish shallow stream. After a hundred meters, they began climbing up a slope, trying not to slip on the loose stones. A few minutes' labor brought them to just below the rounded summit, and there they hesitated for a moment.

If we are in the right place, Merral thought, *then just over the top will be the lake and, on the other side of that, will be the ship.*

Frankie gestured him forward. They crawled up on their hands and knees and, lying uncomfortably on the cold and pebbly ground, peered eastward.

With the image distorted in color and texture by the goggles, it took time for Merral to work out what it was that he was seeing. Before them was the rough descent down to the lake edge, and beyond the dark, immobile waters he could see the other shoreline. In the middle of that, like some sort of strange reclining ebony sculpture, was the intruder vessel.

"The ship." Merral's whispered words rang with soft wonderment and fear. At first, all he could make out was the general shape of the intruder craft. Even when Frankie passed him a fieldscope, he could still make out little more than he had seen on Vero's images. There was the single front leg, the paired and larger rear legs, and between them, the forward-descending entrance ramp. He could see no sign of life but felt that in the irresolvable blackness around the ship there could easily have been any number of sentries.

Merral put down the scope. Although actually seeing this vessel added little new to what he had already observed on the images, there was nevertheless something almost overwhelming about the experience. The intruder ship had been progressively an abstract theory, a computer image, and a crude piece of imagery. Now, at last, it was a solid and tangible reality, and with that the whole operation had assumed a dire immediacy. After all, with a real ship went real battles and real deaths.

Frankie tapped Merral's arm and together they slid down below the crest of the hill.

"Well, it's *there,*" Frankie said in low, awed tones, and Merral knew that he had, in his own way, felt the same arresting intrusion of reality.

"Did you expect something else?" he asked.

"I don't know," Frankie answered, and Merral could make out his shrugging his shoulders. "I suppose, sir, that's the thing about this business. I've given up knowing what to expect. I was concerned, I suppose, that it might have gone. To have been a bad dream."

"No, it's there. But that may be the bad dream."

"Yeah. So it's as we planned then, sir?" Merral identified disquiet in the voice. "It looks awful big. To try and blast that front leg and maybe get a hole in the ramp doorway?"

"Yes," Merral answered, sounding more confident than he felt.

"We can do it. That's what Perena preferred. Her argument was that we were more likely to disable the ship by concentrating on the front. I think she was also worried that there might be fuel at the rear."

Frankie seemed to chew on that. "Yeah, sir. It makes sense. Right; I'll make sure we keep a continuous watch on the ship from here. Get us an optic fiber communications link down to the sled. What watch do you want, sir?"

"Me? I'll take the last hour before dawn. I need to be here to watch the diplomatic team approach anyway."

"Yeah, I worry about them," Frankie said in a sad voice. "I feel they are going to be in trouble."

"Yes, I think so too. And I think they know it. I think they are the bravest of the lot of us."

"True. Anyway, Captain, if it suits you, let's go and get the cable set up to here. Then you can go and snatch some sleep."

◆

Down by the sled, Merral settled down on a more or less flat spot, put his cutter gun within reach, rolled himself in a thermal blanket, and tried to switch his mind off.

Despite his tiredness, he found sleep elusive. The cold, pebbly ground and the inadequate blanket were factors in keeping him awake, but what ultimately kept sleep at bay were the wild swings of emotion he felt. He struggled against the near certainty of a battle and the unnerving possibility that, in the darkness, a sheet-dragon creature circled above them. To seek relief, Merral turned his mind to warm thoughts of Anya and again felt excited that she cared for him and that he cared for her. Yet from that peak of exhilaration, he would soon slide into guilty feelings about Isabella, and then the fear would return. Eventually sleep came, only to be broken after what seemed mere seconds by a gentle shaking and Philip Matakala's apologetic voice in his ear asking him to wake up.

Stiffly, Merral pulled himself to his feet, yawning and rubbing his face, aware he was covered in a cold dew. His watch told him it was almost five. Now, an hour before dawn, the dark of the western sky was already becoming lighter.

Philip had prepared him a cup of coffee, and Merral gratefully drank it and ate some biscuits. Then putting his armored jacket and the goggles back on, he picked up his gun and walked slowly back down the stream valley. Ahead he could easily make out the figure of the watching soldier on the ridge, the circuitry of his goggles painting his warm body orange against the cold blue of the ground. Carefully, Merral climbed to the summit of the mound and crawled forward to get alongside the man who, hearing his footsteps, turned toward him as he approached.

"Morning," Merral said quietly.

"Morning, sir. Good to see you. Very good." Merral recognized who it was and noted the relief in the voice of Lorrin Venn.

"See anything, Lorrin?"

"No, sir, but I feel it." Merral sensed him shudder. "Nasty looking ship. Gives me the creeps." Merral found it hard to remember the bubbly young man whom he had first met and realized that he hadn't heard Lorrin whistle at any time during the night.

"Wish you were back working in Isterrane?"

There was a faint pause. "I won't say, sir, that in the last hour, the idea hasn't come to me," Lorrin answered; then Merral felt he smiled. "But I asked for this. I asked you to get me in on this. And I'll stick with it. . . ."

"That's the spirit, Lorrin. I can't say I'm very happy about it."

"Yes. Well, I suppose back in Isterrane it all seemed . . . well, exciting. Like a sort of grand sports event. Know what I mean, sir? I couldn't miss it, could I?"

"No, I guess you couldn't," Merral replied.

"I've been thinking about this. I mean this is the—I don't know—*strangest* event in the history of the Assembly. This is history in the making. And when it gets talked about in the future, I want to be able to say, 'I was there.' Yet I'm still a bit scared, sir."

"I don't blame you, Lorrin. The key thing is, I suppose, to do what you have to do. That's what I tell myself."

"I'll do my best, sir."

Merral suddenly felt sorry for Lorrin. "I know you will. Now, any signs of life?"

"I think they vented steam a few minutes ago. A cloud of something warm, but otherwise it's quiet. I thought I saw something move around just now below the ship, but I couldn't be sure."

"Nothing on this side then. No birds or bats?"

"No, sir," Lorrin said with just a hint of hesitation. "But I find your eyes play tricks after a while."

"In what way?" Merral asked, feeling that something lay behind his words.

"Well . . . I thought I heard footsteps earlier. Lee Rodwen was with me and he agreed. But there was no sign of anything. Or anybody. But we felt, well . . . watched."

Unsettled by his words, Merral glanced around with the night goggles but saw nothing but cold ground and a gnarled pine tree to his left.

After dismissing Lorrin, Merral stared again at the ship for several minutes but saw nothing new. He found the silence odd; it was a strange and tense quietness, as if some colossal storm was brewing. He slid his goggles up and squinted into the darkness with his unaided eyesight. Above him, the stars were glowing. In the sky ahead, the pure blackness of night was now turning into shades of indigo, and above the jagged horizon the stars were fading out. Indeed, by straining his eyes, Merral could make out the silhouettes of the eastern Rim Ranges standing black against the purpling sky. Wreathes of mist drifted this way and that in the slight westerly breeze.

Merral slid the goggles back down and examined the ship again with the scope. There was no sign of activity. He gave up looking and concentrated on listening, stretching his senses as far as he could, swinging his head this way and that. He wondered whether Lorrin and

Lee had really heard anything. Or had it simply been their imaginations?

He listened carefully, but all he could hear was the faint rustling of the breeze in the branches on the solitary pine tree nearby and the feeble gurgle of water in the stream behind. There was no sound of animal life: no birds, not even the buzz of an insect. Merral felt ill at ease.

Then he looked again at the distant ship and felt suddenly almost overwhelmed by its power and menace. In contrast to that machine, his own force for the initial attack seemed pathetic; a mere sixty men, mostly dragged from college studies barely days ago, with almost every piece of equipment improvised from quarrying, farming, or forestry. True, they had courage and dedication, and Merral knew he could rely on them to do their best, but what he had seemed so puny. *Our only real asset is surprise, and even that might have been compromised.... Surely, we are like a bunch of village children suddenly thrown into playing a Team-Ball game against the Isterrane champions.*

As Merral stared across the still, dark waters of Lake Fallambet Five and considered the sheer inadequacy of his forces, he slipped into silent prayer. Yet, here and now, it seemed that prayer was not easy. Merral was able to say the words in his mind, but as he tried to pray for the day ahead, words were all that they seemed to be. Irritatingly, Anya's form and face seemed to teasingly pop up into his prayers and distract him with guilt and desire. Finally he ended his praying, feeling that there was no answer.

As he considered the situation, Merral felt himself drifting toward self-pity and even anger. Here he was, on the verge of awesome events and about to lead men to possible—even probable—death, and badly in need of God's support. Yet instead, he had silence. *Say something, Lord!* But the silence only continued.

Suddenly Merral heard the tiniest of noises off to the right. He knew with certainty that another man had joined him. He felt a spasm of irritation that he had been so absorbed in his own struggles that he had missed his arrival. Merral swung his head round but, to his surprise, the goggles showed only the cold ground and the single forlorn pine.

I must have imagined it.

As he looked back across the lake to the ship, there was another slight sound from his right. It was as if one of the men was adjusting his position on the ground. Mistrustful now of his goggles, Merral slid them up and peered into the darkness toward where he had heard the sound.

He stopped breathing.

A mere arm's length away from him, a large, dark shape was lying on the ground.

Slowly, taking strained breaths and aware that his hands were shaking, Merral put the goggles back over his eyes. To his surprise, he could make out no form there and no hint of any heat source disturbing the uniform chill blueness of the ground. Alarm threatening to flood his mind, Merral slid the goggles up again and stared to his right. Were his senses playing tricks with him?

The shape was still there and Merral peered at it. He shivered, certain now that something was lying next to him—something the size and shape of a man.

The dark form next to him stirred, and abruptly Merral felt under a gaze that seemed to go right through him. Suddenly he felt terribly exposed, as if he was being examined. An almost irresistible urge to run and hide descended on him.

In the silence the figure spoke. "Man, a time has passed. The war deepens."

"I'm sorry," Merral replied, hearing his voice wobbling with fear. "I can't remember your name."

Even as he spoke, he knew what he heard was not the voice of any man he knew. Indeed, he realized, with a strange and chilling certainty, the voice was not human. It was in one way characterless and neutral, and yet in another it had an extraordinary and unassailable authority.

"You do not know my name."

Merral's throat was suddenly dry. "I mean," he said, swallowing nervously, "you, er, are one of my men?"

"One of *your* men? In no sense."

The words held a rebuke.

"Then who are you?" Merral asked, his hand inching toward his gun. Perhaps, he thought, the enemy was already among them. His fingers closed around the stock. "Who are you?" he repeated.

The voice broke the silence. "Man, you are right to be concerned. I have come as the representative of the King."

Merral felt that the word *King* reverberated strangely, as if it had its own special resonance.

Before Merral could answer, the voice spoke again. "The King who was, and is, and is to come. The one who was slain as a Lamb and rules as a Lion. Does that answer your question?"

"Yes," quavered Merral, realizing that whatever this creature was, it was not an enemy. He felt at once relieved, chastened, and terrified. "But— but, who are you?" he asked.

There was another pause. "I am an envoy. I am sent to you from the Highest."

Suddenly it came to Merral in a flash of comprehension that this had to be the strange being who, only hours before the Gate was destroyed, had appeared to Perena.

"You—you are the one who spoke to Perena Lewitz? the one who warned her about the Gate?"

Slowly, and with only the faintest rustling sound, the dark form seemed to rise up from the ground and stand upright, obscuring the waning stars. Merral peered up at the figure, knowing with a hard certainty that the being that stood before him was gazing down at him with stern, cold, invisible eyes. He suddenly felt small and exposed, as if he were a mouse under an eagle's gaze.

"I did," the voice said.

Merral sensed, with a deepening fear, the head move as if to stare more closely at him. He cringed. *I ought to thank him. I owe him my life.*

"Man, whom do you serve?" the voice asked suddenly, its tone cutting and sharp.

"The King, of course," Merral answered. "It goes without saying. I bear his badge."

In the darkness, he reached out to his shoulder and touched the embossed Lamb and Stars emblem on his armored jacket.

The voice spoke again. "Nothing goes without saying. It never did. And least of all now, with the enemy unchained."

The blackness that marked the figure's head seemed to bend accusingly over him. "So you are his servant?"

"Er, yes. Yes, of course," Merral answered, shivering and wondering why he sounded so guilty.

"So you obey him in all matters?"

The word *all* seemed somehow to have a universal feel to it, as if there was nothing it did not include. Merral felt a new stab of discomfort, as if somewhere, some raw nerve in his soul was being probed.

"Why, yes," he answered, desperately wishing that the conversation might move on to other subjects.

"In *all* matters, Man?" Merral found the coolly knowing tone to the voice profoundly unnerving.

"Well, yes . . . ," Merral answered slowly, aware of something like acid eating into his mind and etching around thoughts of Isabella and Anya.

"So there is nothing that has happened this night of which you are ashamed?"

There was a terrible ring to the words, and Merral quailed at them. He felt as if a spotlight had illuminated the innermost parts of his life.

"Well, I . . . I suppose I may have . . . made an error of judgment."

The only answer was a strange and terrible silence in which Merral felt he had to speak. "I was confused," he said, almost spluttering his words, feeling his face flush. "It's, well, been an awful time. *Awful.*"

"Man, did I ask for your excuses?"

"No . . ." Merral fell silent.

"You broke a promise."

"But that . . . ," Merral hesitated, feeling transfixed by the invisible gaze of this visitor. "Well, you see, Isabella extracted it from me. . . ."

"And what has that do with breaking a promise?"

"Ah, things have been changing in Ynysmant. It has been very hard."

There was a heavy silence before the dark figure spoke again.

"I was sent on the basis that you wanted help. Is that still the case?" Now the words seemed to have a ring of impatience in them.

Suddenly, Merral felt a surge of defiance. He had to resist. "I'm sorry," he said, "but I must say that she manipulated me."

"Really?" There was a strange weariness in the voice. "Your first ancestor used a similar excuse. In the beginning."

"Well, I do feel that Isabella—"

"Man, I was sent to deal with Merral D'Avanos. Not any Isabella."

Merral suddenly felt that being apologetic might be more profitable. This terrible figure had to be placated. "Look, I'm sorry," he said. "What must I do?"

"Man, you must resolve to repair the wrongs you have done. The commitment you made must stand until it is ended—if it is to be ended—by agreement between you. You must also explain the true situation to the one you lied to and encouraged unfairly. And apologize. And apologizing, I must remind you, is not the same as making excuses."

It suddenly occurred to Merral that both actions were horribly unattractive. "Look, is this important, I mean, right now? *Really* important?"

There was a sound like an angry intake of breath. "Of course!" The words were charged with displeasure. "Do not add folly to dishonesty. You have invoked the King's help this day of battle because of his covenant agreement with his people. At the heart of all covenants lies obedience and faithfulness. Yet in these last few hours you have despised both of these in your own life."

From nowhere came the wild thought that he couldn't let Anya go. *I must fight for her.* "But—"

"Enough, Man!" The envoy said, and his dark form loomed over Merral so that the voice almost seemed to buffet him physically. "Choose. If you wish to fight these things in *your* strength, then you may do so." Merral, pressing himself against the ground, found the pause before the voice spoke again as menacing as any words. "But I warn you, you will not win. Not against these foes."

Suddenly the voice sounded as if it was retreating into the distance. "Or if you do win, it will be such a victory that men and women will wish until the end of time that you had lost."

Merral sensed the figure seemed less substantial now, as if it were merely smoke or mist.

"Which will it be, Man?" asked the quieter, fainter voice. He could see a star now where the figure had stood, as if the envoy was fading away.

His mind buffeted by a tumult of emotions, Merral hesitated, unable to choose between his fears and his desires.

"Decide," the voice said, but now it was a drained echo coming from a vast distance. Where the envoy's figure had been, more and more stars were becoming visible.

Suddenly a great and awful fear came into Merral's mind, a terror of an unspeakable darkness and grief. In the fear, he saw that there was only one way forward.

"Please! I'm sorry. I choose the right way," he cried, and this time he was aware his contrition was genuine. "I am truly sorry and I repent. I will try to sort out things with Anya and Isabella."

"Try?" The voice was nearer now and the figure more solid. Stars vanished. "That is inadequate, Man. *Do.* Make things right whatever it costs you. And watch yourself, Merral D'Avanos. The enemy delights in using a man against himself." The voice seemed to resonate strangely. "He seeks your ruin. For him, there are more satisfying and useful ways for your destruction than fire, sword, or tooth."

"I can imagine."

"Imagine?" The rebuke in the tone was tangible. "Man, I have *seen*." There was a knife's edge to the words. "I saw Saul, son of Kish, go from mighty warrior over Israel to the haunted wreckage of a man. And many after him. Lesser and greater. I am an envoy and I am a witness."

Merral, now utterly appalled at the idea that he had tried to withstand this being, felt unable to speak.

"Now listen, Man," the envoy went on. "We have wasted time. The hour of battle is almost upon you. I am to warn you of the thing on the ship."

"The dragon thing?"

"That? That is a servant, no more. It is its master you must fear. That is a spirit, released from the utter depths and now housed in a body crafted for it by some of your race."

"Mine?"

"Yes. But listen. Such beings are powerful and not easily vanquished. They remain linked to their own realm and derive their power from there. Even were that ship to be utterly destroyed, that being would shed its body and persist here as a disembodied form. Your world would not care for that."

"Like a ghost?"

"Their kind has had that name. And others. To destroy it completely, the link with its realm must first be broken. Then, while it is weakened, you can consign it back to the abyss."

Merral felt a cold sweat on his forehead. "And how am I to do that?

"You, and you alone, will enter the ship. You will need courage and arms. Take your gun, a blade, and a charge. I will meet you inside to give you instructions. There, Man, you must fight, and there is no certainty of victory. I do not know the outcome. Only the King does."

Against the lightening sky, Merral felt that he could make out limbs and a head on the envoy's form.

"I want to know—please—will there be casualties?"

"Man, if you want to battle evil without loss, then evil has already won."

"I see. I just wanted to know."

"You have the only guarantees that there are, and those have existed since the founding of the worlds. Have faith in the King, and be true to him and his Word and, in the end, all will be well."

"In the end, yes. But what about in the meantime?"

"That? *That* is mere curiosity." There was almost scorn in the words. "Play your part. See, the sun rises."

The voice had begun to become more distant again. The figure suddenly began to fade away as if it had been merely vapor.

"Merral D'Avanos," came the whisper, "I trust we will meet in the ship."

"Wait!" Merral cried, but there was only silence, and he knew he was now alone.

He stared across the lake, his mind reeling both at the contact he had had and the dreadful revelation about his own behavior. He found himself humbly asking God for forgiveness. *How appalling,* he thought in a mood of bitter astonishment, *that I could have ever behaved like that.*

Then, suddenly aware that dawn was about to break, Merral forced himself to consider the task ahead. Across the western sky the stars were fading out; in the predawn glow he could make out the difference between the lake and the rough land beyond and see the ship with his naked eye. Looking at his watch, he saw that there was just twenty minutes before the hoverer would start its journey up the lake.

He peered again at the ship through the fieldscope, seeing slightly more details of it now. As he looked at it, he felt that Perena's insight had been right: this could never have been an Assembly ship. Not that all Assembly vessels were beautiful; the *Emilia Kay,* for a start, was hardly stunning, but she had a plain functional harmony that was pleasing. This intruder ship, by contrast, had an unattractiveness that seemed almost to be deliberate.

Realizing that dawn was only minutes away, Merral took off the night goggles and laid them aside. From now on, there would be enough natural light. He turned his gaze back to the ship. With a shock, he realized that something was different. He snatched up the fieldscope to see that around the ship there were creatures moving like ants around a fragment of food. It took him a few seconds to work out exactly what was happening and a few more seconds for the implications to sink in. Above the long black hull, camouflage sheeting was being rolled back, and down on the ground, he could make out creatures working on the supporting frame.

Merral grabbed the microphone, fumbled for the call button, and pressed it.

"Frankie!" he snapped, hearing agitation—if not panic—in his voice. "They are preparing the ship for takeoff. Get the men ready for action. Alert Perena and Zak's team, now!"

"Are you sure, sir?"

"Yes!"

"Okay, will do!"

As Merral turned back to the view of the ship, he could hear orders being given. Desperately, he tried to weigh his limited options. Was he to wait for the diplomatic team? Or should they launch their attack now? It was a complication he had not envisaged.

He looked across again to the intruder vessel, hoping against hope that he had been mistaken. Yet, in the growing light, there could be no doubt that they were indeed removing the camouflage. As he watched, Merral noted that the tall, dark ape-creatures were doing most of the lifting with their long forelimbs, while the smaller cockroach-beasts scurried around at their feet, apparently working on lesser tasks. The shapes and characteristic movements of the two intruder types dug up hateful memories to Merral that he tried to suppress.

There was a bleep from beside him and he picked up the handset.

He could hear Frankie breathing heavily. "We are now ready, sir. I guess we can launch within seconds."

"Okay. I don't think they are going to leave just yet. There is still work to do. But it definitely looks like they are getting ready to move. I'll get on board as you come past."

"Fine. I'll have a helmet ready for you, sir." Besides Frankie, Merral could hear men moving.

"Oh, and I want an explosive charge too."

"For you, sir?" Frankie answered, his tone filled with doubt.

"Yes," Merral answered, hearing the reluctance in his own voice. "I'm going to get inside the ship. I may need it."

"Inside?" There was a pause. "Er, sir, did we discuss that?"

"No, Lieutenant, we didn't," Merral said, surprising himself with the sharp authority in his voice.

"Yes, sir," Frankie answered. "A kilo charge with an intermolecular cement pad and a sixty-second fuse—will that be all right? That's all we have."

I have no idea. I haven't a clue. "Ideal. Thanks, and keep the line open."

A sliver of brilliant red light suddenly rose over the horizon, and the rays of the new sun cut through the mist patches on the water. Even as Merral watched, the world seemed to change. The light lit up the hill around him, and he felt grateful for the warmth of its rays. He was suddenly awed by the realization that, with the exception of the space conflicts that ended the Rebellion, this was going to be the first true battle of mankind under a strange sun. Then he pushed the thought aside, telling himself that in reality it wouldn't make the slightest bit of difference.

Merral switched his gaze back to the ship. Here it was now plain, even to the naked eye, that the camouflage was being dismantled. With the fieldscope, Merral could see piles of metal tubes and fabric sheeting accumulating on the sand and stones at the foot of the strange vessel. It must, he decided, be more than coincidence that this was happening only a day after the attack on Felicity. If they knew they were discovered, were they then also prepared against any attack?

Merral tried to count the figures opposite. There were perhaps a dozen or more of the ape-creatures and at least the same number of the cockroach-beasts. Of the winged creature or men there was no evidence. *We are at least matched in numbers, and there may be many more inside.*

Without warning, the creatures burst into action. The fabric sheets and metal frames were hastily thrown aside, and the antlike figures began running about at the foot of the ship. A faint mechanical noise drifting up from the southern part of the lake explained the new activity. The hoverer was on schedule and had already been seen.

Merral stared down the lake. Far away in the middle of the water, the frail white dot of the hoverer was moving up toward them. He reached for the microphone, hoping that, away to the north, the other team was ready.

"Frankie," he said, marveling at how steady his voice sounded, "the diplomatic team is in view and has been seen by the ship."

"They said they were moving, sir. Everybody here is ready to go. Ready for your word."

Merral turned his gaze back to the ship, where there was renewed activity. Some of the creatures had returned to packing the camouflage sheeting while others were bringing a tubular apparatus on a tripod down the ramp and out onto the lake strand.

A weapon, Merral realized with a feeling of horror. He was tempted to call Frankie and have him order the hoverer to turn back. In the end, he resisted the idea. The rules they had agreed upon were plain. There had to be clear evidence of the failure of diplomacy and preferably active aggression by the intruders before any Assembly attack could take place.

With the fieldscope, Merral looked south down the lake, seeing the hoverer moving straight and steady toward the Intruder ship. He could make out the flags flying, the creamy V-shape of the wake behind, and could even make out dark forms of two people standing erect by the hoverer's prow. He lowered the scope, trying to gauge the present distance between the hoverer and the ship. Contact must only be minutes away.

There was a yellow flash on the other side of the lake.

A large, dirty orange sphere of flame rolled from below the ship across the water straight at the approaching hoverer. Trailing white steam behind it, the ball crossed the gap between the ship and the hoverer in under a second. As the burning sphere was on the point of engulfing its target, the hoverer lurched abruptly sideways.

The evasive action came too late.

The flaming ball, almost half the size of the hoverer, struck the side of the hull and rolled over the vessel in a explosion of oily golden light.

Merral, already speaking into the handset, had a confused impression of the white craft being thrown up and sideways, and of tiny figures being flung into the water.

"Hoverer attacked! Hoverer attacked!" he shouted. "Everybody start immediate operations!"

As he spoke, the boom of the explosion reached him. Waiting only a fraction of a second for Frankie to acknowledge his order, Merral flung the handset aside and grabbed his gun.

As he did, out of the corner of his eye he caught a glimpse of another smoking ball of flame being fired from below the intruder ship. Whether it struck what was left of the hoverer Merral never saw, because he was already slithering down the stony slope toward the stream and his men.

Two thoughts hammered together in his brain as he raced down: a cold fury that the intruders had attacked an unarmed boat and a cloying fear that the sleds would suffer the same fate before they were halfway across the lake.

"Let it not be!" he gasped under his breath as he slid down, sending a volley of small stones flying around. "Lord, let us at least have a chance to fight!"

CHAPTER 20

As Merral reached the bottom of the slope, the sled, full of men in uniforms grappling with gear and weapons, came silently skimming down through the shadows toward him. It slowed down briefly. He clambered clumsily on board, and outstretched hands guided him roughly into a seat near the front.

The sled renewed its acceleration down the valley. All around him, Merral glimpsed anonymous-looking, pale, stern-faced men bracing themselves, holding guns, and checking webbing and straps. Lorrin Venn, scared excitement written across his face, passed him a helmet, while someone else fastened a belt around him. As someone passed him a small package labeled with ominous red symbols, Merral heard Frankie, sitting at the front of the sled, yelling into his helmet microphone. Merral, unable to make out his words, presumed he was talking either to the *Emilia Kay* or Zak's team.

Suddenly he turned to Merral. "What happened?" he shouted, tightening his helmet strap.

"They fired a big ball of flame without warning!" Merral yelled back, aware of the men around him on the sled listening. "It exploded over them. They didn't really have a chance! Then they fired again!"

Frankie shook his head angrily and turned to face forward.

The rock-strewn valley was opening up on either side of them now as they raced down, and then suddenly they were out onto the flat delta surface and into the full glare of the rising sun. Philip slowed the sled down to align it with the exact coordinates for the computer-controlled approach.

To the south of them, Merral glimpsed a turbulent column of

dense white and gray smoke spiraling up from the waters of the lake. He tried to derive some comfort from its quantity, telling himself that it looked as if someone at least had survived long enough to trigger the smoke canisters.

"Now!" Frankie shouted. Merral caught a glimpse of Philip hitting a red switch newly welded on the control panel.

The booster pack ignited.

There was a surging, booming roar from the rear of the sled. Merral, pressed back against his seat, felt the hull beginning to vibrate like a beaten drum as the sled raced, with growing speed, over the desolate ground and green reed clumps.

They were still accelerating as they came to the water's edge, and Merral found himself holding on even tighter as the slipstream began to whip past him and snatch at clothing and straps. The sled was impossibly low, and he felt that there was barely a handbreadth between them and the wave crests. Every so often they clipped the top of a wave with a hissing slap and the sled gave a little bound that made Merral's tense stomach quiver again. At any second, he expected the sled to overturn. Glancing back at the shoreline they had come from— already diminishing into the distance—he could see the wake of spray and fumes trailing behind them. *They will have seen us now,* he thought, looking ahead to where the great dark silhouette of the fuselage of the intruder ship was now rising up above the approaching shoreline.

Merral braced himself again, remembering that at any moment the computer would use the gravity-modifying engine to flick the sled sharply to the side. A maneuver, he unhappily reminded himself, that they had never done at anything like this speed and that the sled had never been designed for.

Now!

The sled jerked a dozen meters to the right, bobbed sharply, and struck the wave crests with a great slapping noise. Merral felt that if he hadn't been strapped in he would have been thrown free of his seat. Yelps of exhilaration mixed with alarm went up from the other men.

Over the roar of the motor, Merral could hear the creaking of the titanium skin and girders under the strain of the jump. The sled wobbled, smacked the water again, recovered its equilibrium, and raced onward.

Merral peered ahead, squinting into the dazzling sun, his eyes fixed on the intruder ship still visible only as a vast silhouette.

They were still accelerating but no longer at such a fast rate. Merral saw that they were already halfway across the lake.

They hit a wave. Water flew up everywhere into the sunlight, and for a second, a faint, ghostly rainbow appeared. *A covenant sign,* Merral told himself, his mind numbed by the wild vibration. *We must have hope and have faith.*

The sled shot sideways, this time to the left, and again he found himself pounded back against the seat frame.

Now there was spray all around him, and Merral felt cold water on his face and seeping into his clothes.

From under the rear of the intruder vessel came a bright yellow flash. Then, like an infant sun, a glowing orange disc of fire came streaking straight toward them.

There was shouting around him. Everyone ducked.

Just as it seemed that they would be engulfed by the spinning fireball, the sled suddenly shot to the right. Barely two meters away, the fiery sphere—a man's height or more in diameter—flew past them with an angry hissing noise. The smell of steam and smoke drifted past from its wake.

Merral was suddenly aware of a new grimness on the faces of the men around him. Any remaining exhilaration had been removed by the realization that they had been fired on. The beach was fast approaching, and there were other questions to ask.

Merral wiped cold spray from his eyes and tried to focus on the bouncing image ahead. The black ship now dominated the view, and below it Merral could make out distinct shapes of the long-limbed, slouching ape-creatures. At their feet, cockroach-beasts with their restless rocking movements scuttled around. Merral had a worrying impression that there were more of them than there ought to be. The ship, too, was bigger than he had imagined.

We've miscalculated. His stomach lurched. *It's too late to turn back.*

There was another flash, but this time it came from the nose of the ship and the sphere of flame flew north over the waters. *A second gun,* Merral thought in alarm as he traced the projectile's motion. Its target, another dark dot trailing spray and fumes behind it, was racing onward to the intruder ship.

He jabbed the man next to him. "Look! Zak's team!" he shouted, and as he watched he saw the second sled jink sideways. A moment later, the ball of flame sprinted harmlessly past it.

His own sled lurched violently to the left again, and water flew around them.

He could hear Frankie and Philip shouting together, their voices barely audible over the roar of the booster, the hiss of spray, and the booming slap of the hull against the waves.

Frankie leaned toward Merral, bellowing at him with exaggerated movements of his mouth. "Sir, Philip wants to go straight at the gun! A smoother landing there. Better hang on tight!"

Then there was another burst of light from the rear of the great black ship, and Merral saw a new flaming sphere coming toward them.

No! He suddenly saw with relief that it was aimed to their right and would easily miss them. Then he realized that it had been so directed that when—as must happen any second—the sled made the next lateral slip, their rightward slide would take them into its path. Their tactics had been deduced and already countered.

"Down everyone!" Merral screamed, pressing himself down against the hard wet metal and expecting at any second to be thrown into the water.

Suddenly the sled lurched.

But to the left.

The flaming globe hissed well away from them. Merral made a

mental note to praise whoever had written the program. If he got the chance.

As he looked at the shore, his relief was short-lived. They were barely seconds away from the water's edge, and they were clearly going too fast. The beach was rough and boulder strewn, and the cliff face beyond it seemed horribly close. They had to decelerate.

Merral watched Philip maniacally flicking switches. He was struck by the fact that there was now water slopping around inside the hull and that his feet were already soaked.

The booster cut out.

At that precise moment, Philip tugged on a control panel lever. The nose of the sled rose up into the air and the rear end struck the water with an awesome, juddering crash.

For a fearful instant, Merral, flung viciously against his safety belt, was aware of boiling white water below and pale blue sky above. From all around him came the awful noise of creaking and flexing metal. Just as he was sure they were going to tip over, the nose came down and cracked onto the water in a bone-jarring blow. A fountain of white spray gushed up all around.

The sled ploughed on.

They were slower now. Yet a glance at the shore ahead where the sands were glittering in the new sunlight showed they were still not slow enough. On the intimidating, charcoal black bulk of the ship he could make out details of the fins, ramp, and legs. Beneath the ship, creatures of both sorts were running around across the gleaming sand like animated black paper cutouts, their legs kicking up little sprays of sand as they ran. With a ghastly feeling in the pit of his stomach, Merral realized that there were far too many intruders. They had indeed badly miscalculated.

There was a screaming whine as the engines were thrown into reverse. Out of the corner of his eye, Merral glimpsed red lights flashing furiously on the control panel.

Philip was turning the sled now, swinging it toward the rear of the ship, tilting it like a racing yacht. Now they were aiming straight for where two of the ape-creatures, their odd shapes warped still further by vastly elongated shadows, were swinging the barreled gun toward them.

Sensations now came in so fast that Merral had barely time to assimilate them: rippled sands under the water, little waves breaking against the strand, spray in his face, intense black shadow under the ship, Philip suddenly flicking the gravity-modifying engine switch, the knife edge of fear in his stomach.

The sled struck the water again with a ferocious, deafening smack.

For a second it bounced up and then, lunging forward, thudded heavily onto the shore.

There were now new sensations: the scream of metal on sand and rock, the hissing spray of grit flying everywhere, the mountainous rear of the ship sliding above them like a vast black roof blocking out the sun, and the dull brown pebbly cliff racing toward them.

At the gun, black animal shapes were suddenly trying to throw themselves out of the way.

They struck the gun.

There was a prolonged grinding crash of metal upon metal. With an appalling soft, liquid thud, something large and black and as limp as a child's toy flew overhead, its outstretched limbs flailing against the sun.

The sled slewed and jolted crazily and then, with an insane ear-piercing screech, they came to a halt in a cloud of dust and sand.

For a brief, stunned instant there was a numbed silence.

Then, apparently from everywhere at once, furious shouts and cries erupted. Some—familiar and human—were from the sled as the men tried to leap free. Others—wild and animal—came from underneath the intruder ship.

Merral, partly dazed by the impact, fumbled for his belt release catch and clambered free, trying to orient himself. They had stopped just behind the intruder ship. As he stood unsteadily on the sand he could see, towering above him as high as a five-story building, the curved, blackened rear surface of the ship broken only by three inset thruster nozzles.

The foot of the cliff was less than ten meters to their right. As he realized how close they had come to hitting it, he heard a sudden, bellowed warning.

Something the size of a small man, brown and shining like wet wood, was racing toward him. On the edge of his vision, Merral saw another cockroach-beast coming from his left. Behind that was another. And another.

Merral raised his gun and, trying to steady his shaking hands, flicked off the safety switch. There was a gratifying hum from the stock as the electronics came to life. He sighted on the heaving chest of the cockroach-beast and fired. The gun hissed. Merral saw the hard central ridge of fused plates become momentarily illuminated with a red disc of light. There was a faint wisp of smoke. With a rattling and spluttering scream, the creature toppled over.

As Merral trained his gun on a new target, there were bellows, screeches, and yells all around him, and he was suddenly aware that he was in the midst of a bitter and chaotic hand-to-hand battle. All about him soldiers, ape-creatures, and cockroach-beasts were locked into a melee so intense that it was impossible to work out what was happening. Immediately to his left, a yelling man was kicking wildly at a cockroach-beast slashing at his legs with its bladed fingers. Barely thinking, Merral reversed his gun and swung the butt as hard as he could against the creature's plated head. There was a sharp and sickening crack, and the beast was flung backward onto the ground.

The soldier the beast had been attacking aimed his gun and fired repeatedly at it. There was a smell of blood, steam, and fear.

Another cockroach-beast, its carapace the color of old leaves, leapt ferociously at Merral, who dodged desperately to one side. Its pincer-like digits slid a handbreadth away from his face and clattered harmlessly on his armored jacket.

For a fraction of a second, Merral glimpsed dark eyes glaring at him and the moist, twitching slot of a mouth opening and shutting around yellowing, needlelike teeth.

Thrown off balance, his attacker tumbled to the ground beyond him. With a leap of surprising energy and speed, it sprung back upright and turned to face him, chattering angrily as it flexed its armored legs.

As Merral raised the gun, it jumped at his face. Instinctively, Merral jabbed with the barrel, striking the creature in the neck while it was in midair. The beast toppled back and hit the sand. As it tried to rise, Merral, aiming the gun by intuition, fired twice. With an uncontrollable rattling of limbs, the cockroach-beast fell back onto the bloodied sand.

Almost at his feet, a soldier, his helmet awry, was rolling on the ground, locked in a bitter embrace with a thrashing black ape-creature that almost dwarfed him and whose arms were clamped round his throat. A fellow soldier danced around the struggling pair, stabbing and slashing away with his bush knife at the hairy limbs whenever he could. Beyond him, another man, screaming in fear or anger—or both—was furiously hitting a further ape-creature in the face with the butt of his gun.

As Merral ran over to help, he saw two more ape-creatures running toward him with their elongated arms held high and their teeth bared. He turned, fired, and missed. He found the focus beam switch with wet fingers, slid it to the "wide" setting, and fired again and again. The shots seemed to have no effect and the creatures were almost upon him. Then, as suddenly as if it had been a machine, the leading ape-creature stopped dead in its tracks. Its jaws opened wide in a howl of pain and it began slapping its shoulder, from where Merral saw a trickle of smoke emerging. Suddenly a line of yellow flames flickered along the massive chest and leapt across to the wrist of the beating hand. With a series of pitiful screams, the creature turned and loped frantically toward the lake where it plunged its smoldering body into the waters. The other creature fled back under the hull of the ship.

Suddenly Merral was aware that the men around him were looking for new enemies. The attack was over. Around the sled were strewn the bodies of their attackers; perhaps seven cockroach-beasts and three ape-creatures, looking far less human in death than in life.

Frankie, his face streaked with blood and looking this way and that with a wild-eyed gaze, was gesturing frantically to a stack of metal struts and plates some way back against a pile of boulders near the cliff.

"Back! Over here!" he shouted, his voice hoarse. "Take cover!"

Slowly, their pale faces proclaiming their shock and horror, the men followed his gesture, picking up weapons and helmets as they went. Two were limping, one badly. A sobbing man was led away past Merral, clutching a hand shorn of fingers. An ape-creature writhed momentarily and then lay still.

Guns, chest armor, and surprise gained us this brief victory, Merral thought, a part of his mind marveling at his ability to analyze under stress. A glance around suggested that all of his men lived, but that two at least were injured to the point that they could take no further part in the fighting. *Next time, it may be different.* As the thought came, he realized that the next time might be only seconds away.

Frankie, his trousers torn and dirtied by red smears, ran over to him. "Sir, better take cover with us. . . ." He looked ahead under the ship. "There's dozens more there!" he cried, his voice ringing with alarm.

Merral looked over to see more dark forms emerging off the ramp and gathering in the deep shadows under the hull. Instinctively, he ducked down behind the tilted sled, gesturing to Frankie to join him. As the lieutenant squatted next to him, Merral looked around, trying to take stock of the situation, noting that the remaining men were running or limping to take cover behind the equipment pile.

Frankie stared at Merral, his hands shaking. "I could never have imagined it, sir." He swallowed and looked at Merral with astonished and troubled blue eyes. "Sorry, I'm kinda shaken up. I ended up sticking my gun barrel in the mouth of one of those ape things. I had to pull the trigger. . . ." He closed his eyes and shuddered. "Sir, can you imagine what happened?" he asked.

"Take it easy, Frankie," Merral said, patting him on the arm, feeling faintly ridiculous as he did it. "You've a done a good job so far. Any ideas for the second half of the match?"

Frankie shook his head. "Sir, I'm afraid . . . well, I don't think we can go ahead with the plan—" He looked around. "We are down to twenty-seven, twenty-six men. There's another twenty or so of them and more coming. And that front leg's past them. What do we do, sir?"

There was such a pathetic note in his voice that Merral felt a spasm of pity for him. The exercises at Tanaris had been so simple. This was reality. A situation they were unprepared for, a location away from where they were supposed to be, and an enemy that was more horrible and more numerous than they had expected.

"Zak's team?" Merral asked. "Did you see what happened to them?"

"Zak's team? Oh yeah. I think I saw them land north of the ship, sir. They were being fired on too. And there was a bay there."

"Let's hope they made it," Merral said

Frankie glanced down, saw a smear of blood and black hair on the Lamb and Stars emblem on his armor jacket, and began to rub it clean with a finger.

"Sorry, sir. I guess I look a mess, eh?" Frankie's jaw began moving up and down as if he were chewing something. Then he seemed to snap back into reality. "Sir, there are too many for us to attack."

Merral glanced back to the rest of the team, who were taking cover behind the equipment piles and enlarging depressions in the sand. "True, Frankie. Let's go for Game Plan B."

"Game Plan B, sir? What's that? I don't remember that."

"Easy, Frankie, easy," Merral said, feeling that by trying to calm Frankie he was calming himself. "You get your men to take cover by those boulders. Dig down into the sand like they are doing now, but get them as deep as they can. And use that equipment for cover. If you can keep firing and hitting one or two of them, that will help. Slowly whittle them down until we get more people here."

"Sir, is that okay?" Frankie asked, his eyes wild. "I mean we *are* supposed to take the ship. Orders."

"I know, Frankie. But they aren't going to fly away with everybody outside. Keep everybody there. If they show signs of taking off, then you can risk everything and run and attack the legs."

Frankie's eyelids flickered, then he swallowed, turned around, and began shouting instructions to the men to dig down and make defenses.

Merral looked ahead to the ship. Beyond the massive rear legs with their pipes and pistons, he glimpsed creatures running and hiding behind some of the piles of metal and camouflage sheets near the ramp. He turned his gaze to the lake, taking in the smoke still hanging over the water behind him. Where was the other sled?

Frankie nudged him. "Sir, should I call Perena and warn her?"

"Good idea. Hadn't thought of that. If there are more of those guns around the ship, she could be in trouble." He looked around. "Tell her to come in from the east and land the men on the slope above the ship. But not to approach from the lake."

"Yeah. Land on the cliff top . . . Makes sense. It'll give us some protection from an attack up there. Okay. I'll do it."

"Good," Merral answered, relieved that, in spite of being traumatized, his lieutenant showed signs of being able to think. "If these things get up top, we'll have a problem."

"Yeah, sir. Right. We don't need another attack from there."

As Frankie took out his diary and talked into it, Merral examined the ship further and wondered how he was supposed to make an entrance. The ramp itself was out of the question. It was almost a hundred meters away, and he could see dark forms edging out cautiously in front of it. It would take at least a hundred men to assault that entrance.

But was the ramp the only possible access point? Merral turned his attention to the complex lattices of discolored pistons, struts, and pipes that made up the rear legs. Stained by grease, they ran up some twenty or more meters from the great square feet and extended up inside the fuselage. On the back of the right leg was a narrow metal ladder that ran up from near the ground into fuselage wells where it was screened by some sort of hanging bay doors.

Merral decided there was a reasonable chance that it connected with the ship's interior. Anyway, there seemed no other option. He planned his actions. A short, rapid dash would bring him to a leg; once there, the leg would give him cover as he climbed, and at the top, the hanging doors would give further protection.

Frankie's voice, now slightly brighter, broke into his thoughts. "Sir, I got through. She'll be with us in fifteen minutes and will off-load the men to the east as close to the ship as she can. I guess we stay down here and wait and fire at the creatures, I suppose." He seemed to catch Merral's gaze. "Sir, you're not still going to try and get inside?"

"Yes," Merral answered. "That's what I've been told to do. Can you and the others make a distraction? get those intruders to keep their heads down?"

"Sir, if you think it's wise . . ." Frankie's expression suggested he was of another opinion.

"Wise? I'm not sure," Merral replied, aware as he spoke that someone had run up to join them from where the men were taking cover. He turned, recognizing Lorrin Venn and feeling a great relief that he was not badly injured. However his pale, fraught, and bloodstained face suggested that what was left of Lorrin's enthusiasm had died in the fighting.

"Sir," Lorrin spluttered to Frankie, revealing a torn lip and a chipped tooth, "we reckon there are men there. Under the ship. Wearing some sort of armor and with guns."

As Merral peered into the shadows at the far end of the ship, something whistled past his head. There was a dusty explosion on the cliff wall.

"Lorrin, get down!" he bellowed, ducking down below the sled.

Aware that Lorrin had remained standing, he reached up and jerked the uniformed leg. "Get down!" he repeated.

There was a further whistle and, with it, a soft splattering noise.

The leg shook violently.

Merral stared up to see Lorrin clutching his throat, blood oozing through the closed fingers. With an expression of stupefaction on his face, Lorrin sagged slowly down to his knees as if in slow motion and then collapsed forward. Merral was suddenly conscious of Lorrin's chest heaving under his armor and of Frankie gasping in horror beside him.

Treat it as a logging accident, Merral ordered himself. *Go into the automatic first-aid mode you have been trained for.*

"Lorrin," he said, his voice thick and distant as he fumbled for his medical pack on his belt, "Perena's going to be here soon." He tore the pack open, his fingers jamming against each other. *The ship has good facilities, and Felix Azhadi is a trauma-care expert.*

As he pulled out the bandage, Lorrin thrashed sideways. Merral knew that it was too late for Felix or anybody to save Lorrin now. All he could do was clutch his thrashing wrist.

An only child, Merral suddenly remembered with a deep and piercing bitterness, as Lorrin twitched and kicked his way into death.

There were more fierce whistles overhead now. Something hit the cliff and stone chips flew out in a spray of fragments around them. Behind him, Merral saw some of the remaining men frantically digging deeper into the sand with bare hands and improvised tools. Others were heaving up metal struts to give them more protection.

Frankie, his face a ghastly white, was gaping at the body. He looked at Merral. "Sir, Lorrin's dead?" he gasped, swallowing hard and blinking. "O Lord God . . . Sorry, sorry . . ."

"Yes, Frankie!" Merral said, trying to suppress both guilt and anger. "Now get back there and shoot back!" *Return fire,* the manuals had called it.

"And, Frankie, I'm going for that right rear leg and going up in from there. Tell everybody to aim for the men, not the creatures. The men are the ones with the guns. After you start shooting, I'll count to five slowly, then run." Merral was surprised at how cool his voice sounded. He looked at Frankie, wondering if his words had registered.

"Okay, sir; the right leg. A count of five. And Lorrin?"

Merral stared at the body by him, struck by the bloodied hand lying on the gray sand, its fingers wide open as if ready to receive something.

"Later. He's gone Home."

"Oh, what a mess. Sorry," Frankie muttered, his fists clenching and unclenching, and Merral glimpsed tears in his lieutenant's eyes.

"It is, Frankie. Better get back to your men. Stay low, and when I give you a signal, fire at the intruders. The men mainly."

Frankie seemed to take control of himself. "The men. Okay. Be careful, sir."

"I will be," Merral answered automatically before he realized how stupid it sounded.

He saw Frankie touch Lorrin's outstretched hand. "Sorry," he said in a tone of immense sadness. Then, bent double, he raced back to his men.

Merral stared at the ship, forcing himself to concentrate on the task ahead and not think of Lorrin next to him, dead and silent.

There were shouted orders behind him, and more whistling sounds and small explosions broke out against the cliff. Something, somewhere, clanged off a piece of metal. Merral slung the gun across his shoulder and prepared to run.

He turned and caught Frankie staring at him with an inquiring look from over a bulwark of gray metal plates, stones, and camouflage fabric.

Merral crouched into a running position and raised his thumb.

"Fire!" came the shout, and there was a jumble of hissing sounds behind him. Bitter, angry shrieks came from under the ship. Merral slowly counted to five.

He ran.

He had intended to dodge from side to side, but in the end fear drove him to run as fast and straight as he could. Ducking as low as possible, he raced across the sand, expecting at any moment to feel something hit him. He was aware of the grit under his feet and things whining and whistling past him.

A stone or a ricochet bounced off his armored jacket with a harsh clipping noise. Sand spat up around him. Something seemed to skim by his helmet, and from somewhere there was the smell of burning.

Now, though, the ship's leg was in front of him. Gasping for breath, Merral ran gratefully behind its protective bulk. But he knew he dare not stop.

Urgently, he began pulling himself up the ladder as fast as he could. He was under no illusions that the foot of the leg, midway between his men and the enemy massing around the ramp at the front of the ship, was safe.

Rung by rung, his chest heaving under his armor, Merral clambered upward, aware of the heavy gun tugging at his shoulder and the bush knife clattering against the ladder.

He was no more than a dozen rungs up when he felt the ladder vibrate sharply. He glanced down to see an ape-creature, its black hair lank and wild, climbing up after him with fluid movements of long arms. It turned its face up to him, showing bottomless dark eyes and pale flaring nostrils.

Merral redoubled his speed but, in a second, his ankle was grabbed in a ferocious and tightening grip.

Barely thinking, Merral slipped the gun off his shoulders, grasped the strap and let it drop butt first.

There was the sharp crack of metal on bone as the gun's butt struck the creature's skull. Merral heard a soft groan. The pressure on his ankle was suddenly released, and something large and heavy tumbled down, striking the ladder as it went.

There was a deep thud from the landing leg pad.

Without looking down, Merral shouldered the gun and resumed his hectic scramble upward. Weighed down by his weapon and encumbered by the stiff armored jacket and helmet, he found the climb difficult. Twice he felt his feet slide on the oil-stained rungs. Below him, and from under the ship, he could hear renewed firing and wild screaming in response. Trying to ignore it, Merral kept on climbing.

Suddenly he found himself inside the dark sanctuary of the undercarriage cavity. There, gasping for breath, he paused and listened to the shouts and noises from below. He glimpsed, far below, the still figure of the ape-creature sprawled on the sand at the foot of the ladder. It could almost have been asleep, but the pool of glistening crimson fluid around it denied that interpretation. There had been deaths all round this morning. Merral felt a spasm of pity for the creature he had slain. He wished it were all over. He glanced back to where, beyond the tilted sled and the intruder bodies, he could see his men behind the piles of metal tubing and rocks. They were feverishly scooping and pushing away sand to make their position more fortified. With their backs protected by the cliff, it seemed a reasonably secure position. If there were no further direct assaults, they might be safe until the reserves arrived.

He pulled himself up onto a narrow mesh walkway at the top of the ladder and stood up cautiously, catching his breath and looking around in the gloom. There was a strong smell of grease, and from somewhere came the humming of pumps. Panting from his exertions, he glanced around at the untidy complex of piping and cabling about him. He saw a number of labels in a red spidery script that he had never seen before. Despite the incomprehensibility and ugliness of the lettering, he was struck by what he saw, sensing that there was something about both the writing and the labels that spoke of humanity. Indeed, as he looked around, he felt that the whole structure, with its tubes, pistons, nuts, and bolts, seemed in some way, of human origin. There was nothing here, he was sure, that was alien. *Wrong* perhaps, but not alien.

Pushing such thoughts to one side, Merral concentrated on trying to enter the ship. To his relief he saw that ahead of him the gangway extended to an oval, polished, gray metal door. He approached slowly, fearful that it would be locked or that it might open to reveal attackers. He held the gun at the ready in case the door should suddenly open.

To the right of the door Merral noticed two triangular buttons. A tentative press of one of them caused the panel to slide sideways with a hissing noise. Beyond it was an ill-lit, green-painted corridor that seemed to run sideways across the vessel. As the door opened, Merral was assailed by a stale organic smell, reminiscent of old garden compost but somehow more acrid, that made him wrinkle his nose.

So, I can now enter the ship. Yet he paused.

Somehow, he was reluctant to trade the fresh air and indirect daylight of the undercarriage bay for this fetid, dark tunnel. He steeled himself to enter, but with one hand gripping the edges of the doorway, a thought suddenly struck him.

He could, he realized, simply place his charge here, trigger it, and slip back down the ladder. With this hatch blasted away or—at very least—rendered useless, the intruders would have to stay in the Farholme atmosphere. To Merral, the idea suddenly seemed a compellingly sensible proposal. It avoided the risk of his entering the ship at all. Indeed, it had the great advantage that he could be back with his men in moments. And wasn't that where he belonged? The only problem was that the envoy had ordered him to enter the ship and do battle with the creatures inside. Yet as he thought about that command, a doubt surfaced. After all, he told himself, the envoy had not stated exactly *when* he had to enter the ship. Could it be perhaps that they were to achieve surrender first?

In a second, his initial doubts had multiplied. Who really was the creature that had appeared to him earlier? In fact, was he so sure it was right to obey him? After all, did not the Scriptures say that the devil himself could appear as an angel of light? Perhaps—and the idea came to him forcibly—it was a trick to lure him to his destruction.

Anyway, even if the envoy was not some demonic phenomenon, Merral told himself that it could not be ruled out that he was merely some sort of vision, a figment of his imagination as it labored under the stresses of the day. As he reflected on the idea that the envoy was either an illusion or a demonic visitation, he became aware of an appealing corollary to such interpretations. In either case, he had no obligation to keep the unwelcome promises he had made concerning Anya and Isabella. It was an attractive idea. And yet—

Torn by uncertainty and trying to stave off a decision, Merral leaned farther inside. As he did, he caught his finger on something sharp and felt a sudden stab of pain. He snatched his hand away and sucked the gashed fingertip.

His attention painfully drawn to the door, Merral glanced around the frame, noticing that there were in fact numerous rough metal edges. He was surprised. Assembly practice was always to round and polish smooth all surfaces, whether visible or invisible. Such carelessly raw edges would never have been allowed on a finished product.

In a moment his perspective changed, and he now realized that there was something about this ship that he hated to an intense degree. Fueling that hatred was a certainty that this vessel was at the heart of the corrupting evil that had descended on his land. And as his hatred blossomed, he felt that every one of the dreadful events that had happened since Nativity had ultimately originated from this ship.

Merral suddenly became aware how strange his delay at entering the ship had been. Could it have been that he had been somehow influenced? tempted? Well, he decided, if that was the case then the attempt had failed.

With renewed determination and a new anger, Merral set the cutter gun beam on wide focus and checked that the status light was on red.

Then with a brief prayer and a final glance at the ground far below, he entered the ship.

CHAPTER 21

The moment Merral set foot in the intruder ship he felt that something had changed. It was as if he had left his own world and passed into another—one that was strange and unfriendly. He found it impossible to define why he felt that this was so. The interior of the ship was dark and foul smelling, and there were strange noises, but it was more than that. He was aware that there was something else: something too subtle to be instantly pinned down, but something that was wrong.

His hands clenched on the gun, Merral stood still, looking cautiously around. The dully lit corridor stretched to either side of him, with metal ribs protruding out along each wall and casting deep shadows on the floor. At each end the corridor appeared to join larger longitudinal passageways that ran along each side of the ship. The corridors were higher than he had expected, as if made for giants. Or, he thought darkly, monsters.

Nothing moved. He took another step forward. With a hiss, the door closed behind him. The light and distant sounds of the outside world abruptly vanished.

Merral was suddenly aware of being isolated—more isolated than he had ever been in his life. Struggling to suppress an invading fear, he listened carefully, trying to make sense of the noises that he could hear from within the ship. Some of the noises were mechanical: a faint electrical hum, the sloshing of fluid in pipes, a distant vibration from some pump. Yet there were also other noises less easy to assign an origin to. There was a soft, high-pitched chatter, like that of far-off animals in a zoo, and a low, irregular, insectlike chirping whose source was impossible to locate.

There was a chillness to the ship, an odd, clammy coldness, different from the fresh cold of a Farholme winter. There was something about this austere green corridor and this bleak ship that seemed to speak to Merral of wild, deep, and hostile space. He felt the hairs on the back of his neck rise, and for a moment, he shivered uncontrollably.

"Okay, now which way do I go?" he asked quietly, his voice echoing in the stillness. He realized that he expected no answer.

"Go right, Man."

The voice was just there. Clear, audible, and unmistakably the same voice he had heard on the other side of the lake. Merral looked around, trying in vain to find the source of the voice. Against one of the bracing girders ahead of him was a deeper shadow that he was sure had not been there a moment earlier.

"So you *are* here."

"Man, the King's servants keep their promises," the strangely flat voice said, and Merral sensed the hint of a rebuke. Yet despite it, Merral felt curiously relieved at hearing the envoy's voice.

Then, catching a glimpse of Lorrin's blood, still wet on his sleeve, Merral turned to the shadow. "Lorrin Venn's dead!" he said, and he could hear the bitterness in his voice. "The others are at risk."

"I know. They are my concern too," the voice stated. "Yet evil must be fought, and battles cost. If you want to serve your men and their families best, do what I say. Lorrin played his part and is safe in the Father's house. You are not yet there and there is much to do. This is a most dark and perilous place, and there are many dangers. As you have just found."

"Yes," Merral answered, disturbed but somehow not surprised that the envoy knew of his hesitation.

"Now go right." The tone did not allow for argument.

"Envoy," Merral said, "can you go ahead first?"

"Man, do you not understand?" The voice was sharp. "This is your race's war."

"I see. But I thought you had the power."

"Power has nothing to do with it, Man. It is what is right. Only those that are human can fight for humanity. Even the High King bowed to that law. Or have you forgotten what you learned about the Nativity?"

"I see. I just hadn't seen this as the same. . . ."

"Man, I can only advise you. Am *I* human? Now go right."

The urgency in the voice was such that Merral instantly started right along the corridor.

As he padded along the floor, Merral glanced around constantly, trying to take in his surroundings. The contrast with the *Heinrich Schütz* could not have been more marked. That had been an artistic masterpiece of light and smoothness; this, he sensed, was a coarse, even brutal, assembly of parts.

He had now come to the passageway. Here he stopped and peered cautiously around the corner. As he had suspected, it was a major corridor and seemed to run the entire length of the vessel. It too seemed to be deserted. He listened, aware of a strange, twisting soft breeze that moved around him as if there were pulses of air in the corridor.

"To the front of the ship," came the order.

Merral was suddenly struck by the way that the voice sounded exactly the same here as it had out by the lake. It was as if it was unaffected by the local acoustics. Perena had described how the words of the envoy sounded as if they had been "pressed out of the air." Now he understood her description.

Merral turned left toward the nose of the ship and began moving along the corridor as rapidly and quietly as he could. The light was all wrong: it was not just dull; it was as if it was somehow drained of energy. He thought longingly of sunlight.

In this part of the ship, the outer fuselage was supported by large protruding girders, and feeling that they might provide him some cover, he walked close to them. A hasty glance over his shoulder gave him the impression that a dark shadow glided along after him in the dark margins of the corridor.

Merral, his nerves on edge, was aware of new noises in the ship: a distant clattering, muffled thudding sounds from below, a high-pitched scratching somewhere. A small, eddying spiral of dust flickered around on the floor ahead of him. Despite the coolness in the air, Merral realized that he was sweating profusely.

As he moved down the long, dark passageway, staring nervously into the shadows, his initial impressions about the ship hardened. In addition to the crude, rather unfinished workmanship that was all around, nothing seemed to be as neat as on an Assembly ship. In one place, an indecipherable label seemed to have been slapped on the wall in such a hurry that it was not horizontal. In another place, a panel had been put back so carelessly that a bolt head still protruded. He passed a crumpled fragment of plastic on the floor and the Ancient English word *litter* came to mind. He had a growing feeling too that there was something fundamentally wrong about the whole way the ship was constructed. On Assembly ships, the framework and supporting structures were always hidden. Here they were standing visible. It was almost as if the designers hadn't cared how things looked.

Midway down the corridor Merral stopped, suddenly struck by a new phenomenon. At his feet the metal floor had clearly been badly damaged and then patched up. The job had been done in such a rough and untidy manner that he could feel the join through his boots. He saw that the hull skin and the roof were heavily scarred; through the uneven paint, the sheen of bare metal could be seen in places. Something traumatic had happened here, and sensing it might be important, Merral wondered what. He glanced at a girder nearby to see that fine silver globules were speckled on its surface. Gingerly, mindful of the sharp surfaces, he ran a finger along a raised edge, pulled it away and looked at it. A number of tiny, perfect, shining metal spheres were stuck to it. Rolling them between his fingers, he puzzled briefly over what they meant. Merral walked on a few more steps and paused. Just ahead of him, he heard a fragile metallic tapping sound, like the noise of a tiny hammer striking pipes.

A little more than a meter beyond him something moved. Two gray tendrils, like enormously elongated fingers, crept round a wall strut at the height of his head.

He froze as a dull metal egg-shaped structure, perhaps a meter long, followed after the fingers. Its surface was made up of dozens of facets, almost as if it was some strange crystalline growth.

Merral felt he was being stared at. He raised his gun.

"Wait!" came the sharp command from the envoy, and Merral eased his finger a fraction away from the trigger.

Suddenly the egg-shaped body seemed to rotate on its fingers and, in a fluid, precise movement, swung down two impossibly long legs behind it onto the floor. Then, letting go with the front limbs, it dropped free. With delicate and economic movements of its four extraordinary limbs, the thing moved to the center of the corridor in front of him.

There it rose up so that the body was at the level of Merral's face. *A mechanical insect*, Merral thought, before realizing that the four legs, nowhere larger than a child's wrist, were without visible joints or segments. Indeed, they seemed to have both the suppleness of tentacles and the rigidity of limbs.

The machine—Merral had not the slightest doubt that it was a machine rather than a living thing—moved closer to him with smooth, impeccably coordinated leg movements.

Merral stared at it, trying, through his fear, to make sense of something so totally unfamiliar. As he looked at it, he saw that high on a front facet were two small, glassy black circles that stared at him. The machine bobbed and swayed as if trying to get a thorough look at his face.

As it did, Merral realized, with a further strange assurance, that what he faced was not simply a remote surveillance machine but something with an intelligence of its own. He stared back at it, now able to make out details on the body panels. There was an array of small green lights on one surface, a series of sockets along another, and fine lettering on a third.

The machine spoke, but Merral could make no sense of the jagged syllables. He knew, though, that they were words rather than noise.

"The machine says it doesn't recognize you. It wants your

identity." The envoy's steady voice seemed to come from just over his shoulder.

"What do I do?" Merral whispered back, wondering how you dealt with an intelligent and probably hostile machine, barely an arm's length away from your face. *We should have predicted this,* he told himself with a spasm of recrimination. *We knew the intruders had worked without restrictions. We should have guessed that they would have ignored the notoriously complex Technology Protocol Two about creating autonomous sentient machines.*

"Man, show it the identity disc you bear," said the envoy.

"But the disc isn't mine. We don't have them."

The machine swung its head as if it was trying to find out who he was talking to.

"Do it!"

Merral found the chain around his neck and, jerking it out, held the disc firmly up in front of the machine.

A panel flicked down on the underside of the body, and a tendril, as fine as a man's little finger, uncoiled smoothly out and extended to just in front of Merral's chest. Four delicate digits flowered on its end and grasped the disc with a gentle firmness.

The machine seemed to stare at what it held. "Lucas Hannun Ringell," it pronounced in slow tones. Then, after a moment's hesitation, it carefully enunciated the date of birth, "Three *dash* three *dash* twenty eighty-two."

There was a pause, as if it was thinking or consulting with something.

Suddenly the digits released the disc. The limb whisked back inside the body and the machine stepped back sharply with a simultaneous movement of all four legs.

"*Captain* Lucas Hannun Ringell?" it said, and there was no mistaking the note of questioning in the voice.

Along the length of the corridor, bright red lights began to pulse and a wailing siren sounded.

"Now shoot it," said the envoy.

Merral aimed at the body and squeezed the trigger. There was a brief cherry red glow on an underside plate, and a puff of smoke belched out. A flurry of thin, pale gray shards whistled outwards, clattering against the walls and floor. Fragments of metallic and plastic circuitry popped out. Amid thrashing limbs, the creature banged against the wall and crashed to the ground.

"Sorry," Merral muttered, wondering if he should apologize to intelligent machines. Then, stepping carefully over a still-flicking leg, he moved on down the corridor. He began to stride quickly forward. There was no point in stealth now; the alarm had been triggered, and the next machines or creatures he met would know that he was hostile.

"I should have shot it first," he protested. "The alarms have been sounded."

"No. The ship's defense systems think that Lucas Ringell is loose on the ship. They will divert forces to deal with this most serious threat."

"You mean," Merral spluttered, "you *want* them to come after me?"

"It is necessary. Your men cannot handle the Krallen pack they now face."

"The *what?*" asked Merral, struck by the menacing sound of the term *Krallen pack*.

"You will find out."

"Thanks," Merral said, recognizing in some distant and neutral part of his mind that he was being sarcastic. "I hope you can handle them. But—another thing—how can they imagine Lucas Ringell to be here? They must know that he died millennia ago."

"They think you are like them," the voice said but did not elaborate.

Suddenly the lights flickered, and Merral heard a faint click from his gun. He glanced down to see that there was no status light of any sort on. He stopped, tapping the various switches. But no light turned on. It was as if all the power had vanished from the machine; his weapon was dead.

"My gun's malfunction—," Merral began and stopped, jarred by the realization that the status light on his diary had gone off as well.

The indefinable shadow spoke. "The being at the heart of this ship has power over such things. Shoulder your gun; you may need it later. Move on."

Despite feeling a need to protest, Merral did as he was told. He found his knife, grasped the handle firmly, pointed it away from him, and pressed the release button. With a smooth click, the meter-long, dull gray blade extended. He pressed the retract button, and the blade hissed back into the handle. *At least my knife works.* The idea gave him little reassurance.

He strode on down the corridor. Suddenly he heard distant noises from ahead of him. A cold chill swept over him as he realized that the sounds were getting louder and nearer. The growing noises were matched by the rising vibrations he could feel in the floor. In an instant, Merral had a terrifying vision of something—no, many things—bounding up stairs and along corridors as they raced toward him. He looked around for somewhere to hide.

In seconds, the noise was clear enough for him to make out that it was made up of a collection of strange whistles, hoots, and the clattering of many feet. *The Krallen pack,* he thought, and considered turning and running back the way he had come.

"W-what do I do?" he said.

"Stand still against the wall and say nothing," said the voice close behind him.

Merral turned around to try and see the envoy, but all he could see was a tall, oddly vague blackness behind him. It was as if the envoy existed on some plane that was either too close or too far away for his eyes to focus on.

The noises became louder and the floor rang. Trembling with fright, Merral pressed himself behind a protruding girder on the inner side of the corridor. Resisting the temptation to close his eyes, he peered forward down the corridor.

The lights at the far end were suddenly obscured, and in a second, the passageway was filled with strange gray, athletic creatures racing toward him, some bounding along the floor, others—no less fast—swinging along the roof, whistling and hooting to each other.

Merral's first terrified impressions were of four-legged creatures the size of the very largest dogs but with very un-doglike legs. A pack indeed, he thought, like hounds or wolves. Suddenly, just as the leading creatures were barely a few meters away, Merral sensed the shadow on the edge of his vision moving, and he had the impression of an arm being thrown up above and in front of him. He blinked; he could still see, but everything before him was hazy, as if some gauze sheet now hung in front of his eyes.

"I will hide you," the envoy said. "You are not ready to face these things."

Merral had a sudden vision of himself standing pale faced and wide eyed behind a wing of the envoy's cloak.

With astonishing speed, the pack came to an abrupt halt just in front of Merral. Conscious of his frantically pounding heart, Merral stared at the things that confronted him. There were ten—no, more—a dozen of them. The overriding impression he had was of an overwhelming, intelligent, and disciplined hostility. *These Krallen are not dogs*, he told himself, *they are way beyond that: there is intelligence here—coordination and language.*

Indeed, they didn't really look like dogs. They were too big—they stood chest high to Merral—and their tails were short, muscular, and passed smoothly into their bodies. The limbs were striking, apparently having something of an apelike flexibility, so that the three creatures hanging from the ceiling seemed no less at ease than those standing on the ground. In fact, as Merral stared at them, he decided he wasn't even sure that they were mammals. There was a cold, almost reptilian air to their actions, and their gray skin was hairless and thick. Their heads were roughly triangular, both in cross section and profile, widening to the rear and the bottom. Two small, dark eyes were inset in the upper part of the face and were protected by prominent ridges above and below them. The lower part of the head was dominated by a strong-jawed mouth.

As Merral watched, he saw their heads moving this way and that as if scanning every square centimeter of the corridor for the slightest trace of him. The whistling and hooting they made through half-open mouths kept changing pitch and tone, and Merral sensed that they were sharing puzzlement. His eye was caught by one, which had a wide black depression along its flank as if some flaming object had struck it. He found himself puzzling over why there was no blood and why the creature seemed to be unaffected by such a major wound.

At he stared at it, the nearest Krallen moved closer. It stopped and extended a forelimb, waving it slowly this way and that as if cautiously checking to see if there was something invisible before it. As it did so, Merral was suddenly struck by the feet—or were they hands? They had five big, fingerlike digits, three facing forward and two facing back, and as he watched, Merral saw sharp silvery blades extend from the fingers. *Like a cat,* he thought but checked himself when he realized that not even a lion had claws this long or this sharp. It was strange too how metallic they looked. It opened its jaws and Merral saw, with a strange lack of surprise, that its mouth was filled with sharp, knifelike silver teeth. Hadn't Anya warned of the possibility of designed predators? Surely, Merral decided, these were they.

Seemingly baffled by Merral's disappearance, the creature stopped still and seemed to stare at or through him. Then it spoke—and Merral was in no doubt that the whistles were words—and suddenly two Krallen sprang forward—they were surprisingly light on their feet—and bounded down the corridor in an oddly regimented action. Perhaps ten meters away, they spun round in a perfectly coordinated maneuver and, with their noses to the ground, began to sniff their way toward him.

As Merral watched, horror-struck, peculiarities registered. There was a precise smoothness to the way the Krallen moved that puzzled him. There were curiously regular features on the skin at the shoulders and wrists that almost looked like sockets or mounting brackets. And

Merral was certain that there was something else about them that was odd, something that was very obvious. But he couldn't identify what it was.

What are these things? he wondered in a mixture of terror and perplexity as the two creatures came to within a handbreadth of his feet and began to look up at him with their cold eyes.

Yet as they moved their heads toward him, Merral became aware of the envoy reaching out his hand—he felt he could make out faint fingers—and gently touching the nearest creature on the back of the head.

"*Az izara hamalaraka,*" the envoy said in a soothing tone, and the strange words seem to vibrate quietly in the air. Merral sensed that it was an order.

The Krallen that he was touching gave a slight shudder and uttered a long, descending whistling note. As if it was a mechanical device, it smoothly bent its knees and lowered its head so that it crouched low on the floor. As if some sort of contagion was spreading through the pack, one by one the others followed suit. The three creatures hanging from the roof sprung lightly down to the floor and did the same. Then, as if it was part of a carefully choreographed routine, the strange eyelids on the beasts simultaneously closed shut.

With an astonishing sense of relief, Merral stared at the twelve identical forms lying still on the floor in total silence.

"What did you say?" Merral asked.

"You could translate it as 'go into system shutdown mode.'"

"Oh."

"Forward," said the envoy and seemed to drop his hand. The haze that had been in front of Merral suddenly cleared.

Merral remembered something. "Daniel . . . , " he said. "Didn't God send his angel and shut the mouths of the lions for Daniel?"

"There are precedents. But lions are easier."

Merral stepped forward, gingerly tiptoeing between the still forms. He glanced down, noticing for the first time that the gray skin of the creatures was finely scored so it looked as if was made up of numerous straight-edged patches. *Like tiles*. He noticed another one that had a marked but bloodless gash on it.

"Are they dead?"

"They were never alive."

"What do you mean?" Struck by a thought, Merral glanced back at the others. *Yes, how very odd; they're all identical.*

"They are not animals," the envoy said.

"They aren't?"

"They are made beings. Synthetic creatures. Made of artificial bone and tissue."

Of course, Merral thought with a flood of realization, *that's what was odd about them: they weren't breathing. They had been running and weren't panting.*

"But why?"

"Why make them, you mean? Their makers wanted things that had none of the weaknesses of flesh and blood. The Krallen are stronger than any animal, they are hard to destroy, and they never sleep or tire. A Krallen pack would run across Menaya before it even slowed down."

Merral saw that they had come to some stairs.

"Are there more—"

"Enough! Now ascend, up to the next level. There is much to do."

Merral looked up and down the stairway, realizing that it must go up vertically through most of the ship. The siren was still blaring, and he could hear far-off, angry noises, but there were no noises from nearby.

"Very well," Merral answered, and he began climbing the stairs, keeping close to the wall, aware that close behind him something followed him. Somehow he found the envoy less alarming now. There was still something disconcerting about him, but in this hostile ship he seemed to be almost a friend.

Near the top of the next flight of stairs, Merral stopped and peered carefully over the top of the final step. Another lateral corridor stretched out before him. It was empty. He moved forward along it, hoping that if he was going to meet any opponents, the envoy would protect him again. Against the likes of things such as these Krallen, Merral felt his bush knife would be of little use.

Nearly midway along the corridor, he passed a wide doorway to his right. From the presence of a button pad at its side, he decided that it was an elevator. Next to it and aligned, as far as Merral could determine, with the central axis of the ship, was a large and strangely ornate alcove. He looked at it and saw that it had been blackened, as if a fire had been lit in it. In it was a strange statue made out of a dark gleaming metal.

Merral stepped toward it, realizing as he looked at it that it was a large cast of a human head. Or rather, it had been. Something had happened to make it melt, flow, and drip so that the original features of the face were now impossible to determine. Yet as he looked at the marred sculpture, Merral felt certain that it had been intended to portray strength, power, and authority. For a second, he wondered how such a mishap had happened, before he realized with a shock of identification that the damage might not have been accidental. Indeed, as he gazed at the sculpture, he felt suddenly certain that someone had willfully blasted the bust with some sort of weapon.

Puzzled, Merral stood back and saw, below the recess, an engraved label. The top line of writing was in the unattractive cursive script that he had seen earlier. Here it had been defaced, scored through several times by a knife so that even if he could have understood the letters, he would have struggled to read it. *They have tried to disfigure it,* he thought, puzzling over the oddness of the concept. Then his eye was caught by a second line of text below it, which had escaped damage. It was in a different, more familiar script, and Merral gasped as he realized that it was written in Communal.

"*Zhalatoc, Great Prince of the Lord-Emperor Nezhuala's Dominion.*" He spoke the words aloud, feeling as he did that the strangely discordant names seemed to linger in the air.

He turned, trying—and failing yet again—to focus on the envoy. "What does this mean?" he asked.

"Everything. And, for the moment, nothing. Your business lies within the chamber."

Merral turned and looked at the entrance doorway on the other side of the corridor. What new horrors lay beyond? He walked over to it, noticing an odd-shaped handle and a notice to the right of the door. The first three lines of the notice were in the ugly, wiry red font that he had seen before. Yet below it was a three-line inscription written with a neat electric blue script in Communal. Merral read the words.

Warning!

STEERSMAN CHAMBER

Out of Bounds!

Merral frowned. Although the individual words made sense, the overall meaning eluded him completely. Warning, he understood, but what was a *Steersman? Chamber* was plain, reminding him of Jorgio's ominous caution, but what the last three-word phrase meant was utterly beyond him. As Merral stared at the writing, he felt certain that the odd way the letters were shaped and spaced was one that he associated with the earliest period of the Assembly.

"And what does this mean?" he asked aloud.

"You will learn. But you must go on. Open the door."

Merral turned to the door and grabbed the handle. He hesitated for a second and then tugged at it.

As the handle rotated down, the door beside it slid quietly sideways to reveal a small but high compartment illuminated with a dull green light. Apart from another door on the opposite side, it was empty and featureless. *It's an airlock,* Merral thought.

"Leave your gun here. It will only hinder you."

Merral hesitated for a second and then slipped the useless gun off his shoulder and placed it against the wall as, with a hiss, the door slid closed behind him. His fingers moved toward the bush knife on his belt as he tried to hold back a feeling of panic and oppression.

"Now go through the next door. But remember, there is more than one danger in this place."

Merral walked to the door facing him and grasped the handle beside it.

"Okay," he said, his voice shaking. "Let's get this over with."

CHAPTER 22

The door opened vertically. It had lifted only a fraction before Merral saw a mist seep out from the chamber and felt cold air round his ankles. With the chilled air came a dreadful smell. The whole ship smelled, but this was something stronger: a putrid, rancid combination of a hundred separate odors of death and decay. It was so overwhelming that, for a moment, Merral wondered if the air was breathable.

As the door opened fully and the mist swirled around his legs, he looked around, feeling every muscle tensed for action. He stood at the edge of a large and gloomy chamber. Although the chamber was surprisingly high, wide, and long, it was crowded. Poking through the mist, like islands in some sea, was a scattered miscellany of dark structures—pillars, columns, and slabs—some rising to more than his height. Around the sides of the chamber, numerous fittings—perhaps cabinets or lockers—rose up to the roof, where large beams spanned the ceiling like the ribs of some gargantuan animal. The only lighting came from a dozen or so small, spherical lights of different sizes, ranging in color from orange to an icy blue, that were apparently randomly arranged below the roof. The combination of these strange lights, which seemed to be floating in space, the numerous structures, and the mist made the gloom of the chamber uneven, giving pools of inky shadow and patches of gray twilight. There were sounds too: a soft rattling and chattering, and Merral felt certain that, beyond the range of his hearing, there were other noises. In these sounds, he sensed a strangely tense and expectant tone.

I am awaited.

Shivering from cold and fear, Merral looked around urgently, sensing that he was being watched and aware that any one of a hundred places in this dreadful room could conceal peril. There was far more to this chamber than what he could see, feel, and touch. The darkness was not just the absence of physical light; it was an icy shadow that seemed to cloud his mind. He tried to think of Ynysmant, his family, Anya, and sunlight and open fields and woods, but here they were all distant memories, faint and muted. *Light and life have faded here.* He shuddered.

"Where am I?" he asked aloud and he heard his voice tremble. "Where have I come to?"

The voice behind him spoke slowly. "You have come to the edge of your world and to the entrance of that realm where the light does not come. Now go forward."

Merral took a step forward, and as he did, he crunched something underfoot. He glanced down, kicking with his feet to try and clear the mist, glimpsing white and gray fragments on the floor.

"It's dirty," he said under his breath and stepped forward again, wading through the mist as if he were fording a stream.

Merral saw before him a wide passageway that ran between some of the structures to the center of the chamber. There was more light there, and he could make out a short, strange column rising up out of the vapor. Beyond it was a series of steps that led up to a platform on which there was a seat.

Something sat on the seat; something that he wanted to look away from; something that instead dragged his unwilling eyes toward it. It was tall and thin and had the color of a dead leaf. Its form was human, but as Merral stared at it, he saw it move and knew, with a sure stab of dread, that it was not human. As he gazed reluctantly at the thing at the heart of the chamber, he saw it slowly raise a gaunt brown arm and make some sort of gesture. A command, he realized.

"Be careful," warned the voice behind him.

From somewhere ahead there came the faintest of noises: a soft, rhythmic, swishing sound. Suddenly, in an agony of fear, Merral saw something moving through the vapor toward him from the center of the room. A thing that moved in an unhurried way with a slow rippling of wide wings that caused the vapor to flow off its dark back.

Merral spun round, looking for somewhere to flee.

"Stand firm," came the order.

Merral turned back to face the oncoming creature, realizing through his fear that he faced the same being that had attacked Felicity. Behind the wide wings he could make out a long tail swinging from side to side.

Wanting to run but knowing that he had to stand his ground, Merral pressed the button on the bush knife and the blade shot out. *The teeth are on the underside,* he reminded himself, trying to work out the implications for defending himself.

The thing came closer.

Guided more by instinct than reason, Merral grasped the bush knife's handle firmly in both hands and swung the blade high above his head.

The creature slowed down until it was barely moving, suspended in the midst of the vapor as if it were treading water.

It's planning its attack. I must let it get close, but not too close. And I must strike at just the right moment.

Perhaps two paces away, the sheet-dragon came to a dead stop. Then the wings began to beat slightly faster and the broad front of the creature bent slowly upward so its front edge rose up out of the vapor.

A widely spaced pair of dark beady eyes seemed to survey him. He tensed, barely breathing, and considered stepping forward and striking the creature but held back. The eyes continued their cold gaze and on the upturned tip of the underside he could make out the start of the bleached slit of the long mouth. As the creature bobbed up and down, he could see—just below the vapor's surface—the first pair of clawlike limbs around the mouth.

Suddenly there was movement. The head turned to the right and the beast swung its body around, a triangular wing tilting high up out of the mist as it banked.

It was leaving.

As the dragon turned away, the long tail swinging leisurely round after it, Merral relaxed his muscles. He lowered the blade and began to breathe again.

The tail lashed out.

Merral felt something wrap itself round his knees. He was tugged forward and tumbled into the cold mist. As he fell, the blade flew out of his grasp.

The dragon's body rose up high into the air with surprising speed, twisting as it came up so that the long, pulsing crevasse of the mouth faced him. As he plunged under the cold vapor, it crashed down toward him.

As he hit the floor, Merral rolled to one side. Instinct—or panic—took over, and he scrabbled desperately to his feet just as a great wing lashed down past him, glancing off a shoulder. As it did, the vapor was thrust aside and he saw the blade lying at his feet. He bent down and snatched it. As his fingers closed round the handle, he looked up.

And froze rigid.

An arm's length ahead of him, lifted up by rapidly beating wings, the creature was rearing up vertically out of the vapor. It rose until it hung there, spread out like some monstrous kite, a mere pace away from him. Still bent over, Merral could feel the air from the beating wings brushing past him, was aware of the long tail hanging down into the vapor, the buttonlike eyes staring at him, and—above all—the obscene, wet, vertical slit of a mouth suspended just in front of his face with the eight pairs of claws around it scrabbling in frantic anticipation.

Frozen rigid by terror, he realized that, at any moment, the creature would slide forward and the mouth would be upon him. A part of his brain that had somehow resisted being immobilized by fear told him that, under the vapor, his right hand was holding his bush knife. And another part told him that the creature hadn't realized it.

There was a whisper in his mind: *If I can move fast enough and if my limbs work, I might have the advantage of surprise*. The creature gave an extra little flick of its wings and, as if about to embrace Merral, moved closer.

The mouth gaped wider.

Now.

Merral bounded upright, swung the blade high, and with all the force he could find, chopped downward.

"The Lamb!" he cried.

The blade struck the creature midway between the eyes and kept going, cutting down into the flesh. Merral reeled back under the impact, tearing the blade free.

The creature, nearly bisected by the blow, flopped down into the mist where it thrashed helplessly from side to side.

"And *that*," said Merral in a loud but trembling voice, "was for Felicity." He was surprised at the bitterness in the words.

On the floor, the convulsions of the creature slowly died away, and the mist rolled back over the bloodless corpse.

"Well struck," said the envoy's voice, "but beware the desire for revenge. It has betrayed others. It may betray you."

"Point taken," Merral said, wiping his brow. "But I have a soft spot for horses."

There was a moment's silence. "Continue," said the envoy, as if passing over some matter. "There is still work to do. That column in the center must be destroyed."

"As you say," Merral answered, reluctantly facing the fact that he had yet to deal with whatever lay in the center of this ghastly chamber. He looked around it, hoping that this was the only such creature. As he did, the strange array of lights suspended from the ceiling caught his attention. They reminded him of something—but what? One pair of lights close together made him think of a binary star system.

Suddenly, he realized what the lights were.

"They are stars!" he said aloud. The central light was Alahir; the others were the adjacent stars. Suddenly, the chamber made sense.

"Of course," he said. "A steersman steers. This is a map. They navigate Below-Space."

"Just so," said the envoy. "A useful service, but one that comes at a price."

Merral walked slowly forward between the gray line of structures. What were they? Cupboards, lockers, consoles? He did not want to know what was inside them. Suddenly, out of the corner of his eye, he saw something pinned to a vertical surface. He stopped. It was a dead kestrel, its brown wings pinned out wide as if it had been crucified. Hanging next to it was a half-completed silver filigree frame that matched the bird's body.

Merral nodded in recognition. It seemed years since he and Vero had encountered the dead bird spying on them at Carson's Sill, but the discovery that such a monstrosity had been begotten here was so unsurprising as to be inevitable.

He walked on, the mist swirling around his legs, his footsteps echoing dully in the heavy silence. He was reluctant to even glance at what was ahead. Finally, aware that he was nearly at the strange column and that he had to face what lay beyond it, he lifted his eyes up.

Immediately ahead of him, now perhaps only five paces away, the column poked up out of the vapor. This close to it, Merral could see that it was different than the other structures in the room. Its multisided surfaces were neither dull nor dirty but had an odd gleam to them, as if the structure was made of some polished metal. The column was chest height, and immediately above it, the air seemed to shimmer and twist as if some strange energy flowed through it.

Keeping his eyes fixed on the column, Merral stepped forward again. It had six sides, he saw. Was it a sort of Gate? And if so, where did it lead? He could see too that the column had patterns engraved upon it, extraordinary loops and spirals that, when you looked at them, had an oddly unsettling effect. That this was indeed the source of some awesome and dread power seemed plain.

"Envoy," he asked, "is this science or magic?"

"Both," came the flat answer, "there are depths—and heights—

where they merge. But your task is to destroy it." A faint noise came from beyond the column, and at last Merral summoned the courage to look at the seat and the form the color of dead leaves that sat on it.

Barely a dozen paces away, the large figure with elongated and twisted limbs and a misshapen head with empty eye sockets watched him.

A steersman.

Merral was struck by two successive and contrary impressions: The first was that the steersman was extraordinarily insubstantial. What stared at him from the seat was no more than a dry and hollow husk, something with no more solidity than the discarded carapace of some great insect.

The second impression was very different. Suddenly Merral sensed that he stood before a being of extraordinary age. The creature had seen mountains and even worlds form. And with that age came power and authority. He knew too that the being before him was a mighty king seated on a throne. As that thought came into his mind, Merral noticed that the monstrous head wore a small metal crown. In an instant, his first impression was overturned. It was he, not the steersman, who was ephemeral, and insubstantial. *It is I who am dust.* He trembled.

In that moment of vulnerability, Merral was suddenly aware of the envoy speaking from behind him. "It lies. Go forward in the name of the Lamb and do what must be done. Go."

Reassured, Merral took three steps forward. He closed the bush knife, clipped it back on his belt, and reached for the explosive charge.

As he touched it, he became aware of the steersman moving in its seat, bending forward with stiff limbs, as if turning to stare at him. As if he had opened a door into the face of a winter's gale, a bitter torrent of malice suddenly poured over him.

Overwhelmed, Merral stepped back.

"Man, do not be afraid," the envoy's voice said. "It can do you no harm unless you let it. Trust in him who is the Lord of all realms. Go forward. Plant the charge on the column and trigger it."

"I'll try," Merral said, finding words difficult and taking two steps forward. Another step and the column would be within reach.

Suddenly he was aware of the steersman rising stiffly from its seat like some monstrous, desiccated insect. With a lurching, brittle motion, the thing walked to the column.

Merral stared at the creature that faced him. The face, long and impossibly narrow, seemed paper-thin, and the eye sockets were spaces in which motes of cold dust circulated. In an instant, Merral's contrary impressions resolved themselves. The steersman had both power *and* emptiness: indeed, its very power lay in the emptiness. It was the being that emptied things of life and light and drained all that was good out of them.

Merral tried to suppress his terror. *I must do what I have to do.*

The steersman moved its fingers, and the sound was like the rustling of dead leaves. Without warning, the creature spoke into his mind.

Ringell . . . Ringell . . . they brought you back?

The words were as clear as if they had been spoken, but he knew the jaws of the steersman had not moved.

Merral said nothing but slipped the explosive charge off his belt and felt for the protective wrapping on its back. *I have a task to do, a part to play.*

But you are not Ringell, are you? I was misled.

Forcing himself to concentrate, Merral tore off the wrapping on the red package so the adhesive patch faced toward the column surface. There seemed to be a battle going on in his mind. Light and darkness strove against each other like the interplay of sunlight and shadows as clouds raced over a field. One second, Merral wanted to flee, and the next his desire was to complete his task.

I am the king, said the voice in his mind. *Stop! Obey me!*

"No, you're not," Merral said aloud. "The Assembly stands and her Lord reigns."

Fool! Both the Assembly and her King have forsaken you. I am your king now. Leave while you can.

"Go away," Merral said aloud. "I have a task to do, a part to play."

He pressed the charge against the column, feeling a slight and tingling vibration under his fingertips as the inter-molecular cement bonded. Three seconds would do it.

One, two, three.

Stop! You cannot win! Your isolation is over; the breach in the barrier remains. There will be others who will come in vast ships of unimaginable power. And we will come with them.

"I have a task to do, a part to play," Merral repeated. His stumbling fingers found the protective film over the trigger and he tore it off.

One by one your cozy little worlds will fall. Like leaves in autumn. We will start with Farholme.

Merral found the safety pin, pulled it out, and threw it away into the chill mist at his feet.

We will strip the flesh from your people, turn them against each other, and damn their little souls.

Merral's fingers looped around the firing cord. The words sang in his mind: *I have a task to do, a part to play.*

We will win. We are your inheritors. The uniting of the realms will take place. The end of the Assembly has come.

A task to do, a part to play . . .

Merral pulled the cord.

Nothing happened, and he stared dully at the package, expecting at least some flashing light to tell him the fuse had been ignited.

It's a chemical fuse. He turned and started to run back to the door of the chamber the way he had come. *A sixty-second fuse . . . I should have counted.*

As he raced to the door, the mist parted around him. It seemed thinner now.

The dragon must be just ahead of me. He ran to one side to avoid treading on the body.

Nearly there. Merral glimpsed the tail in the mist at his feet. He stepped over it.

"Look out!" the envoy shouted.

The tail lashed out and snagged his ankle. Merral stumbled and lurched painfully into the nearest structure. He slid to the ground.

Stunned, he lay there for a second before he realized his danger. *I must get up.* He pulled his foot free and staggered back to his feet.

He ran on and lunged through the open doorway into the compartment. He turned, tore at the handle with clumsy fingers, and swung it upward. As the door began sliding down, Merral collapsed backward against the wall and slithered down to the floor.

With what seemed an appalling slowness, the door moved down.

"Come on!" he shouted.

The door began to seat itself into the slot in the floor.

A dazzling flash of white lightning shot under it.

There was a stunning clap of noise, and the whole ship seemed to vibrate. Merral felt things strike the compartment door and slide down. The lights failed and then with a few blinks came back on again.

As the echoes of the blast died away, he rose to his feet. His ears were ringing; he was shivering with cold and ached all over.

"You should have come back well away from the winged creature," said the envoy. Merral tried one more time to see him, but as ever, he was no more than a shadow on the periphery of his vision. *Like an optical illusion: present, but not present.*

"Yes," Merral admitted. "I assumed it was dead."

"It was, but beings such as your enemy can manipulate the dead."

"I see."

"Now, you have one last task."

For a moment, Merral wondered whether to refuse. As he hesitated, he noticed that on his gun the status light now glowed green. He glanced at his belt and saw that his diary was working.

"Okay," he said, aware of the weariness in his voice. "What do I have to do now?"

"You must return and slay the being. Even that blast only stunned it and stripped its body of its protection. Unless you destroy it, it will soon pass into an invisible spirit form. You must use your knife. But be careful."

Merral closed his eyes. *I have come so far. I suppose I must go on.* "Very well," he said.

Once more, he found the door handle and pulled down.

CHAPTER 23

With a series of creaks, the door slid open slowly, letting in a wreath of hot, foul smoke.

Waving his arms to try and dispel the fumes, Merral stepped carefully over the wreckage by the door. He was surprised to find that the chamber was now much better illuminated; the strange lights had gone, and along either side of the roof, strip lights had now come on. The mist had fled and the temperature seemed warmer.

The chamber had been devastated. Almost all the structures in the room had been badly damaged. Paneling hung from the walls, doors of lockers swung open, blackened cabinets were tilted and twisted, and the floor was covered by every kind of debris.

Merral walked forward, stepping carefully around the fragments. The corpse of the dragon could not be seen and he did not seek it. He walked toward the shattered column, aware of the envoy following noiselessly behind him. Even with the gloom lifted, Merral had no desire to linger here; he wanted to be out of the ship and back with his men.

Something white on the floor caught Merral's attention. He shuddered to see that it was the limb bone of some creature. Looking around, he saw there were other bones lying about. Were these the remains of things the dragon had eaten, or had they been used in some dreadful rite? He didn't wish to know and kept moving on.

He found the steersman by the broken metal shards of the column. It was lying sprawled over the remains of the seat, its limbs extended in impossible directions. As Merral approached, he saw it move. As he stared, he was astonished to find that the motion came not from the body, but within it. The pale brown surface seemed to ripple as if an invisible hand was moving matter from one place to another. As Merral watched, he saw the spindly legs shorten and solidify.

"Quickly!" urged the envoy. "Slay it."

But Merral felt reluctant to act. The spectacle unfolding before him was so astonishing that he felt he had to watch.

The movement within the steersman had now shifted to the body: the cavernous abdomen seemed to enlarge and become smoother, as if being inflated, and the skin became softer and lost its dried-parchment look. The creature gave a little lurch and slipped against the ruined chair so that it now sat facing Merral in a broken-necked way.

"Man," came the urgent order, "strike!"

"I will," Merral said as he stared in wonder at what was happening, and he moved his fingers to the handle of the bush knife. But he did no more than that.

Before him, the chest of the steersman was changing in the same way that the legs and abdomen had, becoming smoother and more rounded. The movement shifted to the arms and fingers, and wrists were fleshed out.

Now the neck moved and the head twisted forward. Eyelids extended over the cavernous sockets, cheeks filled out, eyebrows grew. A nose suddenly bulged outwards as if molded by an invisible sculptor, and the dry brown lips became a soft and healthy pink.

"Strike!" the envoy ordered.

Impressed by the urgency in his voice, Merral pressed the button on the handle and the blade raced out. He raised the knife and squinted, aiming for the neck.

The lips moved.

"You have won," the creature said.

Staring at the being that was forming in front of his eyes, Merral relaxed his grip.

"No! Wait!" The voice was human; the words were ragged as if it was still learning to speak.

Merral lowered the blade.

"It was a mistake to come here," the thing said in contrite, apologetic tones. Its words were smoother now, as if the mouth and lips had learned to move in coordination. "You may exact your price from me. As in the old fables."

Memories arose in Merral's mind of the primeval fairy tales of his childhood with their fantastic goblins and sorcerers. The creature shivered, and with a ripple the flesh on the face seemed abruptly to slide into place as if it were a garment that was being adjusted.

"Name anything," the creature continued, almost pathetically. "What do you want?"

Merral, conscious of the dull gray metal blade held in his hand, found himself torn. He wanted to end this horrid thing's existence, and he yearned to hear more. He hesitated, and its form changed further; tissue flowed miraculously from one place to another, and the pale brown skin became softer, paler, and more alive.

Merral glimpsed the dried blood on his sleeve: Lorrin's blood.

A deep anger bubbled up in him. "Thing!" he shouted, his voice unsteady with rage. "The Gate is gone! We are cut off from the Assembly. Everything is—" Emotion choked his words. In his mind, he could see Anya and others: Isabella, Barrand, and Elana. And poor dead Lorrin. "Everything is . . . is rotten!"

"I apologize," came the cool answer. "But you know, these things can be undone."

Merral watched as the creature flexed smooth fingers.

"Undone?"

A golden fuzz of hair was extruding from the skull.

"Strike!" ordered the envoy again, but although Merral tightened the grip of his fingers around the handle, the blade did not move.

"Wait! Please." It was both an order and a plea. New changes flitted across the face. "This voice," the creature asked him, "the one you are listening to. Tell me, please, what do you know of it?"

"I trust him and I have seen what you look like."

"You have been misled by appearances," reasoned the smooth

voice. "And after all, you have not seen him. How do you know what he looks like? No, he wants you locked here on Farholme forever. If you strike me, you will lose all hope of traveling back to the Assembly. And without help, your tiny world will never survive in isolation." There was a pause. First one, then both ears sprouted. "Spare me and we will leave your system, and I will give you the secret you want. Of finding help and getting back. I will give you this ship. I am a steersman."

"Strike, Man! Before it is too late!"

"Oh, Merral," the creature said, its voice now gentle, even humorous. "He just wants to stop you from learning knowledge."

Merral stared at the creature. It was a young man—no, he realized with a mixture of emotions—it was a young woman. The face was shy and graceful and had wide, dark brown eyes. The hair, still growing, was framing the face.

Smooth, pale red lips parted gently in speech. "Merral, this envoy thing is a spoiler. He is himself fleshless, and thus he hates everything associated with life. But then, you know that, don't you?"

The tone was amused, intelligent, and sensible. To his utter amazement, Merral realized how much sense the thing was making. *No, it is not a thing, it is a person—a she.*

The long legs now locked themselves under her body so she seemed to sit cross-legged. The face looked up demurely at Merral as if expecting him to automatically acknowledge the truth of what she said. There were faint flickers of motion along her back as if some invisible sculptor was putting the final touches to his creation. Her hands, finely nailed, came up in a gesture of helplessness and embarrassment over her nakedness. Merral was almost overwhelmed by the vulnerability of this girl.

"You know, he wants to stop your enjoyment," she said, her tone at once wise and sympathetic. She shook her golden hair and it caught the light. "To stop you from doing what is your right. After all, this is *your* planet. Not his." She smiled at him and he felt his heart tremble. "Look, let me help you rebuild your world. I will gladly serve you. Help you in every way." She smiled with a happy innocence. "We can do things. Together."

The single word *together* evoked an extraordinary excitement.

"Do you really promise?" Merral asked, telling himself that listening could do no harm. Indeed, he reminded himself, did he not have a duty to extract the best possible concessions for his world from this being?

"Oh yes," said the earnest voice.

I must give her a new name. Something beautiful, something fitting. As he was thinking about it, he caught another glimpse of the caked blood on his sleeve.

"But Lorrin Venn is dead," he heard himself say.

"I know," she answered thoughtfully, "but only a short time ago. There will have been little biochemical change yet. If you promise to spare me, I can bring him back."

"You can do that?" he gasped.

Then she gazed up at Merral, and he thought how he longed to be immersed in her timeless and beautiful eyes.

"Spare me. I can restore life."

Then she bowed her face toward him submissively, as if to indicate that she was his.

As she bent her head, Merral glimpsed beyond her fine hair something white that had rolled under the chair in the blast. It was a polished, smooth waxen object, like a bowl.

In a moment of appalling knowledge, he knew what it was: the skull of a child.

And in that moment, he knew that she was Death, not Life.

He screamed.

The blade arced straight down. With a terrible sucking noise, it sliced through the smooth flesh of the neck.

Merral closed his eyes briefly as the head hit the floor. Slowly, sobbing with emotion, he opened them. The slack-jawed face was upside down, looking up at him from the ground.

"Man, have it be gone." The envoy's words were formal and unsympathetic.

Then, aware that his hands and legs were shaking, Merral spoke words as they came to him. "Thing! Demon! Whatever name you are known by, I command you by the authority of Jesus, the living King of the heavens and the worlds, be gone, and return to your realm to await your judgment!"

The figure crumbled away as if it were made of sand. A faint column of dust spiraled up into air and then, in an eddy of air, it was gone.

Merral stood there shaking, full of shame, realizing how close he had come to disaster. He wanted to be sick. What was it that the envoy had warned him barely an hour ago? *The enemy seeks your ruin. For him there are more satisfying and useful ways for your destruction than fire, sword, or tooth.*

"I'm sorry," he gasped. "I didn't mean to listen."

The shape of the envoy, although still at the margins of his vision, was somehow more substantial than it had ever been.

"You would have been far wiser not to. Again, you nearly fell."

"I'm truly sorry."

There was only silence in response.

"Is it destroyed?" Merral asked, still shaking.

"It has lost the body fashioned for it and gone back to the abyss."

The horror of the thing, and of what he had had to do to slay it, came back to him and made him shudder afresh.

"Envoy, what was it?" he inquired.

"I do not name it. Its name is best forgotten until the Judgment breaks. It and its kind had been set free. By explorations where mankind was not meant to go, and by men who thought that they could be harnessed."

"And would she have kept her promises?" Merral asked.

"Man, you know so very little," the envoy said, and there was a great sadness in his voice. "Not one of your race ever struck a deal with their sort and did not regret it. I think Lorrin's family would not have long thanked you for what walked in their midst and pretended to be their son. And the Assembly's rejoicing at your arrival through Below-Space would have been very short-lived."

The figure beside him seemed to sigh in an almost human way. "And troubled as your world is now, all this would have been a pleasant dream compared to what you and she would have unleashed together as Lord and Lady of Farholme. Let alone your offspring."

"I see." Suddenly Merral felt very small and very weak.

He turned to the envoy, now certain that he was much less indistinct than he had been.

"The other things. The things the steersman said, in my mind. The breach in the barrier, the end of the Assembly. *Those* things. Are they true?"

"There were lies there, as you know. Yet not all was lies."

"Which bits were true?"

"Ah, Man, that is for you to find out."

"I had a feeling you'd say that."

"But more importantly, next time, obey immediately."

"Next time? I thought it was finished?"

"Finished?" Merral suddenly heard a sound that might have been a laugh. "No, you will know when it is finished. There will be no doubt of that moment."

"What about the evil loose on my world?"

The dark shape at the margins of his vision seemed to suddenly become even more solid, and Merral thought he could make out a strange, archaic coat and a round, wide-brimmed hat that seemed to hide the face.

"No," the figure said slowly, "the war will go on. But with this gone, your world may have some measure of healing."

"Only some measure?" Merral asked sharply, feeling that the sacrifice of Lorrin and the diplomatic team and—for all he knew—another dozen more, merited a greater prize.

"The time for the mending—and ending—of things is not yet. Be content with what the day brings. But you must go."

Suddenly Merral realized that outside the battle still raged. He glanced at his watch; to his amazement he saw that he had been on the ship for only twenty minutes. "Yes, I must."

"You will face opposition outside the door, but they already fear you as Lucas Ringell. When they see you return alive and victorious out of here that fear will be greater. They may use terror, but they are not immune to it themselves. And your gun works now."

"Thank you," answered Merral, collapsing his blade and clipping it back to his belt.

"Man, save your thanks for him who sent me." He paused. "I too serve."

Then Merral turned, ran across the ghastly floor and through the doorway. Any sense of achievement in having killed the thing that had been the source of evil was dampened by the awareness that he had come so close to destruction.

He picked up the gun, and as he did, he turned and looked back. There on the floor of the chamber he saw a tall, straight-backed man, clothed in a black ankle-length coat over black trousers, whose face was hidden by the brim of his hat. He was poking tentatively and thoughtfully at the remains of the column with a black-shoed foot.

As if aware of his gaze, the figure began to turn toward him. Merral, curiously anxious not to see the face under the brim of the hat, turned away.

He slid the gun to "ready," saw the status light go to red, and tugged at the handle of the outer door. As soon as the door began to open, he heard the shrill noise of multiple sirens.

As the door opened farther, he curved his finger around the trigger.

He gasped.

Lined up in front of the defaced bust in two symmetrical and silent rows were at least twenty intruders. The back row was made up of towering ape-creatures, the front by a line of twitching cockroach-beasts.

With a sickening feeling, Merral realized that every single one of them was staring at him.

CHAPTER 24

The door clicked fully open, and as it did, it seemed that for a brief moment time itself froze. As the forty or so weird and hostile eyes gazed at him, two thoughts came to Merral: The first was the bizarre one of how much the sight in front of him resembled some monstrous parody of a formal sports team image. The second was simply this: the time had come to die well.

Then, on the heels of that, came a third thought: He had, first of all, to announce the defeat of the monstrous steersman.

"The steersman is dead! Glory to God and the Lamb who reigns!" Merral cried, in as loud a voice as he could muster. And as he shouted it, he felt astonished at the calmness with which he faced his end.

Then he fired in the air, and amid the crash of falling ceiling panels, the twin lines of the opposition suddenly broke. With a terrible cacophony of wails and yells, the creatures fled left and right in utter panic. Merral fired again into the midst of the fleeing figures on both sides.

The result was an astonishing—and gratifying—mayhem. The smaller cockroach-beasts with their faster initial response were overtaken near the stairways by the longer-limbed ape-creatures. The result was that both sets of terror-struck creatures tried to get down the narrow stairs at once. To his right, Merral saw an ape-creature trip over a cockroach-beast and go flying, taking another of his own kind with him. To his left, two ape-creatures reached the stairwell at exactly the same time, their limbs becoming hopelessly enmeshed, while a cockroach-beast cannoned into the back of their legs. Fighting erupted between them, and he glimpsed a brown-shelled creature tumbling—or being thrown—over the rail.

Merral fired quickly once more at each side, to renewed howls. Noticing that the elevator door was open, he ran in and pressed the lowest of the six buttons.

The doors closed, and with a soft whine, the compartment descended sharply.

Merral realized how desperately he wanted to leave the ship. How many of his men had perished? he asked himself bitterly. They had achieved some sort of victory, but what had been the price?

Suddenly the elevator stopped and the door opened smoothly, revealing a low-roofed and gloomy lateral corridor. Yet for all its gloom, Merral rejoiced when he realized that he could smell fresh air. Furthermore, over the noise of the sirens and the sound of panicked, tumbling feet echoing from the levels above, he could hear sounds and cries from outside.

Merral exited the elevator compartment. As he did, he felt a new and powerful vibration begin. He knew instantly what it was: the engines of the ship were starting up.

"Time to go," Merral said aloud.

To his right, a fresher, cleaner light seemed to be flowing into the corridor. He ran to that end and carefully peered round the corner.

Beyond a pile of equipment and crates, he could see a ramp sloping downward. At its base was a strip of beach where a chaotic mass of cockroach-beasts and ape-creatures milled about.

There were other noises from the ship. Harsh, unintelligible words trumpeted from speakers, and a red strip light began pulsing rapidly along the ceiling. The vibrations reverberating through the ship began to rise in strength and pitch.

Merral moved forward, ducked behind an oil-stained container, and peered round at the ramp. Up it trudged a handful of the ape-creatures, some limping, others showing patches of raw red flesh amid their black hair. At their heels scuttled several cockroach-beasts, one with a severed arm, another trailing a limp leg. Merral noticed that on the ramp there was a trail of red smears. At the end of the sorry line, he caught sight of two heavy, dull gray metallic figures, shorter than the ape-creatures but much taller than the cockroach-beasts. For a moment, he thought that they were yet another race until he realized that what he was seeing was an encrusting armor that covered the figures from head to toe. Underneath their heavy protective suits he knew these were men. One, he noted, had a left arm that hung limp.

Halfway up the ramp, the men stopped, squatted down stiffly, and fired a dozen whistling blasts out at the beach beyond. Then they stood up, turned, and with a heavy, labored tread retreated back up the ramp.

As they passed him, barely three paces away, Merral heard a new noise, a deep mechanical groaning from within the ship. He looked to see that the ramp was beginning to rise.

Without thinking, he threw his gun down and rose to his feet. Then he leaped onto the ramp and began racing down its bloodied surface. Above the sound of his boots pounding on the metal he could hear the shout of harsh voices.

He had been seen.

At the very edge of the ramp, Merral dropped to his knees, grabbed the metal rim, and rolled himself over. He heard the sound of firing. Something whistled over the tips of his fingers so close that he felt its warmth. Aware of the fresh air around him and glimpsing the sand beneath him, he let go.

It was a long drop.

He struck the soft sand with a force that punched the wind out of him. For a moment, he lay there, dazed but grateful to God that he was not going to die on that foul ship. Then he caught a whiff of bitter smoke, heard the cries around him, and saw the shuddering corpse of a cockroach-beast in front of him.

Something hissed over his head, and Merral rolled himself down into a nearby hollow in the sand. High above him there was a clunking sound as the ramp seated itself into the vast black underside of the hull. All around him, the beach surface was shaking with the vibrations from the ship.

As his breath returned to him, he looked around, trying to take stock of the situation. About him lay a scene of devastation, with smoldering debris and the bodies of intruders.

Barely an arm's length away lay the half-burned corpse of an ape-creature, and beyond that another lay immobile at the edge of the blue-gray waters of the lake.

Despite the ramp's closure he saw there were two intruder groups left fighting, one between the twin rear legs and another—nearer to him—just in front of the nose strut. There three armed ape-creatures crouched behind a pile of equipment and fired clumsily.

Heartened, Merral realized that the ongoing defense suggested that both Zak's and Frankie's teams were still in place and attacking.

There was a booming noise from above, and he glanced up to see the sky-blocking mass of the ship visibly vibrating. Underneath him the sand shook in response, and around the legs, gravel and sand spurted up.

Suddenly he realized that, above the noise of the intruder ship, he could hear a new and weightier clamor. Abruptly, the line of sky over the lake darkened, and Merral glimpsed the clean, pale blue underside of the *Emilia Kay* sliding into place over the intruder vessel.

Perena's got them in check.

Suddenly there was shouting.

To his right, helmeted men in green were slithering down the loose cliff face on ropes. The reserve troops.

As if responding to their arrival, Merral heard the rising bellow of rocket engines behind him. The intruder ship jerked into the air a fraction. It hung there for a few seconds before thudding back to the ground. Ahead of him, Merral saw the ape-creatures swing their weapons toward the reserves.

It suddenly dawned on him that it was not yet all over. There was still resistance, all three legs of the ship were intact, and there was no sign of any doors having been blasted open. The mission remained unaccomplished. Aching in a dozen places, Merral rose to his feet, found his bush knife on his belt, and once more opened the blade. Then he charged forward at the nearest ape-creature, his feet sinking into the dark sand as he ran. Suddenly conscious of his approach, the creature swung the gun barrel toward him. Before it could fire, he thrust the barrel aside with his arm. He lunged with the blade at the creature's throat, feeling it strike home through fur and flesh.

With a spluttering cry, the creature fell back, its weapon crashing heavily into the sand.

Merral stepped back, trying to ignore the blood on the blade. Above him the entire hull of the ship was now shuddering. One of the two remaining ape-creatures tottered to the ground. The remaining ape-creature turned toward Merral, cradling a long-barreled weapon in the black fur of its arms. Then its head twitched; a ghastly red circle punched into its face.

"Sir, sir! Are you all right?" a voice shouted.

Merral turned to the soldier, recognizing Barry Narandel of the reserves. "Yes, Barry!" Merral shouted back. He felt he wanted to hug Barry and say how extraordinarily glad he was to see him and his men, but he didn't trust himself. Instead, he gestured to the front of the ship. "We need to get a charge on that leg!" he bellowed.

Barry nodded as a new and more sustained roaring began from the engines above them. Warm air thickened with flying sand and hot fumes billowed around them. Ahead, the front leg juddered afresh, thrashing sand all around as the table-sized metal foot rose up and then bounded back down onto the sand.

"It's about to take off!" Merral shouted over the new roar of sound.

Seizing a red package from one of his men, Barry ran with it to the leg. Just as he was about to climb on to the pad, the entire leg jerked free of the sand.

As the massive metallic foot lifted, a dark gaping hole appeared. Barry's legs slid down into it, dragging him under the overhanging pad.

The charge he was holding flew free and bounced along the ground.

"Get him out!" Merral screamed to the men, over the mounting gale of the engines. He knew they couldn't hear him, but it didn't matter; they were already running to their lieutenant's aid. Merral ran to the charge and snatched it out of the layer of bouncing dirt that now carpeted the ground. Somewhere above him, more jet vents were opening up, and the mixture of dense white smoke and dust made it hard to see anything more than a few paces away. The lake and the cliff seemed to have vanished into a smeared haze.

Ahead of him, in a vibrating blur, Merral could see the landing foot hanging at the height of his waist. He ripped off the backing strip on the charge and, running around the men as they struggled to pull their leader out of the sand, grabbed the side of the foot.

With the flying sand stinging him in the face, Merral reached over and slapped the package as far in on the pad as he could. He tore off the protective film from the firing cord and pulled out the safety pin.

The moment Barry was pulled free he would pull the detonation cord.

Suddenly there was a new shrieking roar from the engines. The ship pivoted sideways, and the suspended foot of the landing gear swung wildly. It struck Merral against his chest armor and sent him reeling. Somehow, he regained his balance. He reached out to regain his hold on the detonation cord, and as he did, the foot dropped down again.

Barry gave a terrible scream and the ground shook.

In a new torrent of sand, noise, and fume the leg lifted up sharply. As it rose past him, Merral lunged forward onto it, catching hold of a metal strut with his left hand and pulling himself onto the pad.

There was a ferocious jolt.

The angular corner of the pad struck under the edge of Merral's armored vest and jerked upward into his abdomen. An explosion of pain engulfed his chest.

Merral gasped, overwhelmed by the agony. *I must hold on!* he told himself over the dreadful pain, the deafening clamor, and the hot, choking smoke.

The ship was moving up.

Merral glanced down, seeing a figure with a red smear around his crushed legs and green-uniformed men standing around him with their pale helmeted faces staring upward. The raging fire in his chest continued to burn, and he could feel a warm liquid trickling down his stomach.

Fighting off an almost irresistible desire to pass out, Merral reached out with his free right hand and with slow, painful movements, found the charge. Even the slightest move seemed to drive a cruel stabbing blade up into his lungs.

He moved his fingers up, centimeter by painful centimeter, until he reached the cord. Then he grasped it between two fingers.

I must be sure I have it firm, he told himself between spasms of pain.

Now was the moment.

Now. But his fingers, apparently part of another man's body, wouldn't respond.

Now! *Now!*

Then, stiffly and reluctantly, they tugged at the cord.

There was a new agonizing jolt as the ship abruptly tilted and slipped sideways. A numbed Merral realized that the intruder vessel was dodging out from under the *Emilia Kay*.

Check, but not yet mate.

As the ship tilted, the sun shone into Merral's face, and blinking madly, he looked downward to see the ground underneath him covered with tiny upright figures, black bodies sprawled out on the sand, and gray plumes of rising smoke.

Suddenly he was aware of a new kind of vibration. He looked up to the dark cavity under the ship's nose and realized the foot he was clinging onto was sliding upward. He glanced back to see that the massive rear undercarriage legs were retracting as well.

Unexpectedly, the ship swung round and went into a shallow dive. To gain speed, he decided.

For a moment, there was blue water below him.

Merral let go.

The next moment he was aware only of the cold air whipping past him, the dazzling sun in his eyes, the Rim Ranges poking up their serrated peaks to the sky, and the awful pain in his chest. Then he closed his eyes.

Something smacked into him.

As he went under the icy water, Merral felt new and agonizing pains in his chest, as if someone was knifing his ribs.

He opened his eyes to see blue water around him and a yellow light far above. He tried to swim up to the light, but the pain was all too much. The coldness of the water made him want to gasp, but he couldn't breathe.

Somehow he rose up through the waters until he was bobbing up into the air and the sunlight.

Gasping in agony for air, Merral looked up and saw the dark bulk of the intruder ship flying onward. He could see the underside smoothing itself out as the legs were withdrawn into the hull. A sudden triple jet of orange flame burst out at the rear, and the vessel began to accelerate away southward down the lake, gaining altitude as it did.

Something is supposed to happen, Merral thought, his mind numbed. *There is supposed to be an explosion.* The ship became a small black pencil heading up into the stratosphere.

Perhaps, after all his efforts, the charge hadn't worked. *How disappointing after all that effort . . .*

A tiny yellow flash rippled under the nose, and fine fragments of dark debris rained downward.

The ship continued accelerating until it was only a charcoal-colored point trailing a dirty streak of smoke above the far end of the lake.

Good-bye. The cold water chilled him. *Good-bye.*

Then, in an instant so quick that it was almost nonexistent, the black point turned into a dazzling disc of clear silver light.

In that briefest fraction of time, the light seemed to equal the sun in its brightness.

Blinking, Merral heard a wild roll of thunder, and moments later a strange, unruly wind ruffled the choppy waters.

The disc of light faded to yellow and then leisurely transformed itself into a smudgy, dirty cloud. For a moment, it crossed Merral's wearied mind that the intruder ship had somehow escaped into Below-Space while still in the atmosphere.

Then he saw the first of the fragments splash down into the lake with a hiss. Soon the whole southern part of the lake was covered by a series of rising steam columns.

Destroyed, destroyed utterly. Perhaps it was best that way.

• ◆ •

It hurt to breathe. Merral noticed a red color in the lake water by his jacket. *I am still bleeding.* The armored jacket seemed to be keeping him afloat. *Just as well. I don't have the strength to take it off.*

Perhaps he would drift ashore. He tried kicking, but he lacked the energy. Anyway, it hurt too much.

The line of the shore was some way away, and he could now see the bulk of the *Emilia Kay* where the intruder ship had once stood. A fair exchange . . .

There were other noises now, but Merral was too tired to bother with them. He felt like sleeping. *I played my part; not well, but I did it.*

Freezing water lapped into his mouth and nose, jarring him momentarily alert.

The wind was getting up. He was aware of a little semicircle of waves radiating out from around him. *Strange,* he thought, in a dreamy haze. *Beware the weather in the Made Worlds.*

Then there was a splashing sound beside him. He knew it was sharks coming after his blood. Why had they ever introduced freshwater sharks into Fallambet Lake Five? He must ask Anya.

How very silly.

Something was now grappling with him, a thing of soft blue

plastic tentacles wrapping round his arms, legs, neck, and head. *An octopus,* he thought stupidly, too tired to resist. Was that better than a shark? He was aware of the tentacles becoming slowly rigid, and he realized he could no longer move.

Suddenly he was conscious of being lifted up, of water running down his chest, of his legs being pulled free from the lake, and of a chill and noisy wind whistling around him.

Still puzzled by the octopus, he looked up to where he could hear a humming. There above him was a white Assembly rescue craft with the cross etched in red on the underside, balancing itself on the four columns of hazy air at each corner. A dark doorway opened above him.

In seconds they were lifting him on board, and the octopus was collapsing and slipping away. Then there were white lights and soft, urgent voices and a delicious warm heat flowing over him.

Merral looked up to see a familiar dark face.

"Welcome aboard, Captain D'Avanos," Vero said with an expansive smile.

Merral cleared his throat, aware that he was safe. "Thank you, Vero. . . . I thought I'd go for a swim."

Merral was aware of conversation, and then an authoritative female voice spoke sternly to him. "Please stay quiet, Captain. Save your energy."

"But, Doctor, I give orders," Merral protested feebly, feeling light-headed.

"But as my patient, you are outranked," she said without humor, and Merral realized that he really wasn't well.

"Vero," he whispered, "shouldn't I be with the men? My men?"

"Zak's taken temporary charge, Merral. But it's all over."

Merral was aware of the rescue craft swaying slightly.

"Did we win?" he asked.

There was a moment's hesitation, and when Vero answered, his voice was subdued. "Win? Yes. I suppose so." He sighed deeply. "It just doesn't feel like it. But the doctor's right; keep quiet."

Then the female voice was back and a bright light scanned his face. "Thank you, Verofaza. You have at least two broken ribs, Captain. Some possible internal damage. You haven't coughed blood?"

"No. I don't think so."

"Good. We will transfer you to the hospital ship. Dr. Azhadi will want to have a look. You'll be back in Isterrane in two hours. Now a slight sedative." There was a cool whisper against his wrist. A soothing feeling drifted up his arm.

Then the motion stopped and a door opened. Abruptly they were lowering him into the sunlight onto a trolley, and from his horizontal position he could see another large white ship nearby with a side hold door open.

As they pushed the hover trolley toward it, he saw a line of green uniformed men forming up. Merral looked at them and saw how they were dirty and bore cuts, scratches, and bandages. As he passed in front of them, a loud ragged cheer went up. Looking away to try and hide his emotions, he saw that on his other side was a line of still, horizontal forms, lying on stretchers with their bodies and faces covered by bloodied sheets.

He blinked away tears.

CHAPTER 25

Merral awoke with infinite slowness, climbing up out of deep sleep into a world of whiteness. Gradually he realized that he was lying amid white sheets in a white-painted room and that sunlight was coming in through white gauze curtains. It took him longer to remember who he was and why his chest hurt. Then he smelled the sterile odor of the hospital and realized that his chest was encased in a light cast.

There was a faint noise to his right. He turned, somewhat stiffly, to see Vero, wearing casual clothes, working on his diary at a table. He looked up and gave Merral a tired but relieved smile.

"So how do you feel?" Vero asked, pulling his chair over to the side of the bed.

"As if I had exchanged one piece of armor for another."

"The two broken ribs. Some minor internal injuries, other wounds and blood loss. And incipient hypothermia. Fallambet Lake Five is not a place to swim, even on the edge of summer."

Merral lay there, images flashing through his mind. "I don't remember coming here. The battle was when?"

"Just over twenty-four hours ago. You were anaesthetized to travel back. You were also exhausted."

He was aware of the equipment around him now. There were monitor screens at the edge of his vision, and he could feel the sensor straps on his ankle and neck.

Vero looked drained.

"The casualties?"

Vero shook his head and was silent for a moment. When he spoke, his voice was burdened. "T-twenty men dead. And of the diplomatic crew, three are missing, assumed dead. That includes Erika and Louis as well as Fred Huang. We recovered the pilot alive but with some burns."

"Nate," Merral said dully. "That was the pilot's name."

"Another twenty wounded, including you. Some more serious. One may die."

"Oh, dear," Merral said, and as he spoke, he realized how inadequate his words were. But then were any words adequate? One third of the attack force was dead or wounded. "I saw Lorrin Venn killed,"

Vero nodded, and Merral thought there were tears in his eyes. "Yes. Philip Matakala told me."

"So Philip survived. And Frankie Thuron?"

"Yes, but with injuries. Zak made it too."

"I thought Zak would."

"He fought well, the men said."

"I'm not surprised. And Barry Narandel? I saw him get his legs crushed."

"We got to him in time. They say he'll walk again but never run."

Merral stared at the ceiling in silence for a long time. "I'm sorry. Desperately sorry. Sometime I want to see a list."

"Whenever you want."

"Thanks. And Perena and Anya are well?" Merral tried to keep his voice neutral.

"Yes. I'm sure you will see both later. The intruder ship, of course, is in a million fragments." Merral looked at his friend and saw that he seemed to be staring into the distance. "I doubt we will recover much of value."

Merral realized how bitterly disappointed Vero was over the loss of the ship.

"Yes. I wish we could have taken the ship. But we misjudged things, Vero, my friend. There were dozens of things on board."

Vero sighed. "Maybe a hundred. And other creatures."

"They were seen?"

"Ah, you know something of this." Vero gave him a sharp look. "It seems that just after you entered the ship a pack of creatures emerged and began to attack Frankie's team. The reports speak of them as being like fierce dogs or lions, with claws and teeth. Intelligent, regimented, and quite unstoppable—"

"Krallen."

"What?"

"They are called Krallen. I met them. I will tell you about them. Another time."

"Ah. Anyway, just as they were about to overwhelm everybody, they suddenly turned and raced back to the ship. After that the resistance was only sporadic. When Perena arrived and the ship began to take off, what was left of the teams made a concerted attack."

"I see."

Vero frowned. "We—no *I*—made an intelligence error. The ship was bigger than we thought. We also assumed that their ships would carry the same numbers as a comparable ship of our own. But somehow there were far more. Their crew compartments must have been horribly crowded."

"Yes, I realize that. It was . . . an *evil* ship."

"So I imagine," Vero said. Then he paused, a look of guilt on his face. "Do you think they were alerted?"

Merral stared at the gauze curtains. "No. They may have realized that we were onto them, but thankfully, I don't think the defenses were especially ready. If they had been, I don't think any of us would have made it to the ship. We were very much the weaker party in numbers and weapons."

"I was worried that the business with Felicity might have been the cause of the casualties."

"Yes. But I'd say it wasn't."

"Thanks."

"But, Vero," Merral added, "we blundered into something that was beyond us all. There was worse on the ship than anything we feared. I met the thing in the chamber."

"The creature that attacked Felicity?"

"That was there. I killed that. But there was also a being there. . . ." Merral realized that he didn't want to talk about what he encountered.

"Yes, you said things in your sleep." Vero raised an eyebrow.

"It was only that I—that we—had help that we didn't have an utter disaster."

"That too, I gathered."

There was a knock at the door, and the tall, erect, and gray-suited figure of Representative Corradon entered the room. As he did, Merral caught a glimpse of two men in unfamiliar blue uniforms standing stiffly outside the door.

"Sorry. I see that this is not a good time," Corradon said with a tone of gentle apology. Merral felt that although the representative looked as if he had not slept for many days, his manner was composed and his expression very much that of a man in control. Vero stood up and made as if to leave.

"I do need to see you, Sentinel," Corradon said, clapping a large hand on Vero's slight shoulder. "Could you wait outside?"

Vero nodded and left, closing the door behind him.

Corradon sat down in the chair by the bed. "I had a long chat with Vero yesterday. He feels very badly about the attack. So do I. But it could have all been much worse. Much worse." Merral watched as the representative allowed himself the luxury of a faint, tentative smile of relief. "We didn't get all we wanted. But we did win a victory."

"Of sorts," Merral added.

"True, but, Merral, we could have had this thing festering in the heart of Menaya forever. Anyway, first things first. On behalf of the people of Farholme, I want to thank you now. There will be other occasions, I have no doubt."

He extended a hand, and more as a courtesy than anything else, Merral shook hands carefully. He was certain he didn't merit the gratitude.

Corradon gave him a half smile. "I gather I can shake your hand. I was told, though, I shouldn't make you laugh."

Merral allowed himself a sigh. "There is, I fear, sir, little danger of that."

The half smile faded away. "I'm sorry."

"So am I. There was a lot of bloodshed yesterday."

"Yes." Corradon's voice was soft and sad. "I gather that you should make a speedy recovery. How do you feel?"

"Drained. I need to think through what I saw. There are things to do. And you, sir? How are you?"

The representative considered matters for a moment. "I feel better than I did. *Reassured*, in some way. At midday today, I am broadcasting to the people of Farholme. And at least now I can tell them the truth: we were invaded and the Gate was destroyed, but the invaders have been routed." He sighed. "Albeit at a high and sad cost. But at least the burden of secrecy is lifted." He turned to look out of the window, and Merral saw his silhouette, confident and strong. *The public profile; if you are to receive bad news, then you would want it from such a man.*

"But there are other things I have to announce," Corradon said, sounding less assured. His strength and confidence seemed only skin-deep. "There are other things I have to say. Of new troubles . . ."

He paused, seemed to struggle with his doubts, and his voice brightened. "Yes, I still desperately wish that I didn't have this job. But I have it and I will try and do it."

Merral found the determination in his voice encouraging.

"Good."

"Thanks. The speech today will have about 100 percent attention. People are getting up especially for it over in Aftarena. And we are beaming the signal to Bannermene so that in a generation's time it will go round the Assembly. I should warn you that your name will be mentioned in it. I will have to say that a hastily summoned task force under your leadership managed to destroy a superior force of invaders—"

"Sir," Merral interrupted, "I would prefer to be anonymous.

Unless you wish to reveal how badly I handled things. I think we must be careful that the glory goes to God."

There was a slight nod of his head. "I understand. But I'm afraid I refuse the first part of your request. You can hardly be anonymous. And as to the second part, this coming Lord's Day is to be a solemn day of gratitude for deliverance and for the remembrance of those who were lost. Today I will also give out the list of casualties."

Twenty dead, Merral thought bitterly and wondered if that would be any consolation to Lorrin's parents or anybody else's. But the implication of Corradon's statement troubled him; once it was made, he would no longer be a private person.

"But before I speak to our world," Corradon continued, interrupting Merral's thoughts, "I want to talk to you about what happened. On the ship. Are you willing to do that?"

"Yes," Merral said, after a moment. "But can I talk to both you and Vero about it? I don't want to repeat myself." He knew he had to speak about what had happened soon, and it might as well be to both Corradon and Vero at once.

"Very well. I will get him."

Corradon rose from his chair and went to the door. He returned with Vero and a nurse.

"Sorry, Merral," the representative said, "medicine takes priority. This gentleman wants to see you. Vero and I need to talk anyway, so please excuse us."

Together they walked over to the window and out onto the balcony. As they pushed aside the flimsy curtains, Merral caught a glimpse of the gleaming blue sea. He had a sudden deep longing to walk lonely beaches on his own.

The nurse helped Merral to sit up, asked him those questions that the machines couldn't answer, and gave him a glass of medicated orange juice. Then, with a respectful glance at Corradon, he left, closing the door carefully behind him.

With the nurse gone, the two men came back in and pulled up chairs around the bed. Vero's face was troubled.

Corradon turned to Merral. "Thank you. There are lots of questions. If we'd have known you were going to get on board we'd have put a shoulder camera on you. Now obviously at some stage there will have to be a full report. And an inquiry. But now . . ." He and Vero shared glances. "Only if you are up to it, of course . . ."

Merral breathed in heavily and instantly regretted it. "Yes, physically. Mentally, I'm not so sure. But it is important. I suppose I should start with the appearance of the envoy."

Then, with interruptions for him to drink, Merral went through what had happened to him and what he had seen on the previous morning. He did not discuss the personal matters that had emerged with the envoy, although he was aware that he had hinted at more than he said.

He was interrupted twice. The first interruption came from Vero when he described the shattered statue and its inscription.

" 'Zhalatoc, Great Prince of Lord-Emperor Nezhuala's Dominion,' " Vero repeated, taking down the spelling and entering it in his diary. He stared at the screen, a range of emotions crossing his face; then he looked up. "As I suspected: two proper names that we have no records of in Assembly history. And you don't need me to tell you that to use the language of 'Great Prince,' 'Lord-Emperor,' and 'Dominion' for anyone other than the Most High is alien to everything the Assembly stands for. But written in our script . . ." His face expressed a deep and worried perplexity. "Who are they? What do they want?"

"And why was the statue defaced?" asked Corradon, anxiety visibly eroding away his look of confidence.

The questions were unanswered, and Merral continued with his account of what had happened in the chamber. He hesitated when he came to what the steersman had seemed to say to him as he had stood before the column. *After all,* he told himself, *it was a voice in my mind.* Yet the words had been so significant and ominous that Merral felt he had no option but to share them. As he described what had been said to him, he was aware that uneasy looks were shared between his visitors.

"Stop!" said Corradon suddenly, and Merral felt that his composure had now all but vanished. "Let me get this right. He said—or you felt he said—'Your isolation is over; the breach in the barrier remains. There will be others who will come in vast ships of unimaginable power.'"

"Yes. 'And we will come with them.'"

"This is—" Corradon's face paled. "No," he said slowly, as if reasserting control over his emotions. "Later. Continue."

Merral ended his account with his wild ride on the leg of the intruder craft. "So I just jumped and hit the water and saw the explosion. And I don't know how long after that I was picked up by the rescue craft."

There was a moment's silence before Corradon spoke. "An extraordinary account," he said, and Merral heard fear in his slow words. "Quite remarkable and, in part, terrifying. There is much more I would like to ask you, but I'm grateful for what I have heard. I have . . ." He shook his head and turned to Vero. "Did you have any questions?"

Vero, who apart from his one interruption had listened in total silence, put his long fingers up around his cheeks. "Dozens. Most can wait. But I do have one or two that I need to ask. Merral, you said the ship was dirty and smelly. Did you see any signs of damage?"

"Other than the statue? Yes, there was one place. Just before I met the thinking machine."

"Go on."

"There was a large hole, oh, the size of that door, now mended, and there looked to have been a fire. Or an explosion. At a temperature high enough to melt metal." Merral paused, remembering the spherical silver globules that he had picked up. "And thinking about it, I'm sure the blast occurred in zero gravity. The melted metal had formed spherical droplets."

A subliminal gesture of acknowledgement seemed to pass between his visitors.

"Why do you ask?" Merral said. "I didn't make anything of it. Not compared to everything else."

Vero answered him. "It's just that the *Emilia Kay*'s cameras got some good images as they hovered over, and there were marks on the hull. Blast marks, someone thinks."

"I see."

"A second question: You said both notices, this odd title and the 'Steersman Chamber' warning, were in Communal?"

"Yes."

"And an early style."

"I'd say so."

"Hmm. How *very* suggestive." Vero's voice was almost inaudible, and Merral saw his expression twisting this way and that in thought.

Corradon looked at Vero as if expecting an explanation. Then he glanced at his watch. "Really, I must go. But briefly, Vero, what do you think?"

Vero nodded, as if agreeing with some unspoken deduction of his own. "Yes . . . sir, it is now absolutely plain that the tale we have of the ending of the Rebellion is inadequate. I was very taken with one incidental detail of Merral's account: the way the robot identified him as *Captain* Lucas Ringell."

"Sorry, Vero, I fail to see the significance of the rank. Other than the fact that it knew of him."

"Sir, as you know, Lucas Ringell is always known to history as *General* Ringell, the final rank he reached. He was promoted on his return to Earth, *after* the ending of the Rebellion." A pensive look came over his face. "Or, what we have always called the ending."

Merral began to understand. "You mean the last the ship, or the robot, knew of him was when he was a captain?"

"Exactly."

Corradon stared at him. "Extraordinary."

Vero nodded. "I am now confident that something—man, computer, or whatever—survived the cleansing of the Centauri base and fled beyond Assembly space."

"And has come back."

"Or its descendants have." Vero's unhappiness showed in his expression. "But in whatever way the forces of the Rebellion survived, the trends that Jannafy encouraged have plainly been continued. There appears to have been no respect of any of the Technology Protocols. There has been a pursuit of all things banned: human genetic modification, machines with a humanoid intelligence, undoubted explorations of Below-Space. And somehow, an alliance with deep evil has been made."

Corradon shook his head as if trying to ignore what he had heard. "These are matters to be pursued at length later. I will mention little of them today. It is already hard enough to say what I have to. But after Merral's account, I am now reassured that this costly battle was worthwhile. And that what I will propose is necessary."

As Merral wondered what he meant, he saw Corradon and Vero look at each other.

"Shall I ask?" the representative muttered, but Vero shook his head.

"Very well." Corradon rose stiffly to his feet. "I must go and prepare for my speech. Anyway, I wish you a speedy recovery, Merral. There is more for us to discuss." He patted Vero on the back and walked toward the door.

"Sir—" Merral raised a hand—"before you go, I have a request. Another one." There was something that had to be said, and now was as good a time as any to say it.

"Which is?"

Merral took a deep and painful breath. "Sir, I wish to resign my commission. I want to return to forestry. To go back to Ynysmant." His voice sounded brittle.

Corradon took a pace back toward the bed, his face full of incredulity. "But why?"

For a moment Merral could not speak, and then the words flowed out in an unstoppable rush. "Because I made errors of judgment.

Because there are men dead. Because we failed to secure the ship. Because I'm not good at it. And, above all, because I hate it. Utterly."

Corradon pursed his lips and stared at him before answering. "You hate it? I'd hope so." He shook his head slowly. "Not good at it? I'd hate to meet anyone who was better than you. And the ship was, at least, utterly destroyed. The dead are . . ." He hesitated and then exhaled heavily. "The dead are a grievous and lamentable loss, but they are hardly your fault. As for your claimed errors of judgment, well, I think they are far outweighed by your wise decisions, your courage, and your skill. But there will be a full inquiry on the battle over the next month. There has to be for the records. And for lessons for the future."

He turned, as if to leave, and then paused, staring at something on the bedside table. He bent over, and for the first time Merral saw the dull silvery disc and chain and realized that the identity tag was gone from round his neck.

"May I?" Corradon asked, and without waiting for an answer, he reverently picked it up and stared intently at it, mouthing the ancient words engraved on it. " 'Lucas Hannun Ringell, Space Frigate *Clearstar*, Assembly Assault Fleet.' How very strange. How very strange indeed."

His blue eyes glanced at Merral. "Well, anyway, if heaven allows any knowledge of these worlds' tribulations, neither Brenito nor General Lucas Ringell will have been displeased with yesterday's events."

"Unfortunately, sir," interjected Merral, trying not to sound rude, "my conduct is judged by a higher authority than either. And there, I feel, I have blame, not just praise."

Corradon nodded, lowering the tag reverently down to the tabletop. "It is perhaps as well, lest this victory breed an overconfidence. But apportion blame fairly, Merral."

"I will, sir. But my resignation?"

"I don't accept it. Sorry." Corradon shrugged.

"Respectfully, sir, I believe that you have to accept it. It's over. The task I was asked to do is done."

"Really?" Corradon exhaled loudly. "Merral, Lucian and I have agreed that the FDU is to be closed down. In fact, I will be announcing that during my speech."

"Good."

"To be replaced by a larger and better-equipped Farholme Defense Force with a range out to the system's edge. With real weapons. And—I was not going to mention this now but I will—I'd like you to head it up. As Commander."

"I don't understand," Merral said, staring at him and Vero, struck by the solemnity on both their faces.

"I will be stating—" the representative seemed to weigh his words—"that we will be enlarging our defense capability. As much as our world's limited manufacturing and technical base can take. It would be an enormous help if you would lead the new force. Indeed, I think it would help stabilize shaken nerves across the planet if I could announce your appointment during my speech." He looked out beyond the curtained window with a burdened gaze. "It is my job to tell the whole of Farholme that not only are we isolated from the Assembly, but we have enemies. That is a heavy task. I would like, in the same breath, to give them the slight comfort of saying their defense is in trustworthy hands."

"No!" Merral snapped. "I see no reason for it. I want to be an *ex*-captain and an *ex*-soldier."

Corradon gave him a wry, sad, and sympathetic smile. "I'm afraid, Merral, you face the same dilemma I have faced. This world is in crisis and it looks for leaders. You and I must do our bit to provide them with what they need." He glanced at his watch. "Look, I must go."

He gestured to Vero. "I give you leave, Sentinel, to tell him what I told you."

Then he walked to the door and opened it. He turned to Merral. "Captain D'Avanos, it would be a great help to me—and to Farholme—if I could have your agreement by noon."

Then with a salute, he left.

Merral turned to Vero and was about to speak to him when the door slid open and an energetic female figure with a shock of tied-back red hair entered.

"Anya!" cried Merral.

Vero, beaming at her, got to his feet. "I'm off for a bit; I need some breakfast. Or lunch. Whatever is appropriate for now. We will continue our conversation, Merral." Then he slipped out of the room.

Anya bent over and kissed Merral lightly on the forehead, pulled up a chair, and sat next to him. She was wearing a rumpled navy waistcoat and unfussy, plain blue trousers, and he felt his resolve weakening.

"So, Tree Man, you survived," she teased him, laughing brightly. "I gather that you float. Hardly surprising." The joking tone did not conceal a deep relief. She took his hand and squeezed it hard.

"Yes," Merral answered slowly, "I survived. But I'm not unscathed." He tried to prepare the words that he had to say, but faced with her in person, he found the idea difficult. He played for time. "So did you catch any creatures?"

"No. Not alive." She wrinkled her face in expressive disgust. "They were all dead. Some of the men say that the few that were left alive committed suicide once the ship took off. But there are about a dozen dead specimens in all. Although being clones, I think we'll only need to look at one of each. And none of this very worrying new type. The predators."

"They aren't creatures. They are machines of some sort."

"Machines? That explain—"

"Anya," interrupted Merral, feeling that he had to speak now or her presence would persuade him to forget what he knew he had to say, "I have an apology and an admission to make."

She looked at him carefully, as if wondering whether it was a joke or not. "Which is what?"

"That, the other night, I wasn't entirely . . ." He could hardly bring himself to speak the word, it was so appalling. "*Honest.*"

"About what?" she said, letting his hand drop.

"About Isabella."

Her face darkened. "But you said . . . you *denied* that there was anything."

Merral felt that this was a new agony. "Yes, Anya, I know. I'm truly sorry."

"You mean that . . . there *is* something?"

"Well, yes. It was, well, something that . . ." He paused. "Something that I slipped into hurriedly, without thinking. An *understanding*. Without parental consent. So, well, I thought it wasn't really valid. And I have regretted it since. But—"

Anya had gotten to her feet now. "But *what?*"

"But, that I—we—never ended . . . Not *mutually*." Merral felt his face burn with shame.

"So you are *not* free." Her words were biting.

He tried to smile. "But I would like to be. Very much."

"It was a *lie*."

The word cut and stung like a lash of hail in the face, and the thought came to Merral that in the last twenty minutes he had been praised by the highest in the land and was now being utterly humiliated.

"Yes, I suppose . . . that's a legitimate word. But I was caught off guard. No, that's an excuse. . . ."

"I can't believe it!" Anya said, her expression a harsh mixture of pain and anger. Merral wondered if it might not have been better to have stayed on the ship and been blown into a billion atoms.

"So what are you going to do?" she snorted, her eyes wide with emotion.

Merral tried to look away. "I'm going back to Ynysmant, and I'm going to talk to Isabella. Ask her to agree to our commitment—such as it is—being concluded. *Mutually*."

He could hardly bear to look at her now. He knew that she was glaring at him.

"And if she refuses?" Anya asked in a sharp, querulous tone.

"I hope that won't happen. But if it does . . . I have no idea," Merral said miserably, thinking that in the last twenty-four hours he had known war, death, and injury, and that this was almost as traumatic as any of them. "I now want to do what is right."

"Now . . . ," she said, and the scorn in her voice cut into him. "Oh, *now* you want to do right!" She stood there shaking her head, her hair somehow having come untied and flowing out wildly.

"Anya," he said, "I do love you."

"And why, oh why, should I believe that?" she exclaimed and then rounded on him. "And anyway, what *you* feel is irrelevant if I can't trust you."

"I'm sorry."

"I hurt," she said, wringing her hands. "I just feel . . ." She shook her head as she tried to find the words. She glared at him, her eyes glistening with tears. "I just don't have the vocabulary. I just feel that . . . I don't trust!" Then she turned sharply on her heels and stormed out angrily.

The door thudded heavily shut behind her.

Merral lay there, grasping the sheets with his eyes shut, wishing it had all never happened, and feeling very sorry for himself.

A few moments later, he heard the door opening, and he opened his eyes to see a young male doctor looking at him in a concerned way. "Oh, Captain D'Avanos. The metabolic monitor system sent me over. Your functions were indicating high stress loads just now. You are, perhaps, in pain?"

Merral stared at him, not sure whether to order him out. In the end, an approximation to civility triumphed. "Thank you. It's not a medical problem. But you can help. Unhitch me from these monitor cables, will you? I want to walk. To the window. I need fresh air."

There was a pause. "Well, we were planning to keep you under observation until tomorrow."

"And what happens if I just pull them off?" countered Merral, hearing a strange brusqueness in his voice.

The doctor looked alarmed. "Oh, I'd rather you didn't. You'll probably damage the sensors, and they are made—*were* made—off system on Ticander. We have only a limited number."

Merral lifted up the sheet, painfully bent down to his ankle, and began undoing the covering bandage. "Well, let's not risk that, shall we? Get them off, please. And can you find me some proper clothes?"

•—•—•

Ten minutes later, the far-from-pleased doctor having departed, Merral walked stiffly over to the balcony rail and leaned against it, trying to avoid the tender part of his chest. As he had suspected, he was high—perhaps six floors up—on the tower that was the Western Isterrane Main Hospital. He looked out southward over the playing fields, green woodlands, and rolling pastures that ended abruptly at the sharp line of the sea cliff. Beyond that, the open vastness of the sea stretched onward to the horizon. Around one of the new sandbanks offshore, he could see the etched lines of white breaking waves, and he could just make out flocks of gulls wheeling. He breathed in and felt he could smell the sea air.

He had hard decisions to make.

He was still pondering them a few minutes later when there was a noise behind him, and he turned to see Vero entering.

Again, he glimpsed the two statue-stiff blue figures outside the door.

There was something in Vero's gait and look that told Merral he had met Anya. The sentinel walked out to the balcony and, standing by him, stared at the view.

"Sorry," he said, but the single word conveyed an intense empathy.

For a long time Merral did not answer. He felt the warm sunlight on him, stared at the curves of the ground ahead and the splendid beech trees clad in the green brilliance of their early summer foliage, and heard the excited screams of the swifts as they swooped around in the air catching insects. He wanted to be a long way away.

At length, he spoke. "Vero, I don't know about you, but since

Nativity I have said 'sorry' to more people than in all the rest of my life."

"Me too. The world has changed in so many ways."

"It is broken, Vero. And I don't know how we rebuild it." Merral's sigh was deep enough to make his chest ache. "It is broken so badly, so thoroughly, that I could weep."

He caught a look of sharp, pained sympathy from Vero. "I know," he said, almost inaudibly.

Merral remembered something. "The men outside, the ones wearing blue. Who are they?"

Vero leaned forward, staring toward the infinite distance of the sea, and when he spoke his tone was distant and drained. "A new organization. Advisor Clemant has come up with it."

"Called what?"

"Police."

Merral closed his eyes briefly as he grappled with the significance of the word. "What?"

"It's not a Communal word. It's an old French and English word. A non-military law-enforcement body. For internal security." The staccato, reluctant phrases displayed his disquiet.

"Oh, I know what it means, Vero. But here? in the Assembly?"

"Yes; Clemant is no fool. He knows what we know. That the old world is gone. And that the new one will be a hard place. The police will be, he says, merely a precautionary and temporary measure. Maybe . . ."

"I know. He hinted at it. Oh, what a mess," Merral muttered, feeling that another new, discordant note had entered his world. *It was never Eden here. At best, maybe it was a sort of harsh New Eden. But it has gone. I miss it already and I fear for its future.*

The noise of schoolchildren playing a Team-Ball match on the fields below dragged him out of his sad reverie. He looked over to where Vero was silently wrapped in his own thoughts.

"What are you supposed to tell me?"

Vero looked up carefully at him, "Do you really want it?"

"It can't make things worse."

Vero's fingers tapped the railing thoughtfully. "It can. I heard a rumor last night and had it confirmed now by Corradon. While we were training at Tanaris, some of the Space Affairs orbital experts began to bring together some of the astronomical work Perena had started. On the records of objects within the Alahir system. They had lots of data that she hadn't been able to access, and they reprocessed all the old records." His voice was emotionless.

"And . . . she was wrong?" Merral asked, feeling that there was now a note of alarm ringing throughout the spaces of his mind.

"No. She wasn't. Her path of the intruder ship was confirmed. Of the first ship."

The adjective exploded into Merral's brain. "The *first?*"

"Yes. The thing is, they found another trace. A few days later."

"Where is it?"

"Ah. The best analysis suggests it appeared in the system a day later and followed the first intruder ship at a distance, as far as the inner asteroid belt, where it changed orbit and stopped." He gave a profound sigh. "Now, as you know, there you—I suppose I ought to now say *we*—have good data and continuous monitoring. It stayed for a week and then headed back out of Assembly space. One day it was going fast toward Fenniran. And the next, it had gone."

The facts were easily absorbed, but Merral struggled to find meaning in them.

"What else can you say about it?" he inquired.

"Only that it was bigger. Much bigger."

Merral clutched the railing as hard as he could, as if by doing so it would somehow impart something of its stability into his own life.

"Jorgio said that the barrier was down. The steersman confirmed it."

"And warned of other ships."

"Indeed. This second ship—any ideas what it was doing?" Merral now understood what Corradon had meant about "lessons for the future," why he wanted an enlarged FDU, and why he had wanted Merral to lead it.

"We don't know for sure," answered Vero, looking up as if he expected a sign in the heavens. "But there is a suspicion that it was chasing the first intruder. That was the idea generated from the orbits alone. The evidence from the ship here, including your report about the damage, confirms that it had been attacked."

"So the inference is what? I'm still partially sedated, remember." *Or am I? Perhaps I am just numbed.*

"That the intruder—call it the first intruder—was fleeing."

"So, although it was hiding in the Lannar Crater, it was not hiding from us."

"Not *primarily* hiding from us. But you see the obvious implications?"

"No. Or rather, I think I do. But be gentle." Merral felt that a whole chorus of alarms was now echoing through his body.

Vero continued in a soft, factual tone. "The idea—the theory—is this: There was a chase, and the first intruder somehow made it into your—*our*—system. The other ship followed it. Only to realize it had stumbled onto something too big. *Us.* The Assembly. It watched for a bit and then went back."

"From where it may return again at any time?"

For a long time Vero said nothing but just stared over at the tiny running figures of the schoolchildren around the ball.

"Yes," he said, and his voice was small. "That's the point. They may be our friends or our enemies. They may be this Dominion under this Lord-Emperor Nezhuala. But we know that they know how to fight. And Corradon and Clemant feel that we ought to be prepared for the worst."

"I see."

"Yes," Vero said, looking at his watch. "But we can talk about it later. Corradon is speaking in an hour. I was going to watch it with Perena." He paused. "And probably Anya. Are you all right here?"

"Me? Yes, I want to think about what I must do. Your news has added a new dimension to the problem. But you, Vero, what will you do?"

"What will I do?" Vero asked slowly, and Merral saw his brown eyes tracing a black swift, effortlessly scything through the air.

"I, like you, thought my task was over. It is not. I need to search every bit of data Brenito left me on the rebellion of Jannafy and see if we can find any clues as to what really happened. And I want to talk to Jorgio again. Oh, and I suppose I must prepare my statement for the inquiry." Then Vero touched Merral's shoulder briefly. "And you, my friend?"

"I have a lot to think about. I want to leave for Ynysmant as soon as I can. I want to write my report while it is fresh in my mind, and I have things to sort out with Isabella."

"Yes." Vero looked at Merral with his deep brown eyes. "I am sympathetic. I have been thinking. About the way we are." He paused. "Can I say something?"

"By all means."

"It is just this: Before all this happened, we took everything for granted. We did what was right because it was pleasing to us. We had, as it were, the wind behind us. Now, all that has changed. The wind is against us. Yet what is right has not changed; it has just become harder to do it."

Merral considered his words. "Yet we must still do what is right, even if it costs us. Yes, that makes sense."

"It's little comfort, I'm afraid. But I must go. I will be in touch."

"And me."

"Give my love to your family and Isabella when you talk to them. I will pray for you."

"Thanks. And I for you."

Then abruptly, as if wishing to conceal some deep emotion, Vero turned and left.

Merral watched him go and then turned back to stare at the view. *I never realized how much I had until I lost it.*

A final whistle blast from the Team-Ball referee drifted up to him, and as he watched, the children began boisterously trooping off the pitch. Merral presumed they were leaving in time to see the historic broadcast. He watched their colorful animated figures moving away to their changing rooms. They were unaware—and would be for a little longer—that a permanent shadow had fallen over their lives.

As Merral watched them, the decision made itself.

He walked slowly back into the room and found his diary among his possessions in a drawer. He took it and strolled unhurriedly back out to the balcony. It would be easier for him to say what he had to say with the view of the woods and the sea in front of him than in the anonymous and universal hospital room.

As Merral switched the diary on, he saw that the restrictions on its use had been lifted. He had had calls from his family and from Isabella. Well, he would answer them in due course. He tapped the screen. "Get me Representative Anwar Corradon please."

A moment later an image of a young man appeared, looking up from a pile of folders.

"I'm sorry. The representative is busy, I'm afraid. This is Jules, his office assistant. As you know, he's speaking in a quarter of an hour. Can you leave a message please?"

"I want you to pass on a message to him now. Urgently."

Jules's face acquired a look of profound disbelief at the idea that anyone could wish such an action at this time. "I'm sorry. But he is engaged in preparing for this rather important broadcast."

Merral tapped on the icon to transmit his name.

The man glanced at his screen and suddenly stiffened, his face flushing. "Oh . . . Captain D'Avanos, sir. I must apologize. I didn't recognize you. The message was . . . ?"

"It is very simple, but he must hear it before the broadcast."

"I'll take it to him now. He's next door. I do so apologize."

"Your apology is accepted. Just tell him this." Merral took a breath, closed his eyes, and then gave Jules the message.

It was just a single sentence.

After he had spoken it, the young man looked at him in perplexity. "Just that?"

"Just that. The exact words. He'll understand. Thank you," Merral said and flicked the diary off. He went into his room, put the diary down on the table, and turned the wallscreen on with the volume low.

Then he went out again on the balcony to continue staring at the view and feeling the sun on his face. There was so much he had to do, and so many perils he had to face.

He was still standing there when the "Hymn of the Assembly" sounded from the screen.

"Time," Merral said aloud to no one, and he turned to go inside and watch the broadcast.

Time for all Farholme to hear that the long peace of the ages was finally over.

Time for them to be told that they faced awesome enemies.

Time too for them to hear that Commander Merral D'Avanos had accepted the burden of being in charge of their defense.

 Born in Wales in 1954, Chris Walley grew up in northern England. He studied earth sciences at university and has a doctorate in geology. He taught at the American University of Beirut in Lebanon from 1980 to 1984 and then returned to Wales to do ten years of consultancy work with the oil industry. He began writing in the late eighties and had two novels, *Heart of Stone* and *Rock of Refuge,* published under the pseudonym of John Haworth. In 1994, along with his family, Chris returned to Lebanon to teach again at AUB. In 1998, he came back to Wales and began to make a new career in writing and editing for the Christian market. He retains his geological interests and is an adjunct professor of geology at Wheaton College. Chris and his wife live in an old cottage on the edge of Swansea and are very much involved in a local Baptist church.

areUthirsty.com

well . . . are you?

degrees OF guilt

Sammy's dead...they each played a part.
Kyra, his twin sister. Miranda, the girl he
loved. And Tyrone, a friend from school.

WHAT'S THE REAL STORY?

There's always more than
one point of view—read all three.

kyra's story
{DANDI DALEY MACKALL}
ISBN 0-8423-8284-4

miranda's story
{MELODY CARLSON}
ISBN 0-8423-8283-6

tyrone's story
{SIGMUND BROUWER}
ISBN 0-8423-8285-2

degreesofguilt.com

degrees° betrayal

Betrayal comes naturally—where you
stand will determine who's to blame—but
there's always more than one side to the story.

Revenge is sweet . . . or is it?

**There's always more than
one point of view—read all three.**

sierra's story
{DANDI DALEY MACKALL}
ISBN 0-8423-8726-9

ryun's story
{JEFF NESBIT}
ISBN 1-4143-0003-4

kenzie's story
{MELODY CARLSON}
ISBN 1-4143-0002-6

degreesofbetrayal.com